For Henry Griffin Stewart Foster

Maira —

Great to meet you. Thanks for picking up on class divisions, wasn't sure I'd pulled that off —

Haylow

a novel

Gray Stewart *July 17, 2017*

Gray Stewart

Livingston Press
at The University of West Alabama

Typesetting and page layout: Joe Taylor
Proofreading: Hannah Evans, Maggie Slimp, Jessica Gonzalez, Jessie Hagler,
Tricia Taylor
Cover design and layout: KDA Communications
Cover photo: Royal Gorge Regional Museum & History Center
Back cover illustration: North Jersey History & Genealogy Center

This is a work of fiction.
Surely you know the rest: any resemblance
to persons living or dead is coincidental.

Livingston Press is part of The University of West Alabama,
and thereby has non-profit status.
Donations are tax-deductible:
brothers and sisters, we need 'em.

first edition
6 5 4 3 3 2 1

Haylow

"La vérité historique est souvent une fable convenue."

—Napoleon Bonapart

Prologue

When Travis Hemperly was twelve-years-old, his father told him about a man who had been chained to a tree and killed with an ax. They were driving south in the Wide Track Pontiac, speeding down I-75 through the flat farmland south of Macon and toward the Florida border. The car didn't have air conditioning, so there was no relief from the July heat and none coming. The sun was high, both windows rolled down, the inside broiling, hot air whipping through. When Travis asked his father why he'd bought a car with no a.c., Henry glared back cross-ways and set his teeth. "Think, son. Think. The compressor alone weighs almost 500 pounds. Don't you know how that would slow a fast car like this down?"

There wasn't much traffic on the highway this far south. A logging truck struggled northbound, pine trunks stacked, debris flying in its wake. A buzzard swooped in a lazy circle, riding the updraft, looking for lunch. The Pontiac's engine drowned out everything. At this speed, Henry had to shout to be heard--and so he did, yelling in bursts of enthusiasm and anger and amazement about shadow societies and puppet masters, about three families who manipulated the global economy and controlled all governments everywhere. And aliens had visited the earth—not aliens from Mexico but from another galaxy. They'd come thousands of years ago, found the Mayans down in the Yucatan, and the Mayans had worshiped them like gods. They even built great stone temples for them and carved pictures of their spaceships into rock. The proof was right there. All you had to do was look. Then the Mayans all disappeared! Vanished, just like that! Every single one of them! No one knows what happened to them to this very day.

But they don't want us to know that, either. They don't want us to know any of it. How do you get people to wake up and see what's happening?

"I don't know," he said, replying to himself. "I don't know what to do."

The speedometer needle dropped back as the effort of his protest killed the Pontiac's momentum. Henry squeezed the steering wheel between his knees and steered with his legs, turning the car by pushing up and down on the balls of his feet. Travis raised his head from the comic book in his lap. The black vinyl seat was slippery with sweat, and his Bermuda shorts left no room for error—any movement and the vinyl burned a brand. He pinched the bridge of his glasses and pulled them off, leaned into the open window and the gust roared in his ears. A green field rushed by, then brown furrows plowed back to the tree line, then more cows—four of them at a feeder, all standing in the same direction.

"There's a man in the Soviet Union who can bend a spoon with his mind and levitate whenever he feels like it."

"It stinks," Travis said.

"Pull your head back inside the window, son." Henry inhaled. "That's manure. They use it to fertilize the crops."

A lull settled in between them. Outside the windshield, there was nothing to see but smashed bugs and the vanishing point. Another insect splotched the glass and Henry triggered the windshield wipers, with grim results. Before too long, Charlie Hemperly's ghost caught up with the car and slipped in through the driver's side window. He squeezed past the headrest and took up his old spot on the back seat. Charlie's funeral had been not two weeks before, his body not two weeks in the ground, and he was just beginning to get a feel for his haunting skills.

"Are we almost there?" Travis asked.

"So, what are you reading?"

"Nothing. Just a comic."

"About three hours. What's it about?"

Travis looked down. On the cover, a white man with rippling

muscles and long blond hair swung a large mallet at an off-stage threat.

"Viking polytheism."

"Huh. Well that's . . . huh," Henry said. He adjusted the rear view mirror, checked his teeth, then reached out for the radio dial. The FM signal hadn't lasted an hour outside of Atlanta, and now all they could get was spotty AM, "Your Cheatin' Heart," and a preacher testifying through the crackle.

A few miles down the road, the Gnat Line swarmed across the interstate. A seasonal hazard this far south, the tiny black bugs clouded the bottom counties in Old Testament plague, waiting to whine into eye orbits and feed on the fleshy corners. Travis and Henry were from the city and unprepared—Travis because he'd never been this far south before, Henry because it had been a while and he'd forgotten. Only a few miles to go before they crossed the line into the swarm. But not yet.

Outside the windshield, an obstacle cropped up down the road. Travis leaned forward and removed his glasses for better vision. A tractor plodded down the right lane, fat tire treads choked with earth and stamping red clay in its wake. The driver sat erect, shoulders back, chin up, a proud sun-baked statue, his straw hat shading dark skin underneath the tatty brim.

For a moment, the space between the Pontiac and the tractor seemed fixed, unbridgeable, the heat between them, an adhesive. The air a coagulant. Henry leaned forward over the steering wheel, his eyes penetrating. He didn't react, didn't hit the breaks or turn the wheels. Then he stepped on the gas, and the distance between them vanished. Travis stamped a foot to the floorboard, shouted and closed his eyes. Just before impact, Henry raised a knee and the steering wheel turned. They swerved into the left lane and blasted past. The tractor's driver didn't turn his head, didn't flinch, and didn't seem to notice them at all. Henry didn't react either, other than to lean back.

"I saw a man who had been chained to a tree and killed with an ax, once."

Travis shifted his legs and the vinyl seared. "Do what?"

"I did. I did. It was down here, at my grandfather's—your great-grandfather's place. My brother and me. Your Uncle George. We were coming back from Valdosta, going back to Granddad's farm, and there were all these cars pulled off to the side of the road, all these people going off into the woods. It was hot, just like this. Granddad pulled over, too, and we got out and followed him. Back not too far, all these people were standing around a tree. A man had been chained to it and someone had taken an ax to him."

"An *ax?*"

Travis tried to imagine it but couldn't. The thought made him numb. Henry nodded his head in confirmation. "Back before the Interstate." The Pontiac accelerated, the hot air through the windows louder now. He turned his head and looked Travis straight in the eye.

"I did."

Heat wobbled up from the asphalt. How horrible a sight it must have been to witness, Travis thought. What a story it must have been to tell. The idea of it grew and stretched until it formed into something tangible, something solid, a high-pitched whine that flew into his ear, a screech of wings in and out, and then there was something in his eye.

Chapter One

Dubois Hall is the first stop on the self-guided tour. It's at the highest point on-campus and an uphill climb from everywhere, but Travis Hemperly likes to start at the beginning, so he hikes up the hill with a map unfolded before him like an accordion. He follows a path not-to-scale, a bold red line that worms its way around the sketched college green and leads him from one landmark to the next. Their illustrations look chubby, as if they've been inflated beyond maximum PSI. Below them, unrolled scrolls provide historical details in loopy calligraphy. *1867: Dubois Hall was the first building erected on the campus. It was built over a Confederate cemetery.* He makes a note of this, pauses to reorient himself, and squints into the morning sun. There it is, at the end of the college green, a slant of hipped roof rising above the giant magnolia trees. On the cover of the map, a tintype photo of Dubois looks like it was taken the day construction was completed: the giant magnolias that now block the view are saplings just planted. Exposed, the center tower rises high in Victorian splendor. The wide veranda is inviting. The latticework is elaborate. Alone in a meadow surrounded by forest, it seems the only building for miles. This must have been quite a socially progressive project, he thinks, building a college for freed slaves on what were then the outskirts of town.

Nowadays, Dubois looks like a firetrap. The eaves droop. The porch sags. Time has siphoned mass and volume from each and every one of the peaked red bricks. It is a splendid dilapidation nevertheless, Travis thinks, the only building on the quad with historical weight—even though the map says it's just a dorm these days. The other buildings around the green represent the twentieth century and crowd out the builder's vision. They elbow and jostle for attention like unruly children, but Dubois still sits at the head of the table.

Travis is out of his element. He has never taught on a historically black campus, has never been a minority on any piece of real estate he has ever set foot on. And he's dressed for the wrong weather, hot as it is. He hasn't worn a necktie on a college campus since . . . ever, he thinks. Not back at the University of Minnesota as a grad student and later as a history instructor. But job interviews call for a certain protocol. True, his element is the college campus, but he takes a slow breath to quiet the jitters. It will all be over in an hour, one way or the other. In sixty minutes, he might be gainfully employed in academia once again and return to the professorate, the one occupation he's really geared for. So far, all signs point to yes. The sky is big and blue, and there is not a cloud in it. A good omen. A good beginning. If he gets the job, he will have to move back South and return to the city of his birth. 'Back home,' he thinks, but feels no connection. He's been gone so long he's even lost the accent.

No one else is about. The students and faculty are getting in a last bit of the summer break before classes begin, no doubt, and he's glad for a little meditation time in this setting. The Olympic Games have just left town, and the physical plant hasn't yet removed the debris. Bunting draped along the wrought iron fence has faded into red, white, and blue litter. Along the street, American flags droop from light poles, exhausted from months of cheering. Travis wonders what Olympic event was held on the campus. Basketball?

Stop Number Two on the map is the Klan Bell. It is big and brass and secured to the earth between two solid posts. An iron wheel, like a ship's wheel, is mounted on the side, the mechanism for turning and ringing. The map explains: *The Alarm Bell was used to warn the students whenever the Ku Klux Klan attacked the campus. Upon its ringing, the entire college gathered at this spot.* He tilts his head at this detail and wonders if it's true, but there it is in print. Cigarette butts litter the ground around the posts. Somebody smokes here. Travis rolls his own and feels the urge but holds off when he hears footsteps.

A young man—a student, surely—rounds the corner of Dubois Hall and strides down the brick pathway, purple windbreaker clashing with his combat fatigues. His paratrooper boots have been spray painted gold. The student hoofs it down the herringbone with a steady, determined step, his bald head shining, recently shaved. His costume makes Travis recall his days as a Viking re-en-actor at L'Anse aux Meadows, back when his hair was long enough to braid. He still feels the loss of his bushy Viking beard, having trimmed it down to a Trotsky mustache and goatee for the inter-view. The semester's imminent beginning is in the air. He is breath-ing the stuff, the growing energy he always senses as the first day of class approaches. He feels a sudden fondness, feels the camaraderie he always does with students at the beginning of a new semester, notches up his necktie and nods hello. The student strides, head forward, eyes forward, staring blankly ahead. When they're so close that they almost bump shoulders, the student breaks wind, with zest. It is a sustained rumba in a key that Travis can't place, a fart that echoes.

He stiffens and braces for the floating stink but only smells cologne, something rugged yet sophisticated. He spins through his mental Rolodex: American history. Brown v. Board. Freedom Summer. "We Shall Overcome." *Scatology Today*. Spastic bowel? He recalls his own undergraduate diet, the lean years of generic mac & cheese and experimental chicken from the A & M. The purple windbreaker advertises a Greek allegiance in gold lettering. Was that a prank? The student plods off, golden shoelaces dancing with each footfall. Then he throws his head back and barks like a dog—a big one with a deep guttural explosion. *Hough! Hough! Hough!*

Somewhere down the hill, another big dog barks back. Travis is a cat man himself and doesn't know his canines, but the bark brings to mind a large pit bull hopefully chained to something heavy. The student in the purple windbreaker heads toward the barking, and the bell tower down the hill begins to bong. It is time for his interview. His apprehension is not tasty, but he swallows it anyway.

Garvey Hall has been banished from the picturesque side of

campus. The Humanities Department has been exiled from the college green, pushed down the hill and up against an abandoned housing project. It is the most unpopular postcard in the campus bookstore. When the students write dispatches back home, they first select postcards of Dubois Hall or the bronze statue in MLK Plaza striding forward and pointing North. Then go cards of the Klan Bell. The Business Department. The Student Center. The Post Office. The Parking Deck. But there is always a surplus of Garvey Hall postcards stuck together at the bottom of the rack. Travis heads down the hill and makes his way over to the liberal arts. They are all shoehorned into the small building: History. English. Music. Art. Philosophy. Foreign Languages—and it's a tight fit. The supply closets are dedicated for office space, these days.

A construction project blocks his route, and it's a big one. A great hole has been chewed from the earth and a chain link fence erected around. Through the wire diamonds: a geology lesson. Sediment changes colors from dark to light, brown earth to red clay, as the strata offer clues to what came before. A Caterpillar excavator scoops dirt, the arm swings, and the load pours into a dump truck bed. A sign on the fence says "Hard Hat Area," and everyone in the pit is following the rules. Four men in yellow hard hats goldbrick over by the front end loader, orange vests hanging open. Travis takes in the construction drama as he skirts the fence to go around. They're building something big here. Whatever it is will dwarf the adjacent humanities building.

Garvey Hall looks like an insect, a big brick bug beetling its way up the hill and trying to return to the postcard of the campus green, but its progress has been stymied by poor diet and lack of exercise and it can't escape the backwash of holly bushes. The bug's head is a theater auditorium, thin windows vertical and two stories tall. The entranceway neck is made of glass and attached to a bloated thorax and abdomen of classrooms and offices. On the roof, men shout to each other in Spanish. Mariachi music adds a happy note as they operate around a roofing kettle of hot tar. Travis wrinkles his nose at the smell and imagines that they are defending the humanities disciplines under siege and keeping watch for the next assault, vats of boiling pitch ready to dump the molten load onto attackers below.

He hustles into the neck of the bug. The hinge on the door is busted and the door slams hard behind him. The glass rattles. In the hallway, the light diminishes as it goes. Fluorescent tubes above are in need of replacement. His worn but freshly polished loafers squeak all the way up the stairwell to the top floor. Do squeaking shoes portend good luck or bad? He can't remember. He is calmer now. Relaxed, even. He is ready. Around the corner, the Chair of the History Department stands beneath an analog clock mounted above a classroom door. Dr. Davis looks exactly like she sounded on the telephone the day before. A diminutive black woman on the gray side of middle age, she is professionally dressed in autumn fashion.

"Did you enjoy the campus, Mr. Hemperly?"

"There is certainly a lot of history here. Thank you for the map."

"No, no," she holds up a flat hand. "You can keep that. I'm sure you noticed the construction." She pulls the door to the classroom open. "Across the parking lot? That will be the new Humanities Tower," she beams.

"Really? That's impressive."

"And long overdue," she adds in collegial commiseration as she gestures inside. Travis says after you but she insists, so he inhales slowly, looks for his center, and enters.

Sunlight dwindles through window glass on the far wall, and the classroom looks drab and neglected like they always do, slowly breaking down as they always are. A few ceiling tiles knocked out of square. Cinder block walls a dehydrated urine, with smudges and scrapes from the usual student abuse, the careless damage from daredevils leaning back in their chairs. Four student desks have been pulled from the ranks and placed before the teacher's desk up front, center stage. They are arranged in confederation against a lone wooden chair, *Propty of Garvey Hall* stenciled on the back. The hot seat, Travis thinks and tamps down the urge for a smoke. He tries to get a feel for the rhythm of the room, but there is no rhythm.

The day before, his telephone conversation with Dr. Davis had been short and to the point. Was he available for an interview tomorrow at ten? The position was a one year non-tenure track appointment, she clarified and apologized for the short notice.

Like most of the faculty, she had left town during the Olympic debacle—the college having canceled summer classes to host the event—and she'd just returned to find a stack of messages on her desk: directives from administration, invitations to exotic conferences out-of-state. And on top of the pile, a curtly-worded resignation letter ("Dear Dr. Davis, I quit."). This was bad news, schedule-wise. Four fall classes were suddenly unstaffed, and the semester began in two weeks. She had to find a replacement immediately. As fortune would and did have it, Travis's application letter and curriculum vita were next on the pile. "Travis Hemperly" sounded like an Anglo name. Dr. Kalamari wouldn't like it, but why not a little diversity? She reached for the phone.

Outside the windows, the construction site fills the glass with a panorama of grinding and banging. The dump truck beeps as it backs up, audible above the noisy window unit, which could use some freon. It's set on High Cool, yet the air rattling from the grill is tepid at best. On the phone, the chair had explained in a way that sounded like an apology that the college was investing in the humanities. The new provost was an economist, she'd said, and he intended to bring the logic of the marketplace to the college. He understood the importance of the liberal arts, as the construction outside demonstrated.

Three members of the History Department faculty have answered the chair's call and made it in for the interview. None of them seem happy to be here. A heavy black man—300 pounds at least—leans against the teacher's desk before the green blackboard. He is casually outfitted in monochrome: a gold velour jogging suit with a racing stripe on each leg to suggest athleticism. A thin woman in denim dress and salt-and-pepper hair sits upright in a student desk. Beside her, a rumpled man with white hair and a hook nose stares blankly out the window. When Travis enters the room, all heads turn. The heavy man stands, and the desk creaks in thanks. Introductions are made all around, greetings and handshakes all around, and Travis curses the fourth cup of coffee he poured before making the drive from the fleabag hotel, tries to hide the tremor in his hand by holding it low for handshakes. Dr. Longman in the gold, Tigony in the denim dress, and Klein with the beard. He repeats the names in his head and hopes that they stick. Firm protestant handshakes all around.

"You must excuse the disarray, Mr. Hemperly," Dr. Davis says. "The Olympic Games have taken over everything. All will be in order before classes begin, of course." She apologizes again for the poor turnout.

Longman's stomach rumbles. "Excuse me," he pats his golden belly. "My new diet disagrees with me." His stomach complains again.

The chair offers the chair. "Please," she says. Travis sits, his back straight and feet firmly on the floor. This is it. On the corkboard square behind the inquisitor's row, a thumbtacked flier announces study abroad opportunities in Europe. A blonde girl, an Asian boy, and a black or perhaps Hispanic student of indeterminate gender smile shoulder-to-shoulder below the Eiffel Tower. Telephone numbers have been torn from convenient tabs. His chair wobbles back then forward on uneven legs, as the others take their seats. For a moment there is only the acrid smell of hot tar. Footsteps pad above the ceiling. He wonders if the roofing crew is hiring.

Dr. Davis settles into a desk beside the others and gets down to it. "First, thank you for coming in on such short notice."

"I appreciate the interview."

He expects to begin with an opening statement, but it doesn't go that way. Klein starts off with a leading question. "Mr. Hemperly, you come to us from the University of Minnesota?" Travis leans forward and touts his alma mater. He tries to use his body language to advantage, sits up straight in the chair, dismisses his natural urge to slouch, but isn't so rigid as to appear uncomfortable. Then he leans forward to show forthright interest. Klein looks down at papers on his desktop. Each of them has a copy of Travis's CV, which is notable for its thinness. His eyes dart, and his cheeks flush. He has recorded his accomplishments as fetchingly as possible, has highlighted his contribution to the discipline of Viking studies and shined light on his budding expertise, but he is at the bottom of his field and has inflated his resume accordingly.

"Tell us about your dissertation," Longman jumps in. A volley from Travis's left flank. This is a well-defended position, and he counters easily. His dissertation charts the Viking Diaspora and catalogues the spread of the Viking peoples across the globe. There are nods all around at this, a point scored in his favor, and he begins to relax. He is in his element, after all. They are all scholars of history come together in their natural habitat. Sharing historical areas, particularly when well-articulated, creates a bonding effect. How far from completion is your dissertation? When do you anticipate completing your doctorate? He's made great advances recently and, while it's always a challenge to find time to write (sympathetic nods to this), he hopes to have a completed manuscript by this time next year. He pinches his nose to hide any sudden spurt of growth.

"And what is . . . L'Anse Aux Meadows?" Klein asks. "I'm not familiar with that institution."

"L'Anse Aux Meadows is a research environment on the coast of Newfoundland," Travis says. "It's an archaeological site preserving and protecting the location where the Norse peoples, the Vikings, arrived on the North American continent." He details the dynamic educational space. The settlement provided him access to an interactive teaching laboratory, a unique opportunity for hands-on education for both student and teacher. "It allowed me to continue my research in the field and was a most enriching opportunity," he nods effusively and milks all he can from the year he spent as a tour guide at a tourist trap.

At the beginning of the previous academic year, there were no teaching jobs available, or at least none for him. The University of Michigan was tightening its belt, and his instructor's position had been eliminated overnight. The notification in his mailbox explained that they had appreciated his service and he was to leave his office key with the department's administrative assistant. Three years and thousands invested into pursuing his degree, and there he was, out on the street. He'd heard stories of peers with newly minted doctoral degrees taking positions in the food service industry. Can I take your order, Ma'am? Travis was stubborn and refused to surrender. Academia didn't want him? Okay. He'd find a way to use his book learning, anyway. He packed-up and left the U.S. for a Canadian work visa and became a re-enactor at the first Viking settlement in North America. L'Anse Aux Meadows was the windy, rocky knob where Leif Erickson beat Columbus to the New World to become the first invader from Europe. Now, a thousand years later, the settlement had been recreated by archaeologists and the Canadian Tourism Commission—and they were hiring Vikings. His hair already grown long as a cost-cutting strategy, he stopped shaving too and spent the past academic year in period costume, lecturing anyone who would listen about the Viking Age and pointing the way to the rest rooms. The tourists were Canadians and Europeans, mostly. Lots of Fair-haired Swedes who mistakenly believed that the settlement had been founded by their ancestors. He was always quick to correct this error: Norwegian Vikings made the discovery. Swedish Vikings went east to Russia—but the tourists never seemed to appreciate this clarification. "I was fortunate to have the opportunity to participate at the Center," he plays it up a little more.

The interrogation returns to the University of Minnesota. They discuss his teaching philosophy, and his experience at the archaeological site goes over big here. He is a dynamic educator, and he rejects dry doctrinaire lectures for participatory exercises. He introduces his students to the World Wide Web—it's the future, after all. His buzzwords sit in their proper order and wave flirtatiously.

Tigony leans forward, eyes narrowing. "Have you ever taught an African American student?"

This one was to be expected, of course. There weren't many black students at UM. There weren't any black tourists at L'Anse aux Meadows. Something deep inside him releases oil. He thinks *not many* but says *of course*. Every instructor must be sensitive to the cultural realities that each student brings into the classroom.

"Are you familiar with the learning styles of different students?" she presses.

Yes, certainly, he says. Every student has his own method of learning, and this must be taken into account for successful pedagogy. This is a basic philosophy of effective teaching, in his opinion. She smiles at his answer approvingly. He sits up and the back of the chair jams into his shoulder blade. The interview is winding-down. He can sense the energy dropping and lets his guard down.

"Mr. Hemperly," Longman clears his throat. "How do you teach the origin of civilization?" Travis senses a loaded question. For a moment, he is inert. His chair wobbles. They all lean forward. Tigony's eyes narrow.

"I don't understand the question," he says. "Nile River valley? Is that what you mean?" His heart rate quickens. Fight-or-flight kicks in. So close. So close.

Dr. Davis speaks up. "Could you please give us a few minutes, Mr. Hemperly?"

And that's it. Klein crosses his arms. Tigony wipes her nose. Longman looks at the floor. Davis stands up. She thanks him again for coming. Would he please wait in the lobby across the hall? Travis doesn't realize that he's falling from the wall until it's too late. Elbowed from behind, knocked from his perch, he is an omelet in the making. Below, the king's men try in vain to calm their restless mounts. Gravity gets its grip. There is nowhere to go but down.

*T*he cinder block walls in the lobby are unblemished by decor or personality. Branching off of the main hall, the small room is Un-. Unoccupied. Undecorated. Uninspiring. Unremarkable. Unseemly, even. The only furniture, a connected section of seating from the Olympic Stadium, logo rings molded into the seat backs. If need be, the History Department could pack-up and clear out in fifteen minutes, leaving few clues: a paper clip wedged between the carpet and baseboard. Tiny scraps of maroon paper. A few fingernails, crudely cut. On the wall above the row of seats, a framed cork-board makes no announcements. Someone has fooled around with the thumbtacks and arranged them into a smiley face. Two red thumbtack eyes and a red thumbtack smile, its grin a mouthful of broken teeth. Travis sits on a stadium seat and waits for the blow off. Thanks for coming in. We'll call you. His insides writhe in gurgling turmoil. In the fixture overhead, all the fluorescent tubes are functional, and the harsh light glares on everything. His interrogators have reconvened in the chair's office, right over there, not twenty feet away. He channels all his thought into hope for a positive outcome and aims it at the solid core door, trying to pierce the veneer, plywood, and ultimately the skulls of the interview committee and sway the discussion in his favor. Disasters are averted at the last second all the time. The speeding truck misses the child on the sled. The right wire is cut on the ticking bomb. He has never been much of a clairvoyant. He's just catastrophizing, he thinks, and it isn't long before the door opens. Klein strides over, arm extended. Tigony behind in poker face.

"A pleasure meeting you," Klein avoids eye contact.

"Yes, a pleasure," Tigony says. They seem sincere enough, Travis thinks.

Behind him, Longman looks like he's put on a few pounds since the interview. "I'll see you next week, Dan." He waves at Klein's back retreating down the hallway, hitches up his pants, and walks over.

The big man leans over face-to-face and winks conspiratorially. "Looks like I have a new office mate. Welcome to Blackademia." And the angels begin to sing, all of them on-key. He has returned to the academy. Best not to react to the blackademia crack, he thinks, so he doesn't.

Suddenly, noise out in the hallway: footfalls echo in the stairwell and then on the hallway linoleum, coming fast. Heavy boots stamping closer. Longman looks toward the commotion and steps backwards to clear the doorway.

A thin black man bursts into the room, dreadlocks stuffed into a knit hat of black, red, and green yarn, the colors of Afrikan revolution. He is dressed for combat from the waist down. His desert camo BDU's are bunched up at his knobby knees. Keys jangle from a string of carabiners dangling from a belt loop.

Longman greets him by title, stands in deference and smiles, but the tardy prof makes only the slightest acknowledgment of his presence, barely a nod. He ignores Tigony and Travis altogether, bustles past in a bee-line to the chair's office, stops abruptly and raises a fist to knock, thinks better of it (apparently) and grabs the door knob.

Travis could sure use that smoke about now. Perhaps there is an emergency? The speedy man barges into the office and slams the door behind him. The cinder block walls and solid core door do their job and muffle all the words, but Travis tries to listen anyway. He leans forward, head cocked in obvious eavesdropping stance. The conversation appears to be one-sided. Tigony flees the lobby. Longman looks up at the ceiling and whistles a ditty at the acoustic ceiling tile. An explanation is appropriate here, Travis thinks, and he tries to catch Longman's eye, but he doesn't accommodate until the awkwardness between them inflates to bursting.

"That was Dr. Kalamari," he finally says, then, just as abruptly, "It was good to meet you. I'll see you next week." Travis blinks, and Longman is gone. He moves fast for such a big man.

The door opens abruptly and Kalamari stands with one hand on the doorknob, half in and half out of the office, both coming and going. He is loud and clear now and complains stridently about Atlanta's rapid transit system. A late bus has caused him to miss the interview, and he insists that they hold another one with him in attendance. The chair raises her voice and demands professionalism. Kalamari stiffens, turns and slams the door behind him. He stands with back toward the office, exhales and balls a trembling fist, then takes notice of Travis for the first time. Keys jingle as he walks over. He looks Travis in the eye. "Welcome, my

European brother." He extends a fist, fingers balled.

Travis stands up, perplexed by the greeting. He's never been to Europe. He considers Kalamari's fist and thinks: Rock, Scissors, Paper?

"Travis Hemperly," he presents himself and offers his hand. There is an awkward moment between them, and then Kalamari daps Travis's protruding thumb, tapping it on the tip.

"Kalamari," Kalamari appraises him with a disappointed down-up glance.

Chapter Two

*I*t's moving day, and bad weather has rolled in from Alabama. The dark clouds are everywhere and cover the apartment building in shadow. It's not raining yet, but just wait. Travis has unhitched the tow dolly with the beater Volvo, backed the U-Haul close to the foyer door, and gotten to the strenuous business of unloading everything he owns. A droning in the background grows louder, and suddenly there's a commotion coming closer. He stops untying the mattress and looks up. The helicopter isn't wasting any time. It's over there above the cotton mill, passes between the two brick smokestacks and buzzes straight toward him. It flies so low that it must be flouting an air traffic law, he thinks, but hey, it's the cops. When directly overhead, it banks, curves, and begins to circle. He gets back to work, drags the mattress forward and down the corrugated ramp hooked below the U-Haul's square maw, puts his shoulder into it and tips it into the state of Minnesota painted on the side of the truck. *Some welcome*, he thinks, profiled from the sky just for moving his things. Or maybe they're not here for him. It's a shabby neighborhood. Maybe they're trying to flush out a perp, someone on the run and sneaking through the hood, sticking to the shadows between the close buildings even now, making his way through the untended azalea hedge at this very moment, handgun drawn.

He steps back onto the ramp and tries to make a show of it and look like the honest citizen he is. I'm pulling the furniture *out*, see? He is a taxpayer. He has a job—even if he won't see his first paycheck for a month. Fall semester at the college begins in a few days, and he's got a lot to do.

The sinister clouds make him prioritize. Wait on the couch and the clothes. If it starts to rain, they'll dry out, but his books will get ruined. Mattress first, books next. They are alphabetized and tightly packed into overloaded cardboard boxes he collected from a NLC store in Saint Anthony (top-shelf vodkas, cheap Romanian wines). All of his clothes are piled into a mound on the smoky couch cushions, hangers tangled. They serve an important function: his television is wedged between the pile of clothes and the fabric arm of the couch, and they have held it securely from Canada to Atlanta. This is the TV set that he bought for fifty bucks from the trunk of a late model Monte Carlo in a strip mall parking lot in Minneapolis. There was no remote, but still. The metal ramp creaks as he walks back up and grabs the side of the mattress. He pulls hard, then harder. Fabric rips. He's accustomed to living in neighborhoods on the skids. Sure, he'd rather not live in a low income / high crime community, but the hype of the Olympic Games hiked apartment prices through the roof and this was the only one he could find that met his price point. This latest residence is a three story brick cube, notable only for its lack of architectural charm. It seems like some kind of zoning failure, jammed between the dilapidated shotgun houses flanking the street. Burglar bars are bolted across the window panes on both the first and second levels. The thieves here must use ladders.

The foyer door is propped open with a cinder block, and it's dark inside. The bulb is bad or the switch is dead, and the unlit stairwell threatens. Obstacles wait in the darkness to trip him up: a reel mower, a bail of rebar, a big box full of boxes. His apartment is at the top of the stairwell. Dragging the mattress up the steps will tear it up even more. He is accustomed to moving alone, has gotten good at it over the years, but this time he could use a little help. He only knows two names in the phone book, however, and neither seem appealing. After Charlie drowned, the family split apart, and the only Hemperlys left in the city are his grandmother and his father. He considers the pay phone on the sidewalk, its blue shell defaced with nonsense graffiti. At 96, he wouldn't feel right about asking her. That left his father. After the long drive from Canada, when the U-Haul passed underneath the perimeter highway and closed in on downtown, Travis tuned in to the turbulent rhetoric of AM radio. Henry Hemperly's voice filled the cab of the truck with the same strident tone he'd always had, even before he got into the talk radio business. Five years and it hadn't changed a note. He was worked up to chest-poking speed about the day's topic, which was, ironically, a historical one: Before the Emancipation Proclamation, female slaves seduced their white masters to improve the gene pool of the black African race. They continued this after slavery, through the rest of the 19th century and across the 20th, and they were doing it to this day. And he was taking callers.

"Hello, Henry, and thanks again for all you do. I listen to your show every day."

"Why, thank you."

Travis frowns at the voice.

"I just wanted to say right-on about this. I mean, I work with some black guys, and don't get me wrong, they're good guys and all. They're not always down on the white man like some are. But sometimes they say things like all black women back then got pregnant being raped. That's just stupid. I mean, slavery was a terrible thing, no doubt. Don't get me wrong. My great-grand-father was in the 8th Ohio at Gettysburg. Not to say anything against the Confederacy. But you know that some of them saw it as a way up. I mean, it was just how it was."

"That's very perceptive of you," his father flattered.

"But, but if you say this sort of thing out loud, they call you a racist."

It wasn't much of a discussion. All of the callers agreed with Henry's explanation for miscegenation. Travis turned the radio off. Old times here were not forgotten. He looked away.

Thunder rumbles up in the clouds, and Travis' shoulders sag as he decides against calling for help. Let it rain. He drags the mattress out and down, balancing the whole of it with his arms spread wide. And then a voice breaks in, someone on the other side of the fabric yelling over the noise of the circling helicopter.

"Hey big man, you need a hand?"

Travis peeks around the edge of the box springs. A beefy, bald white guy in white T-shirt and jeans stands on the other side of the ramp. His arms are decorated with tattoos. Hands, too. His septum is pierced with fierce stainless steel: a thick circular barbell curves beneath his nostrils. He looks up and squints.

"Fuck the police, huh?"

He presents his middle finger, raises it in defiance, and flips off the Atlanta Police Department. Then he takes a long, thirsty look inside the back of the U-Haul. Travis wonders if this is the guy the helicopter is looking for. "I could use a hand getting this upstairs," Travis shouts over the noisy chopper and nods at the mattress. His new neighbor grabs a corner and welcomes him to the neighborhood. Travis can't place his Southern accent.

"Let's go, buddy." The skinhead lifts the close end. At the top of the stair, they duck-walk into the empty apartment. Travis sets his end down on the stained carpet and introduces himself.

"Travis." He extends a hand.

The skinhead looks at it as if confused by the gesture. After a beat, he reaches out. His grip is surprisingly weak, and he doesn't meet Travis' eye.

They call him Rhett, he says. Travis leans the mattress against the nearest wall and takes in the sorry paint job. Whoever did the turnaround doesn't enjoy the work. The roller pattern covers the expanse poorly, and the paint is so watered down it doesn't cover the previous tenant's smell. Rhett seems interested in the place, however. He walks over to the picture window at the front of the room and stops underneath the water damage on the ceiling. "You've sure got a good view of the mill from here." And he does. The abandoned cotton mill is framed in the center of the wide windowpane, an enormous brick building falling apart beside the freight yard. Behind it, two smokestacks stand tall.

"Mind if I look around?" Rhett says, walking past Travis and looking around. "I've never been in this one. The crazy fucker who lived here before drank gin and listened to gospel music all day long. That's all he did. Some Appalachian throwback. All these people here are related, inbred motherfuckers. Hey! You've got a bigger kitchen than me and my old lady. And man, look at your refrigerator. We had to use a cooler last month before that asshole landlord found that wrecked piece of junk we've got in there now."

Travis works a quick equation involving first impressions and salty language, ignores the running commentary and walks to the front of the room. He slides the window open and hopes for fresh air. The helicopter has gone, its noisy racket replaced by the rushing traffic on I-20. The clouds overhead are particularly dark. There's a flash of cloud-to-cloud lightning and then a crack of thunder so loud it makes the floor shake.

"Hey, dude, looks like you've got a roach problem."

"Thanks for helping, Rhett," Travis says and explains that he needs to get back to work and finish the job before the rain begins.

Rhett steps back into the room, all questions now: Who'd he deal with at the rental office? What does he pay for rent? When does his lease run out? Where is he from? Why did he move to the city? He sure is a chatty skinhead, Travis thinks, and not so easy to get rid of. Rhett keeps it up. You're a teacher? No shit. What grade? Where at?

When it comes to this last question, Travis hesitates. They are two different sorts of people, Rhett and he. He doesn't know how the skinhead is oriented to the black community but recalls that there's an element of White Supremacy to their tribe. This could be a problem. He tells him where he is on faculty and wonders if he'll recognize the name. Rhett appraises him with new interest and smooths an eyelash thoughtfully.

"You don't look black to me."

"I just started." Travis shrugs.

"Well, goddamn. How long have you been teaching?"

Suddenly all the neighborly curiosity now just seems like the stalling that it is. The back of the U-Haul is wide open and he's been gone too long. Travis thanks him again for the help, but he's got to get back to it, he says and heads for he door. Through the open window, more thunder rumbles. "It's getting late. I've got a lot to unload before it rains."

Rhett chases him into the stairwell. "Hold up, dude. Hold up." Travis takes the stairs two at a time, inserting distance. Outside, it's beginning to sprinkle. Raindrops spot the parking lot in a pattern that increases. He hurries to the back of the U-Haul, looks over everything. It's all here. No, wait. There's a blank space on the couch next to his bunched up clothes.

"My television!" he shouts, elbows up, both hands grabbing hair. "Someone stole my television!"

Rhett walks up behind. "Huh," he shakes his bald head in unconvincing sympathy. "That sucks. You need to be on-point around here, bro."

Travis's thoughts scatter like spilled marbles. My television, he thinks, my TV, and feels the loss deeply. All of a sudden, everything in the parking lot seems threatening. The rain begins to fall harder. To hell with it, he thinks. I'll lock the back and finish unloading in the morning—a solid plan on paper, the U-haul has a hasp and latch on the roll up door, but a combination lock wasn't included in the deal.. He is back to a familiar problem: he's is in a rundown neighborhood in the middle of a large city, and there's no place to shop close by. It's always a drive.

He glares at his tattooed neighbor/thief and asks if he knows where he can buy a combination lock.

"There's a Super Store in the Value Village down Memorial drive. I'm sure they'll have one—if you don't mind all the niggers."

Well, there it is. In a narrative about the South, this incendiary expletive had to show up sooner or later. Best to go on and get it out of the way. The words tumble from Rhett's mouth one-by-one, each of them evaporating in sequence--except for the one, of course. The bad word, pluralized as it has been, expands and not so much diffuses like a bad smell but swells and spreads as if trying to gain purchase and find increase, seeking and causing action and reaction as it does. Now that it is out and about, it begs a response of some kind from Travis—even if it's a non-response—and Rhett is waiting for it. He has only known this tattooed skinhead for a few minutes. Was this a provocative word choice or well-worn noun from his everyday vocabulary? There's no way to know, and does it even matter? He blinks and considers. His new employment status has reoriented him toward the word and now it demands more assessment, this problematic noun, this ugly adjective, this N-word, this creator of offense and conflict and argument and blood and camaraderie and warning labels and increased ratings.

*T*ravis would rather take the beater Volvo, but his new neighbors would surely have the back of the truck cleaned out before he could return with a combination lock, so he leaves the dirty gray car on the tow dolly and drives the U-Haul east in the rain. It's still light enough to read the historic markers sprouting along Memorial Drive. *Attack From The West. McPherson's Last Ride. An Unexpected Clash.* Few details come to mind about the battle, however. The Confederates lost. The city fell.

Considering the surroundings, the old state road isn't much of a memorial. The battlefield pastures and sniper forests have become more a commemoration to urban blight than the American Civil War. Empty apartment buildings dissolve into the weeds, their windows boarded up with plywood. A succession of strip malls are dedicated to ghetto commerce. Establishments cater to a clientele who purchase cigarettes individually and pay in coin. Buy Here Pay Here Auto. JD's Beauty Supply Wigs Beepers. Super Fried Rice and Shoe Time all have empty parking lots, but it's a walking community by the look of it. At every bus stop, black people wait in the drizzle—African Americans, he revises and reminds himself to upgrade his vocabulary in this regard. On a billboard across the street, the cartoon mascot of the Olympic Games—what is that thing?—marches with plucky determination over to the adjoining billboard and inspects a snarling rapper's expensive dental work.

Rhett was true to his word when he said Travis couldn't miss the Value Village. It is an enormous strip mall up ahead on the right, neon sign blazing. The asphalt parking lot is vast, and there are plenty of places to park. The centerpiece of the strip mall is the Super Store, an immense building, square footage-wise. It dwarfs both LaShaun's Video-Fingernails and Bobo's Big and Tall that bookend either side. Why on earth did they build this here? He wonders. It seems a very bad investment by an overly optimistic entrepreneur. The Olympic Games must have had a hand in it.

Travis parks the U-Haul underneath a light pole, locks the cab behind him, and runs through the rain toward the welcoming glass doors, the bright light inside beaconing dry comfort. Next to one of the pillars out front, an old black man (African American. African American.) holds a Styrofoam cup in his hand. White hair. White beard. Wide-brimmed hat that's seen hard times. Rumpled button-down. Threadbare vest. Patched pants and a rope for a belt. It's a sad thing to see someone his age having to beg, he thinks. The old man mumbles lippity-clippity, clippity-lippity in a conversation Travis can't understand. His tipped cup is a universal code, however. Travis slides a hand into pocket and digs for change, scoops the coins, and drops the Canadian currency into the cup. "That's all I've got," he says, which is true. He hustles toward the entrance and the old man doffs his hat and gets back to mumbling.

The automatic doors slide, and the pressure change makes his ears pop. The enormity of the place makes him stop dead center in the doorway. It's larger than any store he's ever been inside of or even imagined. They could build airliners in here, he thinks. They could build another building in here. His mind is boggled and he doesn't know where to begin. He stands on the mat and blocks the way inside, until a nudge at his back as a heavy woman in a wig encourages him with her shopping cart. As his new neighbor rudely suggested, all of the customers are indeed African American. He is new to this, being the only white person in the room, and it makes him self-conscious. Despite the empty parking lot, the place is full of shoppers. He wonders if they are taking note of his race. No one stares, but still. More shoppers come in behind and encourage him forward, and he is pushed into the store.

Where to begin? This store is so large he could walk the aisles for an hour and still miss what he needs. There must be an information counter around here, somewhere, and once he finds it the helpful associate provides directions. He follows them the best he can: past the motorcycles, next to Nursery/Baby Care, left at the food court and down past house parts. He turns the corner, and there they are, a wall full of combination locks of every size and color. There is a padlock for every purpose. Secure your home, protect your belongings, place a lock on everything you own. There are too many of them, he thinks, too big a selection. It makes him feel uncomfortable. The confusion makes him cross his arms as he scans the wall. Presently another cart turns the corner and moves down the aisle toward him, and he notices right away that the shopper is white. A beat later he recognizes her face.

Of all the things he would have expected to happen next, this would have been the last. It's been, what? Ten years? She was a vision from his undergraduate years at the University of Georgia. They'd met in that auditorium class on 18th Century British Death Notices. She was an English major and unlike any woman he had ever met. She was a poet, she had the soul of a poet, she had explained—although she wasn't into publication. Together they'd had only one meeting that would meet the standard of romance (and even then, only tentatively), he feels his heart thumping in his chest.

Suddenly, he is transported from the houseware section to the quad before the library, lying on his belly in the grass and listening to her read "The Love Song of J. Alfred Prufrock" beneath a water oak, one hand on a page of the literary anthology, another gesturing in dramatic, if meaningless, punctuation, giving it her all as students lugged their book bags up and down the green. After the T. S. Eliot cover poem she switched to one of her own works, reciting an ode to the darting squirrels. Travis was smitten:

> *Over in the weedy cemetery*
> *Behind the church tower belfry*
> *The headstones jut up through the dust*
> *Monuments of lives turned to rust*
> *I kneeled before her grave*
> *The mother I was unable to save.*
> *And as the wind blew throughout the land*
> *A daisy reached up and shook my hand.*

Her eyes shined, welling up with tears. She was so good. A

breeze lifted strands of her hair, orange leaves rattled past, and her words touched his heart. He didn't understand it but was mesmerized anyway, and something new clicked into place. His life had changed, even if it hadn't worked out.

And now here she is, the poet ten years later. She looks exactly the same. Her face is a little thinner, maybe. A shock of gray at her widow's peak. Her jet-black hair is pulled back into a high ponytail, just like she used to wear it. Travis is immediately aware of his belly overlapping his belt. His sketchy diet has altered his body over the years. Will she remember me? He sucks in his gut. She doesn't notice him and in fact looks sedated as she leans forward and pushes the cart slowly, her arms crossed on the grab rail.

He takes a step closer. "Margarette Ragsdale."

She looks up. Her eyes puzzle and then focus.

"Travis Hemperly," she says and then comes a sly smile.

She hugs him, both hands around his back. Her face is hot. Her ring finger is unadorned. There is not a thing on it, nothing to indicate a significant other waiting at home with the kids, only a silver ring on her middle finger, a platinum bat with wings wide. The bat signal comes to mind. It complements the look of her black blouse and long black skirt, flowing. In her shopping cart: tapered candles, a single goldfish in a plastic bag fat with water, and underneath, a hundred pound bag of dog food. And she has changed her name, she says. She is Meggan, now. He snatches the nearest Master Lock, goes with the moment, and falls in beside her. They walk the aisles together, make small talk and catch up as people do. Did you see any of the Olympics? A few, she said. Freebie tickets to the lesser events were easy enough to come by. No, she hadn't married. Travis cannot believe his luck, and he forgets to inhale now and then, running out of breath awkwardly. They check out together and he shoulders the big bag of dog food, both acting the gentleman and trying to make it look like an easy lift. They stroll out side by side, pushing the cart together. The rain has let up and Meggan points out her car in the lot. The old panhandler still stands beside the pillar, and when they get to him, he raises the Styrofoam cup.

"He'p ole Remus dis ebnin', Miss mam?"

Meggan pulls a folded bill from her cleavage and gives him a smile as she drops it in. The old man tips his hat and gives Travis the stink eye.

Chapter Three

*I*t's late. Travis snores on his back in the middle of the mattress on the bedroom floor, covers pulled close for protection, when a crash from the living room brings him back to awareness. Wood cracks and splinters as the deadbolt gives way and the door jamb breaks. The door itself swings wide and hits the wall, the brass plate knob punching a hole in the drywall. He struggles to move and tries to get up, but he can't. He can't even open his eyes, can't raise his eyelids, although he gives it a mighty effort. Footsteps pound into the apartment, coming closer. Lots of them, two, three, four intruders not bothering to be quiet about it. They go for the boxes, snatch the duct tape from the cardboard and his library spills out. If he survives, he'll have to re-alphabetize the books they leave behind. Are they looking for the hard copy of his dissertation manuscript? They're in the kitchen, rifling through the refrigerator. What a disappointment that must be. And Meggan is there, too, standing over by the light switch and flipping it. Lights on. Lights off. Lights on. How'd she get here? The intruders are louder now and closer. They'll reach the bedroom in a matter of seconds, stab him, shoot him, hit him in the head with a tire iron. He tries again to wake up, puts everything he has into it, tries to roll off of the bed and hide behind it, but he still can't move. Thunder rumbles and then the flash. He tries to yell, to scream for help, but only a small sound comes out—a little rattle of breath that barely carries. This is it. He is going to die, murdered in his own bed, having moved into one sketchy neighborhood too many. How disappointing to have this happen, just as the warm Southern sun was starting to shine on him. His return to academia. Running into Meggan. Sorrow swells. Such a loss, he thinks. The profound sadness of it all follows him back down.

Chapter Four

My, oh my, Remus thinks. *What a wonderful day*—and certainly it is, with the sky big and blue and not a cloud in it. On the power line over the street, two bluebirds chatter and whistle, wishing him a happy good morning. He looks over their way and smiles broadly, his remaining teeth on display. "How y'all doing this mawnin'?"

Remus has returned to Mr. Chandler's house like he does every once in a while. He left the Union Mission first thing in the morning, but it took him some time to walk over. He waits in the small parking lot across from the Wren's Nest, Styrofoam cup in hand. His joints are stiff after the long walk, but he's an old man, after all. The people are just beginning to get out and about the West End of town, going to work or just going. A MARTA bus grinds past, rolling towards the skyscrapers downtown. On a sunny day like today, it's hard not to whistle a happy tune, and so he does. Plenty of sunshine is heading his way.

The lot is mostly empty, two cars side-by-side and facing the street. Two cars means two drivers and no telling how many children. Folks bring their little ones to the Wren's Nest to listen to Remus tell his stories—although they won't actually let him to do the telling, anymore. They won't even let him on the grounds. Ever since the restraining order, he can't get any closer than the parking lot right here, so he stays put. Living on the street has made him a patient man. Standing and waiting is what he mostly does. His Styrofoam cup is empty except for the Canadian coins they didn't take at the shelter. He bides his time until the children get their fill of Brer Rabbit playing his tricks, waits for the parents to bring them down the front porch steps and back over here to their cars.

These days, a new crop of storytellers tell his tales. There's one of them over in the parlor across the street right now, telling the children about Brer Rabbit and Brer Fox and all the critters. He's heard them do it, too, listened to how they say what they say he said. They mean well, he knows this. They don't mean any disrespect, but they just don't do it right. They don't get the words right. They done cleaned up his grammar, too. But he takes it all in stride—how could he not on such a beautiful day?

Mr. Chandler's house is a museum now, and it's never looked better—and who would know this if not Remus? The Wren's Nest is not as famous as it used to be, either. They fixed it up for those games, painted it and fixed the broken stairs. Gave it a new roof, too. The little cottage is set back from the street, and doesn't it look cheerful with the sun dappling the latticework on the porch? It's always been a happy house. All the joy that has come from this home, no wonder people still come to visit. He misses telling the stories, Brer Rabbit going down the road lippity-clippity. Brer Fox waiting in the shadows. The Tar Baby sitting on his log. He hasn't seen them in he doesn't know how long. It's a wonder where they got off to.

After freedom time, Mr. Chandler wrote all Remus' tales down for the newspaper. Before Remus knew it, everyone knew who he was. They even used to tell about him to the children in the schools. Who wouldn't like that? He'd even come across his own face from time to time, set up on some sign or a picture drawing in the newspaper. Every time he thinks back and remembers, he gets a warm feeling, but when he really puts his mind to it, to how he can be standing right here in this parking lot on this sunny day and at the same time be across the street and inside the stories themselves, sitting on the cane-bottomed chair and telling the stories to the little boy, he doesn't know what to think. It is confusing.

He's not the only one fallen on hard times. None of them are famous like they used to be—Uncle Ben with his rice, Aunt Jemima with her flapjacks, and that Cream of Wheat waiter with the good teeth. At least they still have their jobs, he thinks. He should have gotten a better agent. At least he had it better than those two cement statues, the grinning boy eating the big watermelon and his brother with the fishing pole. He hadn't seen them for he didn't know how long. The only one he sees anymore is the lawn jockey, and half the time he's been painted white. Remus doesn't have to wait too long before the visitors leave the Wren's Nest house, a white woman carrying a little girl out onto the front porch and two boys following, a black man behind leading his boy by the hand and walking carefully down the steps. The two white boys are being boys. One hits the other and then the chase begins, the taller one running over to the mailbox where the bird used to build its nest, the white lady hollering. She catches up and gives them a piece of her mind then makes them look both ways before they cross the street. Remus calculates and takes a step toward the shiny car, but when she goes for the other, he has to move fast. He's not quick these days, but she has to wrestle with the car seats so he has time to get over.

"Howdy, Mrs. Ma'am," he extends the cup. "He'p ole Remus dis mawnin'?"

She leans into the car and hollers at the boys, who quiet down, their eyes wide at him through the window glass. When she turns, she doesn't look him in the eye and he doesn't look her in the eye, neither. She acts like she's scared of old Remus, and he doesn't know what to think of that. He'd just asked her for a case quarter. She gets into the front seat, opens the console box, and rummages. Here you go she says, her arm out the window, and the coin drops into the cup. Then she tells the boys to lock the doors, and it doesn't take her long to crank the car and leave the lot. And here comes the other visitor. The man and his boy, both of them high yellow and wearing neckties like they were going to church. The boy even wears a coat and has an American flag on the lapel. Remus hustles over to the driver's door of the shiny car and greets them too.

"Nice wedder dis mawnin'," he says, and it is a beautiful day, no one can disagree. He does better on days like today. People are more generous. You think that it'd be the other way around, that when people saw him standing in a rainstorm they'd be more inclined, but almost nobody rolls their window down. The father encourages the little boy, who steps forward and isn't he cute dressed up like that? He reaches into his pants pocket and out comes a coin purse. The boy smiles at him, unbuttons the coin purse, two fingers in, and he drops a case quarter into the cup.

"Much oblige, honey," he smiles. Now he can get a donut down at the Krispy Kreme. Everything is satisfactual. He waves as they back up and drive away, and then he's alone in the parking lot, no people, no cars either, and he begins to whistle. Zip-a-Dee-doo-Dah. And look at that. The two bluebirds on the power line begin to chirp along, fly down from the line and whirl around his head, joining in.

Chapter Five

*T*ravis drives to campus around noon. He peels from the rushing interstate, steers the beater Volvo onto the exit ramp, and coasts toward the traffic signal at the intersection. Seven cars are stopped at the red light. A young black man in a black suit and red bow tie stands in the curb grass, holds up a plastic bag full of fruit and waggles it at the driver's side windows. Bananas, apples, peaches, it looks like. His hair is cut close to his skull, and his glasses have thick black rims. He lifts the bag higher and shakes it at the rolled-up window of the closest car, waits a few seconds then steps toward the next, lifts it up, shakes again, waits, turns, and walks down the line, coming closer. Travis glances up at the traffic signal. It's still red but glows yellow in the cross street lane. The light will change before he arrives, and Travis isn't big on fruit anyway. When it turns to green, the vendor turns away and marches back to the beginning of the line. No takers this time.

Travis drives down the hill and toward the college. Classes begin tomorrow, and his courses remain unplanned, his syllabi unfinished. Students tend to think they are getting their money's worth if given handouts, however, so he's got some printing to do. He'll have to figure out how the History Department works and learn his way around, figure out where his classes are going to be held and how to get to them, that sort of thing. The Volvo glides onto campus. Students with book bags travel the sidewalks and criss-cross the street. Travis becomes aware that everyone within eyesight is black, and he is not. He steers toward the south gate, rolls to a stop at the guard shack and explains that he is a new member of the faculty. The campus cop leans forward, elbows on the half door, and looks him over with a skeptical eye before waving him through. He'll need to get a parking pass before next time, he is told, and a photo ID for proper identification.

The beater Volvo rolls on, taking the speed humps with suspension creaking and chassis bouncing. Travis slows for the jaywalkers and the car creeps alongside Garvey Hall. Again he is aware of his melanin deficiency and wonders if anyone notices that he isn't a person of any color whatsoever, but no one looks at him—and why should they? He's just another car on the road. Still, he feels on display and the race thing is in front of him again. It's best to clear his head of this type of thinking, he thinks. After all, he's got enough to do without adding racial paranoia to the list.

He turns right and rolls slowly along the row of parked cars, but there are no open spaces. The construction site next to the humanities building has eaten most of the parking lot and reduced the available spaces by half. It looks like all the faculty has turned out today, or at least their automobiles have. There sure are a lot of Volvos. A colleague crosses the street before him, a bald man in flowing brown dashiki, and enters Garvey Hall. Travis is wearing Western business attire. The labored knot of his blue necktie is cinched tight, and his haircut is so fresh he still has trimmings on his neckline. He leans over the steering wheel, looks right then left, and drives farther from Garvey than he would like, slowly rolling toward the distant reaches and the no-man's land of student dorm parking—which is jammed full as well. When the beater Volvo comes to the end of the student lot, he takes another lap, circles around for one more pass at the faculty parking. In the boredom of the hunt, his wandering thoughts return to his chance meeting the night before with Margarette. Or Meggan, as she calls herself now. The thought of her makes his heart feel light. If he can't find a place to park near the building, he'll walk. He can use the exercise.

The Humanities building comes around again. The azalea hedges up against the yellow brick need trimming and surround it with rowdy green froth. And look, look, look: there's an open parking space, after all. What luck, he thinks. It is the closest space to the building, too. How'd he miss it before? He turns the steering wheel sharply and claims the spot, parking carefully between the boundary lines.

To his left, the construction fence borders the interrupted sidewalk. Behind it, the pit of dirt is larger than when he had his interview. Excavator treads stamp the earth with overlaid tracks. A front-end loader grinds away at the gash in the ground and fills the air with puffs of diesel exhaust. A stern Do Not Enter sign is wired to the vertical weave of the fence, excess wire woven back and forth through the diamonds. On a big board over by the open gate, a four-color illustration of the new Humanities Tower rises toward fluffy white clouds. Progress, Travis thinks. It is good to see the humanities get their due. He is once again impressed with the size of the construction. The new Humanities Tower will dwarf the surrounding campus buildings, which aren't all that tall to begin with. Four stories, tops. It's hard to tell for sure from the picture, but it looks like the tower will rise up ten stories or more, the design a cross between a skyscraper and a cathedral.

Travis exits the car with an armload of books and looks skyward to where the new building will blot out the sun. He imagines the illustrated neo deco curves and graceful vertical flutes. There is no architectural continuity on the campus. The tower will not fit in at all with the hodge-podge of architectural periods represented by the surrounding buildings, erected during whatever decades the administration could get the funds together. The flat-roofed military barracks of the 1950s. The domed roof of a circular building, something from the '60s designed with an eye toward the space age.

A maroon Volvo rolls up, new and sparkling, and blocks him in. The driver lays on the horn as his window rolls down. Behind the wheel sits a white man with a gray goatee, and Travis feels a sudden racial solidarity that surprises him and brings first a cheerful then an awkward thought. The older man gives him a scowl, his glasses resting on the tip of his nose. The whiskers on his chin are ungroomed. Travis puts a smile on and says good morning.

His new colleague leans his head out of the car window. "That's my parking space," he points a finger, jabbing it at the beater Volvo. He gives Travis a stern look through fashionable frames.

Travis glances back at his car. The space is unmarked, other than the oil stain. He can see no number or letter to indicate that it has been reserved. It occurs to him that his car could use a wash.

"I'm sorry," he steps forward. "I'm a new History Department hire." He shifts the books to one arm and offers a hand. "Travis Hemperly."

"Young man, I've been employed here for thirty-three years. You have parked in my parking space."

A breeze caresses Travis' palm, cooling it with rejected collegiality. Seconds tick by, and after it has been made clear to him that his colleague isn't going to shake, he lowers his hand. "Well, I apologize," he says, his voice faltering. "I wasn't told that there was an assigned parking order."

The unkind professor pulls his head back into his car, and the driver's side window slides up and shuts. The engine of the maroon Volvo revs expectantly. Travis's shoulders droop. This isn't much of a welcome, he thinks. He turns back to his own Volvo feeling both chastened and bruised. The other car backs up to allow him room to exit. Travis backs out, clears the space, and waves as he passes but the driver doubles down on the snub and doesn't respond. The beater Volvo limps back to the student parking lot in defeat. He loops around again, one, two, three times, but there are no empty spaces for him—although he thinks he might be able to squeeze in next to the big green dumpster. It is overflowing with flattened cardboard boxes. The beater Volvo squeezes into the small space. He collects the books from the floorboard, tucks them under his arm, and exits into a stink that makes his nose wrinkle. He has to suck in his gut to squeeze through the door. A slick, rainbow-colored juice leaks from the dumpster's bottom and floods the parking space. There is no way to avoid stepping in the goo.

Inside the glass doors of the humanities building, the air is cool and a little musty. The mildew in the stairwell makes Travis' nose twitch. The History Department has taken over the third floor, squashing the English, Music, Art, Foreign Language and

Philosophy Departments into the two floors beneath. The stairwell echoes all the way up.

Some interior decorating has gone on in the lobby since his interview. There is now a receptionist's desk, although there is nothing on the desktop and no chair, either. On the walls, framed photos of black VIP's are on display, none of them familiar to him. The bulletin board over the stadium seating is still empty, the cork-board still blank. Next to the chair's office door is a portrait of a heavy black man with a fat face. His baroque martial regalia makes him look like a third-world dictator, Travis thinks. And hey, he does recognize these two. Martin Luther King and Malcolm X shake hands in a photo op and share a laugh, chuckling at who-knows-what? The photographer, perhaps. As to the others, he doesn't have a clue. He notes that he needs to return later and study up. His assigned office is down the narrow hallway, and it is easy to find—although it is not his office per se. During the orientation, Dr. Davis had mentioned that he was being assigned to a shared space.

The wooden door to Room 333 is closed and locked. A brass plaque announces Professor Abraham Baldwin Longman in bold calligraphy, and underneath, Travis' name has been misspelled in dot-matrix print on a letter sized piece of paper that has been taped to the door. He knocks three times but it is apparently empty, so he sets down the load of books and jingles his keys, pushes the wrong one into the doorknob and it sticks fast. He has to jerk it out with force and finds the correct key on the ring, but still has no luck. It won't turn. Maybe they changed the locks? He fiddles at it for a while, jiggling the key, notches clashing. From the next office over, a head sticks out of the door, summoned by all the distress no doubt, but before he can ask for help, it withdraws quickly and the door slams shut. Travis steps over and knocks on the door, three raps with his knuckles. He waits patiently, but no one answers.

A sigh is in order. Perhaps Mercury is in retrograde today? It occurs to him that, although this thought comes to mind occasionally, he has no idea what it means. It's just something that Margarette used to say—Meggan now, he corrects and reinforces:

Meggan, Meggan, Meggan. He looks down the hallway. There are half a dozen office doors on either side, all of them closed. He picks up the stack of books and heads back the way he came, knocking on each door and waiting patiently before moving on to the next, standing before each and listening for signs of life. Out of eyesight but within earshot, someone in the lobby hums in baritone, a tune that Travis recognizes. *Amazing Grace, how sweet the sound.* Help has arrived. Around the corner, A. B. Longman has pulled a wheeled cart up to the bulletin board. He leans over the stadium seating and posts black & white photographs onto the cork-board, a thumbtack in each corner. He stands upright, hitches up his pants, and studies his work.

"Good morning, Dr. Longman." Travis extends a hand.

The big man turns. Thumbtacks are held between his lips, three silver disks that dot an ellipsis.

Longman spits the tacks into an open palm.

"Greetings, my officemate. How was the move?" He advances his fist full of thumbtacks and daps the top of Travis's offered hand.

"Well enough, thanks. I'm glad I ran into you. I'm having trouble opening the office door. Is there a trick to it?"

"Have you got a minute? Give me a hand with this and then we'll see what we can do." Longman points to a collection of Xeroxed black & white photos on the cart top. Travis says he is glad to help and sets his armload of books on the receptionist's desk.

"Great. Pick out a pic." Longman winks and points at the stack of photos.

Travis reaches for the photograph on the top of the stack. A lynched figure hangs from a tree limb, a black man with his head lolled to the side. His overalls are stained with grease, dirt, or blood, Travis can't tell. He bites his tongue. "Uh . . . this one?" He offers Longman the photo.

"Any one of them is fine. They're all the same." On the bulletin board, lynching photos are posted in no particular order, the borders of the cork-board matted with ribbed maroon crepe paper. Dead black men, sometimes alone, sometimes in groups of two or three, hang at the same vertical angle. Most are suspended from trees. One hangs from a train trestle, a horrid charred corpse before cross-timbers.

Travis stands frozen before the board for a few heartbeats before blinking and breaking the spell. He isn't sure how to react, but something is in order. He settles on: "These are interesting photographs," then reconsiders. That didn't sound quite right. Too understated. He tries again. "They're terrible photos." That doesn't sound right either. It sounds like he's calling the photographer's skill into question.

"So, are you finding your way around?" Longman pushes a thumbtack into the next photo.

"So far, thanks." His voice is hitched up a little.

Longman offers small talk. "I'm the chair of the Bulletin Board Committee." He stands back and again evaluates his work. "Does that look straight?"

"It looks good to me. I mean, yes, it looks straight."

"Well, all righty, then." He gets back to humming. *That saved a wretch like me.*

Travis picks up the next photo. This victim had avoided getting strung up in a tree but is just as dead. He is pulled snug against the base of a large pine trunk. A chain is wrapped around him twice, once across his waist, the other across his neck. His head is hung down, his torso sagging down against the chains. Palmetto fronds poke up from sandy patches and cypress trees in the background. It looks like a swamp. Travis holds the photo closer and something stirs, but he doesn't remember yet.

Chapter Six

The sun is down and the stars are up. Meggan is in the back yard, doing her Wicca thing over by the bifurcated oak tree. There is a lot to look at up in the sky tonight, a lot of action going on in the cosmos. Hale-Bop is now visible to the naked eye. The comet has grown brighter each night for a month, and its white tail splashes the stars behind, propelling it toward the full moon. Venus and Mars are in conjunction between the twin trunks of the tree. All of this astronomical activity must mean something, so it seems like the right night for an appeal to the universe. She unties her skirt in the blue moonlight, drops it into the pile with the rest of her clothes and strides with purpose over to the oak tree. The moonlight makes her skin glow blue, too, and this suits her. She has been feeling a little blue today, feeling like the water sign she is, feeling like a Pisces. A quick prayer to the Goddess helps her find her center, just a few words about balance and the changing season, and then she begins a respectful dance. Her sturdy hips twist this way and that, both arms outstretched. Leaves crunch underneath her bare feet as she circles the oak. Fall is on the way.

Ying and Yang join in from a distance, their barking muffled behind the sliding glass door onto the deck. She has confined her two boys in the kitchen this time. They both stand upright on their hind legs, paws flat against the pane, complaining. She feels the separation and the barrier between them deep inside. Their separation pains her, but this is the right decision. She has the scars to prove it. The wound on her left breast is still red and swollen, a deep scratch from Ying. He was just giving her love, she knew. They get so excited that they just won't behave. Meggan concentrates on the moment, but it's hard to be present in the inner city with all the attendant bustle and noise. The cars on the interstate behind the retaining wall rush day and night, a steady stream that's not so hard to imagine as a rushing river. It helps create a peaceful vibe, but then a siren begins to wail on Memorial Drive and comes closer, doing its damage and derailing her meditation. The fire engine or ambulance or whatever it is yelps, its air horn honks, and it passes and diminishes. She waits for the relative quiet to return with the breeze cool on her back. Goose pimples rise. It's a help to be present and conscious of breathing, so she inhales deeply and slowly, counting off eight seconds, holds it, then empties her lungs and repeats. She finds her center. The heavy weight on her shoulders begins to lift, if just for a few inches. She curls her toes in the dry leaves. Breathing comes deeper and easier, and she muses on the possibility of change. Her troubles lift higher and drift a few feet up, near the bigger branches. Her mind relaxes and lets go, her intuition swells, feels for answers, asks for direction.

You can't have change without change, that's what Peter always used to say. It's funny applying his words to this situation, both heeding his council and cutting him loose according to his own advice. But it's undeniable that this is a time for transformation. The winds of change are blowing in from the East at a gentle five to eight mph. Autumn is on the way. The leaves on the sassafras tree next to the deck have turned from green to red to gold in a week. It is hard to let go of the past. She will see Peter again in a few days. Wednesday is visitation day at the prison farm, rain or shine. Last year, she made the drive in the snow, but the weather had closed the prison facility. And then she immediately blocks the thought—and this surprises her. She has never done that before.

The scratch from Ying is a check mark in the moonlight. She reflects on her usual love / hate relationship with her breasts and becomes aware of their weight. This curse from her father's side of the family, the Neanderthal branch. Since she was thirteen years old, every man she has ever met has spoken to the center of her sternum. Except Peter. He loves her for who she is, or who he thinks she is, or always said he did. He has been away two years now, and she's been loyal, only leaves the house when necessary, doesn't meet other people and holds onto him and what they had. But they have been apart for so long now that they are becoming different people.

Meggan becomes aware that she isn't centered, not at all. Daily life inevitably intrudes. Why is it so easy to drift?

She has given Peter everything. Even her therapist says it's a damn shame the way things turned out. But the universe provides. All you have to do is be open to it. She didn't know what to make of running into Travis Hemperly the other night. Was it just coincidence or a door opening? The unexpected encounter has reminded her of who she used to be before, when poetry was her calling and life was full of possibility. There's no telling if he will actually call. Maybe he was just being polite by asking for her phone number, a way of friendly parting and nothing more. Some men do that. She doesn't know what she will say if he does, but the thought is there anyway, and so she dances around the tree and tries to feel and let the cosmos have a little say-so. Maybe she's been wrong all along. She circles the twin trunks, the moon a little higher now, and the comet bright and big and bringing something with it, surely. A few laps around the trunk and she returns to calm space, closes her eyes and feels the grounding earth underneath her feet. The interstate *is* a river.

Chapter Seven

*T*he Neo-Egyptian obelisk over in MLK Plaza rises up into a blue sky with fluffy clouds plodding behind, snapshot-ready for new students and proud parents alike. Three stories tall, it's the ideal backdrop for a photo to show the folks back home. Hieroglyphic hocus-pocus is carved all the way up to the concrete apex pointing the way to the crescent moon, which has hung around well past daybreak to watch all the action. The monument sure looks exotic next to the shoe box geometry of the administration building. And there's more to it than concrete. Inside, bells hang in cobwebbed ranks and bide their time. Soon. A gizmo will click and whir, gears will spin, cogs will turn tooth-by-tooth. The bells will swing back, clappers will fall, strike their sides, ring the hour and begin the first class of the school year.

Everything is in place, more or less. The Olympic Games cleared out the month before, and only a few signs of its rowdy visit remain. Squares of sod cover the trampled earth in green grids. The blue port-o-lets are still there, ten inviting units cozy up to the new gym, plastic latches lifted to green. No waiting. The classrooms have been repaired from last semester's abuse, spiffed up with a wipe-down of industrial strength fluid that fills them with the suspicious lemony odor of industrial sanitation. Students hustle to class, going this way and that. The faculty are on campus too, their courses prepped, their syllabi picked up from the print shop, their office hours posted. The Great Chalk Drought of '95 stretches into its second year. Already professors hoard the chalk sticks, snap them in two and hide them around classrooms for future lectures. The dorms have been occupied for a week. Class registration is a downhill run for some, an uphill climb for others, Sisyphus style. *No, not here. You need the Dean's signature. Who told you that? You've got to see the Registrar first. This class has a prerequisite. That's the wrong form. If you can talk the professor into giving you an overload, you're good to go.* There is a back-up at the bookstore. Students line up single file out of the door and around the corner. *How can a damn book be this expensive?*

They arrive from all over the city. New SUVs wheel through the south gate, yesterday's Turtle Wax crusting in the hard-to-reach spots. Family sedans and sport scars. Some ride the MARTA rail in from the perimeter highway or take the bus across town. There's no place to park. A pickup truck jumps the curb. It is hip to hop. Thugz Hondaz buzz bass. *Fuck the police and Bone said it with authority 'cause the niggas on the street is a majority . . .* campus security steps forward. You can't park here. No, not there either. Freshman are required to live in the dorms, so they have a short commute. Upperclassmen flaunt their superior knowledge of how the place works. A freshman asks a super-senior for directions to Garvey Hall and is misinformed.

The two doves on the power line look peaceful. Mulish clouds drag shadows across the beleaguered humanities building and the sun shines on the busy construction next to it. The school motto is in a dead language across the banner on Garvey Hall. *Illegitimi Non Carborundum.* A crowd gathers at the entrance, a commotion by the glass doors. Some students wear back-to-school slacks and neck ties, some wear blue jeans, XXX-L t-shirts untucked. Look up there! A window washer hangs in rappelling harness from a thin line of PMI and dangles three stories above the faculty parking lot. He scrapes the grimy windowpanes clear with a squeegee, a five-gallon bucket swinging by his side. Everyone has the same thought. What if he falls? Anything is possible. Even the most jaded senior is a little jazzed. A megaphone speaks Greek to business majors. Alphas and Omegas rally behind alliterated encouragement taped to tasseled tables. *Be the Best and the Brightest!* On the far side of the parking lot, the curious stand close to the cyclone fence surrounding the construction site and watch the progress through the wire diamonds. A cement mixer in the hole beeps backward as wet concrete rotates in its orange abdomen.

And holy mackerel, look at the women on the strip. Everyone is here. I love Atlanta. You can't believe your luck. Spiced air shimmers down on a delicious breeze. A drama major, blouse tight, pushes the air in front of her as she promenades toward the library. Testosterone surges forward. Hey shawty! She ignores the Nubian princess platitudes, and the rejection triggers talk-down. Yo dog, bitch is wack. A freshman just in from the suburbs of Denver means to reply "I'm sayin'" but it comes out "really, dude." Inside the library, a student worker pushes a cart with a wobbly wheel between the bookshelves. She pulls a hardback from the load of books to be re-cataloged—PG 20398.B1147.28a 1964—replaces it in the wrong slot, and it vanishes into the stacks forever. Around the corner, a Womanism major sits in a cubbyhole, three books open on the desktop. She finds male bias in everything she reads. See, there it is again. A Junior Glee Club falsetto lowers his voice and mans it up. A senior tells HERstory, but no one listens. A disoriented Islamic student kneels in the laundry room and prays toward the West. A PK on the DL goes AWOL. You realize that you've lost your schedule. It was right here, now it's gone. A freshman and his family have just arrived from Cleveland, and they stand in MLK Plaza. His heart pounds in his throat as he poses beneath the bronze statue of Martin Luther King, Jr., who strides forward and points at Garvey Hall across the street. He is the first member of his family to go to college. He might just hyperventilate. His grandmother aims the Polaroid, waits for the young man in the maroon shirt to walk past. A little more to the left, son. Right there. We're so proud. The football team breaks from a prayer huddle. *This going to be the year!* A transfer student from Brooklyn crabs backward in the bucket, tail to the pail, claws raised in defense. All this money for tuition and no cable *or* air conditioning. As hot as it is. I didn't have to go here. Yale offered me a scholarship. Sure, the food is good now, but wait until the parents leave. At the west gate guard shack, a campus cop ogles cleavage through sunglasses.

Two sophomore street soldiers on soul-patrol, both clad in camouflage BDU's and black shirts in case the revolution breaks out, tape a flier next to the Klan Bell: WE ARE AFRICAN PERI-OD! They gin up insurrection against the New World Order and glare narrowly at the fashionably dressed assimilated brother, the Jack & Jill Negro over there in khakis and polo shirt. They rue the treachery of the Ice People. That's why the roofs are flat here, my brother. They built them that way to give the Man a landing pad when he choppers in to put us down. The target of their ridicule hoists a book bag full of new texts and gives them the high hat. He hustles toward the humanities building to catch a favorite professor before class and feels the glare of the guys over there by the Klan Bell, the brothers who wear their politics in their hairstyles. Their nubby dreadlocks make them look ridiculous, make us all look bad.

Today is Fried Chicken Wednesday. In the cafeteria, aproned caf staff flip thighs and breasts in popping grease and consider their cholesterol levels. The president has emerged from his lair and is out in the open in Brooks Brothers suit and straw boater, giving students the glad hand. He embraces returning alumni. So good to see you. Don't leave us for so long. Remember where you came from. Your donations will always be welcome. He smiles through the faltering laughter. An accountant in the administration building misplaces a decimal point and miscounts a bean. The provost sneaks a fart. Kwazi Kalamari shakes his head at classroom assignments pinned to the bulletin board in the History Department lobby and considers complaining to the chair. Dan Klien sits in the fire hazard that is his office, three decades of papers stacked toward the ceiling awaiting archival that he'll get around to one day. The rising decibel of anti-Semitic rhetoric out in the Lobby Of Black Rage makes him pause from reading the Op-Ed section of today's *New York Times*. "The Jews own everything! Jews! J-E-W-S!" Suddenly, the dimensions of his tiny office remind him of his visit to the Auschwitz crematorium. A. B. Longman rolls his chair up to the edge of his desk, hard copy manuscript before him. His shoulders slump from the pressure to publish. The effort stains his white shirt yellow underneath his armpits. *If only I could drop this weight.* He wrings his hands over a cliché and rewrites the sentence yet again. Anne Tigony sits before the monitor screen of the History Department computer, her fingers on the keyboard as she searches for a document. This World Wide Web is really something.

Travis Hemperly cuts through the crowd by the glass door and tries to beat the clock to his first class. He has a nagging feeling that he has forgotten something. As he passes the students, he is very aware of his Nordic features and how he is the only former faux-Viking in all the hubbub. The humanities building still looks like a big brick bug and has made no progress up the hill. His first class is somewhere in the thorax. He hustles through a muster of Omegas in purple windbreakers and golden boots, shoelaces untied. These guys again. They bark like dogs. Off in the distance, four deep woofs call and they respond in kind. *Hough! Hough! Hough!* He skirts the dog fight. They punctuate their boisterous camaraderie with the N-word. *Stock options are what you want with a compensation package, nigga.* The N-word once again. Travis stares dead into the doorway and pretends not to hear.

Outside the college gates, the poor and bleeding panhandle and wait. The Atlanta Public Housing Authority has the campus surrounded. This is the West End, Southwest Atlanta—aka the SWATS—where the untouchables have been banished for the good of the larger community. The down-on-their-luck stand on the side of the road and display reading material for passing cars. WILL WORK FOR FOOD PLESE HELP GOD BLESS. Always the same lopsided print. In the projects across from the campus gate, something else just went wrong. *Johnetta, go get the light bulb.* An empty Forty lies on its side, having crawled from its paper sack shell and expired in the heat. Remus's shadow falls across the bottle, his mouth dry, his whistle parched. He pulls a coin from the Styrofoam cup to read the date as always. *What is this? Where's the bird?* A little further into the West End, connoisseurs of crack rock negotiate transactions at convenient intersections. Ill-gotten gains change hands. You can make a crack pipe from a Coke can.

A wrought iron fence marks the campus boundary line along the streets, no signs posted forbidding entry of the locals. Everybody just knows. A non-matriculator slips in anyway, a young guy.

He traverses the campus green and strides down the hill and into the churning confusion of students. Something about him doesn't quite fit this puzzle. Socio-economic disparity is on full display for all to see. His clothing is slept in and wrinkled. His afro has a blow-out. He has a golden tooth. And he smells funky. He walks into the center of the back-to-school fashion show, draws it all up in his nostrils, hawks loudly and spits a gremlin of phlegm to remind everyone what's what. The projectile of spittle sails in a graceful parabola and dashes a wet skid on the sidewalk in the middle of the moving students who all put extra effort into ignoring him.

When the Egyptian obelisk begins to ring, they do not ask for whom the bell tolls. This is it. Parting words and laughter. Book bags sling over shoulders. Groups separate and scatter. You look good in the reflection of the glass door. Tubes of fluorescent light buzz all the way down the hallway. Footsteps echo up the stairwell. The fresh paint underfoot is already scuffed. The wall clock at the end of the hallway next to the elevator can't be right. Look in the door. The freshmen are already at their desks, sitting in ranks, waiting. Outside, a few upperclassmen linger and lollygag, their circadian clocks set on CPT. The devil loses his temper and begins to beat his wife. The biggest ray of sunlight you've ever seen blazes out into blue sky from behind that big white cloud over there, but it begins to rain anyway. The doves leave the line and flap for cover. A light shower spots the sidewalk and picks up fast. Dawdlers scramble for shelter. It's the first day of class.

Chapter Eight

$\mathcal{T}$ ravis has skinny white-boy legs. They are thin and pasty-pale, his muscles untaxed beneath the hairy limbs. There was a time not too many years ago when they were firm and athletic with an honest-to-god suntan. He was lean and naturally fit then, a runner in those days, too full of the stuff of youth to realize that things might change one day. But now he is all too aware of this reduced state, suitable for walking forward and backwards maybe, but that was about it. And not very far. His wrinkled and retracted penis, a nub of manhood in its bird's nest of scraggly hair, is barely visible below the crescent of his bulging belly. Gravity reaches up from the core of the spinning planet, yanks his shoulders forward into poor posture, slows his vertical growth, counteracts all that childhood spinach and pulls him down and back into the dust and earth beneath it. At some point in time that he hadn't noticed— maybe he'd been asleep—the balance of power had shifted. The golden scales had tipped, and his entire body began to sag and droop. He looks down at his bean-pole legs with a sad face and thinks that it's time to get back into shape.

But first, he has to teach this class.

He has been working furiously for two weeks for this moment, to stand in front of the classroom once again and teach. And now that he is here, he realizes suddenly that he isn't wearing any clothing. Not a stitch. He can't believe that he forgot to get dressed this morning. The night before, he'd laid the clothes out across the boxes of unpacked books. The charcoal sport coat and his best necktie—the blue silk one. And here he is, buck naked and standing in front of a classroom full of students, most of them male. He can't believe that no one pointed it out.

They don't seem to notice, however, so he just goes with it. They squeeze into the cramped confines of the institutional ranks, six rows across and five deep, and leave the sorry-excuses-for-desks to their less punctual peers—the desks that wobble, that have had their desktops defaced with decades of pen scribble. The students wearing neckties stand out. And the young man in orange dashiki on the front row wears a scowl. In front of Travis sits the end result of four hundred years of miscegenation. How easily they could be ordered by quantity of melanin, lined up from darkest to lightest in comparative analysis. He does not recognize this, however. At the moment, he is untroubled by the complexities of racial awareness and is as oblivious to it as they are cognizant of it. If he was to consider the racial dynamic, all he would see would be twenty-five black students, adjective emphasized. He doesn't sense the us-versus-him vibe hanging above the desks, doesn't recognize that it demands a certain code of behavior with which he is vaguely familiar, but he hasn't been keeping up with the proper etiquette. He hasn't been reading the newsletters. The Canadian post office is taking its time processing the change-of-address form he submitted weeks before, and *The Daily Caucasoid* hasn't caught up with him yet.

And then there is the noise to contend with. The construction drama outside the window is so loud that not even the rattle and roar of the air conditioning unit can drown it out. A tower, a construction crane ten stories tall, has been erected since his interview. The boom makes a smooth turn, and a stack of I-beams sails from there to there. But none of the students notice. Everyone is attentive. They look Travis over and try to get a feel for what sort of professor he will be, and there is a frozen moment where he does not speak and neither do they. Everyone wants to make a good impression. He begins with an informal and open question, wants them to participate. He wants to make learning appealing.

"Before we begin, do you have anything that you would like to talk about?"

He lobs the question at them, and it hits the floor with a thud that only he hears.

No one says a word. The silence stretches far enough to become awkward, and then the student in the dashiki collects his books, stands up in quickening disgust and stomps across the room and out the door, which slams behind him.

At this point, Travis remembers and puts it all together.

It's the pine tree and palmetto fronds that do it. It's the memory of the fronds that do it, strangely enough, not the commanding detail of the dead man chained to the tree. If the photo on the bulletin board had not had them in the background, he would be explaining his way through the Fertile Crescent right now, complete with handouts that are still warm from the copy machine. But something has clicked into place, and suddenly he remembers a story that his father told him many years before, an unsettling story so long forgotten that it might have just been a dream.

After the student storms out, the room is charged with a different energy. He has never had a student walk out of his classroom before, dissatisfied with his performance only one sentence into the semester. Everyone waits to see how he will react. He is momentarily discombobulated as they lean forward in their desks with new interest. His wits return and he tries to come up with a response that will turn this negative into a positive but can't come up with anything to say, up here on trial. He could just ignore it, but there's a problem there, too, and he hopes that a kindhearted student will feel the negative energy and do something to lighten the vibe. And there he is, sitting on the back row, raising his hand high, fingers wide.

"Why are you teaching here?" he asks.

Nowhere in the marketing literature promoting the college to the African American demographic does it state that the entire faculty is of African descent. There is no graph, no pie chart, no list that divides faculty according to race or ethnicity or gender. They are referred to as a dedicated collective. They are all part of the same college family. There were no photos of white faculty in the college's promotional material, true. There weren't any white coaches in the Negro Leagues, were there? Some things don't need to be said. If A = historically black college and B = black students, then C = black faculty. A + B = C. It's a simple equation. Someone must have made a mistake. If they wanted to be taught by a white professor they would have gone to a majority white college. And now they're sitting here facing this white man standing before the chalk board, and he's not even wearing any clothing.

A. B. Longman's girth swells from behind the lectern in front of the class, his tri-cornered hat set at a jaunty angle above his powdered wig, and he thinks: to aks or not to aks?—that is the question. The choice is before him once again, and here it is not fifteen minutes into the hour. He flips a mental coin. It's a good launch. His thumb hits the hypothetical silver at just the right angle, just on the edge, and it flips up high, turning over and over: Aks/ask? Aks/ask? Aks/ask? The right choice eludes him this time around and he pinches his nose, pulls the tip twice. It is always like this. He'll be plowing ahead, lecture full-on, moving the class through the series of conquests and colonizations that is this semester's version of history: Ancient Egypt, the Greeks, the Romans, the African continent, wherever he has chosen to stand on the line of time for the moment, and at some point he will have to make this call. Always does. The simple interrogative sentence began easily enough. The question formed inside his brain with no political motive, no agenda. They were just some words coming out of his head. The synapses in his brain fire and the electric thought travels down his brain stem to his vocal cords. They begin to vibrate. The thought takes audible form and leaves his mouth.

"Let me . . ."

And there it is. He hadn't expected it to come up so soon. *Hablo tu algo. Laisses-moi te toser une.* Both arms rest on the podium and it creaks as he leans forward. He has to make a decision here. He has to choose a side. It's the first day of class, and he hasn't gotten a feel for them yet, their social orientation, their economic status and corresponding level of identity awareness, hegemony being what it is. He has only their legal appellations to go by, many of them Jack & Jill patrician. There isn't a neo-African name on the list. These monikers, these sound waves that they respond to and claim as their own. But this class roster is a list of unremarkable names. He has already forgotten them all, even though he called the roll aloud not five minutes before. Are they mostly from the 'burbs, children of the affluent and graduates of majority white high schools who need to hear a little of the Vernacular from an authority figure? Or is this group closer to the urban school system disaster? Will they benefit more from hearing one of their own who says that it's okay to ask? No big deal. Look down at your forearm. It hasn't lightened an inch. You remain unassimilated. It's just a word.

Twenty-five students sit in the desks in front of him, counting down to the last day that they will give much thought to world history for the rest of their lives. This is it for many of them, history-wise. The administration has recently altered the curriculum, despite the noisy protests of the history faculty, and the two-semester sequence of world history has been dropped to one. Not that there was enough time to cover the history of all the world in two semesters, but the recent reduction has cut in half the time he has to give them a basis for an understanding of the entire past of their species, and now he cannot sleep at night. Forty class periods of fifty minutes each and then they will have fulfilled the curriculum's history requirement, and they'll stand on the foundation of whatever interpretation of the past has taken root and suits their fancy. Two thousand minutes and counting, to provide a substantial overview of all human history from the beginning. And this is only if they attend all of his classes and pay attention. He could give a satisfactory history of the college in forty classes, he thinks. Maybe give an overview of the city. It's only been around for one hundred and fifty years. The sesquicentennial celebration was just last year. He participated in the festivities himself. He would even be willing to broaden it out to the borders of the state. There was a lot to cover between the Atlantic and the Chattahoochee River since the beginning of so-called history and 1996. He would have to water it down and move quickly, but he could still sleep at night. But the entire history of the world? The further he reaches out geographically and the farther he stretches back down the time line, the more general the material has to become. There is no possible way to fit it all in. Whole civilizations and cultures and eras get left out. The students' understanding of the past is shaped not by what they learn in school but by Hollywood films, historical figures played by overpaid actors wearing funny clothes. Or from something on the small screen, costume dramas on a budget, something squeezed between commercial breaks. Not history but historyish. Only forty class periods. So he finds himself teaching History's Greatest Hits—along with a few off-canon tracks for his own amusement. What does it matter, really? These are freshmen. He can tell them anything as long as he keeps a straight face and stays within the boundaries of what they generally know. He can take side-trips and create whole cultures. Spend five minutes and then move on to something more canonical. Why not Herodotus's *History*? The Amazons with their bows and radical mastectomies. The Hyperboreans with their goat hooves and thousand year life spans. Atlantis sinks beneath the waves, scuttled by the wrath of the deities of the day, and the students dutifully write it all down in spiral notebooks, loose-leafed paper clipped into binders with stainless steel rings, copying his lecture word-for-word. This might be on a test, you never know. He cajoles and coaxes and wheedles and pontificates. He educates. They have been raised on *Sesame Street* and video games, for crying out loud. Flashy colors and loud sounds are appealing. A blinking light would be a help. The thought of living a substantial and profound life will never occur to most of them. If his presentation turns into dry lecture, a regurgitation of material from old coffee stained notes, a catalogue of names and dates, their collective subconscious minds will reach for the remote, clutch the channel changer, go for the Gameboy. Gentlemen, start your doodles. He prods them forward and tries to make them think. He stands before them, a black man in colonial chapeau, testing to see which students get the incongruity.

And there is always, always the problem of code shifting. He is a consummate code shifter, the fastest on campus. He picks up languages and dialects like candy, always has. He is fluent in Hip-hop. He can go from pedagogic discourse and pedantic diction to urban slang to white middle-class how-de-do in nothing flat. He adjusts posture and demeanor and appearance according-ly, stands upright and clean-shaven, breath mint dissolving on his tongue or slouches back in his chair with hand on crotch in ghetto solidarity. Context, context, context. It is a survival skill, this multilingual dexterity. Audience, alas, is important. If they are to make the assent up the ladder, they will have to know how to express themselves in a professional manner. They will have to become articulate in some form of professional vocabulary, be it legal or medical or corporate or academic (not so many of these nowadays, surrounded with examples of modest compen-sation as they are). They will have to be mindful of when and when not to employ the Vernacular. Some of them believe that they will have to talk white, and that's a hurdle. But most have long figured this out. They are social animals. They watch tele-vision. They have been surrounded by these words all of their lives. They have the luxury of being able to enjoy a liquid iden-tity. Some aren't so comfortable with the Vernacular and some are a little too comfortable with it for their own good. But they are Black in America. They will be evaluated by how they say what they say, and it doesn't matter who they are talking to or to whom they are talking. Simple speech is a political act. And so they code shift, and that's the key he uses to unlock the closed door before him. He wants them to live not just successful lives but profound lives, even if it is only an armchair profundity. He wants to give them a taste of it, wants to lead them all the way to Who. Their parents and their peers and the church and pop culture duke it out over their souls to tell them *what* they are. Not who but *what*.

And his thinking comes full circle as it always does, the silver coin reaches its apogee, tumbling over and over and then drops flat into his palm and he has his answer. Irony is the word of the day, after all. It is written in chalk on the green blackboard be-hind him. He straightens his tri-corn hat, fingers the felt jutting out above his nose.

"Let me aks you something."

Once again, Dr. Anne Tigony has to decide whether her duty lies to herself or to her state. With blue lights flashing in the rear-view mirror, she pulls her car over to the shoulder of the interstate and rolls to a stop while the morning's rush hour traffic speeds by, relieved that it isn't their turn. The posted speed limit is 55 mph. She can't plead that she can't read the signs. They are clear as day. But she is late for class, what was she going to do? she pleads. I'm a teacher. I'm late for class. Please officer, can you let me go with a warning? But the State trooper tells her that the law is the law. He is just there to enforce it. As he walks back to his squad car, her driver's license cupped in his palm, she pounds the steering wheel with her fist and mutters something vulgar. Raindrops begin to dot the windshield, a small shower, gray clouds overhead. When she finally hustles into the room, the class is half over.

"Dear sweet ones, I apologize for my tardiness."

The students have waited for her to arrive, but the initial first-day-of-class energy has dissipated, budding interest has grown into boredom and metastasized into impatience. Just last week, during Freshman Orientation, the provost of the college stressed repeatedly that first impressions are important. To be early is to be on time. To be on time is to be late. African Americans have to excel to compete with their white peers, who benefit from a privilege that is both unearned and entrenched. This was just the way it is. And now here they sit, all of them having arrived early as instructed, and the white professor isn't even on time. Isn't there a rule that you only have to wait ten minutes for a professor to arrive? Five minutes for an instructor? Isn't it in the handbook somewhere? But the department's administrative assistant had poked her head into the doorway and told them to wait. Dr. Tigony would arrive soon.

Not ten minutes later, she hurries through the door, denim dress whipping, sets her tote bag on the desktop, and introduces herself. Welcome to Freshman English Composition. She apologizes again for her tardy arrival and it speaks well of their character that they would wait for her so long. They have much to do today and are going to have to hurry in the time they've got remaining. The students sit dutifully, open vessels ranked in rows of five, and she wants to make a life-long impression. She reaches into the bag with both hands and retrieves a garden trowel in her left hand and a small wooden coffin in her right. It's one foot long, the one that she purchased last Christmas for her niece's Barbie Doll collection but decided to keep for this purpose. They clatter onto the desktop and out next comes a yellow legal pad and then a Bic pen. The students lean forward. She has captured their interest. A click of the pen and she scribbles a single word. Then she tears the sheet from the pad, folds it in half to cover the word, and steps forward.

"We are going to begin with an ending," she says and holds the folded paper aloft. "I've written a word here that I'm going to pass around the class. You know the word. I want this to be the last time you use this word. I want this to be the last time you even think about this word." She presents it to the closest student on the front row. "Please read this and pass around the room." He takes it, unfolds it, scowls.

"Dear one, I understand the conflict that it creates, the turmoil that it creates inside of you, inside of all of us." He passes it to the desk behind, and the word makes its way around the room, a few students giggling, she notes. But most sit impassively and a few with thoughtful looks. They are engaged.

"Today, we are going to bury this word. Forever. We are going to attend its funeral." Students pass the piece of paper back to her, and she drops the word into the coffin with little ceremony. "We need to reassemble outside as quickly as possible. Follow me. You can leave your belongings. This will only take a few minutes."

The students shift around, a few looking at each other, and they're game. They leave their seats and enter the hallway.

Tigony leads, the trowel in one hand, the coffin in the other. "Let's reassemble outside the door." She shepherds them out of the building and into the small courtyard. The bronze statue of the Reverend Dr. Martin Luther King, Jr. stands on his marble pedestal across the street, pointing to the Garvey Hall offices above. She leads them over to the closest giant magnolia, a few of its large, stiff leaves scattered on the ground underneath.

"Gather round," she instructs, a few stragglers still walking through the door. It's rained recently and the grass is damp but not the earth underneath. She bends down to the exposed dirt and root. Her first inclination is to ask a student to dig the hole, but that would recreate the age-old dynamic, the ugly order of a white overseer ordering a person of color to manual labor, so she digs the hole herself, putting her back into it.

"Okay," she stands upright, dirt on her dress. She's broken a sweat with the effort, can feel it on her back between her shoulder blades, and feels gratified for it. She holds the little casket aloft. "Take a last look," she tells them, shows it around. The crude rectangle, the mini-grave, open beneath her, and waiting. No pall bearers necessary. The students close in, a few in the back joking around. Always, always the students in the back who joke, it doesn't matter how solemn the event, she thinks. She lowers the casket slowly with both hands. It fits easily into the grave. A few scrapes with the trowel to cover the hole with dirt, and she packs it down.

"Now and forevermore, we declare this word dead and buried." She wipes the dust from her hands. That's that.

"You might have to dig a deeper grave," one of the students in the back quips. One of the jokers.

It happens slowly. First one student lifts his head from crossed arms on the desktop and ratchets upright. Another closes his notebook and tucks his ink pen behind his ear. A third reaches for a book bag that hangs in limp harrumph over the back of his desk. They can feel time. All have been alerted by the buzz of a visceral alarm clock lodged deep within their guts. After a lifetime of classroom incarceration, their circadian rhythms are sensitive to the fifty minute mark, and their innards have realized that this class period has run its allotted course. A Pavlovian response without the tinkling bell, they know it's time to go. Soon the whole room is jostling about and trying to send the time's-up signal to the wound-up Prof.

Kwazi Kalamari sums-up his lecture. "They have lied to you about your history, brothers. Lied, lied, lied."

He strides back and forth before the chalkboard in a tirade of summation, his natty gray dreadlocks bouncing like twined yarn. His bad back gives him a militant posture. The ashy calluses on his palms come from a lifetime of digging earthworks, of hastily shoveling shallow trenches to build temporary fortifications before the enemy tops the rise, always better equipped and with superior forces, always having advantage of the higher ground and a supply line that stretches for miles. He digs in and makes his stand here in the classroom, confronts the freshmen with their mixed-up world views, gets a sense of who feels the plight of the people and who has been mowing the lawn, unaware of his yard-boy status.

"Your ancestors built America. Built it with their sweat, their blood, and their lives! They died for you!"

He looks over the class for new recruits. The conscription list has grown short and the need is greater than ever. The ranks thin every day. Comrades are killed by bullets or drugs, locked up in prison or abandon the fight, leave their posts and light out for the shopping mall. It has become a war of attrition. He tries to hold the line and keep it together while mustering reinforcements, and so he teaches them their history and calls for volunteers. A few lean forward with bated interest, but the majority stir into the fuss of decampment. It seems like five hundred years of slavery and oppression would be a hard thing to forget to remember, but the students overlook it easily enough. And it gets worse every year. How do you counteract a lifetime of programming? Some of them have been assimilated beyond help. It takes sacrifice, and that is precisely what they are unwilling to do. They are so comfortable in their suburban neighborhoods and designer clothes that they might as well be white for all the good they would ever do the people. Yet he tries anyway. He gives it everything he has—and here they are, not even paying attention.

"Everything you know is wrong!" he says, arm raised high, index finger extended and shaking admonition.

Kalamari is a veteran of the fight. He enlisted when a young man, the same age as the students seated before him. The Movement is in the history books now and he has entered them himself, if only a footnote. Just look in the text on the desktop over there, the one with the black binding, on page 472. He was there at the beginning before it even had a name, was there for the boycotts. The sit-ins. The mass meetings. As it turned out, the revolution was televised, after all—not some feeble halfhearted protest like today but a true social uprising that gained momentum every news cycle. He was there during Freedom Summer, there on Bloody Sunday, there on the Edmund Pettis Bridge, on the front line of social change, marching across the span, stepping forward with the crowd, arms linked and singing "We Shall Overcome." Off key. Like he actually believed it would happen. They returned to the hotel and gathered around the television to watch the protest on the nightly news, and what came on? Two white men orbiting the Earth. Kalamari—a Gemini himself—sat on the bed, jaw dropped. Yes, they televised the revolution, but only for about a minute—and only at the end of the broadcast. The white man boasted about Emancipation and how they fought and died to end slavery and free his people, but his people weren't free. They were dying in the ghettos every day. No jobs. No money. No future. Martin and Malcolm were killed and then another Kennedy and the popular uprising became less popular and receded into the Reagan '80s. The machinations of J. Edgar Hoover dismantled the Movement and the CIA began to distribute crack rock and HIV to the inner cities. They created AIDS in their laboratories to kill the black man, turning his manhood—the only thing he had left—into a weapon against his own people. His people weren't free. Eventually the clouds of disillusion had blown in and cast their oppressive gloom, a generation had grown into the middle class, and they had lost the initiative.

"Everything we do is based upon what they think!" Kalamari

does an about-face and paces to the other side of the room. Only a few students take notes. The rest are packed and leaning toward the door, ready to bolt. They have been Anglicized. The European take on the world is so pervasive that it is deeply entrenched even here. Most of his colleagues, brothers and sisters in the struggle, even buy into it. The Diaspora drifts in all directions, he tells them. Follow your people. The only European history he teaches in his class is the Black Death. These students are African and will never be empowered until they see the world from an African perspective. Man came from Africa. Civilization came from Africa. Egypt is in Africa, not the white man's Fertile Crescent. And even Egypt, the word itself, is a white lie. The name of the country is Kemet, ancient Kemet, not this English word Egypt. They rename everything to wipe away what came before them.

The Americas were discovered by Africans, by his ancestors, not the criminal Columbus. Egyptians sailed their reed boats across the Atlantic to the new world hundreds of years before. These students have been misled about who they are since they started going to school, have been trained to look at the world through the same corrupt European lens, and now his class will be the last chance for them to find their African consciousness. After that, there is nothing between them and the big white lie. White history, white economy, white philosophy. White everything.

The bell tower tolls, signals the end of the class period and the students jump to gather their stuff. They make for a hasty exit, and this makes his shoulders droop with depleted morale. He is not just serving the history curriculum, not just espousing a profession. He is fighting for the existence of his race. There is nothing more important, so he rallies one more time.

"Brothers!" he shouts to get their attention, heads them off, blocks the door, and orders them to gather in the corner of the room, all of them. This creates much hesitation on their part. They stand in interrupted exit, unsure what to do. Kalamari commands: they can't leave the room until after they have complied, until after he has shown them. They follow along tentatively, move into the cinder block angle of the back wall, all twenty-five of them shifting, a few awkward giggles from the unfamiliar compression of personal space. Kalamari joins them, turns his back to them and against them, his arms outstretched as he pushes back and squeezes them all into the corner, shoulder-to-shoulder and tight together.

"This is what it was like in the slave castles, my brothers. Imagine being like this, squeezed like this with hundreds of brothers in a room, not for days but for weeks. You had to stand in your own feces, wade in your own shit up to your knees. That was what it was like. Never forget this, brothers. Never forget."

Chapter Nine

So, had Travis's father witnessed a lynching, or at least the aftermath of a lynching? The question knocks around in his head all the way down the crowded hallway. Most of the pieces suggest that he had, but his father hadn't called it that at the time, and Travis hadn't thought to ask. He was only a child and didn't understand the lay of the land, race-wise. The tale wasn't in the family canon and now was little more than a few images in his head, not a full-fledged memory: his father and uncle standing in the shadow of the wood, their faces frozen in disgust or horror or surprise, the great-grandfather he had never met, and the victim chained to the tree in anonymous silhouette. That was all, not much more than an anecdote, a half-remembered incident, the beginning of a story or maybe the end of one, but no striding narrative. It is not so easy a thing to picture now that he tries.

He has the right tools to work with today, so he selects the proper instruments and fleshes out the memory, puts it in the appropriate historical context and hangs a gaudy cloak of precise detail onto its shoulders. The clip rolls and the scene is set definitively in the summertime now, in peak-heat July, with all that oppressive humidity to work with metaphorically and cicadas available for background music. Clouds block the sun in heavy-handed symbolism. The victim, racial category still unchecked, slumps against the pine bark (for it is a Standing Pine that he is chained to now, the details crystallizing as Travis colors-in the narrative, even at this late a date). His father hadn't said that the man chained to the tree was black, and the lack of ethnic cue had implied a lazy commonality, so he had assumed that the dead man was kin, race-wise. Back then, people were white. Black people were black. That's the way it worked. If the victim hadn't been white, his father would have said so, wouldn't he?

Travis enters the slow flow of students and keeps a low profile as he drifts along, two textbooks and extra syllabi tucked tightly underneath his arm. The students file from the classrooms and move up and down the hall in the cross-currents. They have ten minutes to get to their next class, the same as everywhere. He dips his paddle and makes course corrections as needed. His post-class slouch evolves into *homo erectus* posture, and he walks the line between authority and courtesy as he navigates down this corridor of a sudden and different politics. Back at the University of Minnesota, the students in the class change hubbub were mostly white. They were merely obstacles to avoid along his paddle to point B or C. Travis moved down those hallways in anonymity, pushing his way through the crowd unfocused on race or ethnicity or gender or anything of political nature other than what was on his mind at the moment: the merit of his last lecture or lack of it, how he should have worked on his dissertation that morning, the upcoming disappointment of the bologna sandwich in the paper sack on his desk.

This day he wants to leave the stream as soon as he can. He angles toward the approaching entrance to the History Department lobby, digs in hard so as not to overshoot. An animated debate spills from the door jamb: Is Oprah a sell-out? He doesn't mean to eavesdrop, but the argument is passionate, the voices loud, and the conversation hard to ignore. Both sides present animated cases, lay tagged exhibits on the tabletop for the pensive jury to review. When he steps into the room, the dispute cuts off mid-rejoinder and the three students over by the lynching photos clam up in a sudden and awkward silence, surprised by his unexpected appearance and abrupt ethnicity. In the display case behind them, the lynched dangle forever from tree limbs and train trestles, but it is the snapshot of the dead figure chained to the tree that captures his attention now. He recalls few specifics of the long-ago trip to south Georgia clearly. The blazing sun and the heat. The gnats in his ears. His father in another sand trap, hacking away at the taunting golf ball and the sand spray flying. He had enjoyed working the tines of the level rake through the sand pit, clawing serrated grooves through the grains and then smoothing the sand with the flat end. He hadn't imagined the trip south. It had actually happened. He still had a photograph somewhere of his father smiling in front of the clubhouse, before the tournament soured his mood. The trip *had* actually taken place, but the ax murder story? Did that really happen? It was so long ago now that it seems as if it could have been something his imagination cooked up. It was just a false memory, the muddle of an ABC TV movie of the week and Faulkner novel from that Southern literature elective he took as an undergraduate. It was nothing but an archetypal tale of the South in his subconscious brought to life by anxiety and the unfamiliar ethnic context.

After his brother drowned—which never really felt like a death as he had not so much died as vanished into the choppy lake and not returned—the closest Travis had ever come to death had been about sixty yards, he figured, that day on-site, when he saw it standing on the rocky shore, its tattered black cloak blowing in the salty arctic breeze off of the bay, its skeletal finger pointing Bergman-like at the tourist from Nova Scotia who had just collapsed beside House J, the smithy. Travis had been drawing water from the brook when the man near the turf house clutched his sternum and reached for the woman, his wife, whoever she was, standing beside him, his eyes wide and bulging before he dropped dead into the pit. Travis galloped over in his Viking get-up, leather sheathes dangling from his waist, and was the first staff member to reach the fallen tourist. The woman kneeled against the dead man's shoulder and screamed for Travis to help, please help, but he didn't know what to do once he got there. The Nova Scotian wasn't breathing, his face was blue, and Travis considered techniques of cardiopulmonary resuscitation that he had seen on television. Wasn't he supposed to breathe into the guy's mouth? The spittle hanging from his salt and pepper mustache advised against it, and he began flapping his arms and yelling for help. "Get the warden over here!" Certificates confirming their training in emergencies such as this were mounted on the back wall of the tourist center. The ambulance didn't arrive for a while, the M.D. who happened to be among the tourists that day did what he could, and Travis backed away from the dead man and up against the Norsemen turf house dwelling with the other re-enactors, content to coordinate crowd control, keep the curious tourists back, and smoke cigarettes until the ambulance left for the hospital, its lights flashing as it pulled away, siren off.

But an ax murder? He didn't know how to relate to such a grim scene, not then and not now. His brother's body had never been recovered, and he had no image, not even the ghost of an image, to haunt him in its casket repose. The tourist had been hauled away with the usual flurry of first world concern, taken to an antiseptic environment of waiting professionals and whatever goes on in a county morgue, but an ax murder? Travis steps up to the display case, and the mental image of hacked red meat makes him queasy. The black and white photo is grainy and faded with age. Photocopying has blurred the details, but they all fit. The sandy ground, the Spanish moss hanging, the palmetto fronds with jabbing, rapier tips. The heat invisible and the gnats too small or quick to capture on film but he inserts them anyway. He leans closer and looks for trauma, tries to insert gruesome wounds. Where should he put the ax falls? In the chest? The neck? The head? There is no mutilation visible in the photo, although the resolution is so poor and the image so degraded that its blend of blacks and whites and grays lends itself to interpretation.

Dr. Davis steps into the lobby from her office, a beatific smile beaming through teeth whitened by cream applied in frothy grimace throughout the summer months. Not a single disaster has occurred the entire morning, not one. All of the students are registered, every one of them, and not a single schedule has been dropped or even challenged. All of the courses have classrooms in which to be taught. Not even her colleagues have complained. No one has directed as much as a surly word in her direction, not even Dr. Kalamari. Just a few students popping in to say hello. And there is the new hire, standing over by the three majors and looking at Professor Longman's exhibit on the bulletin board. She walks over and greets him.

"Professor Hemperly. How are things going thus far?"

All is well, he says and recaps his class briefly, remarks on the quality of the students, although they were a quiet bunch for the most part, and he omits one part. He omits the early walk-out. It is good to be before a class again. Civilization has pulled him back to its bosom. Just a month before he had been at his professional wits' end, all this time and money spent on his education only to find that it left him unprepared to do pretty much anything else. There wasn't much of a future in being a Viking. He had become ensconced in academia, not the Ivory Tower itself but in the cinder block parapet beneath it, and he hadn't noticed the chasm that had opened up between him and the rest of humankind. The non-matriculators, former students all—for all had been students to some degree, the people that he and those like him had educated, tested, and evaluated before they left for lives outside of learning, whatever that entailed. He doesn't tell her this, of course. Instead, he asks her for a key to the faculty men's room down the hall.

The door to Garvey 333 is wide open, and he stops in the doorway. He shares the small office with a big colleague, whose bulk displaces a significant amount of volume along with the two catty-cornered desks, the low bookshelf, the file cabinet. That's about it other than the wall of hats, a dozen of them hanging from nails in rows of three. Hats across eras and social class. Top hat. Porter's hat. Captain's hat. Ball cap. Limp silk doo-rag. Tri-corn. A. B. Longman stands before the bookcase, a hammer in his hand, and he takes a step back to admire the new wall hanging above it: a brand-spanking new rebel flag hangs big and shiny on the wall. *Oh come on*, Travis thinks. *This is a bit much*. The lynching photos, the student walk-out, and now this. The frumpy Confederate flag is a dramatic addition to the sparsely decorated office, its stars and bars of Confederate defiance nailed to the cinder block, gold tassels around the border hanging in limp defeat. Is he is being hazed?

"What do you think?" Longman's deep baritone asks as he

drops the claw hammer onto the desktop.

"Well . . ." Travis grasps. "The State flag controversy?"

"Exactly! You should have seen the look on the face of the cashier at the Army Navy store where I purchased it. I thought it would be a good reference point for discussion."

"It's certainly topical. Did you have to hang it over my side of the bookshelf?"

Kwazi Kalamari sticks his head into the office, still clothed in urban camouflage. No yarn hat today though, and his dreadlocks hang long. Longman sees him first.

"Hey, Dr. K. How are you doing today?"

Kalamari pulls his glasses down the bridge of his nose and takes in the flag. "I'm *free*." He studies it with a scowl.

Travis sets the books down on the empty desktop. "I just got here," he offers in explanation.

Longman lifts the hammer from the desk, smiles and takes the credit.

"I don't approve, Brother Longman, not even in jest. This symbol of oppression has spilled so much of our people's blood."

Travis feels squeezed. Three people in the little office add too much volume to it and displaces a large quantity of breathable air from the room. He inhales what he can and looks out the window pane for escape. Underneath the big blue sky, students criss-cross MLK plaza. The Egyptian obelisk rises dramatically, hieroglyphs rising to ancient gods. To the left, the larger-than-life statue of Martin Luther King strides forward on his pedestal, his bronzed arm raised and pointing an accusing finger at Travis from across the street.

"You know my work, Dr. K."

"I prefer Dr. Kalamari, *Mr.* Longman."

Longman drops his eyes and apologizes for stepping from his station, obsequious and deferential. He turns to Travis. "I wrote a paper last year arguing that African-Americans should appropriate the St. Andrews Cross for themselves. We should wear it proudly as a symbol of what we've overcome."

"And where did you publish that paper?" Kalamari asks.

Longman ignores the dig. The sudden outbreak of office politics makes Travis feel like an intruder. His colleagues have a history that he does not know, insider dialogue he does not understand. Perhaps there is an opportunity here to bond and make a connection, even if a slight and superficial one, but they continue their conversation over and around him. Kalamari signifies. Longman signifies back. Best to leave them to it. So he does.

Chapter Ten

*H*arleys, Harleys everywhere and not a place to park. When Travis returns to the apartment later that afternoon, the parking lot is full of motorcycles. Six big cruisers lean side-by-side, all at the same tilt. Five skinheads, two with mutton chops, stand a few feet away from the lined-up bikes and drink PBR from an unchilled box. The case of beer at their feet looks as if it has been torn open by a thirsty monster, the cardboard ripped and mangled but still holding the dwindling cans together somehow. It isn't cold or even cool but looks like it could be by the jean jackets that they all wear in denim solidarity, standing in a huddle around today's project: a motorcycle separate from the rest, parts removed, black oil pooling underneath. Rhett squats before the iron barrel engine and ratchets a socket wrench.

Travis parks the Volvo on the street, parallel to the curb, removes his necktie, pockets it in his sport coat and locks the door with the key. He can get all the books and papers up to his apartment in one load if he hurries, but the skinheads are between him and the foyer door, and he foresees a confrontation. He doesn't know if they are soft suburban skinheads from outside the perimeter highway or are of the harder neo-Nazi variety, but if the latter's the case he figures that Rhett has spread the word about his employer. They are bikers, dressed as bikers dress, club membership sewn into the fabric. It is their lot to jeer and hassle in their rockabilly sideburns and belittle tax-paying citizens with regulation haircuts such as himself, but when he steps within taunting range they just murmur *How's it going?* Rhett waves the greasy wrench and offers him a beer.

"How'd it go, professor?"

These people stole his television, his shiny, pretty television.

They are in the beginning of their relationship and defining how it will proceed. He wants to handle it in a way that stops the thieving and burglary right now, but feels burdened by appearance. He has an education. He teaches. He owns a car. He dresses for work. All point to the same thing, he thinks: please rob me. He can dress down after and on the weekends, but the damage has already been done. He doesn't know motorcycles from Adam and none of them seem Viking-history-inclined. Nice for Rhett to offer a beer and he doesn't want to refuse the peace pipe, but the books in the crook of his arm are getting heavy. Keep it short and friendly. "Can I take it with me?" he asks. "Got a lot of work to do." He indicates the armload of texts slipping, his vice grip loosening.

"Sure," Rhett says. "Hey Fuckhead, give the professor a beer."

A fat biker with heavy beard, his future as a shopping mall Santa assured, reaches for the box and tosses a can. Travis catches it (Thank God, he thinks, humiliation in front of other males avoided—no small feat with an armload of books) but they aren't looking at him and don't see him catch it. No cool points earned. Santa points at the spark plug. "That's upside down, dumb ass." Chuckles all around, Rhett included. He is determined to fix the bike come hell or high water, or so he claims. Travis says thanks and excuses himself then regrets the polite exit. He doesn't want to look like a punk, and somehow social etiquette seems the wrong choice here. He'll have to drop some curse words next time to make up.

The stairwell is still dark—*they can spruce up the outside of the building but not replace a light bulb?* he thinks as he lugs the books up the steps, and the dark encourages recall. The lynching photo returns, the victim chained to the tree, and it's heavier now, this memory, metaphorically speaking. He has considered calling his father on the telephone all day to confirm that he actually told him about it—and now that he's back at his place, he'd rather do anything but pick up the phone. So he does. He eats a leftover taco. Rolls a cigarette. Starts to plan a class. Smokes the cigarette. Clips his fingernails, sits on the couch and stares out the window. The sun lowers between the smokestacks, and the sky above the mill turns a deepening purple. It is time. But first, to the kitchen for some alcohol for fortification. He opens the fridge. In the center of the top shelf, the lone can of PBR and the dip for the chips. And what's that? He bends over, head into the bright cold air to get a close-up of the black dots scattered in a line across the glass shelf, trekking across the tundra to reach the salsa. Ants, expired in the cold and laid out in traffic pattern, bumper-to-bumper and frozen to a standstill.

He grabs the beer, pops the top, and returns to the couch. The telephone is plugged into the jack next to the stack of boxes, a cheap pushbutton base and handset with a Minnesota Vikings sticker on the receiver. In his wallet is a list of telephone numbers, such is his memory, and his father's number is somewhere near the bottom. Henry Hemperly had always been an unreliable narrator—another reason Travis questions the ax murder story—and he is concerned about what this foretells about his own future mental state. They've got the same DNA. His intellect is his currency, job wise, and he is afraid that, despite all his efforts, he won't be able to avoid the cliché of turning into his parent. Nothing he can do about it other than fret and wait for his mind to unravel. Case in point: the last time they spoke face-to-face, Henry told him something that Travis wished he'd kept to himself. They'd met for pizza before Travis moved to Minnesota, and both were making an effort at it despite the whole dead brother/son issue, when Henry pulled another slice from the pie and munched off into that place Travis had come to dread: the increasingly peculiar landscape of his faith.

After Charlie drowned and the family fell apart, Henry had returned to the church of his childhood for solace, which had been a good thing for every one. For a while. But more and more he had followed a path visible only to him and others born again. Travis, not having a strong investment in organized religion one way or the other, had learned not to engage when the conversation veered onto that path. Wiser to just sit on his hands and listen, which is what he started to do on this occasion when Henry began to testify about the miracle visited upon him the weekend before. This was the real deal, he said. The genuine article. No hyperbole here. He wasn't talking about a traffic accident or lucky golf shot. He meant an Old Testament style miracle from God in heaven. Divine intervention and all that went with it. Henry explained that he had been considering joining a country club for a while. He was getting older and had felt the pull of long fairways, short grass greens and all the accompanying social status, but doing so brought emotional turmoil as it echoed his life before the drowning and the divorce. Lots of baggage here, the kind of stuff that's easier to avoid than face. Ever since he received the invitation—not such an easy thing to get in the first place—he'd gone back and forth about what to do. Who would pass it up? But he couldn't make a decision, so he'd turned it over to a higher power. He had placed the choice into the hands of the Lord and left it up to His greater wisdom. Despite the strength of his faith, he hadn't really expected anything to happen. Surely the Lord had his eye on larger concerns. Travis nodded at this. But that turned out not to be the case. He pulled another slice from the circular pan, mozzarella stretching. Travis sat on hands and held his breath.

"Last Saturday morning, when I went out to move the sprinklers, there were colored golf balls all over the front yard. Hundreds of them."

At this point, a long pause settled in. The words were out there in the ether, but they escaped Travis. His father was completely serious. No blink of eyelid, no sideways smile to telegraph that he was putting on. Henry sat across the booth, straight-faced and working his jaw. It wasn't so much the miracle itself that bothered Travis as it was the physical evidence of it. Having been raised in the South, he knew his gospel. Moses led the Israelites across the parted sea, but it closed up soon after to drown the pursuing Egyptians. There was the burning bush, but it had gone up in smoke, nothing left but charred twigs and ash. Christ himself left no footprints on the water for forensics teams to cast in plaster. All water turned to wine had been drunk—the rarest of vintages. Another glass, please. Miracles occurred all the time in the Testaments, but they were plot elements, Travis thought, and didn't leave evidence.

Sure, sometimes he'd hear about a silhouette of Christ in a potato chip or up on a billboard of spaghetti noodles, something open to interpretation that demanded a leap of faith, but physical evidence left behind? Colored golf balls? Hundreds of them? This was a miracle that begged too many questions. Did he pick them up? Had they improved his game? What brand would God select, anyway? Would they be logo-less, or did he have his own typescript? And what colors were they? A heavenly pastel or hard primary colors, the basics? He didn't want to insult his father's faith. Had he been on his toes, he wouldn't have asked him to elaborate, would have just nodded and changed the subject. But he didn't. Whether from a morbid fascination or a lapse of good sense, he prodded for more and asked an obvious question. Why would the creator of the universe want his father to join a country club in the first place? Because, his father said, he had played the course as a guest and been appalled by the crude language of the members, vulgar and profane at the same time. That's why. Understand son, it takes courage to testify, he said. It takes steel in the spine to stand up and point to where the culture has gone down the wrong path and there is no influence at this club that he could see to counter the slide, no one to suggest that the offensive language was untoward in any way. The slippery slope of sin is strong. Allowed to go unchecked, the profanity will lead to deceit then infidelity then theft and murder and all the rest. And some of these men even belonged to his church. It was a tricky thing to do these days, to influence spiritual belief without putting people off and seeming pious, which can only make things worse and push them farther from righteousness.

His father had put Travis in a tight spot. Either the miracle was real, or he was crazy. But at least he's paying for lunch, so Travis never asked the questions begged, never knew whether his father had collected them from the yard, what became of them, whether he had played them—talk about a lucky golf ball. The concept was too big for him to wrap his head around, so he sat quietly in the booth, son not challenging father, and finished his pizza while Henry segued into an update about the old Chris Craft cabin cruiser, about its latest and final sinking, as if he assumed that Travis was following his abrupt *non sequitur* from heavenly miracle to pleasure cruising. The golf balls had stayed with Travis for a decade just like the ax murder story had stayed with him for longer, scattered across the green suburban grass of his imagination, wet with the morning dew.

After the PBR is finished and three more cigarettes rolled and smoked, he sighs and reaches for the telephone. The call travels by landline outside of the metro area, across the perimeter highway and out into the galaxy of sprawl beyond. His father's broadcasting voice answers on the third ring, but when he realizes who is on the phone, it quickly cracks, and Travis is flummoxed by the emotion.

"Travis? Travis? Hello son! Are you, where, is everything okay?"

Travis is unprepared for this, and it is awkward going. His rejection of the Hemperly side of the family was aided by distance and circumstance, but now that he is back South for at least one academic year, he is bound to have to face up to some of his transgressions. He has called for one reason and one reason only. He wants to ask his father about the story of the ax murder. He wants to know if it was a lynching, wants to know the race of the victim. That's it. Otherwise he wouldn't have made the call. It's a simple question: was the victim black or white? He isn't sure how to get around to asking, and so they catch up and his father's rush of emotion, the sincerity of his fumbling words and loss of radio voice make the call disarming. Maybe he should have written a letter.

His father asks specific questions. Yes, he is living inside the perimeter, has rented an apartment in Cabbagetown. No, he doesn't think it's dangerous living downtown. When he tells his father where he is teaching, that he has gotten a job at one of the city's Historically Black Colleges, the conversation grinds to a halt. The pause grows into a gap before his father breaks the silence and says that's great. That's great. It's a fine school, then he changes the topic to his radio show which is going well, as popular as ever. They are talking about syndication: A.M. markets in South Carolina, Alabama, and Mississippi. And then on to Travis's grandmother, and guilt rises. He had heard through the grapevine that his father and brother had moved her into an elderly condo complex in-town, had finally pried the car keys from her fingers after her last accident. Selling the house had been difficult for all involved, and initially she had put up a fight but was now settling into the condo. Piedmont Lake was a nice place. It was clean and the residents were the right kind of people, he said. On his end of the phone, Travis goes for Oh Brother body language and rolls his eyes at the ceiling. Considering the water spots on the clumsy paint job, he's not living in right people territory himself. But it sounds fancy. They serve breakfast, lunch, and dinner every day in a ballroom, had even moved the chandeliers from the Biltmore Hotel to hang from the high ceilings. Her health is good. She's amazing, but go visit her, son. Travis says he will. His golf game is better than ever—he almost hit his age the other day, would have done it if he had had a little more luck with his chipping and putting. The broadcasting job allows him to spend lots of time on the course. And there's his segue.

"Say dad, do you remember when we went to south Georgia when I was twelve or thirteen, when you played in the State Amateur Tournament?"

"That was a long time ago," Henry chuckles.

"I was thinking about it today, and I remembered that on the drive down you told me that when you were young, you'd seen a man who'd been chained to a tree and killed with an ax."

The other end of the phone is silent for a few beats, but it's hard to read the pause.

"Well I remember the trip son, but I don't remember telling you anything like that." His father isn't using his radio voice and doesn't sound insincere, but it's hard to tell. "Good Lord, why son?"

Travis has no answer. He hadn't anticipated a denial. This is awkward. It didn't really happen? The memory seemed real enough but there was a question mark there too. It was so long ago. So he plays it off that he was just wondering, that he had thought he remembered it and then tries to change the subject himself but the conversation has reached its apex, traveled its parabolic arc and descends rapidly into polite sentences with little substance. The broadcaster's voice returns and a distance begins to widen between them. I can't tell you how happy I am to hear from you, son. We need to have lunch. Come on out to the club sometime. And go visit your grandmother.

The call ends and that's that. He hangs up, sits back on the couch, needs to drive up the street for more Bugler tobacco, but he has one more call to make.

He has waited for an appropriate number of days to pass before calling her. He doesn't want to telegraph too much interest, after all. Margarette. Mary. Margie. Marge. Molly. Meg. Meggan. Her birth name—Margaret—unfolds like a multi-tool. It is a Swiss Army Knife of a name, easily adjustable to reflect whomever she found herself to be on any particular day. It was a first draft of a name, inviting revision as needed, never straying so far from the core of its root, her mother's name: Margaret— its popularity having long faded over the fickle years to become cobwebbed and grandmotherish. You didn't meet a lot of Margarets these days, so it sat at the lunch table alone and waited to become the popular girl once again. When he had known her at UGA, she had been Margerétte, a variation of the name with a little dash of Latin spice added to perk it up into her poet persona. Over the years the name had continued its agile metamorphosis, only returning to its original state in official documentation. In her church phase, she was Mary. In her athletic phase, with her head phones and jogging bra, she was the more sprightly Meg. Molly in her flapper phase, a retro-trend that she tried to jump start singlehandedly but never caught on. Now, ten years later, she was Meggan, not the poet. But she still had the same peculiar light in her green eyes. Other than the gray she hadn't aged. She looked the same as the last time he'd seen her, the night they climbed the basketball coliseum dome.

She was about to leave the university for good, had finally

graduated and landed a job in Atlanta. That last night, she had planted a seed in his mind and then driven onto State 29 and out of his life, her diploma picked-up from the registrar's office, her car packed and gassed and ready for the drive to the city. They'd gone to listen to music at the 40 Watt and then a bottle of champagne after to toast. But not just anywhere. A little B & E was necessary to make it memorable, and they sneaked onto the grounds of the basketball coliseum in the full-moon dark, both of them a little drunk and Travis toting a bottle of sweating champagne. They broke campus, city, and county laws, stuck close to the night shadows, and kept an eye out for the patrolling campus cop cars. When the coast was clear, they climbed the concrete arch of the north buttress, survived a besotted stumble up the tricky slope without falling, squeezed through the bent grate, and then they were on top. The stars more brilliant now in the shadows above the street lights, and they settled down near the edge—not too close to fall off but close enough to risk it. The lights of the little college town flickered on the ridge a mile north, its magical quality not lost on Travis and enhanced by both the alcohol and his growing and yet-to-be-diagnosed nearsightedness. They drained the bottle in ten minutes, making toasts to the university. The bars. T. S. Eliot and Sylvia Plath. Travis twisted the cork back into the bottle and sealed in the moment. He placed it on the edge of the dome roof where, if he looked up from the street, he would be able to see it later. She recited her latest poem, something about sorrow and loss. The roof of the dome glowed in the moonlight, a geodesic planetoid tumbling beneath the star field overhead. Orion's Belt moved west across the sky and dragged all the other stars along with it, and they kissed for the first time, gently at first with soft lips and then with more heat. It was the only perfect moment he had ever known, and he hitched her to it like a mule to plod forever down the road behind him, hauling a wagon load of romantic ideal, always back there somewhere.

"Hello?" Her voice is tentative on the other end.

"Meggan? Hi. It's Travis."

"Hey!"

Twelve years of up-on-pedestal idealization makes his heart flutter. The Gregorian chanting on her end of the telephone drops to a low drone as she turns down the volume. Travis thinks that maybe things will work out for him after all.

Chapter Eleven

*T*ravis hasn't looked at the photo in years but knows it's somewhere in the vodka box over in the corner, lost among the hundreds of other pictures he has hauled with him for more than a decade now. He has kept them for reasons that he does not understand, a spotty chronicle of his life, testament to his development from infant (lots of these) to today (not so many). The final few are from grad school graduation, hooded in doctoral regalia and fleeing the stage, diploma cover under arm. And only one in Viking garb, mouth open, eyes closed, cigarette poised in incongruity, the photographic eye losing interest in him as he aged, all that promise squandered. Why waste the film? He rarely looks at them. Perhaps he is a pack-rat? He considers, but one glance over at the boxes in the corner—his still unpacked stuff—the sagging couch and the mattress and box springs on the gray carpet in the other room—make him feel like a poor representative of that order. He's not much of a hoarder. He is not a collector, other than well, okay, the books, but he's learned to travel lightly. He has been teaching history from a suitcase in an adjunct scramble for long enough to know that it's just easier when moving day comes around again. He counts his pennies and doesn't accumulate a detritus of knick-knacks. He does not own colorful shot glasses of cities he has visited. He has not purchased Elvis memorabilia. He does not own Black Americana salt & pepper shakers or kitschy Christian iconography. He does not search through antique stalls looking for strip-tease ink pens or deco ashtrays or purple-prismed bottles unearthed by privy dig. But maybe one day, he hopes.

The photographs themselves, the forensic evidence of his life, are not cataloged or organized in any way. They are mixed arbitrarily in envelopes with fading logos, artifacts that record the evolution of the photograph developing industry since his childhood: Kodak, Photo-mate, Wolf Camera, Eckerd Drugs, Wal*mart. When he moves to his next transitory address, he'll refrain from tossing them out once again, but he seldom looks at them, because doing so inevitably results in coming across a photograph of his brother, and then he has to contend with all of the unpleasant turmoil that comes with it, but this morning he needs a little something. Margarétte—Meggan now—is the foreground, but his mental image of her is hazy, even though he saw her the week before, and he wants to reconcile the soft-focus dream in his head with the actual image captured on film, even if it's an old one. He rifles through the envelopes, stays on task, avoids getting lost in the nostalgia photos rouse. When he finally finds it, it is stuck to a postcard of the coliseum dome, a blatant "excuse-me-will-you-please-take-our-picture?" picture. They both look like tourists, even though they had only made the trip up to Blood Mountain in the piedmont from Athens.

Travis and Margarette stand on a fieldstone walkway, Rabun Gap deep and green behind them and the Blue Ridge Mountains rolling in easy humps underneath the overcast, the gray clouds. An obliging tourist from Tennessee snapped their picture, the two of them standing side-by-side before the scenic overlook. It is his only picture of her, his only physical evidence of their short time together, and he regrets its neglect. He pulls the picture and postcard apart carefully, tries to unstick them without doing damage, but the postcard takes a piece of gray cloud with it anyway. She looks the same with her raven hair and high ponytail, but man has he aged. His hairline has receded, and he's wider now with a gut and a goatee. He was a runner back then, had run a road race that morning and is wearing the evidence in the picture. His 10k T-shirt is crisp and clean with the new-shirt vertical folds still visible in the fabric, and look at his full head of hair and his big happy open-mouthed smile showing all of his teeth as he pulls her close, lassos her with his arm around her shoulders, her mouth set in a grimace and her arms flat at her sides.

Last night he had a vivid dream and remembers it this morning. He was young and fit again, just as he had been in the photo. His dream sense felt his body the way it used to be, filling up a reduced and right amount of physical space and displacing the same amount of atmosphere he had prior to its aging and thickening, before all the food and inactivity made it exceed its design limits. But this is the body that he was born into, and these days it seems to have ideas of its own. After a shower, he looks at his dripping reflection in the medicine cabinet mirror and decides that it is time to get back into shape, to lose the weight, maybe grow his hair out a little bit and return, or at least take a step toward, his former self in the photo, now pinned to the refrigerator with a maple leaf magnet.

He has until the weekend before he will see her. That's four days—almost five. Maybe he can drop a few pounds, some water weight at least. Time is working with him today as well—he doesn't have to be on campus until noon and can get in a run around the neighborhood. So he finds his running shoes in a book box, knocks them together to clear the dust. They don't look too bad, are only five or six years old. The inside tread has flattened and worn down at the heel, too, from his lopsided gate. Not too bad. Just do it. Thus, he re-enters the sweaty, optimistic world of physical fitness with both eyes on the upcoming dinner date. He still can't believe his good luck at having run into her after all these years. He doesn't buy into karma or astrology or fortune cookies or any of that. There is only luck. It is dispensed worldwide in uneven quantities with no regard to need or necessity or desire. It doesn't matter how good you are or how hard you pray, he thinks. There is no explaining it. Things happen for reasons of their own or no reason at all. And now, two portions of luck have been parceled out to him unexpectedly, because that's how it works. It is up to him to capitalize on them, to turn them into hard currency and make a profit from his good fortune, so he slips on a ratty pair of running shorts, pulls athletic socks over his unsightly bunions, laces-up a pair of running shoes, and leaves his apartment before the sun has risen and the neighborhood has begun to stir and come to life.

The Travis back in the photo shunned the J-word and looked

askance at those who used it. But as he plods alongside the rail yard wall he realizes that is exactly what he is doing: Jogging. He is not actually moving fast enough to be running. He is a jogger these days, and the demotion makes him feel reduced, a little marginalized and second rate, no longer able to keep up with the younger and more spirited. All of his students could out pace him without breaking a sweat. His feet no longer spring gracefully in forward stride, first the heel and then toe propelling him forward and faster. Those days are gone. Now they hit the pavement flat and heavy, telegraphing with each footfall that they have arrived and that it is time for him to stop this nonsense. The cigarettes haven't helped, and he spits nicotine phlegm at the high concrete wall as he plods along. The sun is up now, half of a red ball on the horizon, the clouds a deep pink, almost purple. His feet already hurt from the pounding. After three blocks he stops and walks for a bit, still pacing along the wall that separates the little mill village from the rail yard next to it. On the other side, all sorts of industrial violence. He can only guess its purpose. Heavy metal collides with heavier metal, and a tremendous crash shakes the ground and echoes, a tractor trailer of freight dropped down onto a flatcar stack. The noise of in-town living is his soundtrack. The banging and clanging throughout the night wakes him, but he's beginning to get used to all the noise, that and the MARTA rail train across the rail yard with its soothing rattle, the elevated commuter cars sliding over concrete stilts in a gleaming graffitiless procession.

He catches his breath and picks up his pace again. To his right, shotgun shacks decay. All of them are damaged in some way, paint—where there is paint—peeling, porch roofs collapsing, tar paper torn away, asbestos tiles cracked. There isn't much to the little mill village, and he has learned his way around in no time at all. The clapboard shotguns are built so close together, all of them wood suffused with termites, an outright curiosity that the entire neighborhood didn't burn to the ground a century before. These diverting thoughts blur his awareness of pain. But not for long. Soon all he can think about is how badly he wants to stop running, but he compels himself forward, exerts willpower, albeit at low voltage. He'll stop when he vomits, he tells himself. That shouldn't be too long. The concrete sidewalks are unforgiving. The soles of his shoes do little to cushion the blows, and his knees begin to protest, too. The asphalt won't be as bad on them, he thinks and crosses the weedy grass strip, steps off of the granite curbstone and into the bike lane, a white strip protecting from the traffic. Shoes scrape down the asphalt pavement as he jogs the empty street with an ear out for cars coming up from behind and wary of the oncoming, too, but no one is out this early in the morning. And it works.

A few blocks ahead, there is a tunnel underneath the rail yard, and he picks up his pace toward it when hypoxia gets its grip, and Travis's brain begins to starve for O^2, which is a help, a little delirium to occupy thoughts that become bleary and diffuse. Knees hurt. Red sky at dawn. Graffiti nonsense. The Volvo's radio speakers are blown. He does not understand what is broken, and he hasn't had the inclination or the cash to replace them, so he just keeps the radio volume low so that they don't buzz too badly.

The car approaching from behind doesn't employ this strategy. The boom of bass reverberates through busted speakers and bounces off the rail yard wall as the car slides up from behind. Travis moves closer to the curb. The boom and rattle of gangster rap overtakes him. Over his shoulder, a jacked-up late model Chevy with a spray can paint job rounds the dogleg trolley corner, wide rims spinning. The car is all blown speaker buzz. Can't even hear the engine. The vinyl top of the Chevy is peeling away, the windows rolled up and tinted dark, the driver a shadow outline as it passes and makes a turn into the tunnel, boom echo fading.

His shoe bumps the curbstone, and he pulls it back together. After his father denied telling the ax murder tale, Travis had let the question drop, but now it comes back to nag. His father had sounded sincere. Did he just forget? How could you forget something like that? He should have asked him in person, looked him in the eye and read his body language. He plods down the street and mulls it over one more time, thoughts freer with oxygen depletion. The lynching photo is in his head, the dead man chained to the tree, the spectators in their hats, and suddenly it hits him: His father hadn't been alone. His uncle was there too. If the story is a false memory, it's a false memory with leads. My uncle, he thinks. Uncle George had been there, too. That was part of the memory. He can ask him. Two sources. Maybe three. Maybe his grandmother can shine some light on this as well. Three sources to triangulate and corroborate. He can't believe that he didn't think of this before. The door isn't closed. This perks him up and his pace picks up, too.

The mouth of the tunnel isn't far ahead, and sound inside amplifies and echoes. A sudden thumping grows louder quickly. The rap car has returned, and the bass buzz from the wrecked speakers pound from the tunnel and into the morning light. It rolls from the arch, rims spinning, doesn't heed the stop sign and turns toward him, not slowing much at all. Tires squeal and the engine accelerates above the thump. Travis squints into the tinted windows. Still nothing but a shadow. The late model V-8 engine roars as the car comes fast. Travis scrambles to get out of the street and up onto the sidewalk. He makes it, but not by much as the driver swerves toward him and tires scrape the curb to send a clear message. It speeds away, bass fading, license plate receding fast. His glasses are back at the apartment but he tries to focus and give it a shot, squints at the tag to report to the cops, this attempted hit and run, but there is only a cardboard sign wedged into the center of the bumper. Tag Appied For.

Chapter Twelve

*H*enry Hemperly sits alone in the booth in the late p.m., a one-man show. He broadcasts from outside the perimeter highway at 50,000 watts and spreads the message to folks tuned in. Every time he swivels the chair he thinks the same thing: tell them again to lubricate the casters. The wheels squeak so loudly that his audience can hear it on the air. The repair is so simple. WD 40, 3 & 1 Oil, a little graphite—any of those will do the trick, but no matter how many work orders he fills out, they won't do it. They're not fixing it on purpose, he thinks. The janitor is black, and he's got it out for him. He clears his throat and leans toward the boom mic.

"There's no doubt about it. Our Confederate heritage is being erased."

His voice pitches up to suggest outrage, but his heart is just not in it this evening and he sags back into the cushion. The day before, he was surprised by a phone call from his surviving son, and he's been off his stride ever since. He hasn't been able to sleep for one and can't concentrate, two. Prayer is the answer, of course, and he's been at it for a while, praying for Travis to reach out, praying with whole heart—not just in random moments driving or doing the dishes. He kneels nightly, gets down on his knees by the bedside, elbows on the quilt, hands clasped, eyes closed, mind focused, and gives it everything he's got. Please. A phone call. A postcard. Something. He has been doing this for he doesn't know how long. Now that the call has finally come, he doesn't know what to do. He put so much effort into trying to make it happen that he hadn't considered what to say once the phone rang.

They didn't talk for long—five minutes, tops—before the awkward pauses began. Travis hung up not long after. Henry has replayed the conversation in slow motion ever since, has broken it down, analyzed it to death and now he has it memorized. The initial surprise. The flood of emotion. The between-the-lines finger pointing, both of them speaking on top of each other. Go ahead. No, you go ahead. Charlie was there from the first word, his ghost traveling the AT&T lines. He haunted Henry to bed, causing a restless night, sheets kicked off and trapped in the depression in the middle of the mattress. This morning after breakfast, he phoned Pastor Thimble about it. He even wandered off-topic during last night's show and mentioned on air that his son had moved back to the city to teach at the black college—to the surprise of his listeners and Arnie in the control booth, who grinned and gave him the thumbs up through the window. He thought that Henry had invented having a son as a ruse to blunt the complaints, but Arnie is a racist and an unbeliever with a foul mouth. He's a good golfer, though.

It's been a difficult day, yes, and the chair squeaks again. Sometimes Charlie is far in the back of his thoughts, the accident so distant a memory that it is almost not there at all, and on these days Henry has a sense that the past hasn't ruined the present. And then there are days like today and he is back on the lake once again, stuck in the moment and standing on the deck of the cabin cruiser with his arms crossed, the wind strange on the water, the dry leaves rustling on the tree line island way over there behind the tiny buoy. One phone call has brought it all back. There is no getting around it. He killed his youngest son. Killed one son and lost the second. He has lived with this burden for twenty years, even though he knows in his heart that he has been forgiven. It's not enough though. Try as he might he cannot forgive himself. His entire life is summed up by a single moment, a decision that turned out badly for all aboard that day. He is standing on the deck of the Criss Craft beside the engine hood with arms still crossed, the wind still strange, having just tossed Charlie into the lake after surprising him, picking him up and throwing him over the transom and into the dark green water. Henry's ankles lock as the boat bobs underneath his flip flops. Beth's mouth is wide open just before the scream. Travis is skinny in cut-offs and tossing Cracker

Jacks to the freeloading crow. Charlie didn't even try to swim. He didn't do anything, not even a doggie paddle. He just hit the water spread eagled, eyes wide, mouth open, and disappeared beneath the chop, swallowed up by the big lake. This was how Dad had taught Henry to get over his fear of the water, how Granddad had taught Dad. The sink-or-swim method was a rite of passage in the Hemperly clan, although Charlie had been the first one in the family to actually sink.

Every time the accident returns to the foreground, it always follows the same path and arrives at the same question: why didn't Charlie try? How could he not have made an effort? When Travis's time had come five years before, the Criss Craft was mothballed, docked and dusty in yet another extended state of disrepair, lashed to its slip in Holiday Marina and floating but not going anywhere. They had driven up from Atlanta that Saturday to work on the bilge pump, and during a break he crept up behind his firstborn standing at the far end of the dock and spitting into the water to lure bream to the surface. Henry caught him by surprise and pushed him with both hands into the shallow cove. Travis responded appropriately, like he had when his father had given him the push, swallowing water and crying but getting the point. He splashed about and stayed afloat and learned to swim that weekend. When Charlie's time came, he did nothing. He didn't even yell. He just flew over the rail, hit the water, then the splash, and he was gone.

The door to the booth cracks open, and Arnie's head sticks in with urgent whisper. "Henry! Dead air! Dead air!"

Henry snaps back to the present, fuzz in the headphones, and he shakes it off and gives Arnie the thumbs-up. The casters squeal as he turns the chair. Where was he? The pad on the cart player lists the night's topic and supporting points. A grunt to clear his throat.

"I hope that pause allowed the message to sink in," he ad libs. "It's the truth. Our Confederate heritage is being erased—intentionally and methodically by the dark forces of the Atlanta City Council. Next bullet: Monuments to our Confederate dead have been pushed aside one after the other and our heritage pushed with them. Next bullet: Now I know what you're thinking: here he goes, talking about the state flag again. But not at all, not at all, no sir. The flag is but a symbol, a representation of a way of life. People who attack our heritage have defined that way of life as being evil, and they say that the symbol represents slavery and oppression, and folks, we have let them do it. Tonight I want to talk about what the symbol really stands for." Arnie nods through the glass. Henry makes his case. "Valor. Honor. Chivalry. Righteousness. These words have no meaning to the youth of today, to the young people who are our future. They are bombarded by so much moral corruption and sexual depravity and yes I'll say it: sin. I'm not a preacher and I'm not preaching to you, but call in and tell me if you think there's a better word. They are bombarded by so much perversion and sleaze that they do not know right from wrong. They have no moral compass."

Charlie sinks back down. Henry finds his stride, builds up steam, and his voice sounds red in the face. "The culture has lost its way. All you need for proof is to look inside the perimeter highway. I was born and raised in Atlanta back when it was a decent place to live, back before we let them take it over. I know some of you are thinking that it's always been a hell hole, but that's not true. It used to be a good place to raise a family. I know I'm not supposed to say this, but the blacks are destroying the fabric of our society, and it is spreading like a cancer. Somebody has to say it. They have normalized thievery and drugs and lying and fornication as part of their culture. They have brought chaos and anarchy. Just listen to their music. Violence. Hedonism. Misogyny. Miscegenation. Yet when you point out the obvious, they call you a racist. Well folks, it is time for us to fight back. What we need, and what I advocate to you this evening, is a return to a Confederate Value System. Gentility must not just be protected, it must be expanded. We need to return to the principals of valor, honor, chivalry, and righteousness. We need to hold a moral fidelity to these high ideals."

Arnie appears in the glass again, pointing at his wrist watch.

Government regulation demands that he announce the time and call sign every hour on the hour, and he has forgotten again. "You're tuned in to WCTR—Confederate Talk Radio—and this is tonight's discussion topic." He punches the blinking button below the rotary dial. "Caller, go ahead."

A male voice speaks up. Industry thumps in the background. "Hello, Henry. I thank you for your show and appreciate you taking my call."

"Thanks for tuning in."

"I've been telling everybody who will listen ever since it happened and even filled out a report with the APD—like that'll do any good. I never go in to Atlanta unless I absolutely have to, but last June my wife kept bothering me for us to make the trip in to see an Olympic event, so we drove in to watch one of the swim events at Tech—the U.S. and Paraguay—and as everyone knows parking is a nightmare down there. We finally found a lot but it was a good ways from the pavilion and no shuttle so we had to walk. Anyway, this black guy in an orange vest motioned us in off the street and charged us $20 to park—outrageous I know, but I paid it 'cause we were tired of driving around. Anyway, come to find out that it was just an empty lot. The other cars parked there for free. It was pure theft—a mugging really. He might as well have had a gun. We could have been killed. And here I was, telling her that downtown wasn't that bad. Anyway, I don't know if this fits into your topic tonight but I just wanted to get the word out to people so they'll be careful. If you go downtown, don't trust any black man who says he's running a parking lot. Too many people stay silent about this sort of thing. This is why the country has gone to hell."

"Well, it most certainly does," Henry nods. "And it speaks specifically to tonight's topic and underscores my point. We have to restore the character of our nation. This unfortunate person's behavior was certainly not honorable and he is hardly living a righteous life by stealing from the uninformed. He took advantage of you and stole your hard-earned money, and we all know what he spent it on. Had he lived by the code he would have welcomed you to the city and offered his assistance, not taken advantage of you—and let me take this moment to be clear: this value system is not purely a 'white' value system. The blacks will be the biggest beneficiaries by adopting it themselves—Again the four points: Valor. Honor. Chivalry. Righteousness. Thanks for calling." He punches the button. It sticks. The chair squeaks. He punches again. "Next caller, go ahead."

The lyrics come loud: "Fuck the police and Bone said it with authority 'cause the niggas on the streets is . . . !"

"Oh-kay!" Henry cuts the call and shakes his head. Where the heck is Arnie? Do I have to do everything around here myself? he thinks and pulls the mic closer. "I think that proves my point right there. Next caller, go ahead."

"Hello, Henry. Great show tonight. I think you've really tapped into something here. I want to thank you for telling the truth. Too many people shut themselves at home, watch TV and pretend that everything is hunky-dory, and all the while the government is failing. Schools are failing. Churches are failing. Families are failing. Our entire culture is in crisis. It takes courage to stand up and say the things you're saying. We've got to do something soon to save this country, otherwise it's going to be too late, if it isn't already."

"Yes sir." The chair squeals. "All the examples you cited—I don't agree with you that the churches are failing—the inner city churches, maybe. But the others. Just think about it. Think if all people everywhere—white, black, red, yellow, green, whatever—lived by such a code of civil behavior. Imagine crime dropping off to nothing. We wouldn't need police departments or the taxes to support them. Everyone would be better off."

"The rule of law."

"The rule of law," Henry nods and confirms.

"This could become a movement."

"It's exciting to think about, isn't it?—and it's such a simple concept."

Tonight's show is going better than Henry expected. He feels validated and thinks of the possibilities, considers a marketing campaign. Thoughts of bumper stickers and residuals bring a warm feeling. He pauses a sec in case the caller wants to continue, but he only asks about the squeal. "Just some technical difficulty," Henry says. "You know how fast technology changes. Please remember us on our next members drive so we can keep the equipment up-to-date. Thanks for calling," he punches the button. "Next caller, go ahead."

"Hello, Henry. Thanks for taking my call. This isn't about your topic, but I wanted to ask you anyway. You said last night that your son teaches at a black college and I think that's very commendable."

"Why, thank you."

"What I wanted to ask was, what's that like for him? How do they treat him, especially with a father as dedicated to our Confederate heritage as you are?"

Broadcasting is an easy gig. Henry has been hosting his call-in show for two years now, and how many topics has he put together on the drive over? More than he would admit. There's not much to it. He comes up with an issue that will keep his listeners riled-up and then manages their calls and keeps them stoked so they'll keep tuning in. He could do the show in his sleep if need be. But this question is unexpected. He doesn't talk about his private life on the air even though he introduced it himself inadvertently on the last show. When he mentioned it, he was still lightheaded from the phone call, was still processing and praying about it. Had he had a little distance, he would never have brought it up, and he did not intend for it to become a regular topic of conversation. He has never had a problem finding words before, but now nothing comes. It's a simple question, but he has no answer.

After Charlie went under, it took him a good ten seconds to realize that something had gone wrong. Certainly the boy was just clowning around under the surface. Beth was up fast off the seat cushions, hands on the rail and leaning over, then her red fingernails dug into his shoulder, as she screamed at his crew cut. Travis behind in the mate's seat yelling too: *Dad! Dad!* And then everything slowed down. The pitch of the boat. The chop of the waves. The flap of the freeloading crow. Henry drew a big breath, plopped one foot on the engine hood for spring and he was over the side, arms straight out before him, hands together and pointing directly at the widening circle where Charlie had disappeared. Hands arms head into warm water, the rush of bubbles as he clawed handfuls back and fought his way down, pulling himself deeper into the green, the sun dazzle fading with every stroke, and the water cold now. Before him: nothing, the darkening abyss total, the pressure building in his ears, the pain sharper with each pull downward, the water colder and colder still, the force of it squeezing his head, his lungs tightening and then heaving, and he was out of air. Charlie had a twenty-foot head start, a straight-down projectile now falling to the lake bed one hundred feet below the boat and toward the ruins of a little hamlet submerged when the dam was built and the foothills flooded. He descended toward a building still standing, the roof of a small church. His body struck behind the leaning steeple, his shoulder crashing into and through the rotting timbers and scattering deep-water catfish. Despite the two day search by State Patrol divers, he was not recovered.

Arnie at the window, face puzzled, finger tapping.

Henry is shaken. He removes his reading glasses, wipes his eye with the back of his hand and waves him off. "What was the question?"

"How do they treat him? The blacks. Your son?"

"You'll have to ask him," his voice hoarse and he cuts the caller off abruptly. He doesn't want to offend a listener but needs to nip this in the bud now. He punches the button and clears his throat. "Next caller, go ahead."

"Thanks for taking my call." A lady's voice. "I've been listening to what you've been saying about your 'Confederate Value System,' and I'm just calling to tell you that you are a complete jackass."

Henry chokes, stabs a finger at the lit button to disconnect. "Bye-bye, little lady," he croaks, the caller banished from the airwaves. Talk about a slap in the face. It takes him a moment to regain his composure. Lots of dead air in tonight's broadcast. Arnie's head in the window mouthing foul language. Henry fumbles, leans over the boom mic. "I see that one of our friends inside the perimeter is listening in tonight. You hear her language. You see how she behaves. Another angry lesbian, no doubt. This is what has happened to womanhood. These people are so fanatical they can't even participate in civil discourse. I'm here trying to offer real solutions to real problems. In this country we have something called the First Amendment, missy. I know we're all familiar with it here—all our regular listeners, anyway. It's what the Founding Father's fought and died for. His index finger punches the lit button. "Next caller, go ahead."

"Like your pathetic signal could even reach the city." Her voice still in his ear. "Does the FCC know about you? It's 1996, asshole. Catch up with the rest of us."

Something has gone wrong. Henry punches the button one, two, three times, but the light still glows. How many times has he told them to upgrade the equipment? They had a surplus after the last fundraising drive, but what did they spend it on? T-shirts and coozies.

"All you're doing is using coded racist language. What's next? 'Was slavery really wrong? Are women really people?'" Henry tries to get a word in edgewise but she talks over him. "Let me explain it to you: the Civil War ended one hundred and thirty-two years ago. The South lost. What is it about that that you don't understand?"

Arnie in the window. He slices his hand across his throat and sends the kill sign. Henry puts his hands in the air, both palms up and points at the telephone.

"You're just a racist with a low IQ and a microphone. What gives you the right to be so socially irresponsible? How dare you! Your only value system is the value system of the affluent white male. You don't have the intellect to comprehend anything else. Why don't you volunteer sometime and actually do something that helps the community?"

Henry engages: "There it is, folks. The classic liberal response to any situation is to cry racism. You might want to do your homework and know what you're talking about before you attack others, little lady. I'm volunteering my time to help the community. All of us on air here at WCTR are. We are all in the trenches here. It's because of our hard work that you're able to sit at home drinking your latte and eating your cheese."

"You're crazy. That doesn't even make sense. Do you even know a single black person? The guy earlier said you had a son. Now that's a scary thought, people like you breeding—and he's teaching African-American students too?! No wonder nothing changes."

And she hangs up.

Henry is discombobulated. The phone lights up, blinking buttons of support, he knows. Whenever there's a slip and someone like this gets through, he can depend on his regular listeners to get his back. "Reminds me of my ex-wife," he quips and wipes egg from his face. It shouldn't be so hard. All he wants to do is help. His audience, his golfing buddies, they all talk of the city as if it is a hopeless wasteland, overrun by the blacks and the gays and nothing but a danger and a tax burden. Sodom, Gomorrah, Atlanta, the tri-cities of moral corruption. But he was born and raised downtown, as were his parents and his sons, and he still feels the connection, more so as the years pass. The city was small and civil then, and downtown was honest and safe. It was a good life. And it can be so again, one day. All they have to do is move back inside the perimeter, build private schools for their children until enough blacks move out so that the public school system can be fixed. It's going to be a big job, but he is confident in his vision. It is his way of giving back. The Value System is just the beginning.

Quittin' time comes late, and Henry is exhausted. It's been a long one this evening, and it has really taken it out of him. He signs off, ends tonight's show by waxing poetic about how the Confederate Value System will allow his listeners to maximize their cash flow, and hands over the noisy chair to the Hunley guy on the late-late shift—a chubby fellow wearing a butternut uniform, and sporting both a beard and a tasseled sailor's cap. *Don't give him a chance to talk about that submarine*, he thinks, *or I'll never get out of here.* Arnie has long left the building, has turned out all the lights in the little office, and Henry rummages through the file cabinet and then the desk for yet another work order. He just can't understand it—not their failure to fix the chair, but their failure to fix themselves. The three hundred-or-so years of bondage were unfortunate, but that was a long time ago. Why don't they seize what's before them today? Why don't they make more of an effort? The structure of civilized society is before them—a great gift. Why don't they take it? He pulls one, two, three ink pens from the Cyclorama coffee cup before he finds one that writes and drops the order in the mail cubby with the Janitor label. This time, his request is more emphatic, all capitals and underlined. A firmer hand. No "please" this time. His keys jingle as he unlocks the glass door and steps into the office park.

The night is clear. The moon is full. All the grounds are manicured, a soft breeze and fresh cut grass when he inhales. The center boulevard is lined with peach trees in the blue moonlight, all at the proper height. His Lexus is the only car in the lot—the Hunley guy lives close by and rides his unicycle—and it cranks on the first turn. He backs up, turns, rolls the short distance to the exit arrow and hits the break at the red light to the street, settles back into the bucket seat and the weight of it all settles onto his shoulders. Outside the windshield: nothing on the right, nothing on the left, the road wide open before him. Both lanes well lit by the street lamps in receding pools. The engine idles. Across the street, all lots are empty. No one in the office park this late, the moon up high, and the traffic light still red. He sags back, head on the headrest. Jesus has finally answered his prayer, and now he has a chance to make things right with his son. Thank you Jesus. *Footprints.* Charlie is long dead, the family split long ago, and he is alone now despite the women in the singles class with their *maybe we can work something out* eye signals and Dot from over near the clubhouse. His mother is amazing, that's what everyone always says, and he finds comfort in her long years, but she is beginning to slip. George is up in the mountains and won't come down. There's no one else to take care of her. Maybe a drive into the city to see her this weekend. Maybe it will be one of her good days. He hasn't played the course at the club with his golfing buddies since before the Olympics. They're not family, though. Family. Travis said that he would call back, said that he'd think about meeting at the club for lunch sometime. You've got it all, Henry, that's what they say. His pastor said it this morning, or implied it, and Henry let him think it but he'd trade it all. All of it. He does have his audience, his regular callers. Steffen. Thomas. He feels a connection with them, a genuine fondness despite the limitations of these phone-only friendships, and there sure are a lot of smashed bugs on the windshield, time to go by the car wash again and if he gets there before noon on Saturday it's only five dollars, although they don't do the inside but he can vacuum—gosh, this is a long light.

Chapter Thirteen

*T*he provost steps from the administration building and out into the morning sunshine blanketing MLK Plaza. Students criss-cross the concrete expanse in the frenzied ten-minute change between classes. They navigate around the statue of Dr. King, the Egyptian obelisk rising up behind, more students across the street hurrying to class before the bell rings the hour, all hustling to be on time as he mandates every chance he gets in front of them with a microphone.

His shortened stride betrays his preoccupation. There is something weighing on his mind, and the fresh air will do him good. Walking the campus benefits his soul. It always has. Today's issue is a minor annoyance, to be sure, just something he overheard. Still, it bugs him. He doesn't concern himself with people who bad mouth him behind his back, those spiteful casters of aspersions. A man in his position of power is bound to ruffle feathers now and again. He just prefers not to overhear it, which is what happened earlier this morning when he walked up behind the dean of student services—a non-alumni.

Let's start with "good," he thinks. He has no truck with this adjective and agrees wholeheartedly. He is a good man. He is in good standing with official offices. His credit rating is excellent. He has obeyed federal, state and municipal laws all of his life. He's been a deacon at the AME for a decade. By any measure, he is a good man.

"Old," on the other hand, sticks in his craw. Who wants to be called old? He looks good for his age and certainly doesn't feel old, just a pain now and then. After a certain point, age is relative anyway. There's a gray area. For that reason, he disagrees with the application of this word to his personage. Sure, to his granddaughter he must have the taint of elder years apparent in his hair, which went from kinky black to woolly white overnight, it seemed. His goatee followed suit. He just doesn't consider himself old—although he can understand how some would apply the word to him.

And finally the most problematic descriptor: the erroneous noun "boy." It is thorny on several levels, of course. He's hardly a boy in any sense of the word. As a racial epithet, not even the white folk use the term these days, not like they used to. He has risen to the top of his profession and is a solid tax-paying citizen. No one would reference him as a boy, not chronologically, not racially. But the three words together ring in his ears as he strolls across the plaza. The phrase suggests that he has not earned what he has received, that connections and back-room cigar-chomping have somehow lessoned his accomplishments. This is not so. Sometimes a cigar is just a cigar. Just because he is on the national board of directors of his fraternity does not mean that he has not earned his achievements fairly and squarely. Still, the phrase haunts. It's hard to shake.

Across the street, the broad side of Garvey Hall stretches up the hill, the glass entranceway connecting the classrooms to the theater in full view. Students hurry back and forth along the sidewalk in front of the building, and inside the glass entrance, too, a flurry of activity. Behind the humanities building, the construction is coming along nicely. The I-beam frame is up, the shape of the tower now outlined. Such a grand new building for the campus, he thinks. Such a waste of space to have it dedicated to the humanities. Business is his business, and the business department is ascendant, he's made sure of that since he was kicked upstairs to administrative affairs. All the struggle for all these years, and only now is black America entering the segregated halls of commerce in a significant way.

Atlanta might be a chocolate city, but the white business structure still holds power. It is time for all of that to change. Their time to perform in the corporate arena has arrived. The dream will be deferred until they manage to do this, and they won't manage to do this until the college puts the focus where it needs to be. He shakes his head at the construction. Being well-rounded is all well-and-good, but it wasn't going to solve the problems facing the community. Why didn't more people understand this? They need more CEOs, not more poets.

He steps across the street and enters the dwindling stream as the obelisk behind him begins to toll the commencement of the next class hour, ambles down the sidewalk and skirts the giant magnolias as late students twist and turn in front of him, and he directs a disapproving eye to each. He makes an announcement: "To be early is to be on time, to be on time is to be late," broadcasting the message of reinforcement to ears in range. Everyone accelerates. Distance widens between them. It only takes a few words to make the students flee. Call him what they will, he commands their respect, and this settles his mind. Everything is falling into place. The trains are beginning to run on time.

He rounds the corner, his mood lightened now, so much so that he feels like whistling, although he would never do so in public, and then the needle scratches the vinyl and brings him to a sudden halt. Twenty feet ahead, a short Ku Klux Klansman in full regalia stands outside the back entrance to Garvey Hall. He is wearing the whole ensemble, toga sheet and pointed hood with eye holes cut. Paratrooper boots and a protest sign held in left hand, a homemade declaration in black Magic Marker: WHITE SUPREMACY! Gray dreadlocks fall from underneath the back of the hood. What the hell is this? the provost thinks and reaches for a name. It's the one with the dreadlocks. Kalamari.

A student steps from the door, and the klansman begins to heckle.

"Hey, boy!" he yells with heavy country accent and pointing finger. The student glances at him, one of those turn-of-the-head sidelong glances, before straightening up and walking on, ignoring the taunt, "I'm talking to you, boy!" the klansman yells. "You better listen to me, nigger. We gonna' pay you a visit tonight!"

The student ignores him and hustles off to class. A small crowd gathers in front of Woodson hall thirty feet west, five students stopped to watch and more on the way. He's attracting a crowd when they should be going to class. Two students step from the parking lot, book bags both and one wears a necktie. The klansman turns. "You two niggers better watch out. You'd better stay away from white women."

"Too late, dog," says the young student in the necktie. The other busts out a laugh as they maneuver around him and through the door.

"You think you're smart, boy," he yells after them. "I'm gonna' string you up!"

Someone in the crowd in front of Woodson says something, and there's a big laugh all around. "Hey, cracker!" one yells, but they straighten up when they notice the provost.

The provost steps forward. "Kalamari!"

The klansman turns. "Who you callin' Kalamari, boy?" he says in the same hostile cornpone voice, but then a muted explanation, "This is a dramatic exercise to encourage vigilance." He follows with an urgent whisper: "And you're blowing my cover."

"Kalamari, stop this nonsense. You're making the students late for class." He turns to the crowd in front of Woodson and says it again: "Gentlemen, to be early is to be on time, to be on time is to be late." Before he finishes the sentence, they begin to scatter and head off in different directions.

Kalamari lowers the sign, removes the hood and shakes his head, dreadlocks swinging free. He glares at the provost and his eyes narrow. They lock eyes, and the provost stares him down. He thrills at moments like this, whenever he can go one-on-one with a member of the faculty. They always defer to power, especially the humanities faculty, every one of them a sheep. The best Kalamari can manage is a strained: "The most valuable lessons don't always come from the classroom."

"Today they do," the provost says and makes it clear by his tone. Kalamari is a hard one to figure, he thinks. Had he been provost at the time of his tenure review, he wouldn't have been granted permanent status. Not a chance. Of this he is sure. It is beyond understanding why he has stayed on faculty even with tenure. The provost has seen to it personally that his salary has remained in the low tens. Still, he stays. How do you get rid of these people? Kalamari retorts to the command with a weak invocation of academic freedom, but the provost is finished here and isn't going to entertain a silly conversation. "See to it that you don't disrupt the students' schedules."

And with that he walks away, leaving Kalamari standing with hood in hand, when he hears the aspersion cast once again, even though it's a mumble. The words bounce off of his back. His character is not impugned. They can grouse all they want, but they still fear him, locked into their little-people patterns, as they are. Three steps and his shoe moves into the shadow of the new construction rising before him, the building taking shape and beginning to tower, the vertical girders, iron clanging, blowtorch on the fourth floor blasting sparks, shooting a twinkling shower in his direction. Such a waste, he thinks, such a waste, and he suppresses a covetous instinct. The construction was approved and initiated by the previous administration, a project conceived by a different leadership with a different vision, a limited vision chained to the past. The blowtorch does its hot work, a surge in the shower of sparks, and one of them beats the odds, claims a longer life and stays lit while the others wink out. It catches on the wind and drifts down from the heights. He follows it falling, coming closer, when it ignites an idea within him. Something that hadn't occurred to him before. He is in the position of power now, and power has its privileges. The challenge is how to use the privilege, and he warms at the revelation. He releases a sigh, a long, slow exhale. Getting out and about always frees his thinking, and this was certainly a walk worth taking. His head drops back and he looks up high, takes another gander at the rising beams, imagines the building completed, imagines the building as it should be, and he cannot deny that on this day, without a doubt, it is good to be provost.

Chapter Fourteen

*I*f a smile is but a frown turned upside down, the chair has gone South—as people in the North say. Dr. Davis was inclined to dismiss the first phone call, the first complaint, as just one of those things. Parents complain from time to time, call on the telephone or come in person. Those who believe that they have clout go around her now and again, go over her head and straight to the top of the administration building across the street. But addressing parental complaints is one of her duties. Such flames are usually fanned by concerned mothers. She is a both a mother and a grandmother and understands. They worry about their children, most of who are away from home for the first time, and there is cause for concern.

But this is something different. A small fire has ignited in her office before she even enters the room, a parent on the telephone—the phone itself ringing insistently as she hurries to turn the key in the lock and get inside with books and carryall and drop them in the corner chair and then over to the phone before it stops ringing. Anger on the line. No pleasant introduction, not even a good morning, just a demand for answers that she does not have. She has no explanation, she tells the fuming voice. She has known Dr. Kalamari for many years, and no one has ever made this sort of complaint. No, she's sure, she says. She placates the parent who hangs up less heated but leaves a veiled threat anyway. The seat cushion embraces her as she relaxes back into the chair, receiver hot in hand, cord stretching, and she exhales. The blinking yellow light alerts her to voice messages. She punches in the code and finds two more complaints, just as angry for the same reason. And it's not even nine o'clock.

She knows his schedule and waits for him to arrive for his

early class, and hears him enter the building and the junior faculty greeting him along the way. But he did not respond to the note that she left him herself in his mailbox: *Dr. Kalamari: See me immediately. Dr. Davis.* The message could not have been more concise or clear, but he did not come to her office before his class. Is he avoiding her, she wonders or is it just the usual resentment of female supervision? Perhaps he *is* hiding something, but she decides to give him the benefit of the doubt. Perhaps he is in a rush to prepare for his class. Still, she keeps an eye on the wall clock above the bookshelf and when he is due to return after the hour is up, she leaves the desk, stands in the lobby doorway off the hallway, and waits. Her colleagues each have their own way of walking, their footfalls giving their approach or retreat away (except, mysteriously, for professor Longman who makes no sound, as big as he is), and she has always been surprised at the predictability of their schedules, their movements. Kalamari's gate is unmistakable, his pace quick, his boots clomping heavily above the din of noisy students changing classes. He enters the lobby of the history department. He wears a white robe today, a change from his usual camouflage pants, but he pulls the robe over his head and wads it up and she sees that he is wearing his usual wardrobe underneath.

"Dr. Kalamari. A moment in my office." She doesn't say please, back turned now.

His heavy boots follow, and he walks in, dragging a protest sign, his pace a little slower today and his forehead wrinkled in the preoccupation of post-class wind-down.

"The door," she says.

"Good morning to you, too, Sister Davis." He pulls the knob behind him, shutting the lobby out, steps to her desk, drops the robe into the chair on the right and sits on the left, not saying a word—unusual for him. He usually tries to dominate the conversation immediately. No pleasantries are traded between them, no collegial patter whatsoever. Tension thrums.

"Dr. Kalamari. I've received some complaints this morning, three parents by telephone and two written from students in your 101."

"Yes?" He examines his fingernails.

"The complaints say that you have been touching the students."

"What are you suggesting?" his voice calm and eyes still appraising cuticles. He opens his mouth and sustains a yawn.

"I'm not suggesting anything, Dr. Kalamari, but I have complaints here. I have documentation to which I must respond. And Legal Affairs has called." This gets his attention.

"Who wrote them?" Kalamari stands and demands. "Let me see those." He snatches the two letters, glances over them, balls them up with both hands. "Nonsense." He aims for the trash can. Shoots. Scores.

"Dr. Kalamari! Remove those immediately. This is not a frivolous matter."

"Sister Davis, this is just a misunderstanding," he defends, but he does pull the crumpled paper from the can, tosses it back onto her desktop and sits. The ball of complaint bounces to the telephone, ricochets, and rolls to a stop. She opens the wad, pats them flat, and reads: "'This note is to alert you to the fact that Dr. Kalamari has been placing his hands on the students in his history 101 class in an inappropriate manner.' Explain this misunderstanding to me."

"Sister Davis, I believe the note is speaking to an exercise I use in that class. I try to recreate the conditions of the Middle Passage. It's a helpful exercise to reconnect them to the injustice of slavery."

She lifts the other complaint, limp and crinkled, clears her throat and reads. "Dr. Kalamari grabbed my manhood. He makes us lie on the dirty floor and then he gets on top of us and rolls around and feels us."

Kalamari jumps up out of the chair. "These students have become too disconnected from their history!" His hands on her desktop now and he leans closer, speaks louder. "How do *you* teach them about their history? Assign them a chapter to read?"

"Dr. Kalamari, I appreciate your efforts to make your class dynamic, but you will stop touching the students immediately. Surely there is a way to do this without angering parents and involving Legal Affairs."

"Physical contact is an important part of the message!"

"Not anymore."

"Who are you to tell me how to teach my class?" he snaps. "My methods are effective, sister. We are not picking cotton here. We are fighting for the survival of our people. I will not abandon our cause just because some handkerchief head can't stand up to our oppressors."

"Dr. Kalamari, there is no need to insult me for doing my job. You will comport yourself in a professional manner or I will add another reprimand to your file."

"'Comport myself'?" he sneers. "Sister, you have been working in the big house for too long." He stands and snatches his books from the chair, turns his back, and heads for the door.

"Dr. Kalamari," she implores. "Be reasonable."

He stops in the doorway. "Reasonable? Sister, it was reason that enslaved our people in the first place!" He slams the door behind him. The door jamb shakes.

The crumpled complaints gripe from the desktop, and she considers poor judgment on her part—not just now but last spring. The choices we make, she thinks. When the position of chair opened suddenly the year before—the previous chair disappearing mid-semester among rumors of corruption, something about an extracurricular soccer team—the provost offered her the position. She had accepted it, because the increase in salary would allow her to cut back on her moonlighting but mostly because she would be the first female chair of the department in the college's 110 year history, and she was unable to turn down the opportunity to contribute to such a moment of social progress, however small. She was well aware of the biases and predilections of her male colleagues but hadn't anticipated such an abrasive reaction to her supervision. None of them had wanted the position for themselves and were comfortable maintaining their established schedules, so she didn't expect the discontent. The choices we make, she thinks again, and now has to decide what to do about this latest fire, larger now after talking to Dr. Kalamari. The telephone begins to ring, an angry tone, and then bursts into flames. Again. She sighs heavily and reaches for the hand towel in the bowl on the window ledge behind her, pulls it from the water, rag dripping, wrings it once, and beats the flames back before picking up the receiver.

Chapter Fifteen

T *he neon penis sashays green into the room . . .*

Meggan doesn't believe in revision and never has. Each poem comes to her complete, pure, perfect, and rewriting just contaminates. She sits in her cubical, her back to the open end, and writes on a legal pad, just like she used to, writes with a green Bic pen, just like she used to and allows her script to loop and flow. How long has it been since she's written in longhand? Cursive is unfamiliar to her now. She covers the work protectively, blocks the pad with her body should any of her nosy co-workers snoop in. It used to give her so much joy, writing a poem with a pen on paper, the direct physical connection between her soul and the page, but she has been using a computer and writing service-oriented prose for so long that it has killed the skill. She has lost touch with her feel for the music of the words, their rhythm, their beauty, and now that she tries she can't make them come.

Nothing.

She has lost it all.

It is over.

Chapter Sixteen

A.B. Longman sits at the kitchen table. He reaches for another Premium Saltine and thinks: The earth is missing its moon. The tellurium on the tabletop is old and broken, the tilted globe dated 1880. He collects orreries, or tries. Planetaria are hard to come by here in the States, fine machines of the solar system made of brass and wood, artifacts of another age. While European intellects were puzzling out the solar system, their New World counterparts were busy enslaving Africans and warring with the Indians. It was shipped by Royal Mail from Birmingham, England to his condo uptown—a gift for himself that he bought after the last course he moonlighted at Ft. Mac. It's not a bad gig, teaching world history on the side to the U.S. Army, motivated as they are. The brass base of the gizmo is damaged. The gears are tarnished. The moon is long gone. Who knows when it broke from its metal arm and rolled away? The earth is a century out of date, a brown and fading orb. The sun is in sad shape too. He needs to replace the candle in the center, the mighty star dwindled down to a wax stub—hardly a deity worth worshiping. One day he will restore it, replace the missing moon to orbit the planet and pull the tides once again, but it is not high on the list at the moment. It is another project for another day.

He pushes the plate of Hamburger Helper aside and considers not for the first time that he needs to upgrade his diet. Too much of his food comes packaged with NASCAR endorsement, white men in jump suits with sponsor's badges sewn on and a race car parked behind. He enjoys fine food and has a refined palate, but the other is so easy. And then there is the racial component, of course, more or less balanced by a little Louis Armstrong on the CD player, some Dixieland Jazz: brass horns, a little pomp and strut marching the streets of the Jim Crow French Quarter. He recalls fondly his days at Xavier, tried to make a go of it in the Crescent City, but New Orleans has been on the decline since the Civil War, and he couldn't find a job that didn't require him to spend his days in a kitchen—he spends enough time in his own kitchen as it is. So he packed up and moved to Atlanta, moved to where the money was. And here he sits in another daydream escape, thinking again of home. The food. The feel.

Then an orienting thought comes from the command center: snap out of it, Longman! Time to get back to work, so he sits up straight and scoots the chair closer to the table. The evening's project is scattered before him in pieces. He has trimmed the sails and hull halves carefully from their polystyrene sprues, the decks and masts and crows' nests, too. They lie disassembled on the tabletop: the three ships that started all the trouble. He has everything he needs: Plastic cement. Fine paint brushes—two of them. Little bottles of paint. Brown. White. Yellow. Red. He has paint thinner and an X-acto knife, too. Still, it is difficult for him to start the project. He has never completely understood his perfectionist inclination and has tried to incorporate sloppiness into his life. He tries to apply the glue with abandon. But potential mistakes make him fret and procrastinate. He tries to ignore the pest anxiety, tries not to care that the Christian crosses he paints red onto the sails of the little Spanish caravels will sway outside the lines and look lopsided. He intends to put them on public display, too, even if only in the office. His colleagues will view his work and draw conclusions about his skill and intellect and moral character, and this stymies his progress. It never fails that he finds himself focusing too intensely on what is before him, looking at it from too many angles, thinking about it too rapidly until his thoughts become chaos. It's just a plastic model kit. For Pete's sake, he tells himself. Relax.

He inhales a long, deep breath and considers context. He is sitting here today in this comfortable chair because of Contact. The collision of the old world and the new changed everything. The most profound and violent event in human history is acknowledged by a speed bump of a holiday, and ranks down at the

117

bottom of the Hallmark line, he is certain. Columbus Day. The beginning of slavery time, and no real reason to celebrate. It fits into the holiday hierarchy somewhere below President's Day. Perhaps a sub-layered guilt stirs in the majority after all. He doesn't take the stand as some do, does not call for the elimination of the holiday itself, not at all, but he does lobby for a different sort of celebration, has done so in a paper still unpublished. A period of observance is certainly called for, but parades send the wrong message. Deflate the happy balloons and light the solemn candles. Passover is a good model, the children of Abraham cowering in their homes as death drifts along the streets and alleyways, God's terrible wrath come to visit the unbelievers. No, do not celebrate the beginning of the New World. Meditate on the death of the Old. He has tried to change the trajectory of the understanding of Contact, has gotten some ground at the college but this is the Negro Leagues and his scholarship is aiming for the Majors. Still Columbus day remains on the calendars, an entrenched yet ho-hum holiday. Majority white schools continue to teach that Contact was a positive development in world affairs, the banks and the federal government enjoy a three day weekend, and then Tuesday arrives and the modern western tradition rolls on.

When he teaches Contact, Cristóbal Colón, and the invasion of the New World, he does so without malice, is careful that his presentations are not dogmatic or didactic. He is pragmatic about it, strives to maintain a level head, but it's hard not to sound like he is being judgmental about the Europeans and what came after. He tries to walk the line and be fair, but inevitably he feels like a hypocrite. Exploitation, enslavement, and murder are document-ed parts of the narrative, and the students get stirred up about it from time to time, but truth-be-told, he is ambivalent about the way things turned out. He keeps this to himself, but his personal feelings tend to change according to the side of the bed he has gotten up on any particular day. He can't maintain the outrage for long, certainly no longer than it takes to reach his next first world meal. The plate of leftovers is a testament to New World perk. Brown the beef, add the noodles, dump the flavor packet on top, a little water, and simmer. Beats the hell out of homemade fufu. Sure, he decries the invasion and discovery of the so-called New World now and again, and when this mood takes him he does so with gusto and gets it out of his system. But on sunny days, when he considers his circumstances and puts his life experience in perspective he has to acknowledge that he himself has done pretty well, considering. He makes his living off of the fallout from the grief and suffering of his ancestors. If not for Contact, American slavery would not have existed. The college wouldn't exist. His dissertation topic wouldn't exist. His social standing wouldn't exist. He has made the pilgrimage. He has been to Africa. He will not return. And besides, he would not survive long without this first world stability. He needs access to first world medications on a daily basis. His blood pressure. His heart. His weight has become a problem now, too. The modern world is okay by him.

The Niña, Pinta, and Santa Maria sail across their box tops and toward the edge of the flat earth. Their illustrations are just romantic imaginings. Who knows what they really looked like? They're just making it up, stamping out colorful images to grab the customer's eye, putting the pieces in a pretty box with instructions, sealing it in cellophane and sending it to the shelves. He doesn't begrudge anyone for the way things turned out. He takes things as they come, plays the hand he has been dealt. But today he dwells on a different time line, imagines what would have happened if the three plastic ships had never weighed anchor, had remained in Spain and never caught the tide before the sunrise, had never set sail West at all and had remained in the squalid horror show that was 15th century Europe, their keels covered in barnacles and rotting. The Black Plague. The Inquisition. What if this Christian-based capitalism had not grown West and become the dominant economic engine? What if the Europeans had come to their own ugly and inevitable vermin-filled end and an indigenous world view had grown to champion the globe instead?

The thought of it delays the project a little longer. It's never too late to procrastinate. He reaches across the table for the tellurium on its tarnished stand, grips the brass bar and broken wooden handle (he'll have to replace that as well). The cogs are stubborn and need oil. It is not so easy to crank the mechanism, but with a little more effort the gears begin to click. The earth revolves in fits and starts around the extinguished sun, the heliocentric universe a little worse for wear but still operating as the planet turns on its tilted axis. It orbits through the moonless seasons and another year: The Americas, Europe, Africa, Russia, China and then back around. The people of the earth spin by. No clouds on the planet today. There is sun for everyone everywhere, he thinks. He smiles, turns the crank, and watches time fly.

Chapter Seventeen

$\mathcal{R}$osa Lee Hemperly has traveled through time, has journeyed ninety-six years into the future and landed in the vestibule of this nice dining room. She sits in a high-backed leather chair next to the fireplace. How nice, she thinks. They've turned on the logs. The heat feels good, strokes her arms and warms her cheeks. Her hands stay cold these days, and it's a bother. The younger residents file by with canes and walkers, and some of them drive up on motorized scooters and park by the baby grand. They are well-groomed and dapper, have just come from church and are ready for lunch. She didn't go to Druid Hills this morning. Or did she? And she thinks about the new young preacher with the thin brown hair giving his sermon from behind the pulpit, his voice echoing up to the cross-hatched tile on the sanctuary ceiling and the golden curtains behind him where the choir used to sit. Or did Pastor Thimble give the lesson? She thinks that maybe he did but then remembers his funeral, remembers standing at his graveside service out at Westview. People from all over had driven in and gathered in black around the maroon tent and gray headstones, the biggest crowd she'd ever seen in a cemetery. What a loss it was for her Sunday school class, for the whole congregation. And now that she thinks about it, a Coca-Cola sure would be nice.

She looks around for Gladys, but Gladys isn't there. Isn't that always the way? She doesn't feel hungry but is dressed for lunch anyway and hopes that Henry is coming today. Sometimes he does that, he and that pretty girl make the drive in. Georgie, well, she can't remember the last time. He's always so busy with all those fish. But her sons have always been close. At night they guard her above her headboard in black and white—a portrait of both is framed in gold-leaf and hung on the wall behind her bed: Georgie, Henry. She had them taken special when they graduated from high school in turn, each of them with fresh haircuts and wearing his best suit and tie from Rich's downtown. She sleeps soundly beneath her boys, and has done so for seventy-five years.

A crowd collects before the hostess station, everyone lined up next to the sign with the smiling nigra holding the tray. They wait their turn while the fat girl escorts them to the linen-covered tables all around the big open dining room. It seems like they'd get one that was more able. Rosa Lee smiles at other residents waiting in line, and the new girl she sat next to at the hair dresser's just the other day gives a wave and blows a kiss. When the boys made her sell the house and move here, she pitched a fit and threatened to take them out of the will, but as much as she hated to admit it, they'd been right. Most of her new neighbors are lovely people. She even knows a few of them already from the Prado House and Druid Hills. She would never tell the boys this, but she is glad that she isn't in that big house alone anymore.

In the dining room, the tinkling of silverware echoes up to the chandeliers, and she wonders which table has been reserved for her today. She likes to sit on the window side so that she can see the patio and feel the sunlight, but not at the little tables for two against the wall, tables for the poor dears who eat alone. The fat girl seats them at the little tables next to the window bank that spans the room, and they slump their heads down at their plates and chew. Rosa Lee does not go to the dining room unescorted. She opts to stay in her condo and dine on Ritz Crackers and gin-soaked raisins. But today she has company, family coming to visit. Otherwise, why did Gladys help her get dressed and walk her to this chair? She doesn't know who is going to meet her for lunch today but hopes again that it is Henry. She is warm, the chair is comfortable, and everything around her is pleasant. And then a silver scooter rounds the corner, hums over fast, and runs right into her foot.

Rosa Lee cries out in alarm and her heart pounds in her blouse. This is just terrible. The scooter has stopped and that's a relief, but she feels unsettled by the fright. She knows the woman in the driver's seat, knows her from Druid Hills, and hasn't cared for her since FDR. Bossy, showy, and loud, Ina Musket grips the handlebars with both hands like she is driving a motorcycle. She meant to do that, Rosa Lee thinks.

"Why, Rosa Lee! Did I hit you, honey? I am so sorry!" Ina dismounts her ride. "I hope I didn't hurt you, you poor dear. Is your foot okay?"

"Heavens-to-Betsy, Ina. You nearly scared me to death!"

Rosa Lee looks down at the rude scuff on her beige loafer. Her foot doesn't feel worse than usual—but her feet hurt all the time, so it's hard to judge.

"I don't know, dear." She rubs her heel. "I think I'd better have it looked at."

"I am so sorry. Richard just bought me this new scooter, and it's just so complicated that I haven't yet learned how to drive it. That brake pedal is so far away. You really should get you one of these, honey. They make it so much easier to get around these long halls, and I know your condo is all the way at the end, down near those awful train tracks. And you've got such a long way to go with that walker, you poor dear."

Rosa Lee's walker stands at the ready, grazing next to the arm-chair and munching fleur-de-lis from the carpet, waiting for her to mount and stump down the road, a horse cart plodding along as speeding automobiles and auto-trucks roar by, their tires churning dirt and sand up into her face, all over her new blouse, and just ruining her hair. She wants Henry to buy her a scooter, too, thinks about how they were the first family on the street in the Prado house to own a television, the Halicrafter that Georgie helped her buy. She has asked Henry to get her one, or she needs to ask him to get her one. Maybe he will surprise her with one today. She hopes so.

Guilt. Remorse. Shame. They haunt Travis as he turns into the long drive of the assisted living complex. His grandmother is almost one hundred years old, a living artifact of a century of Atlanta history. What an accomplishment to survive for this long, and it certainly demands more acknowledgment than he has given it. Such a long life lived deserves more respect. Annual celebrations attended. Regular genuflection. Something more than his extended absence and the half dozen yellow roses in green wrapping paper lying in the lap of the passenger seat. He has not seen her in . . . how long has it been? A few visits since he left the South but not for long, not for a while, and just when passing through. The roses have bloomed, lost their smell, and won't last long. But hey, they were on sale.

Try as he might, when he considers her age and how long she has lived, he always considers his age, and he wonders if his DNA is as durable, if lucky heredity will extend his own allotted lifespan. Now that he thinks about it, he can't explain his grandsonly neglect to his satisfaction. Just busy. Out of state, out of mind. He has had access to a telephone most of the time but didn't think to call. The guilt trip was easy to ignore when he lived a country away and on his own time. You know people for a while, things change, and then you don't. But this is different. Maybe he's just looking at it through the wrong end of the binoculars. This is an opportunity to correct the longstanding wrong. No sense in dwelling on the bad grandson aspect of the whole thing. But even after all the soul searching and this reasonable conclusion, he can't shake the feeling that he's just come to pump the old lady for information.

The beater Volvo winds down the long private drive, a railing on his right and a lake to his left—although it's really more of a mud-hole, a man-made pond encircled by a paved path for the elderly to exercise, although today the only takers are a squad of mangy ducks crossing the track and waddling down into the waterhole. They squabble and quack through the rolled down window. The last time he had seen her, she had still lived in the Prado house, just as she always had. Always occupying the same space with the same 1940s vintage furniture—did they splurge to celebrate the end of the war? The mahogany tables with claw feet and plenitude of ornate ashtrays and lighters—although she didn't smoke herself. The low white couch covered in plastic with the abstract painting of the barn above it. At least he thought it was a barn. One of his Uncle George's early works. It's a little jarring to find her in this different environment, institutional despite the effort to jazz-up the building with wide windows and slim balconies. The architect either had an eye for blandness or was only mildly interested in the project.

Most of his childhood memories are long gone. When recalling the past, he's never sure what was real and what is imagined. His profession encourages him to separate fact from fiction, to know what's what in his daily life, as well as in the classroom and in scholarship. Still, his past comes through in fragments. His brother's death. The family falling apart. Healthier not to dwell on the unpleasant. But he does have an overriding impression of his grandmother, and a warm one, too. He was somewhere in the three to five range, he figures, sitting next to her on a couch as she read to him from *Uncle Remus: His Songs and His Sayings*, the same copy that he later pilfered from the attic, signed by Joel Chandler Harris himself. It's still packed in the boxes of books back at the apartment. His grandmother reading aloud in her best Negro dialect as filtered through white Atlanta drawl:

"'*Mawnin!' sez Brer Rabbit, sezee—'nice wedder dis mawnin',' sezee,*" she said.

"*Tar-Baby ain't sayin' nothin', en Brer Fox, he lay low.*

"'*How duz yo' sym'tums seem ter segashuate?' sez Brer Rabbit, sezee,*" she said.

"*Brer Fox, he wink his eye slow, en lay low, en de Tar-Baby, she ain't sayin' nothin'.*

"'*You er stuck up, dat's w'at you is,' says Brer Rabbit, sezee. "'I'm gwine ter larn you how ter talk ter 'spectubble folks ef hit's de las'ack,' sez Brer Rabbit, sezee. 'Ef you don't take off dat hat en tell me howdy, I'm gwine ter bus' you wide open, sezee,'*" she said.

She delivered the mangled dialect with an eye-rolling over-the-top minstrel pantomime and followed up with her habitual snort, a most unladylike drawing up of mucus that made his stomach queasy, but it was a nice memory anyway and he feels a fondness for his grandmother, which leads him back to guilt, back to where he started.

There is an open parking space close to the entrance awning. Travis backs the beater Volvo between two wide Cadillacs, the front of the car facing the street should he need to make a quick getaway. How lucky to get a close spot, he thinks and steps out of the car and into something slippery.

The pavement, the parking lot, the drive, even the sidewalk, are dotted with guano deposits that wait like unexploded ordinance. Good lord, he thinks, what do they feed these ducks? Across the pond, a train chugs across a trestle, its horn blaring at the crossing ahead. Travis reaches back for the bunch of yellow roses, bending over the seat in a compromising position, his sport coat hanging, mulling over which explanation to use to justify his sorry-excuse-for-a-grandson neglect and is completely unaware of the danger behind him. Three mallards have sneaked up over the lip of the pond, sentries on the lookout for invading grandchildren. They waddle like lightning up and over the grassy bank, their webbed feet smudging fast tracks behind as they charge his chinos. The lead duck, a female bigger and fatter than the other two but somehow faster, targets the back of his knee at the bend, her battle-scarred beak going for the soft flesh (this spot most effective in bringing the giants down, the vital organs now accessible). Travis's head bangs the door jamb, and he crumples into the open doorway as they charge from each flank, attacking and quacking. He flaps and kicks at the marauding ducks, but they are too fast for his boot and take defensive positions just out of range. The boss mallard feigns left with her beak and then right, taunting, showing no fear, her two cronies up against her rump and quacking encouragement.

Travis covers his head and prepares for the end. What a way to go, he thinks, but the duck's blood lust abates with a sudden new interest. The lead mallard steps back and extends her long neck, her throat gone full vertical, jerks her head to the right, eyes wide. One long quack from open beak and mallard two and three waddle back at the command and they all turn in choreographed grace and bolt between the Cadillacs and back toward the pond.

Travis extracts himself from the doorway and massages the

back of his knee. That hurt. His savior strides out into the drive and walks slowly down the row of Cadillac trunks, an elderly black man, hat brim pulled forward over sparse gray hair, his tan vinyl jacket with the name of the place stitched in sumptuous looping cursive over his heart. Beneath his arm he cradles a box of duck food in a fullback tuck that he has stepped and fetched from all the way around back, lugging the thirty-pound sack to the pond. Perhaps that explains the guano. Maybe he supplements the pellets with a laxative. The kitchen staff donate leftover prunes to add for good measure. The ducks stand in respectful anticipation, line up with their beaks turned in eyes-right salute as their keeper nods a greeting. They know this ritual well. All residents on the property, the feeble and the fowl, are on the same feeding schedule. Travis stands up, shakes it off, and adjusts his sport coat. "Thanks for rescuing me," he says and adds a halfhearted chuckle.

"Yas sur," the old man answers in Jim Crow obsequiousness and steps out into the lane, his head dropped down toward the giddy ducks.

Travis startles, surprised. *Yas Sur?* Is he serious? The old man won't look him in the eye or even the face, and he keeps his head bowed, the crown of his hat forward, and there's that uncomfortable feeling again. He wants to say something but doesn't know what. He wants to tell him that it isn't like that, fumbles a few words, wants to tell him that he works at the college, that his students are black. But there is no sign of insincerity on his part, no ironic detachment. His is an authentic and longstanding deference. The old man turns his back and walks away, digging a hand into the box and sprinkling duck chow between his fingers onto the asphalt and then into the manicured fescue green, his head lowered and shoulders down in slump, leading the ducks back to the mud-hole pond.

Under the shadow of the awning, and all the way to the entrance: two wooden doors, big brass handles, and Travis grips the one on the left. Chilled air on his face, the temperature different from the rest of the world. He's not sure what he expected to find, but this isn't it, he thinks as he limps down the plush wall-to-wall. Elderly residents here and there, moving up and down the long wide boulevard of a central hallway, moving according to the rules of the road, oncoming traffic to the left, outgoing on the right. Walkers gripped, scooters humming and passing. The place is swank with clean and fragrant carpeting, dark mahogany wood paneling and real live plants. There isn't a hint of urine anywhere. It seems more country club than nursing home. He considers his shabby apartment and feels under-dressed, his sport coat wrinkled and loafers un-shined. The place is so big with hallways feeding into the main channel here that it would be easy to get lost, best to ask for directions. Besides, he doesn't want to wander around, who knows what he'll run into around a corner in this place? The blonde woman behind the reception desk is helpful, if a little long winded, her Blanch Dubois drawl eventually leading him to the dining room.

His grandmother is easy to spot even after the years, sitting beside a faux fireplace and talking to another elderly resident, someone else's grandmother. She's shorter than she used to be but looks the same for the most part, with the same old explosion of hair flash-frozen in mid-kaboom, although it has passed beyond gray now and gone entirely white. Her eyes are clear and blue, and her satin blouse is bright burgundy and stain free. He gets his excuses ready to go and walks up and into interruption range.

"Hello, Grandma Rosa Lee." He gives his best smile and nods to her companion.

"Travis! Where have you been!" she snaps, not a delighted-to-see-him response at all but a strict admonishment, the same as back when, as if he were late to the dinner table after too much playtime. She presents her cheek. He bends over and gives a peck.

"Well, I've been up North," he says.

"Up North? What on earth for?"

"I've been working." He smiles at the other woman, who looks over his wardrobe and gives him a *tsk-tsk* look. "In Canada."

"*Canada?*" She puts a hand to her chest. "Goodness gracious, honey. Why?"

"That's where the job was. I'm sorry that I haven't been able to get back down, but I've been busy." And this is mostly true.

"Well, you must have been busy, honey, not to have time to visit with your grandmother. Were you just going to wait until I was in the grave, or would you have been too busy then, too? Where's that pretty girl? Did you marry her?"

Travis has no idea who she's talking about and offers the roses. "No, ma'am. She's still up North." Good days and bad. That's what his father said. She seems to have her wits about her and a little more guilt seeps into his bloodstream. He's glad to see her. He is. He really is.

"Thank goodness you finally cut that hair. Now you need to shave that beard." Travis raises palm to chin and grooms. "Ina, this is my Grandson Travis. He's Henry's son."

Ina offers her hand and says that she is pleased to meet him.

He takes her limp hand, says he is pleased to make her acquaintance. It occurs to him that he has never actually said those words before, that he is pleased to make an acquaintance. He's butted into their conversation, and their body language suggests that there's still some unfinished business between them.

"Is anyone joining *you* for lunch today, Ina?" Rosa Lee asks with a few bats of the eyelids for innocence.

Ina's lips tighten. "Well, you know, dear. My Richard is so busy with his practice. He's been so successful that he's hardly had time to come up for air." The fleshy wattle underneath her chin wags when she speaks.

It seems to Travis that he's stepped into the middle of a skirmish and is standing directly in the line of fire.

"That's a shame, honey," Rosa Lee says and drives the knife deeper with, "You poor dear." Ina retorts with a weak recitation of her son's credentials. He was the official dermatologist of the Olympic Games, after all. And then she changes the subject.

"And what do you do, Mr. Hemperly?"

"I'm in education." He downplays with his usual answer. He doesn't say, "I teach" or even the starchy and contraction-free "I am a professor," missing entirely that formal titles and pecking order are currency in this dining room. "I teach history," he goes ahead and answers the follow-up.

"History? What grade?"

After all the effort he's put into his professorial image, he thinks. Bifocals on his nose, leather patches on sport coat, mustache and goatee trimmed. The only way for him to look more like a college professor would be to have a pipe between his teeth. There is polite conversation, and then there is grilling, and this feels more like the latter. Ina is blunt and asks where he teaches. He tells her that he teaches on the college level.

"Where do you profess?" She puts emphasis on the last word in a way that makes it sound like a dig.

Travis hesitates. There is a certain order to this place. In the hallway, here, over in the banquet room, all of the residents are white and of Anglo Saxon descent and probably protestant. Beyond the hostess desk, they sit dressed in formal wear, coats and neckties beneath two enormous chandeliers hanging down from the high ceiling, lots of room, an elegant ballroom effect. The grand chandeliers really sell it. They sit at linen-draped tabletops, two-tops and four-tops, as the black help in serving livery—old school maid outfit, black dress/white apron—carry trays of food in and out of the swinging door to the kitchen. This is an old dichotomy, the historian inside thinks, what they have been accustomed to over their long years. When he tells her where he teaches, she reaches up and adjusts her eyeglasses, fine tuning for better focus.

"Isn't that a Colored school?" she asks, face full of new wrinkles suggesting puzzlement.

"Yes, ma'am. They call it the black Harvard." The provost mentioned this at the faculty meeting, and the idea stuck in Travis's head, so he put it aside for use in just this sort of situation.

"The black *Harvard*?" A thin smile at this.

"Yes, ma'am."

"Well, isn't that interesting," she says, and there's only one way to read that tone. The best strategy is to end this thread of conversation. He doesn't like where it's going, so he suggests they move into the dining room and offers his arm to his grandmother. She steadies herself up from the chair, tells him to leave the walker, stands up straight, more-or-less, and they make their way to the hostess station. Travis stops by a stand with a blown-up photograph of a smiling elderly black man. It is the same guy who rescued him from the ducks. He is dressed in serving livery and holds a silver serving tray, a big welcoming smile for the photographer. The only writing on the sign, three words, large for weak eyes and stacked in vertical order:

SIMPLICITY.
SATISFACTION.
SERVICE.

It looks like he's come to the right place.

He gestures deferentially for Ida to move along to the hostess station and makes polite small talk, tells his grandmother how young she looks, how good her hair looks today, compliments the surroundings, the impressive dining room and the gold grand chandeliers.

Ina provides historical trivia: they used to hang in the Biltmore Hotel, and Travis knows the building. It's over on West Peachtree, was the place to be back in the day if they were them, so that's where they were, attending galas, balls, débutantes, and tea dances, all sorts of high society events that he'd never been to himself. He drove past it on the way over, the giant hotel long abandoned, another grand building gone to seed, upper windows broken out, lower windows boarded up, torn handbills pasted to the plywood, a black man snarling through golden teeth. Rosa Lee introduces her grandson to all involved and reintroduces him to Ina, who smiles at the goof. For some reason, the hostess is white. She maneuvers between the tables and back to collect the next diner waiting in line. When it is finally their turn, she greets his grandmother and with a big malevolent smile tells Travis that he cannot come into the dining room without a necktie. Travis reaches for his throat, fingers his unbuttoned shirt collar.

"You don't have a tie, honey?" his grandmother asks with surprise, just noticing.

It hadn't occurred to him to wear one. He didn't realize he was going to a luncheon at the Biltmore, albeit an imaginary one.

"Can't you make an exception, honey?" Rosa Lee touches her sternum. "He's my grandson, Henry's son come to visit."

The hostess doesn't budge. This is her gate, and she is keeping it, and she points to the sign on her stand that lays down the law. There are rules to this place, and the fifth is that no one will be seated without proper attire.

"Give him the tie, dear," Ina comes to the rescue.

Wouldn't you know it? The solution was in who you knew. Lucky to have Ina next in line. The hostess draws a long and disapproving breath, her helmet of blonde hair rising, and she pulls a necktie from the cubby inside of her stand. Travis thanks her and stretches it between his hands to examine. It is the most unfortunate piece of clothing he has ever seen, a green silk job with a cartoon figure, what is it? A blue slug with big eyes. It marches across the green silk and farts stars.

"That's the Olympic mascot," Rosa Lee informs and beams with civic pride. "Isn't he cute?"

*T*ravis returns from the men's room, necktie blaring. The dress code now satisfied, the hostess seats them in the center of the dining room beneath one of the enormous chandeliers. In the center of the table, rising from the floral display, a silver stand holds a white card with his surname written on it: Hemperly in cursive script with a doozy of a flourish on the H. He pulls a high-backed chair away from the table and angles his grandmother on his arm.

"Thank you, honey." Rosa Lee sits.

"Yes, ma'am."

She still wears her wedding ring, although her husband, Travis's grandfather, passed away before he was born. It gleams on her ring finger as she unrolls a green napkin and releases a knife, fork, and spoon, and arranges them in particular order on her place mat. Travis adjusts his silly tie and takes his seat, scooting up to the table. The chandelier overhead is shaped like an egg, strands of twinkling light curve from top to bottom. It wheels and sparkles slowly, and his proximity reminds him of the chandelier scene in the 1925 version of *The Phantom of the Opera*, with Lon Chaney and his skull face and dramatic gestures and the great opera house chandelier falling down into the audience. Travis scoots his chair over, hoping to avoid a direct hit. He wonders if his grandmother saw the film when it was first released.

"Did I hear you say that you taught at a black school, honey?"

The dynamic of the old South gets a little louder in the room. These are the people who sat at the front of the bus before segregation, back when white people used to ride the bus—it's mostly a segregated activity these days from what he can tell. They have certain expectations. He is a son of the South, too, but has never been much on the politics of all that. Yes ma'am, he says, and aren't these some chandeliers? Did they really come from the Biltmore Hotel? His grandmother stays on message.

"Well, how can they afford to go to college?"

Wasn't he the one who was supposed to be asking questions? he thinks and wonders how to answer this. There's no way to explain. She's still sharp for her nineties but apparently has not been keeping up with social trends. So he settles on "I don't know."

"Well, I'll be," she says and shakes her head. "Can they read?"

This conversation is not going in the right direction. "Yes, ma'am, they can read," he says and thinks: well, when they want to. On a good day, about half of his students actually read his homework assignments. Best to move on to another topic.

"Grandma Rosa Lee, can you tell me about my great-grandfather?"

"Who are you talking about, honey?"

"Well, the one who owned property in south Georgia. Didn't I have a great-grandfather who owned land down there?"

"You mean down in Haylow. The turpentine farm. Suitcase Charlie. I called him Dad, but they called him Suitcase Charlie."

"Suitcase Charlie?" Travis lifted an eyebrow. That's colorful.

A bit of family lore that hadn't been passed on.

"Charles Hemperly. They called him Suitcase Charlie."

"Why?" He asks the obvious question.

"Oh, he used to go between Atlanta and Haylow, took the train. They said he lived out of a suitcase. He used to stay in the front room of the Prado House when he was up here for the legislature."

The legislature? He thinks, and the surprise is so strong that it emerges as dialogue. "The legislature? He was in government?" It seems like the sort of information that would be part of his family knowledge base, a legacy figure in the Hemperly line, but he has never heard anyone speak of him before now.

"Well, part of the time, when he wasn't down there running that farm. He was a state representative. They have a picture of him hanging down at the capitol. You don't know this, honey?"

"No, ma'am."

"Well, why not?" she looks him over with a critical eye. "You've gotten fat. When was the last time you came to see me?"

Travis thinks: too much information too fast. Sure, he hadn't been close to this side of the family, but how could he not know this? No one ever mentioned it, not that he remembered. His Uncle George had some position with the Democratic Party up in D.C. at one time, but that was different. All he wanted to know was whether his father had seen a lynching. This thing is taking on a life of its own. Another mystery? An oversight? Something dubious wearing a white sheet and holding a torch? His grandmother smiles and waves her hand vigorously at someone behind him. Over by the window bank, Ina sits alone at a two-top, forking through a dome of squash. When she sees his grandmother wave, she drops her head.

"So what was Halo?" Travis homophones.

"That was where he had the farm. In Haylow. That turpentine farm."

"Turpentine?" Travis says. He hasn't heard this either, even though she speaks of it as if it was the sort of place everyone knows, as if it all was common knowledge. Behind her, a trim black woman wearing serving livery appears with a pitcher of water.

"Good aft'noon, Mrs. Rosa." She pours and water fills the glass.

"Oh, Gladys. Hello, honey. This is my grandson come to visit. He's Henry's oldest."

Henry's only, Travis thinks and says hello. Her name tag reads *Octavia*. He smiles at her, but she looks bored and not at him, sets the water pitcher on the table, and pulls out a pad and pencil from her apron. Gladys/Octavia says she is pleased to meet him, and her accent becomes even more down home.

"What 'chall gonna have today? Y'all ready to order?"

"I know what I want." His grandmother hasn't peeked at the menu. Travis sneaks a look at the order pad. It's a pre-printed menu, and her order is already circled.

"Do y'all have okra today, honey?"

"Yes, ma'am. You know we do. Just for you."

"I'll have the smothered chicken and okra. Chow-chow and hop 'n john."

Food both Southern and easy on the teeth. He nurses the wound from his grandmother's insult. He is not fat, he thinks, but he orders the house salad anyway and calculates: maybe he can work in a jog before picking up Meggan this evening.

"What would y'all like to drink? Some sweet tea, Mrs. Rosa? I knows how you loves yo' sweet tea."

"I think I'll have a Co-Cola today, dear," his grandmother says.

"Ooo-wee, Mrs. Rosa Lee! You getting feisty today. Mr. Travis?"

"Water is fine, thank you." He tries to catch her eye, but she is just going through the motions and he doesn't register. Their order taken, she retreats to the kitchen door. Travis gets back to business.

"So in Halo, did my father ever go down there?"

"Down to Haylow? I don't think so, honey. I don't think so. I wouldn't have let him."

"Why not?"

"Your uncle George went down there. I let him go. Worst mistake I ever made. That's where he took up smoking, you know. You don't smoke, do you, honey?"

"No, ma'am."

"It was the mistake of my life, I think. One that I've always regretted. I let Dad talk me into letting Georgie go down there and spend a summer. And I knew he didn't have any business going down there, but it was his grandfather, and I hated to say he couldn't go and he wanted to go so bad, so I let him. He'd never had a cigarette in his life until he went down there. That's when he started smoking. Worst mistake I ever made. You don't smoke, do you, honey?"

"No, ma'am," Travis says. Lie number two. "When was Uncle George there?" Maybe he can pinpoint the year. Travis mines her spotty memory for whatever he can get.

"He would have been a teenager then. Your father was just a little boy. That was during the war."

"And my father didn't go down there?" He circles around again.

"I don't think so, honey. I wouldn't have let him."

"Why not?"

"It was . . ." she pauses and fumbles a few words. "It was just a terrible place, down there in that swamp. You know it's all swamp down there. What do they call it?" And Dad was there, too. Your great-grandfather. I called him Dad."

"The Okefenokee," Travis says. "Why was it terrible? Suitcase Charlie, I mean." All sorts of scenarios present themselves in his head. The bulletin board in the lobby of the history department, white klan robes and orange fire from torches and everyone on horseback, robes flowing in slow motion, hoofs receding on a sand road.

"Oh, he was as mean as a snake." She scowls at this. "He was the most . . . He was just a skunk. Oh, good Lord. I shouldn't say that. He was always good to me. Always good to me. Why are you worried about it, honey?"

"I'm not worried. I was just curious."

For all the opulence in the room, the sparkling off the enormous chandeliers, the baby grand piano and the white tablecloths and formal place settings and the dressed diners and the uniformed waitresses serving the tables, their meal is delivered so quickly that its abrupt arrival spoils the classy vibe. The setting, the dress requirement, the overall climate of the room all suggest some sort of delay between the ordering of the food and the appearance of it, if only to give the impression that unseen chefs labor in the back preparing meals with care in a fresh and friendly manner, but Gladys/Octavia returns with their plates so quickly that he doesn't see how they had time to dish it up. This stuff must have been waiting and ready to go. But his grandmother doesn't seem to notice, just remarks on the lickety-split service. Gladys/Octavia serves them both, lifts the stainless steel cover from his grandmother's soft chicken. The iceberg lettuce is wet in the bowl, two red cherry tomatoes and a dollop of ranch dressing. He should have ordered oil and vinegar, but sometimes it's hard.

"So where are you staying at, honey?"

She is from Atlanta, his grandmother. She was raised here and has spent her entire life here, and she knows the residential housing patterns, the good neighborhoods from the bad, knows where the railroad tracks are and which side of them is the wrong one. Travis opts not to tell her that he lives in Cabbagetown, synonymous as the name is with poverty and instead tells her that he lives next to Oakland Cemetery, which is the truth. It's just across the street. More historic ambiance. Atlanta's first cemetery, built on the outskirts of town which today puts it smack in the middle of downtown. He hasn't been there but knows that the old cemetery is full of monuments to the city's original elite. He's seen pictures: tall stone obelisks and mausoleums and old oak trees throwing shade over the weedy plots. Margaret Mitchell, Bobby Jones, and the confederate dead. Travis drives by it every morning on his way to campus and every evening on his way home. His grandmother's eyes brighten at the mention of Oakland.

"Why, honey, the old family plot is there. I'm eligible to be buried there myself."

Eligible? He thinks and isn't sure what she means. Sounds like a country club, not a graveyard. But it is bad to think of such things under these circumstances, surrounded by so many people who are in their winter years.

Then the baby grand begins to play, a flourish up the entire scale and then back down as someone, a woman sitting on the piano bench, runs her fingers over the keys. The notes echo up to the high ceiling and applause smatters, the room clapping, and his grandmother claps too. The piano gleams as if it has just been polished, catches the chandelier light and shines. Ina sits at the keys, head down at the ivories in concentration. A fluid melody rings from the horizontal chords, resonates through the body of the piano as she plays a classical riff Travis doesn't recognize, then she begins to play a familiar tune, that old standard: the Birthday Song. "Happy Birthday to You" trundles across the room, and Ina's church choir falsetto echoes up to the chandeliers. Everyone joins in and sings along, all heads turned to the birthday board beside the piano. But it is blank. No name is posted to prompt them today, and when the lyrics reach the spot for the birthday boy or girl, "Happy Birthday to . . . ," everyone stops singing, voices quiet, all ears turned to discover who had made it one more year.

Ina belts it out: "Rosa Lee Hemperly!"

Everyone claps, their applause echoing as all the diners turn toward their table. His grandmother's mouth drops open in befuddlement.

"Is today . . . ?" Travis says in alarm.

"But today isn't my birthday? Is it, honey?" Her eyebrows up, eyes wide and she stutters. "My birthday is in . . . today isn't my birthday, I don't think."

Travis stumbles over words. When is her birthday, anyway? Surely, his father and uncle wouldn't forget.

His grandmother looks into the clapping crowd, eyes wide, a doe in the high beams. The chandeliers turn and sparkles wheel around the room.

Chapter Eighteen

One pound. That's it. That's all Travis has lost after five days of hard effort. He stands on the scale next to the bathtub shower, head dropped down to the LED. He has just returned through the tunnel and to his apartment, and his sides ache when he inhales. He lifts a running shoe from the pad, and his weight plummets, then blinking and back to zero. Time for a new battery. Maybe it's not reading right. Perhaps running in the late afternoon is a mistake, is worse on his body somehow. Anyway, a pound. He'll take what he can get.

He'd hoped to settle the lynching question at lunch, get it out of the way and focus on more important things like the night ahead, but now it's a bigger puzzle, his grandmother having dumped more pieces into the box. There's something not right about his not knowing about his great-grandfather, about his career in state government. Sure, he's been disconnected from this side of the family for a while now, but he knew them well enough to know that they boasted when they could. Name dropping is an important element when ranking the social pecking order, and it gets fiercer the lower your position. His grandmother didn't budge from insisting that she didn't think his father visited the family farm in Halo. She'd offered other vague reasons. The weather was horrible. The place was dangerous. There was too much temptation for a young boy and too many snakes besides. But she was almost a century old. Her memory was suspect by default. His own recall wasn't anything to brag about. Every semester he taught, he found himself sticking more and more to the script he'd established as a grad student. And he isn't sure what to make of the new detail, the great-grandfather with the colorful nickname. Is there a skeleton or two in a closet somewhere and are bones beginning to rattle? Being a member of the legislature wasn't Governor, but still it seemed the sort of post that would earn a chapter in family folklore—particularly if his portrait hangs in the state capitol. Now that he considers it, his family history begins with his grandmother emerging from the ruins of the Great Depression, head held high, arms herding her two boys forward. How far back does this go? Were there Confederates in the family? Probably yes. He needs to attend to his own personal history, give the Viking Age the weekend off and figure this out. And he has come full-circle: once again he isn't sure if he was ever told the tale about the murder to begin with. It is frustrating.

But not so frustrating that he doesn't know what time it is. He keeps an eye on the microwave clock in the kitchen as he preps and gets ready. It's been a while since he has been on a proper date, out to dinner and trying to make a good impression and all of that, and as he roots through the clothes closet, hanger scraping down the wooden dowel, he wishes he was more fashionable, more in-season. His clothing comes in thick or thin, prepared for summer or winter and he gets through the in-between seasons by being a little hot or a little cold. He'll go with the winter sport coat, willing to suffer for black.

Meggan lives close, a few rundown neighborhoods to the east, not too far from the Super Store where they ran into each other, according to her directions, and he finds her house easily enough—the mailbox with the gargoyle like she said—and he parks the Volvo in the drive behind her Galaxie (haven't seen one of those in a while, he thinks), its tires between the broken concrete strips, grass in the middle. And guess what? He is nervous. Stop that, he tells his trembling hand. He is a thirty-five-year-old history professor, in full command of his area and confident, he conducts a full load of classes and has published his scholarship and contributed to the great academic dialogue, if in journals that are hard to find and mostly unread, and despite these accomplishments, his pulse is quick and he forgets to breathe. This is unexpected, and he hopes it doesn't show. He doesn't want to appear to be a dolt, so he puts his best foot forward outside of the car and into a pad of crabgrass, steps across the fieldstone to the front door arch, and the door begins to bark at him.

Dogs. Plural. One with a high-pitched yap, the other a deep aggressive yulp. He has never liked dogs, their dumb slobbering and panting and their obsequious and provincial behavior, drinkers of cheap beer all, and always trying to get at him with their teeth. He prefers the cat, felines with their aloof distance and fine-wine-only attitude. But he sucks it up, gets ready to fake it, and knocks on the door four times. It cracks open with a blast of barking and the hounds are almost released as their snouts lunge out. Nails scrape the hardwoods and dig for purchase.

"Ying! Yang! Behave, boys. Behave!"

Meggan does her best to hold them back, wedges her shoulder in the opening to block the charge, her hand grabbing each collar. Travis takes a step back. Then the door slams shut.

That was fast, he thinks. Scampering and clawing and barking and shushing recede into the house and then all is quiet, and he feels on display, standing on the concrete pad under the doorway arch like a traveling salesman with the door just slammed. His pulse is still up, and he tries to make the man on the outside match the man on the inside. He reaches out to the metal moon & stars wind chime, gives it a poke, and the silver tubes clink and tinkle. It's a nice neighborhood, though, modest working class brick homes, generous front lawns all mowed and manicured. Meggan's, not so much. The white woman has the shabbiest yard on the street, overgrown where there is growth. Most of the lawn is a contest between competing weeds. Dandelions. Crabgrass. Poke salad. The usual suspects. In the elm tree beside the trampoline next door, a bird chirps in a persistent rhythm, like a car alarm. Footsteps approach on hardwood and then the door opens wide.

"Sorry about that," she says. "They get so excited."

She is dressed for mourning, black blouse, black skirt, black sandals, the best looking woman at the funeral, he thinks. Her hair is down, her lips deep red, a focal point. His stomach says a few words.

"You didn't have to do that. I love dogs."

"They can be such a handful. Come in, come in." He steps through the threshold and she gives him a quick embrace—a good sign, he thinks. "Let me give you the cook's tour." Her back to him, and boy does she look great. Good call on the black sport coat, he thinks.

It's a small house, the front room decorated with hand-me-down furniture or maybe collected from antique mall raids: mahogany tables, a buffet, a stiff and formal couch, more of his grandmother's idea of furnishing than someone of their era. Still, he's one to talk with his vacant spaces. The rooms full of quaint furniture bring a comforting stability to the little house and to Meggan, too. A quick scan of horizontal surfaces and wall hangings for evidence of male companions. No framed photos propped on the tabletops for display. There is only the oil portrait of a woman striking a stately and pale pose in black ball gown above the fireplace mantel, having just stepped from the clam shell. Her mother?

The tour doesn't take long. The living room. The bedroom. The other bedroom. The bathroom. The kitchen has been updated. Mardi Gras tile. Black granite counter-top with porcelain sink. Outside the sliding door and on the deck, two dogs stand on their hind legs and shout at him through the muffling glass. A Chow mutt and a Jack Russell. Big dog, little dog. Black dog, white dog.

"That's it," she says, arms spread wide over the butcher block table in the center. "Not a lot of square footage, I know, but I bought it for next-to-nothing before the Games started, and prices have been going up and up ever since. I tell everyone I know, if you want to buy a house in-town, you'd better buy it now."

"That was lucky," he says. "How much?"

"Vodka?" her eyebrows up as she reaches for the bottle next to the Mammy cookie jar.

Not a lot of traffic on the interstate this evening, the setting sun a big red ball sinking under the overpass up ahead. There was a time when Travis had wondered if his dating life had seen its sunset, too. Somehow he had grown beyond the activity, or maybe it had just left him behind for younger, stronger candidates. It was just the way things turned out. Once he was out of graduate school, the energy changed and relationships with women became a different sort of business. The women he met these days weren't looking for company, they were looking for a provider, and despite his dogged years of adjunct scramble and digging ditches in the hot academic sun, he didn't fit that bill. After a while he had just stopped trying. He didn't have that much game, to begin with.

But he feels different this evening. The shots of vodka have helped. He isn't much of a drinker, maybe a beer or glass of wine now and then and he can't remember the last time he's drunk straight alcohol. The hard booze makes him feel warm and pleasant, if a little unsteady. He opens her door for her and when they get on the interstate, he makes sure he sticks with the speed limit in the slow lane. It's a short drive anyway, just a few exits down. He has done his homework this evening, has checked the restaurant reviews in the local freebie rag, done a little creative loafing and selected a trendy dinner spot for tonight. The Olympic Games have brought better dining options into the inner city, gourmet chefs building their reputations inside industrial spaces. The article said business was robust through the Olympic summer, but now that the crowds have left town, the restaurateurs are duking it out with each other for the diminished clientele. Reservations are no longer necessary.

There is a good view of downtown from the freeway. Atlanta rises before them, a century and more of brick walk-ups, high rises, and sky scrapers, all clumped together and growing straight up, just like on the postcards. Travis drives, his hands on two and ten, and tells Meggan a joke that isn't funny, but she laughs anyway, and the beater Volvo drifts into the road shoulder and the tires grind. Pay attention, Travis. The road moves back into the center of the windshield, steady in the lane, and there on the right is his father's gigantic head on an upcoming billboard. For crying out loud, he blinks and shakes his own head, but it is still there, ten feet tall and gritting his teeth like he does when he's pissed off. He's aged well, Travis thinks. Some gray in his sideburns and his face a little fatter, but that's Dad, no question.

"Do you ever listen to his broadcasts?" he nods at the bill-board.

She tilts her head to see. "No," she answers, still grinning. "Who's he?"

"Oh, you know," Travis turns it down a notch and tries not to sound so much like a professor. "Just one of those talk radio guys. He talks about the Civil War."

"I don't really do politics. You mean like in Bosnia?"

"I haven't been to the Stove Works," he tacks, "But I've read good things."

"They've got a bar, don't they? I'm ready for another snort."

That's a word he hasn't heard for a while, he thinks and turns on the blinker well before the exit ramp.

They see the smoke first. Three thin streams rise and dissipate over behind the graffiti wall. The Atlanta Stove Works building takes up an entire block or did at one time, the industrial brick now fading, green hipped roof with wide eaves, the Victorian typography: *Atlanta Stove Works* still readable across the wall facing the street. Most of the building is rented out as studio space for in-town artists who are beginning to flock to the affordable prices, or so said the article that sold him on this idea. The restaurant itself has been squeezed into the close end where the forge used to be. Small brick chimneys rise in close intervals around the corner angle of the building. They are spaced a few feet apart, three of them smoldering with black smoke.

"Do they really cook on wood stoves?" she asks.

"That's what I read." He counts a dozen little chimneys. Alongside the parking lot, kudzu vines climb the phone poles and go for the power lines. Stacked logs rise along the street side, a firewood wall. He avoids valet parking, steers the beater Volvo into the peasant lot over by the log wall, and when they are out of the car the stacked logs measure up to his chin. A dark-skinned man in overalls splits logs on a tree stump beside the exit over there. He takes a break, wipes sweat from his face with a red rag, looks at the wheelbarrow full of kindling and wood chips. He sets a log upright on the stump, hefts the ax, and swings it in an arc. The heavy blade comes down hard.

"I've always loved that smell," Meggan inhales wood smoke and goes with small talk. "It reminds me of campfires in the mountains."

It's not too far a hike to the restaurant, across the lot, up the stairs and to the left, past the open-air artist spaces, the individual studios receding to the end of the block. Look at the goldfish in the fountain! Meggan points and leans, fingers in the water and the koi dart away. A hostess greets them, a young woman with mocha-latté skin, sleeveless red shirt and toned athletic arms. She holds the door open, indigo ink tattoos on her quadriceps, a red and white checkered head rag covering her hair, frizzy little dread-locks sticking from underneath. "Welcome to the Atlanta Stove Works," she smiles. "Two for dinner?" And do they have a reserva-tion? A quick survey of the open dining room shows a handful of patrons, three tables taken with the rest wide open. Travis asks for a table alongside the glass wall overlooking the train tracks, a little romantic ambiance, he calculates, plus the article recommended sitting as far from the wood stoves as possible. A dozen of them line the wall, pot bellies with four iron burners, black metal pipes rising from their centers and plugging into the brick wall behind, connecting to the chimneys outside. He can feel the heat from here, and only two wood stoves are lit and in use. Two chefs, both a velvety milk chocolate in white aprons and chefs caps work over iron skillets that sizzle and pop. The hostess says that she will see if she can arrange a window seat and offers them the bar while they wait.

And what a bar it is, a period piece made of oak with brass foot-rail and even a spittoon at the base, bottles of different liquors stacking up across the wide mirror behind reflecting their faces and the back of the bartender's head. Travis pulls a stool back with a gallant flourish and Meggan takes a seat. They are the only patrons in this part of the restaurant, and the bartender is there and ready to serve them immediately, a young desert-colored man with starched white button-down shirt. A riverboat gambler's mustache rides his upper lip. He drops two bev naps before they get settled on the stools. Travis removes his sport coat.

"Is there any place I can hang this?" he asks. "It's a little warm."

"Certainly, sir," the bartender gestures to the empty coat rack. He asks them what cocktails they would enjoy this evening, his voice pleasant, if a little condescending.

"Stoli martini dirty up dry extra olives," Meggan says in a rush to get the words out, adjusts her skirt and gives him a bright smile.

"And you, sir?"

Travis isn't sure which way to go here. He doesn't know his cocktails and her ease with the vocabulary makes him feel second string. "Funny, that's how I like mine. I'll have the same," and he hopes the fraudulent serendipity will hint at star-crossed compatibility. The bartender gets busy, crushed ice wet in martini glasses, and Travis looks the restaurant over. They haven't made a real connection yet and the conversation proceeds through pages of lame dialogue. They discuss the Olympics to death. She rented out the other bedroom to a reporter from Oaxaca. She doesn't offer a gender and Travis wonders. Eventually he gets around to asking her if she still writes poetry, and the conversation grinds to a halt. An uncomfortable pause here. Meggan drops her head. No, she says. No. She gave it up years ago, not long after leaving UGA.

"Why?" Travis blurts, surprise and disbelief a slap in the face. It didn't seem the sort of thing that she would be able to quit. She was a poet. Weren't poets driven by a deep passion that they couldn't undo? How could she just stop? He had always imagined it a calling of sorts, not the sort of thing that could be denied. It is their dharma. She hangs her head, the first glitch of the evening.

"I'm sure you could pick it back up. You were so good." He touches her shoulder with encouragement.

She sighs and begins an abrupt recitation, sampling from T. S. Eliot, just like she used to: "And indeed there will be time / To wonder, 'Do I dare?' and, 'Do I dare?'" That's what I wonder myself," she says and then shouts: "Do I dare disturb the universe?!"

The bartender shakes the cocktail shaker, ice crunching up and down, an alarmed look on his face. Hers is a grand performance, a stage recitation by a diva past her prime and returning to the dialogue that made her famous before the long slide into dark obscurity, back to doing her own laundry and cutting coupons just like the little people. Meggan's eyes shine. She drops down a few stanzas in explanation.

"'*I have seen the moment of my greatness flicker, / And I have seen the eternal Footman hold my coat, and snicker, / And in short, I was afraid.*' Where's my martini?!"

Travis recalls the poem but not the martini line. It's been a while, though, and his single applause fills the empty bar with two hands clapping. The bartender arrives with the blended tonics. Two martini glasses down on the napkins, the glass sides sweating the clear cool liquor, and then the extra, a rocks glass with a small glass urn of extra cocktail in watery ice. Meggan grabs the thin stem and draws a long sip before he can call a toast. Travis raises his martini glass, the vodka well-chilled with wafer ice flow on the surface, green olives impaled by a yellow sword. There's something else, too—tiny black specks dotting the surface. He dabs a finger and studies. What is this? . . . Soot?

The guy from outside wheelbarrows more wood from time to time and refills the aluminum tubs beside the stoves. Meggan doesn't waste time on her martini, drains the glass and the carafe not long after. Travis tries to keep pace, keeping an eye on her descending line of booze, and as soon as he catches up, the hostess is there to lead them to their table over by the glass wall. The railroad tracks outside look long abandoned with weeds between the creosote ties and rusted rails, kudzu advancing. There is even more soot in the dining room and it dusts the wooden tabletops. It's not long before Meggan is drunk. A second martini at dinner (Travis passed on this one) and then soldiering on through a bottle of zinfandel. But it helps lubricate the conversation, and things are going well enough. The small talk blooms into sincere give-and-take. He gets the catfish, she the chicken, both dishes fried in lard in metal skillets popping on the potbellied stove right over there. Greens on the side with a dollop of pimento cheese. Each table has a personal chef and waiter combined who attends to their desires and cooks the meal close by. The food is good, his restaurant research paid off, and the atmosphere historical and interesting because of it. And they catch the sunset from here. It's dark by the time the food arrives. Outside, the mood lighting is dramatic, blue in the trees across the tracks, and the upper canopy glows softly or magically or hauntingly or unnaturally, he can't decide which. Fireflies blink above the abandoned rails, the natural world showing off with a little magic of its own, a little organic razzle dazzle. They swarm from the kudzu, the vines now closer across the creosote and gravel, he could swear, the broad leaves bright green and on the march.

Up to this point, most of the conversation has been nostalgic, but then with more wine turns personal. She and her ex split the month before, and she's glad to finally—finally—be rid of him. His crack addiction eventually became too much to bear. She has sent him back to Utah and to his mother in flyover country, the crack cocaine presumably harder to obtain under her watchful, Mormon eye. Everyone hopes that this will help him kick the addiction once and for all, and Travis wonders who everyone is. But she is glad to have that behind her. She is finding herself again after ten years devoted to a lost cause and moving forward with her life.

Talk about good timing. Travis glows and envisions a good future. He is teaching again and out with the woman of his dreams. He's certainly a better potential catch than a failed artist and crack addict. Perhaps it's the alcohol, but he can't believe how things are coming together for him. Meggan steers the conversation in a new direction from time to time, pushing forward a new digression, this time interrupting his lecture about how the site at L'Anse aux Meadows was discovered and recognized as the definitive site of Lief Erickson's landfall and discovery of the new world. She reaches her hand across the table, fingers wide.

"Hold my hand." It's a command. Every other finger has a

silver ring below the bottom knuckle. Thumb, bird finger, pinkie. "Come on, give me your hand."

Travis reaches and their fingers interlock. Her hand is warm. She grips tightly, mashing rings into flesh, and looks him steadily in the eye.

"This is what I need," she says, her eyes intense. "I need to need to feel passion. I need to need to touch you. I need to need to hold you. I need to need your lips on mine, on my neck, my nipples."

Travis's free hand shoots up. "Check!" Their waiter hustles over from the hot row of stoves. A small change in her eye, her lashes narrowing.

"You don't get it," she says and lets go.

Outside the window, the fireflies flash and show-off, no longer so magical, just insects now. An abdomen glows yellow phosphorescent and bright then fades and the bug disappears, travels, and lights up again a few feet away, sweeping above the lush kudzu leaves that hide the hungry vines as they creep closer to devour the building.

Chapter Nineteen

*N*orth. South. East. West. Travis stands beside a concrete bench and studies the map on the station wall across the rail train pit. It's a simpleton's sketch of the city, not drawn to scale, and it exaggerates the lay of the land. The North-South line is orange, the East-West line is blue. That's all there is to it. The MARTA rail lines stretch to the four cardinal points, runs to the loop of the perimeter highway that encircles the city and separates the outer suburbs from in-town. Destination points are limited. There are no branch lines forking off, no other primary colors put to informative use. He wonders what riders do when they need to go North-North West or South-South East. Bus transfers? he guesses but isn't sure how that works.

An arrow points straight up to a big N, and so he knows where he is. He appreciates the simplicity of it all. The map says he only has to travel a few stops down before he exits for the state capitol. His apartment isn't that far from downtown but he decided not to drive, so he walked the mile to the MARTA rail station. Bad weather has once again rolled in from Alabama and the dark clouds overhead have threatened since breakfast. A block from the station, the bottom fell out. Good thing he brought an umbrella.

Downtown is a mystery to him. He doesn't know his way around and doesn't want to be lost in his own city. Driving the beater Volvo would be a hassle, an inconvenience involving honking traffic and one-way streets, parking meters and parking lots, poor black people bumming change, confusion in general. Taking the train seemed a good idea, so he stands on the platform with the collecting travelers and waits for the rail cars. Once again, he realizes that he is the only person in sight with a melanin deficiency, and the unfavorable ratio makes him take a step back from the pit. He doesn't want to get pushed in, after all. His loafers scrape the terracotta tile, and he drops his shoulders and attempts to look bored and not so much like an outsider. He's getting used to being the only white guy in the room. *I know my way around, thanks, just looking at the artwork.*

Across the pit, the large map fills an aluminum frame and is protected by Plexiglas from the weather and vandals, but that hasn't deterred the graffiti artists. Spray paint sales are up, apparently. The subway ad next to it welcomes the world to the Olympic Games in seven languages, even though they packed up and left town a month ago. There are rules here in this place of transit. Travis doesn't know the drill but tries to blend in anyway. He doesn't know the ins and outs of mass transit, and even though this is a mundane pedestrian activity—passengers and pigeons waiting—there is something exciting about hanging out in this dramatic space, this lair of the trains. He's part of the urban drama now, even if his part is just a walk-on. Blue collar black people take the weight off on benches or lean against the tile wall, transferring to the train or waiting for the next cross-town bus. Most of them look bored. The woman with the headscarf on the close bench reads a book and two guys in Falcon starter jackets laugh over by the elevator door, but most of the passengers stare down the track at the rainy maw at the far end of the station. Travis studies the trash pile swept into the corner underneath the security camera and thinks: *Is that a turd?*

He moves on to find a better spot to stand. The other riders have staked their boundaries and claimed territory, everyone busy ignoring each other as he strolls down the platform next to the caution strip. Most seem to be coming to or from work. Professions are in evidence. Many of them commute in uniform. A woman on a bench represents for McDonald's. It seems it must be an indignity to have to wear the poor fitting polyester uniform out in public. Why add to the degradation by wearing the hat? He paces the perimeter of the pit, and a heavy woman with shiny black wig eyes him with distrust. She grabs the paper hoop handles of her shopping bag and pulls it closer, slides it the remaining two inches to her olive rain-slicker. The two guys beside the elevator door wear puffy starter jackets—although it's not really cold yet. They look him over, whisper and laugh. Eye contact is brief—that is one of the rules. A blast of wind barrels through the east end of the tunnel and everyone leans west. Across the pit, a brunette sits on a bench, a hardback book in her lap, her wet umbrella open on the tile before her and drying. So there are two of us now, he thinks. She looks up and their eyes meet, a quick acknowledgment, just a glance and small nod hello and then her head drops back down to the page. No lingering.

Before he and Meggan had parted with a so-so kiss at the barking door, he pitched a second date and suggested a day trip up to the mountains. Meggan grew quiet and looked at the trampoline in her neighbor's side yard. Why don't they drive up the Blue Ridge Parkway the next weekend to look at the leaves? They could join the leaf-looker invasion from Atlanta and zig-zag through the switchbacks to see the fall colors, the forest canopy turning orange and yellow and red. He wants to drop by George's place on the lake and ask him about Haylow. A trip together would kill two birds with one stone. He can get an answer to the nagging question and spend some extended time with her outside the city and in the romantic mountain setting, hopefully cultivating their connection with a memory or two. Maybe an introduction to a family member who owns lakeside property would leave the impression of financial stability on his part. Despite her out-on-the-town sophistication and flare, she seemed a bit of a shut-in. She had three deadbolt locks on the front door of her house to bolt her inside with those dogs. He can't remember which one is Ying and which is Yang, dumb names for dogs and wrong anyway.

"What about the boys?"

"I'll clean out the back seat. Come on," he encouraged. "It will be good to get them out of the house."

"Let me think about it," her front teeth biting bottom lip.

Taking a trip to the mountains for the day shouldn't be so much of a struggle. There was something standing between them that Travis couldn't see, a ghost with a suitcase, perhaps? The old crack addict boyfriend? That didn't make any sense. He'd been locked up for two years. How far could that go? Whatever it was, he was determined to get around it. He'll push that door until it opens. When he checked his e-mail on the history department's computer and found her e-mail among the list of home-going notices, read its short message—"Let's go. Call me."—he had been encouraged.

Another blast of wind blows through the station. Down the track, two headlights shine in the steady rain, coming closer. The Westbound train toots twice and brakes squeal as it rolls in and rumbles toward his spot on the platform. Shoes vibrate. The waiting travelers make moves of departure, standing wearily from their seats or stepping closer to the caution line, no one in a hurry today. Travis calculates where the train will come to a stop. The starter jacket crew laughs loudly behind him. The doors slide open. No one exits.

Inside the car, the a.c. is roaring. There are plenty of open seats. He evaluates: the side seat by the door or a window with a view? He chooses a double-seat, slides over to the window, and puts the dripping umbrella next to him to discourage sharing. The two guys in starter jackets step into the car and stand up front, one of them holding onto a pole. They speak a rowdy brogue that he can't understand. They are loud and not like his students at all, he thinks, at least when they are around him. He tries to interpret the off-syllables and dropped endings of their private dialect but can make little sense of it until one of them yells, "Motherfucker!" and Travis feels a small pleasure that comes with successful translation. The doors shut and the train sighs before rolling west.

The world is big and wet outside the window. Purple storm clouds halt to shower the city, dropping their ballast but still not rising. The freight yard alongside the rail car track is flooded, blue and orange containers stacked on flatcars and then his neighborhood slides into view, the little shotgun houses and shabby cottages all slide past and recede into the trees that are losing their leaves. He cranes his neck, looks for the roof of his apartment building.

Is that it? Then the cotton mill glides up, its two brick smokestacks towering.

From the back of the car, a man staggers closer, lurching a little as he reaches for a grab rail. He walks right up to Travis and sits in the sideways booth in front of him, their knees almost touching. Travis adjusts. He had selected this seat strategically and positioned the wet umbrella to send a message. The man's hair is wet and stringy, a Jheri curl. He holds what looks like a mobile cellular telephone and speaks rapidly into it. He seems an unlikely cell phone owner, Travis thinks. He's only seen them used by M.D.'s. The antenna has a blue light that blinks up the stalk in stages. Is it a toy? Despite the gloomy weather, he wishes that he had sunglasses, and his peripheral vision strains to maximum. It doesn't matter where he is, the Twin Cities, Chicago, Atlanta. Travis knows what is coming. The guy is going to hit him up for change. Maybe it's his sport coat, maybe because he is white. He will tell him a sad story, a tale of hard luck and then ask for a donation. Travis knows the drama well and has memorized his lines. He considers possible replies. "I've got nothing for you but respect," or maybe, "You've got a mobile phone. Why don't you lend *me* a quarter?" He wonders what the angle will be. Race-guilt? Class guilt? Discomfort from the invasion of personal space? He guesses that race is the wedge today, the hustle here, and he doesn't appreciate being profiled like this, never has. He teaches at a historically black college and his paycheck is modest, and now this guy is shaking him down for part of it. It seems unfair. Appeals for change are part of the day-to-day, an urban tax upon his income. The frequent appeals for change have made him alter his methods of commercial transaction over the past few weeks, and he no longer carries change with him so that he can say that his pockets are empty with a clear conscience. He can even turn his pockets inside out in sad proof. But then he realizes that today he has pocket change. His pocket is full of quarters at this very moment from the token machine at the station. He only had a five when he bought the token, fed the bill into the ticket dispenser and the quarters rained down into the change bin.

The guy holds the big fake phone to his ear with one hand and lets the other assist with talking, gesturing and tapping and pointing as the conversation becomes more heated and detailed, a laundry list of woe. It is a down-on-his-luck family narrative, full of conflict and struggle. Travis could get up and move but doesn't want to do that, doesn't want to be perceived as leaving because of the signal it will send to the other passengers. He doesn't want to confirm a prejudice in their eyes, should they be looking for one. So, he sits. If the guy was white, he thinks, he would have moved already.

"My family has seen a lot of tragedy lately," the guy says into the phone. "My mama was hit by a bus coming home from church on Sunday. She's down at Grady now with a broke hip. My wife was in a bad accident and had a nervous breakdown. They got her up on the 9th floor. My brother, he got knocked in the head by DeKalb County and they got him locked up. I'm supposed to be in the V.A. This shit is messed up for real."

The litany of challenges continues as he details his blues for his imaginary friend on the other end. He's got an interesting angle, Travis thinks.

"Okay, okay, okay. I'll hit you back later. Gotta go," and just like that the list of hardship ends. The blue lights stop climbing the stalk of the antenna and blink out. Here it comes, Travis thinks. He prepares to speak his line. "Say brother, you like barbeque?"

His eyes are bloodshot eyes, his breath stale and acidic. This was not the question Travis expected. Barbeque? He doesn't ask for money, only introduces himself as a tour guide to the city. He says he worked as a tour guide during the Olympics.

"This is my city, brotherman. Been here all my life. I could tell stories," he says, and proceeds to do so. He led groups all over downtown, from Peachtree Center to Auburn Avenue. The guy tells him a good spot for ribs, gives him an insider tip. Then he stands abruptly and pulls out the phone. The antenna lights up. He jumps into the middle of a conversation, walking away gesturing with his hands and the antenna blinking, as he opens the door to enter the forward car. Travis feels gypped. The play ended before he could say his line. He'd decided to give him the token change after all, and he didn't even ask.

The train slides into King Memorial station, and an old black man steps on board at the front of the car. He is disheveled with a white beard and a shabby hat. His vest hangs open. He looks familiar but Travis can't place him. The two starter jackets turn.

"Hep ole Remus dis aft'noon?" He raises his Styrofoam cup toward them.

"Aw, hell naw!" The starter jacket holding the pole pushes the old man roughly toward the door, and he stumbles back onto the platform. The door slides shut. The rail-car begins to move, and the station glides by, the old man bending over to pick up his hat. The starter jackets laugh and add commentary to the incident that Travis still can't interpret. He feels assaulted, himself, he thinks. He wishes he had been able to help the old man, but what's he going to do?

*T*he state capitol is one block up the hill from the station exit. Travis exits a turnstile, opens his umbrella, and walks into the wall of water falling from the overhang and toward the gold dome shining in the rain. There it is, he thinks. The main cog in the big machine of the state. It sits upon what was clearly a high point at some point, but the geography is now so obscured by competing architecture and pavement everywhere and the automobile traffic around it that the original lay of the land has been upended. He has admired this state capitol, with its appropriately fluted Corinthian columns and heavy granite block, covered by a golden dome and topped by a granite woman in loose toga, her slender arms holding both sword and torch, flames up high to light the way. Cannon barrels sight in the passing traffic on Martin Luther King Boulevard. On the high flagpole, the state flag with Saint Andrew's Cross is hanging limply, and the grounds are surrounded by statues of bygone politicos gesticulating in the drizzle. A bearded Confederate general astride bony horse, a white man turning green. Historic markers sprout from the grounds, too, a bumper crop this year. Golden paragraphs describe in detail the Confederate resistance, the same as the monuments on Memorial Drive. On a day with better weather he would make the rounds, stand before them and take in the info, but the storm is picking up. He climbs the long steps and hurries into the building, shaking water from the umbrella.

There is the issue of security, another legacy of the Olympic Games. Two state patrolmen—both female, both black—are on duty beside the security arch which beeps when he walks through. He needs to empty his pockets completely sir and walk through again. He tries to lighten the mood, mentions the rain and how it's a good day for indoor duty, but they are not easygoing and not a word or look in return. The patrolman on the stool offers him the blue bowl with his keys and all the quarters, and then he's in.

State capitols. What can you say? They are clean. Their rotundas echo. Lucrative arrangements with granite contractors have been involved. Travis enters the rotunda and looks up. The domed ceiling is high above, each floor overhead outlined by a circle of railing. One, two, three levels. The rain beating the high arched windows amplify the soundscape. Former strong men of state history are well represented. Portraits of past governors and random legislators hang from walls, all of them sporting the popular facial hair of their era. Dr. Martin Luther King, Jr., is prominently represented in the rotunda, a marble bust on a marble platform. The history of the state is well documented, excepting the absence of Cherokee and Creek Indians (their portraits having been removed). The information desk is the first thing he comes to, but no one is in the chair. The clock says that it's noon, a little after lunchtime. Other than the security detail, Travis has seen no one. There are no tourists about or government employees either, although he can hear their footsteps. On a floor above, a deep country drawl discusses state business and then laughs. Farther away, the sound of children. Everything echoes.

He begins a systematic search for his great-grandfather's portrait. He uses the information desk as a starting point and views every painting up and down every hall and alley and nook and cranny, careful not to miss anything. He begins by observing each portrait, reading the accompanying plaque and spending a moment giving some respect to each, but this quickly devolves into a museum shuffle, so he begins to skip the portraits in 19th and 18th century dress, crossing them off the list with a glance.

His footsteps echo. The search for his great-grandfather is a slow one, and it takes a while to walk each floor. His portrait isn't on the first. Or the second. Or the third. Travis begins to wonder if it's still on display. The closer he gets to the top of the dome, the louder the high voices become, children on field trip. Children: the bane of museum visits, always crowding the best exhibits and breaking his concentration with their oohing and aahing. He catches up with them on the top floor at the state flora and fauna exhibit. Black and white children of elementary school age surround glass cases of state birds and other wildlife unlucky enough to have been designated as representatives of the state, taxidermied regional wildlife on display. A brown thrasher perches on a dogwood tree limb. An Eastern cottontail in a straw hutch. A red fox in pine straws looks back over its shoulder. The two headed snake is a big draw. The kids crowd around its glass case and exclaim at the mutated reptile, the product of chemical dumping, perhaps? Over by the far wall, a miniature artist has been at work, recreating a turpentine mill in a small scale. The large diorama is sprawled across two tabletops placed end-to-end, a crude rectangular building of vertical wood planks. One long side is open to the elements. No doors necessary. The tin roof is detailed with rust. The turpentine mill runs the length of the wall and is encased in the same finger-smudged glass as the stuffed wildlife behind him, but none of the children seem interested in the display. An informative plaque explains the what, where, and why. The miniature artist had talent, and it's even more realistic when he removes his glasses and studies it in soft focus. So this was the family business, he thinks--at least when there was a family business, back before the Hemperlys left the farm for city life.

The mill is more evolved architecturally than the turf houses of the Vikings—better tools to work with after a century of progress, after all—but it's still pretty primitive. Two paper-mâché laborers, both white men in overalls, work around the long shed, rolling wooden barrels up the ramp of a platform to load them into a wagon behind two mules. There's even a little snake curled in the grassy marsh in the corner, watching the action. Hard labor under a hot sun, it looks like. Had Suitcase Charlie had an eye toward legacy and empire building, Travis might just be in the turpentine business right now. How different a life that would be. There were no black action figures, no black laborers on the diorama payroll. Maybe they're all chained to trees or hanging from limbs in the painted forest backdrop? None that he can see.

After a while, the small of his back begins to protest with the march. He gets back on task and turns toward the last hallway open to the public. If it isn't down this passageway, it isn't on exhibit, Travis thinks. His footsteps reverberate as the shouts and laughs recede. It occurs to him that this hallway is the least prominent place to hang portraits in the entire building, a hall of lesser fame perhaps. Perhaps there isn't a portrait and never was, he thinks. His grandmother could have made it up, an elderly woman exaggerating the family accomplishments to impress the other residents. A little revisionist history to spice up a dinner conversation. But the portrait is there after all. It is the last one down the small hall, mounted in a gilt gold frame, his great-grandfather having been exiled to the end of the line and displayed beside a custodial closet.

His great-grandfather was a severe looking gent. His hard face is in profile, half of it hidden in shadow. And the painting contains potential bad news for Travis: he's bald on top. Travis reaches for his own hairline but stops short. Best not to dislodge more hair. Something about the man looks off, and it isn't just the odd profile. He's dapper but no dandy, donned in a black suit, white shirt, navy tie, white hankie crisply folded in front breast pocket. The word *curmudgeonly* comes to mind. In every other portrait— and he's looked at every single one of them so has some authority here—the subjects appear to have tried to look their best for posterity's sake. But his great-grandfather's put-upon expression looks impatient and just sick of the whole thing. The plaque explains:

Charles Hemperly, Sr.
Longest Running Member, State House of Representatives
Clinch County 1913-1954

Travis is glad to confirm that his grandmother's memory was accurate about the portrait. Maybe she was a reliable narrator, after all. She seemed sincere when she said that she couldn't remember if his father visited the turpentine farm. Travis has no firsthand knowledge about south Georgia, the people, the politics. He's only been that one time as a child, and all he recalls is the heat and the gnats. He doesn't want to fill in the blanks of this story with the standard Southern narrative, good old boys and their lynchings, and all of that. His great-grandfather is in the historical record now, even if he's been relegated to an untraveled hallway. Now that he has found the portrait, he doesn't know what he expected to glean from it, if anything. Suitcase Charlie has brought him to a literal dead end. Still, the less he finds, the more he suspects that the dead man chained to the tree in his father's story had been black. He's looking for the truth, of course, but the more he thinks about it, the more he wants to find evidence of a lynching. His great-grandfather hangs on the wall before him, unsmiling and offering no clues. He just snarls at the janitor's closet.

Chapter Twenty

$\mathcal{K}$wasi Kalamari shops at the people's market, not the corporate grocery stores where the white people buy their food and the black bourgeois, too, selecting their prime cuts of unclean beef wrapped in white paper by the butcher and bottles of merlot and pinot grigio recommended by the wine steward on duty. He rejects the A stores uptown, eschews the Harris Teeter. The Kroger. The A&P. Just the thought of giving them his hard-earned dollars leaves a sour taste, and he will have none of it, no. He spends his money with his people on their side of town at the GiantFood. The name hangs below the roofline in large yellow block print, a second-hand sign with a few fluorescent rods dead and unreplaced, not such an easy thing to do from the gravel roof top— the only access. It's not such an easy thing to unclasp and lift the five foot letters up and back and reach the burnt-out tubes. In the evening, when the manager flips the switch to illuminate the sign, antFood lights up in misspelled marquee. This always gets a laugh around the neighborhood, gets mentioned every night. "Going to the Antfood?" "Come on, let's go on down to the Antfood!" He has overheard this with depressing regularity, a sad testament to their position in society, to their low social status, he thinks, and wonders how many of his brothers and sisters get the irony. They have been mis-educated. Deprived of proper schooling, they live on the margins. They are no more consequential than ants themselves and about as aware.

He always takes the cross-town bus, and so he does this morning, carrying the four cardboard boxes and the banner. It's an unwieldy, yet manageable load, though he has to turn sideways to get down the aisle, his lank gray dreadlocks brushing the chrome handholds on each seat back, the load in both arms pressing into the red Massi warrior tunic that he picked-up on his last trip to Tanzania. This Saturday morning provides plenty of seating choices. There are only five passengers crossing town this a.m., each sitting equidistant from the other. Disconnected. He greets the driver, deposits the sufficient coin, and feels blessed when he sees that his preferred seat is vacant, the port window on the back bench. Boots grip the rubber skids as the bus rocks forward and he claims his spot, pushing the stacked boxes below the window with cool air blowing in through the vertical slit. The seat cushion is good for his bad back. A pinched and aggravated nerve in his spine makes him sit upright, and he sits stiffly, his posture erect and pressing back firmly, as always, to keep an eye out and be ready in case any shit goes down. But it never does. No knuckleheads onboard today. Sirens do not pull the bus over to the curbside, and the Man does not rush in with handgun drawn. All is quiet. In the seat in front of him, a young brother with a close haircut slumps a shoulder against the window and looks up at an advertisement. A bullet list details the opportunities awaiting him should he pursue a career as a medical billing specialist.

Kalamari leans over, dreadlocks hanging, and reaches out. "Mass transit is the most socially responsible mode of travel, don't you agree, my brother?"

The question lands next to the tear on the orange vinyl and melts quickly despite the cool weather. The young brother doesn't answer, and the pause grows into non-response and stretches further until he feels as if he is being ignored, his gesture of brotherhood rejected.

"Don't know about that, dog. I'd rather have me a car."

Thus engaged, Kalamari makes his case. He details the damage that mass automotive commuting has brought to the inner city. The toxic haze polluting the skyline. The resulting separation and isolation from healthy social interaction and public discourse, but the young brother doesn't contribute to the conversation. He just reaches for the pull cord above the window to signal his stop and doesn't excuse himself when he leaves the seat. Alone and bruised, Kalamari turns inward and concentrates on the urban blight sliding by outside the finger-smudged window glass.

The Olympic Games have changed the city. All the way down Peachtree Street old brick buildings are coming down and sky-scrapers are going up. Just the other day, *The Atlanta Journal* print-ed a computer-enhanced photograph depicting downtown by the turn of the century, a photo that begged questions. How could so many skyscrapers be erected in four short years? This big city future stirs-up mixed emotions. He is glad that all vestiges of the old South are being wiped away, yet the glass and steel monuments to capitalism trouble him, and a foreboding makes his stomach queasy.

The bus rolls on through a canyon of construction and comes upon the newly renovated Margaret Mitchell house. Of all the buildings, he thinks. This one should be gone with the wind. But there it sits, its two stories freshly painted and hipped roof newly tiled and looking better than it ever has before, not a dump, but a museum now. The white people queue outside the entrance one-by-one in a line stretching all the way to the sidewalk and wait to spend their disposable incomes and gain entrance to see where the infamous novel itself was written. When he thinks of *Gone with the Wind*, he thinks of the film and when he thinks of the film, he thinks of Hattie McDaniel. Of Butterfly McQueen. The humilia-tion they must have felt, Oscar or no Oscar. *"Lawzy, we got to have a doctor. I don't know nothin' 'bout birthin' babies!"* Few books have inflict-ed more harm on his people. And their former owners wait in line to celebrate their states rights Dixieland of gentlemen merchants, women in hoop skirts and all those happy slaves with burlap bags bent over in the heat and plucking the fluffy white cotton bolls. And then they teach this preferred social order to their children. Kalamari looks away and up the aisle, jaw clenched, teeth tight as the bus grinds down the hill and on toward the south side.

The GiantFood sits at the center of poverty. It's the only gro-cery for miles, a marketplace for people who don't own cars but have to eat anyway. They have been segregated, isolated, and ig-nored by everyone but the Atlanta Police Department, who patrol the street heavily. The white people stay away. They rarely come to this neighborhood in person and only pass through when lost, having taken the wrong exit off of the interstate while trying to find the Olympic stadium. He has seen them driving slowly, hands at two and ten, eyes wide and looking for a safe place to turn around. But despite their physical absence, they are always present anyway. The blonde on the billboard above the gas pumps across the street. The freckle-faced redheaded children framed in the window of the storefront—Scottish by the looks of their long faces, their dropping chins. These are the people whose elders were in the Ku Klux Klan. It is obscene that they are here, he thinks, these photographs of happy white people spending money and applying the slow steady pressure of assimilation. Sadly, most of the people don't know this or don't care. They do not know their rich history. They don't know where they came from, and they will never be free until they do. He will change them one at a time if necessary, so he pulls the cord and rings the bell and exits the bus at the stop. His chin serves as support, his gray beard on the top box as he carries the stack across the parking lot and into the grocery store.

Kalamari has made the proper arrangements with the day-shift manager beforehand, and he is more than helpful. He even supplies a table for the merchandise and instructs a bag boy to carry it outside. But when the glass exit door slides open and he leads the brother with the table to his assigned spot, it is already occupied. An old man with rickety teeth stands by the cinder block wall. The Styrofoam cup in his hand tilts to accept contributions. Kalamari takes note. This is the first panhandler he has seen since the homeless were run out of town before the Games began. His woolly white hair is pulled here and there, and the way his full beard grows in reminds him of his father, reminds him of his father's sacrifice, how hard he worked to put him through school. "As many degrees as you can earn," he promised, and he paid for them all.

The old man works his jaw and mumbles steadily. "Lippity-clippity, clippity-lippity." His clothes make the air prickly.

"Hello, sir," Kalamari pinches his nose and contains a sniff. "We'll need this space here. I've got to open for business."

The old man looks him over, eyes his black paratrooper boots, camouflage BDUs and squints at his loose red tunic. "You s'ppose' ter be sum kind er African?" he croaks, his speech a gravelly process, and he stakes a claim before Kalamari can answer.

"Take yo'sef' sumwhar else. I'uz year fus'."

"I'm sorry, my elder, but I've made prior arrangements with the management. I was instructed to set up in this location." He lifts both hands palm's up and makes an it's-out-of-my-hands gesture.

"My elder?" the old man spits a hock of phlegm to the pavement. On cue, the door slides open and the manager tramps out onto the rubber pad.

"I've told you before," he snaps. "No loitering!" He points at the metal sign confirming the regulation. "Go on off! Don't come back here!"

"Show me sum respec'!" the old man threatens with the Styrofoam cup.

"It's okay, brothers. It's alright," Kalamari pats the air with his hands and tamps down the conflict. There is too much tension between his people. Their unyielding oppression has created pathological behaviors, and in this way lies madness. It is all around him, just under the surface, so he calms the situation, tells the manager that he will handle it and thanks him again. The old man scowls and mumbles again, "Lippity-clippity, clippity-lippity." He gives the ground but not much of it, takes a few steps to the low wall bordering the parking lot and hoists himself up onto the cinder block ledge with a huff, his legs swinging, his back to the Chinese take-out place.

The bag boy angles the table and pulls the metal legs down. They lock with a click, and it occurs to Kalamari that the title is demeaning. Bag boy. Bag man would be a better choice but is also problematic as it suggests illicit activity or homelessness. The manager had called him that, called him a bag boy to his face, and this must inflict a psychic wound—something under the surface that festers and rots. It kills the spirit. Once the table stands steady, he clasps his hand in thanks, looks him square in the eye and tells him to stay strong, but the young brother just tells him to have a nice day sir and enters the exit back into the building. He'll have to speak to someone before he leaves, makes a mental note of it and turns his thoughts back to the matter at hand.

He has chosen the right day, and they are coming.

The right demographic shops on Saturdays. Mothers bring their children with them, keeping them in line while pushing their shopping carts up and down the back and forth grocery aisles. He sets up and prepares for his first customer, opens the boxes with his father's pocket knife and distributes the coloring books across the tabletop in an attractive fan display. *African Kings & Queens!* is his best effort and so he arranges it first, opening the top copy to a two-page spread. On the left page: a generic pharaoh and wife look regal in the foreground. On the right: the Pyramids of Giza fill the background. Customer traffic will move from the left side of the table to the right, he figures, and he wants to start with his best. Next comes *Africans Discovered America!,* a work of which he is equally fond. He likes the drama of the narrative and enjoyed illustrating the intentional crossing of the Atlantic and the Olmecs worshiping his ancestors. This his most inspired of the four. It only took him a weekend to draft the entire book, illustrations and all. Third is the less dramatic and more abstract *African Positivity!,* which turned out okay, although now that he reconsiders it, he wishes he'd toned down the central character's smile on certain pages. Last, he arranges *We Still Ain't Free!* at the end of the table, an experimental effort told entirely in the Vernacular. It is the most dogmatic of the set and the least unified. He had a printing deadline to meet and didn't have enough time to realize its full promise and make the illustrations really sing. Boxes of Crayola crayons—the classic eight pack—are stacked behind the merchandise in a cardboard ziggurat. They are free when all four are purchased. This is the hook, devised to attract the parents. He markets his wares with an encouraging banner taped along the horizontal edge of the table with blue tape, a message attracting customers in red, black and green script: *Mother Africa! Free Crayons!* Everything is in place, and Kalamari is open for business. He stands at parade rest behind the table and surveys the grounds with an optimistic gaze. The people criss-cross the parking lot from store to street. Two knuckleheads laugh on the corner. A woman with two boys—both of them coloring book age—enters the store at the far end near the Sock Man's tarpaulin. The old man on the wall behind him has produced a paper sack with a bottle in it, and he takes a swig, elbow up. Lazy clouds drift east and the sun shines through. Kalamari has never initiated a capitalist venture before. Until this idea came to him in a dream, he had never considered being a merchant himself. He doesn't know the particulars of supply and demand in this case but is confident in his merchandise and imagines a crowd before the table, mothers and children wide-eyed and grabbing—and he doesn't have to wait long before his first customer arrives. The exit door slides open. He straightens up and adjusts his tunic. A thick dark-skinned sister in a voluminous blue dress pushes a grocery cart out of the store. The damaged cage is loaded down, and plastic grocery bags are piled on top of more plastic grocery bags. One of the wheels is stuck and scrapes across the asphalt. A little girl sits in the basket seat, both legs swinging through the holes, her hair braided with pink and white clips.

"Hello, Sister!" Kalamari starts. "How are y'all doing on this blessed day?"

"Ain't that the truth," she says and smiles at the sun.

"Hello there, little sister." He grins at the girl. "Do you like coloring books?"

He smiles his biggest and she doesn't say a word, just fixes large brown eyes on his dreadlocks and leans back into her mother's bosom. She sticks a blue toy, the Olympic mascot, back into her mouth.

"What you got here?" The woman eyes the banner.

"Some coloring books for the children." He spreads his arms wide over the display, palms up. "Coloring books about our people. We need to teach them about who they are. You know the schools. You know how they do."

"Hmm-hmm," she hums and pushes the grocery cart closer. The stuck wheel scratches parallel to the table, and she squints at the colorful covers and the stack of crayons. Her brow knits as she scans the books.

"Buy all four and you get a free box of crayons," Kalamari offers and is surprised how easily marketing patter rolls off of his tongue. He directs her attention to *African Kings & Queens!* Kalamari has filled in part of the page himself, mixed colors and created new hues. The remainder is uncolored to suggest possibility. "This book tells about ancient Kemet and the great kings and queens."

"Kemet?" An eyebrow goes for the sun.

"So-called Egypt." Kalamari scowls. "Kemet was the first civilization, a great civilization and the foundation of our people. The African was the first to invent science, engineering, and writing and to discover medicine, architecture, astronomy, and agriculture," he counts through the familiar list. "It is important that we teach the children this."

The little girl grabs for her mother. "Are you an African?" her eyes widen on his dreadlocks.

"Why, we're all African, little sister."

"He ain't no damn African!" the old man shouts from the wall and cackles.

Kalamari frowns and turns. "We are *all* part of the Diaspora, my brother. We are all children of Mother Africa."

"You a crazy nigger. Ain't no damn African, neither!" He shakes a finger up and down on each word: "Don't you be tellin' dat lil' gal no story."

"Brother, your language," Kalamari slides his eyeglasses down the bridge of his nose. "We have a responsibility. We need to set an example." He looks him in the eye to make himself clear.

The old man leans forward and hacks a cough. "My *language*? You ain't fum 'round year, is you, boy?"

The little girl looks up at her mother and pink and white clips jump.

"They just playing, baby," she lays a hand on her cheek. "Don't pay them no mind."

Kalamari turns his back to the old fool, corrects himself for thinking this way and forgives the old man. This old brother doesn't understand what he is doing. He doesn't understand the impact his behavior has on those around him. A sadness wells, a grief that lingers, and their disconnection vexes him. A cloud moves in and shadows the parking lot. Out on the street, the traffic light changes to green and the cars accelerate to the next red light. The Man arrives in a white Crown Vic, black sidewalls shining and blue strobe lights off. The big police cruiser prowls into the parking lot and parks in the handicapped space beside the entrance. The big sister puts her palm on the table.

"How much for one?" she looks him squarely in the face.

"Only two dollars each. No tax."

"You want one, baby?" The girl smiles big from the basket, nods her head, and her braids swing.

"Ain't no damn African." Mumbling and taunting from the wall.

"Go ahead and pick you one, then," she pulls a crumpled bill from her cleavage, considers it, reaches for another and hands them across the table. The little girl leans over the edge of the cart, her brow down in deliberation, and looks from cover to cover. Kalamari smiles when her eyes brighten. She points her finger at *African Positivity!*

"Excellent choice," he says and immediately regrets his clichéd hyperbole. The inflated language of marketing runs so deep, he thinks. "Good choice," he adjusts as the vocabulary of commerce fumbles in his head. His instinct tells him to make the customer feel good about the purchase. He lifts the flimsy book to her outstretched hand, and she grabs it by the spine.

"Thank y'all so much and have a blessed day," he smiles, his first transaction completed, his first book sold. The sun rolls from behind the clouds and warms his face.

"We need that box of crayons," she points at the rising stack.

"Yes ma'am." He serves it on up. "That'll be a dollar, sister." This is too easy, he thinks and imagines that he will be sold out by noon. He has squared off against the global capitalist octopus for so long that he thought this would be a difficult process, full of ethical compromises that he could not make. Maybe there is a way to make capitalism work after all.

"It says 'free crayons,'" The woman nods at the banner, and her voice rises with a little heat.

He knows what it says, he thinks. He wrote the sign. That doesn't mean he can give everyone a free box of Crayolas. Kalamari clears his throat. "That's only when you buy all four." His voice is not so strong, and he adds "Sister," and smiles hopefully and calculates. He won't break even giving the crayons away. He had argued the printer down on price-per-unit but had to order eight thousand copies. The boxes are stacked in his office beside the tall file cabinet.

"Says 'free crayons.'" She points. "Right here. Don't say free crayons with all four." Hands on hips suggest litigation.

Kalamari takes offense at her rude confrontation and feels flabbergasted. Here he is, on his first day of entrepreneurship and already a complaint.

"How's the child supposed to color without crayons?" she demands.

He stands his ground. "Crayons a dollar right here," he points down at the stack. "It's for the people, for the consciousness of our people," he reasons. "They don't print these for free, my sister."

"Don't got no more money to give. That's my last two dollars, right there," she points at the crumpled bills in his hand, her finger poking the air accusingly as if he has swindled her. "And don't you 'sister' me."

"Give dat lil' gal sum crayons befo' I come over der en beat yo' no-African ass," the old man yells from the wall. An appreciative nod from the woman and she extends a flat and expectant palm. He considers refusing again, standing his ground, staying the course, but only for an instant and he crumbles. He should have made it clear on the sign. Live and learn, he thinks and reluctantly pulls a box from the top of the ziggurat. She plucks the pack from his fingers and shakes her head.

"Mmm-umm-mmm."

The two crumpled bills on the tabletop look like trash. The high from his first sale evaporates and Kalamari wants to take a shower and wash himself clean. He should have made it clear on the banner, then there wouldn't have been a problem. He wants to explain himself, explain his position further, but he just thanks her again and feels cheated. She throws her head up, pushes the cart off in a huff, and doesn't look back. The stuck wheel scratches across the asphalt all the way to the bus stop shed. At least the little girl is happy. She swings her legs and leafs through the pages, studies his artwork and smiles with delight. He gives her a wave but she doesn't notice, engrossed as she is. But she appreciates his work, and for a moment, that is something. The bile resides. There are just a few bugs to work out, nothing more, he thinks, and plucks another box of crayons from the pile, dismantling the temple further. He opens the tabbed top. Red, black, green, brown, orange, yellow, blue, white. Which should he choose? Yellow seems best for this purpose. Kalamari steps around to the banner and crouches. He reaches a flat hand behind the paper for support, but it is not so easy to write on the paper from this angle. He considers whether to print in upper or lower case, and then writes as small as the crayon will allow: *with purchase of all four.

Sneakers plop on the pavement as the old man drops from the wall, steadies himself against the cinder block and steps to the table. His head swivels across the coloring book display and stops on the two crumpled dollar bills.

"W'at you got year, Mr. Man?"

"Coloring books for the children," Kalamari stands tall. "I'm trying to do my part, brother. I'm trying to teach them their history."

"Well dat's alright. Dat's alright." The old man looks from book to book and nods. He raises the paper sack, the glass neck of a half pint poking from the bag, and extends his arm. "Go on," he offers. "Get you sum."

Out on the street, a bus pulls to the stop and sighs. Double doors fold and passengers jostle and disembark: three children and their mother and all of them laughing. A breeze at Kalamari's back brings the egg roll reek from next door and ruffles pages on the open coloring book. The two police officers—brothers in crisp uniforms both—exit the squad car and slam the doors. The rim of the bottle is wet and shines. The old man waits, his lips cracked and crusty, his eyes red. Both of his pupils are blown wide. Kalamari considers the list of potential contagions, and it is a long one. His body is a temple. He doesn't drink. He doesn't smoke. He maintains a strict Vegan diet and cleanses his colon with each new moon. Still, he hesitates to decline the offer. He reaches the toe of his boot across the asphalt and feels for the boundary line between them. All he has to do is raise his arm, grasp the bottle and take a little swig in solidarity, just a sip to honor this gesture of brotherhood offered freely. The paper sack covers the label and the rest of it too. There's no telling what's in there, what it might do to his body, to his mind. Caution tugs him back. Better safe than sorry.

"I don't drink, my brother. And neither should you. You need to keep your mind and body clean. Drinking is bad for your health. It's bad for your liver. Our people have enough problems as it is, particularly when it comes to healthcare."

The old man spits on the pavement. "Know w'at yo' trouble is, boy? You don't know whar you came fum."

Of all the things to say.

Personally, Kalamari is a pacifist. From time to time a conflict appears before him and interrupts his peace with its attendant negative energy, and whenever this happens he responds best when allowed a little room, a little time to think things through. But this time around his gut gets the upper hand, and he acts before he can control the urge. He snatches the paper sack from the old man's hand and up-ends the bottle. Gravity is working perfectly this day and does its thing: the liquor dumps out and down and splashes the asphalt wet.

"You done done it now!" the old man lunges, swipes at his face and keeps coming. Kalamari has never actually been in a physical altercation. He has never been in a fight before, not during his childhood, not during the Movement. He never developed the skill and his hand-eye coordination has never been very good. The old man grabs the paper sack and pulls. "Belingy-bang-dang! Gim me my bag!"

It's a short tussle. They fumble back and forth, both gripping the paper sack and the bottle in it, and it occurs to him that he might receive an injury of some sort, a cut, a bruise. He lets loose, but before he can step back, the beefy blue arm of the law encircles his neck in chokehold. The other officer grabs the old man.

"Hold up, sir. Hold up now!"

"Dis year nigger des grab my bag!"

The cop holds Kalamari immobile, and he remembers his father's words: Don't tempt the law. He relaxes and submits, his head twisted and ear mashed into the blue uniform, his nose touching the name tag pinned to the officer's chest: C. Wilson. Kalamari tries reason.

"Officer Wilson!" he pleads, his voice thin through constricted windpipe. "The children . . . We should be setting an example . . ."

The man relaxes his hold and Kalamari jerks his head away. Or tries to. His longest dreadlock is lodged tightly into the silver badge of the Atlanta Police Department pinned on Wilson's chest. Follicles yank. Kalamari yelps *youch!* and steps back, pushes back, his head back against the blue shirt and tries to quit the pulling. Wilson stumbles and Kalamari follows, flails his arms and pops the cop in the face with his fist. Fingers grab his neck in a fierce grip and pull his head, his hair to the limit. Suddenly, senses disappear: Sight. Sound. Smell. Taste. All gone. There is only pain, so white hot and exquisite that time stops and holds as his scalp, his hair, the deep roots tear and the dreadlock detaches and dangles, still tangled in the badge. Sight-sound-smell-taste all return with a loud bang as his face hits the table, and he can taste the crayons. Fingers tighten and squeeze, his neck, his throat, his arm twisted behind his back as his cheek pushes into pyramids.

"Let me tell you something about setting an example."

Kalamari's nose crumples the rough paper, face mashed, mouth open, eyes ahead at the GiantFood exit. Sunshine and shadow in the glass. The door slides open. A woman and two boys step forward and out, plump plastic bags hanging in their hands. The tallest lifts his arm, finger pointing, eyes wide.

"Look!"

Chapter Twenty-one

$\mathcal{A}$. $\mathcal{B}$. Longman has come to terms with the way things turned out. He toiled at the shipyards for a week, sanding and gluing and painting when he should have been grading the stacks of student papers over on the butcher block table. It was hard to let go, as always, hard to abandon the project and set them free. He could have done a better job, and this weighs heavily on his already heavy shoulders. The imprint of brush strokes is clearly visible and the rigging is smudged with glue. He should have used an airbrush. He doesn't own one and doesn't know how they operate, but still. Now his efforts will be on public display right here in the office, sailing across the top of the bookshelf. Maybe his students won't notice the flubs. Maybe they won't notice the three ships at all, as crowded as it is in here and as inattentive to detail as they tend to be.

Hemperly isn't in yet, a pity. No other witnesses at the dry-docks today. Their christening will be a private affair, and he launches them to little ceremony, carefully lifting each caravel from its respective box and setting it down on top of the bookshelf just so, keel rippling the calm water underneath the rebel flag. It's a blustery fall morning and a good day for sailing. As soon as he releases the Niña (the Niña always comes first. He can't help it. It's too ingrained), the plastic sails catch the wind, billow full and the ship puts out to sea. Longman launches the other two without fanfare and takes a step back to admire—a small step for [a] man, not much room in here—and the edge of the desk grinds against his tailbone. The Niña, Pinta, and Santa Maria tack in single file toward the end of the bookcase and the drop-off abyss near the window. Above them, the Saint Andrews Cross blares in all of its obnoxious glory, the stars on their bars, and as a whole he is pleased with the way the shrine is coming together. In the clarifying light of comparative analysis, his work stands up pretty well, and concern over his skills as a shipwright begins to fade. I mean, really. Could the flag be any tackier? It assaults his sensibilities of beauty and harmony. It's just plain gaudy, the visual equivalent of fingernails scraping across a chalkboard—and he's familiar with the trauma that inflicts upon one's soul, having scraped his nails across a chalkboard not an hour before. The flag doesn't offend him because of the race thing. He isn't annoyed by its symbolism or the ugly weight of history and all of that. Its affront is greater, and his beef poetic: it speaks strongly to the bo-hunk aesthetics of those whom embrace it. It is appropriate for a pickup truck bumper or a muscle car hood or a front door mat but little else. Those who get worked up by this sort of thing, students, colleagues, Kalamari, Tigony, decry the racist aspect of its display, and when these emotions swell, he plays along, plays his role, but he's never been able to tap into the same font of anger that they enjoy and in fact has argued that the flag's presence is an asset to the Struggle. It provides a focus and a platform. If there is more driving their protest than self-therapy, and they really want to rouse the rabble, they should remember their Fredrick Douglass: Agitate, agitate, agitate.

Hemperly usually returns to the office after his first class. And it's about that time. This is not an unpleasant realization for Longman. He doesn't mind sharing the office, as long as his desk is by the window, and he's come to like his colleague over the past two weeks—which is a growing concern. Their close proximity has allowed a tentative friendship to rise and take a few steps forward, if just baby steps. Hemperly displays an endearing absentmindedness, and his tendency to talk to himself makes him seem unguarded and genuine somehow. He is nonthreatening in an academic way. But these things never last. It's just a matter of time before he crackers-out like they always do. Longman's instinct is to give the Other as much credit as he can up front and then adjust accordingly. He agrees with the teaching philosophy of the ancient Chinese: teach the kids first-thing that all people are by nature good. He truly believes this. But he can't deny experience and the way racial dynamics usually play out. Just when he begins to feel comfortable and easy around him, when he relaxes his shoulders and drops his guard, Hemperly will say something outrageous and knock down all the built-up trust, something that will slap him in the face, and he'll feel the fool for letting Lucy hold the football once again. And Hemperly won't notice, as they always don't. He'll be oblivious to whatever condescending observation he has made, blind to whatever grossly generalized dynamic he has presented. Perhaps he will share his personal narrative and let Longman know that he has a black friend—although he won't say "black." He'll signify and use the seven-syllable "Af/ri/can A/mer/i/can" as his white colleagues always do in liberal code for enlightened thinking. Longman rarely employs "African American" for this very reason. It crawled out of the afro politics of the 1970s, and he's always found the pop-culture protest antics of that decade a little silly. He sticks to the clean and easy one-syllable adjective: "Black." Let the white folks bushwhack through the syllables. He's going to take the easy route and go around. Call it a rhetorical reparation.

He scoots around his desk and steps to the file cabinet squeezed beside Hemperly's desk. His colleague has the desktop of a new hire. It has a wealth of clean horizontal space—which is a premium around here, and Longman suppresses a covetous instinct. The 4x5 expanse of Verneer is almost virginal. Nothing but a telephone, a purple tape dispenser, and a bargain-bin stapler—all lined up neatly way over there along the far edge. To say that there is a mountain of books and papers on his own desk would be a gross exaggeration, but there *is* a respectable series of hillocks and no room to work, not the room he needs. It shouldn't be too much of an imposition to borrow the space for a while. Hemperly clearly isn't using it. Longman turns to the file cabinet and enjoys the perks of seniority: no bending over for him. The two top drawers are his. The bottom two he cleaned out for Hemperly, and while doing so he came across the posters for the nigger panel and so knows just where to look.

He bends for the bottom handle with effort. The drawer

scrapes open, and there they are. He proposed the panel to the Dr. Davis back when he was a new hire himself: Invite the college and community to discuss the history of the word and its evolution across time, its cultural impact and exploitation as the ultimate power word. She liked the idea, but Longman didn't understand the politics of the Department or realize his place in the pecking order, the bottom. She created a committee of two: Dr. Kalamari to chair and get the lion's share of the credit, and him to do all the work. The most time-consuming of that was the marketing, as it necessitated promotion of the panel to both college and community, which meant posters, a mention on public access radio, and an article in the school newspaper. If not a feather in his cap, at least it was documentation for his tenure dossier. The file is stuffed full of posters and programs for each of the five years that the Department has held the panel and is fat with extras. He always has the print shop print too many copies, despite the downward trend in attendance, trying to balance his hopes for a good turnout with the realities of an activity that most students regard as a mandatory late afternoon assignment that interrupts the dinner hour. His expectations have always been outsized, and in truth it's never a complete washout. There are always a few lively voices in the audience, but the decreasing interest is increasingly palpable, at least to him, and he now has the distinct impression that the subject is something that an older generation is fostering upon a younger audience who doesn't give a hoot about anything other than getting their names on the sign-up sheet to get credit for attending. The discussion, if that's what it is, might be new to the freshmen students who make up most of the audience, but it's become rote for the panel, always the same old participants, and they stay true to type up on the stage sitting in folding chairs behind a folding table: Kalamari always takes the stance that the black communities should embrace the word but it should be verboten to the white folk. Tigony always abhors and thinks that the word should be dead and buried. Klein has had a scheduling conflict every year. And Longman? He tries to think outside of the box (although he dislikes the clichéd phrase, as using it is an example of not thinking outside of the box.) Last year, when he proposed taking a page from the ancient Hebrews and treating the word with the same reverence that they gave the proper name of God (can't speak it, can't write it, but it's cool to use a different word that means the same thing, something fancier than the "N-Word," something Tetragrammatonish) both the audience and his colleagues beside him grew silent. Somewhere in the back of the room, someone dropped a straight pin and it clattered onto the hardwood floor.

He spreads the posters in chronological order across Hemperly's desktop and marvels at how uninspiring he finds them. His imagination should have a little more mojo this early in the day, he thinks. Everything is marketing these days, and the poster is his primary platform to sell the event. He has created a new title each year to re-brand the panel, to sell it with increasingly provocative headlines, used color to his advantage and had them printed on eye-catching paper. Neon orange. Neon Blue. Neon green. The trick is to get the students to notice it in the first place as they trod up the stairwell or pee into a urinal.

The Politics of "Nigger":
Its Historical and Rhetorical Impact on American Culture

"Nigger":
History of Hate or Vernacular Verbiage?

"Nigger": The Black Man's Burden?

"NIGGA": Friend or Foe?

"NIGGA": I'M TALKIN' TO YOU, SUCKA!

Just looking at them makes him weary. Back when it was fresh on his mind and the topic interesting to him, it was easy to channel his energy into lively debate. The students can tell when he is truly invested, when he is representing the academic ideal promised in the marketing literature and when he's just going through the motions. But after five years, it has become repetitive and feels more like a side-show. They will hold the panel. It will be sparsely attended. It will generate heat but no light. And then he'll do it again next year. He considers recycling one of the posters, update the time and the date and leave it at that. Why re-invent the wheel? It'd save a lot of time. All he'd have to do is walk over to the print shop, no need to give it another go.

Hemperly is a concentration breaker this morning. His shoes squeak. Longman hears him enter the lobby, and here he comes down the hallway. He steps through the threshold, footprints tracking up the nice clean floor. His load of books looks heavy.

"*Hola,*" Longman gives a greeting and wonders if he'll notice the armada.

"*Hola. Buenos dias . . . me Espanol es . . . , como se dice* 'rusty' *en Espanol?*"

"*Guten morgen?*"

"My German, too." Travis looks across his desk, eyes on the posters.

"Mind if I use your desktop for a minute?" Longman points at the floor. "You've got something on your shoes."

"Had to come through the construction." He stamps his heels on the linoleum, breaking off red clay. "It's a mess out. No way to get around the run-off in the lot. The desk is all yours," he says, pivots, and sets the books on top of the pile of papers on the microwave oven in the corner. "What are you working on?"

Longman gets an idea. "Have you ever called a person of color a 'nigger'?"

"*What?*" Travis starts. "Of course not."

"Why not? You're from the South, right?"

"Well, I haven't lived here for a long time. But that doesn't matter. It's not language I would use. And I think I'm offended."

"What language do you use?"

"What do you mean?"

"When referring to people of color. When we're not around."

". . . African American."

"Really?"

"Yes."

"What do you call us in your internal dialogue? In your head?" Longman points an index finger to his ear and makes the loopy circle.

". . . the same thing."

"*Really?*"

"Yes."

"Have you ever thought the word 'nigger' in your head?"

"No."

"Honest Injun?"

"*Yes.*"

"You're thinking it now."

"You put it there."

"Ever used it in a joke?

"No."

"Even when you were young?"

Travis crosses his arms. "This is making me uncomfortable."

"Why?"

"It just is. Where are you going with this?"

"I've got a proposal for you." Longman prepares to make the pitch. New blood. That's just what the panel needs. Why didn't he think of it before? Hemperly is no eager newly minted historian still warm from grad school, but he is younger than everyone else around here. And hungrier. Maybe including him will reignite his own interest in the topic. At the very least, it will shake things up. Kalamari dislikes him, so that'll introduce an element of conflict. Who knows where this could go?

Chapter Twenty-two

Meggan lies flat on her back in the center of the bed, and thinks: The bad thing about crying in bed is that the tears run into your ears. And they do, rolling across her cheeks and into her auditory canals, first one then the other. She puts a hand on her forehead, and her headache pulses on her palm. She doesn't know what to do, can't decide which way to go. She had stayed with Pete through it all, even after they locked him up. She had given him everything. And why? Because he asked her. Because she believed in him and she loved him with her whole heart and still does. She didn't have a choice in the matter. No, this didn't mean that she was a doormat. He was just The One. Even after things got ugly, when he would come home cranked-up and angry and start shouting at the boys. She knew it was the addiction talking. But the incarceration had shaken her. She didn't feel older but the evidence was there in the mirror. It was there every morning, noon, and night: the shock of gray above her widow's peak that looked like she had been smacked on the head with a paintbrush. She hasn't lost her looks yet, but sees it on the horizon. She doesn't turn heads the way she used to, for men or women. When she's out and about and passes someone somewhere, doesn't matter who, doesn't matter where, she follows their eye line to see what they're looking at—which used to be her, but not these days. She has taken to wearing low-cut blouses or unbuttoning an extra shirt button. That worked for a while. The thirties are making her invisible. She might as well cut her hair short and bulk up on Cheetoes in front of the TV.

At least she's got her boys. She digs a finger in her ear, clears it, and then the other. They know when she's sad, and they always know how to cheer her up. And here they come. Yang is heavier, and his nails on the hardwood floor make a deeper sound (and a deeper gouge, but it's his house, too). Ying is a little bit of a pup and won't fatten up, and this bothers her, but the vet says he doesn't have worms. Heavy scrape, light scrape, first on the kitchen tile and then on the hardwoods. Yang wins the race and jumps up onto the bed, goes straight for her face and begins licking her cheek and making that sound in his throat. Ying isn't big enough to make the jump, and he's up on his hind legs, paws on the comforter, and complaining. *Help me up! Help me up!*

"Boys, boys, boys." She sits upright to help Ying up, and they come for a hug and smother, giving love. She wraps her arms around them both, pulls them closer and falls back, her head on the pillow. There's no denying it: they smell bad. But it's not their fault. She hasn't given them a bath for a month or more. It's way overdue.

"Stinky fellas," she rubs their backs fast and hard. "Stinky, stinky fellas. How about a bath? You want mommy to give you a bath?"

You stay with someone for ten years and they become part of you. You become part of who they are, too. She and Pete were connected—not with ethereal strands of light but with thick if invisible cables that were plugged into her head and heart. Even in the really bad days, they slept together intertwined, wrapped around each other, both of them the perfect size for the other in their embrace and the same temperature, too. She was lucky.

The time blinks on the alarm clock on the night stand. She can't remember playing snooze tag. No wonder they're so antsy. She sits up and they hop about on the comforter. Ying dribbles in the brilliant shaft of light coming from the window behind the bed, shining across the comforter and all the way over to the vanity mirror. It's a sunny day out, but the weather is beginning to cool. She always sleeps in the nude and likes the chill. This might be the last time the boys get a bath outside before the winter comes. Meggan rolls over, gets out of the bed, wipes her cheeks and gets in a good stretch, assumes downward dog and holds the pose. She hasn't practiced yoga since the boys ate the mat.

"Okay, okay, okay." She throws on some panties, jeans, and one of Pete's paint-splattered sweatshirts, then heads for the kitchen and the coffeemaker on the counter. The custom roast is in a large jar over the microwave, and the smell of the ground coffee beans brings comfort. Five scoops, and when the machine begins to glug, she considers Travis. She remembers him fondly, if not strongly, from her college days. And he seems responsible. He has a job and is a college professor no less. Back at UGA she had imagined she'd marry an English professor one day, back when she still wrote poetry, but that was a different life, a different Margaret. Things never go as planned, at least not for her. Now, all she has is the boys, the children she had with Pete. Both of them from the pound on the same day. She picked Ying, he picked the Yang. She loves them totally, but she's had an increasing feeling that they're not enough. And that takes her back to Travis. It was a ho-hum date, and he's not much of a kisser, but he sure tried hard. That was something.

Ying likes his coffee with milk and sugar. Yang only drinks decaf and so is out of luck this morning. She had ignored his whining, but he gives a sharp bark to get her attention. They are demanding and know what they want. She bends to reach his coffee dish and pulls the milk from the fridge, mixes his coffee in the blue bowl and throws in a few cubes of ice. Ying vibrates with excitement and dribbles on the tile.

"Your coffee, sir."

How did it happen that her choice had dwindled down to two? A moment of wistful reminiscence wells and she wonders how she became the girl, the woman now standing here in this kitchen. All of her sisters in the Zeta house resented her, every single one. Every time the phone in the foyer rang, the house mother would yell up: another call for her. But they didn't turn out so well either. All of her girlfriends are married, none happy. Pete comes up for parole in two years. Travis has a faint odor that she's not sure about. Ying laps at the coffee with his tongue like a dog. Café au lait splashes out of the bowl and onto the tile. The sliding doors. Pine straw on the patio furniture. Morning sun through the paw prints. Dust motes and dog hair.

Chapter Twenty-three

*T*ravis can go this way or that. This morning he decides to go that way and run through Oakland Cemetery, mostly because he's never gone that way before. All the effort over the past few weeks has paid off, and he is no longer a lowly jogger. He now trots along at a respectable speed that most fair-minded observers would describe as running. He's not going to win the marathon but can maintain a modest pace for a few miles. Let the feeble jog and hobble—he's not done yet. And he's feeling pretty good these days. His classes are under control, and he's learned his way around the Department if not the college. He's beginning to hit a stride. Meggan agreed to join him for the drive up to the mountains this weekend, too. His uncle was big-hearted on the phone. *"Come on up. Y'all can have the downstairs."*

He's had an itch to visit the cemetery ever since his grandmother boasted that she was eligible to be buried there. Apparently there is a pecking order for the dead. He wants to see the family plot, too, so he leaves the apartment and runs west. The old grounds of headstones, monuments, and mausoleums rambles over a large tree-covered piece of real estate next to Cabbagetown, his shabby neighborhood. The entrance is at the far end and he'll have to circumnavigate, a mile or more he figures, so he crosses the bumper-to-bumper traffic at the bend in the road, all the cars heading to their nine-to-fives, skirts between a UPS truck and a Fed Ex truck, and treads along the herringbone brick sidewalk. The historic district air is double strength this morning, as he's partaking of two different historic zones at once, but this morning it just tastes like auto exhaust, a harsh gathering of something at the back of his throat that he ejects now and again, turns his head to the road and spits quickly. He trots west along the cemetery wall, the mortar between the brick crumbling back to sand, and his thoughts begin to shake out. This will be the last run he'll get in before the trip to the mountains. Thoughts of Meggan lift his spirits and then he puzzles over dog hair. He doesn't know how it's possible, but he found dog hair in his running shoes this morning when he laced them up after coffee. How could that possibly happen? His loafers, he could see, but his kicks? They haven't been in the same room together, much less the same part of town together.

Kicks?

Where did that come from?

He puzzles over the word, a new addition to his vocabulary, and then realizes that he's picked it up from his students—a bonus to teaching. He is able to stay current on the latest teen slang. And his students are black, so he's hit the mother lode. It makes him feel cutting-edge. He gets to drop newfangled language before it is inevitably appropriated by the white kids and moves to the suburbs.

"I'm just running along in my kicks."

The musing about language naturally segues into the upcoming panel. He likes Longman but is sore at him, too. Travis doesn't appreciate the way he backed him up against the wall with the interrogation about his orientation to the N-word. He calls black people "black" and always has, until he began teaching at the college. He still has a little egg on his face for not just explaining that to him, but the awkwardness of the confrontation made him tell an obvious lie. It still feels like an assault somehow. But the invitation to join the panel had ameliorated whatever bruise Travis received, and he's glad to have the opportunity to participate, although he doesn't know what he has to add to the discussion. His students say the N-word every day, although they drop the hard R and use it like he used "man" when he was their age and had his own teen vocabulary. He thinks it through: Hey, man. Cool, man. Later, man. Yo, N-word. Word, N-word. Peace, N-word. Yo, nigga. Word, nigga. Later, nigga. He pads up the broken brick and turns down the side road to the cemetery entrance, saying the words aloud: "Hey, man. Yo, N-word. Yo, nigga." And the first two come out easily enough but he can't get a grasp on "nigga" and it sounds funny.

The entrance to the cemetery is a brick arch, its wrought iron gates swung open. The roads were laid out with horse-and-carriage traffic in mind and seem a tight fit for a car. Surrounding him is a literal city of the dead, and he appreciates the phrase differently now. Everything about Oakland is old. The oak trees—the place is well named—are enormous and gnarled, white oaks with trunks as wide as his arms outstretched. History underground, Travis thinks. All around him monuments rise. Those who built them must have made a pretty penny. Mausoleums and memorials compete for the first place award in grandiosity, not like the ranks of comparable headstones out at Westview where Charlie is buried, Charlie with his brass plaque flat on the ground. Some are quite impressive, stately columns and intricate wrought iron, an entryway here, a stone angel alighting there, wings outstretched and eyes downcast. And some are just Atlanta-tacky, gaudy and ostentatious displays of wealth, spires that are competing phallic symbols. This is not your average graveyard, he thinks. It's a mini-metropolis built by engineers who had a vague understanding of classical Greek and Roman architecture, as good a snapshot as any into the culture that you could take, he thinks, the historian inside surging. Old money v. new. The hierarchy of disposable income, and established in granite block, no less.

To the north, the downtown skyline is an odd replication with its skyscrapers collected and competing and the gold dome of the capitol building in the foreground. Beyond the cemetery's brick wall border, the rail yard bangs and clangs. Two short blasts from a locomotive horn echoes, and then a bell begins to ding as a diesel engine accelerates. The noise of industry makes the cemetery seem, well, dead. Crowded but empty. Cold stone. He's apparently the only live visitor, just him, the wealthy dead, and the rail yard clatter.

He downshifts to a jog and makes his way over to what must be the administrative building: a squat two story structure, stuccoed brick painted white recently. There's a bell tower on top and a parapet on the right. There are people here after all, and Oakland doesn't have a parking lot. Sedans and SUVs are parked haphazardly on the shoulders of the carriage road, pulled off the asphalt and leaning into drainage gutters, the old bricks thick with moss. Drainage technology from the 19th century. Travis walks underneath the porta cochere and down the short gallery to the main entrance. This is some way in. Ornate. Victorian. Stained glass. Brass knob with angel. When the door opens, a bell tinkles. A whiff of feminine douche escapes, and he didn't expect a gift shop. Everything in the small room is for sale. Figurines in such numbers have always made Travis uncomfortable, and they've got him surrounded. Trinkets and tchotchkes rank across the mahogany tabletops, a squad of the same Confederate soldier, sabers raised. Black Americana sitting on the edge of the shelf and enjoying watermelon. Figurines of a dead lion—lots of these—atop stars and bars from broken flag shaft, the fallen Confederacy immortalized. And over there on the counter, the blue Olympic mascot is in mourning. A row of whatever it is, diapers black, eyes downcast and shedding tears.

The sexton steps to the counter from a doorway behind, a man not old yet but getting close. Not dark-skinned, not mulatto, but somewhere in between. Hairline receding and hair graying. His black turtleneck is rolled down. His spectacles have small oval lenses. His disapproving look reminds Travis that he's wearing running shorts and a t-shirt. Underdressed. He's unexpectedly crossed the boundary into the rarified air of the Old South once again. His faux pas hangs heavy in the air.

"Good morning, sir." The sexton has a clipped voice. "May I help you?"

Travis introduces himself and makes quick explanation of his attire. He is out getting some exercise and his arrival is spontaneous. He offers an apology for his unintended disrespect. Code of the South. He says that he is looking for his family plot and asserts his birthright with confidence. He employs a polite lie and explains that he hasn't visited for a while. Could you please help me find its location? And he has said the magic words. He's a member. The sexton brightens and smiles, and the words begin to flow. He waves away Travis's ill-suited clothing. We have joggers and walkers all the time, he says graciously. It is a pleasure to meet you, he says, his eyes alight and handshake firm. Yes, of course. Follow me. Follow me. He motions him back into the office behind the counter. Travis steps around and into the dimly lit room. Rich wood paneling. Imposing period desk, brass desk lamp with a slight tarnish. On the wall, old framed photos of the cemetery. The city. White men he does not recognize with flamboyant facial hair that suggests they were involved in the Civil War. The sexton speaks with the pointed enthusiasm of someone who delights in his line of work, yet rarely has the opportunity to do so. His customer base has died off, he says, with more longing than gallows humor. The cemetery is almost full. All of the plots were sold by the turn of the century. There is only the rare funeral now and again when someone with a long lifespan has space left in a plot likely purchased in the 19th century. He opens a card box, the metal lid falling back, wets his thumb and flips through the dividers to the H.

"Hemperly, Hemply, Hemperly. Let me see." And then he asks for a given name. Travis is stumped.

"Try Charles," he guesses.

"Charles Hemperly, right here," the sexton says and pulls a card.

"You have more than one Hemperly?"

"No, no. Just this one. Just this one." He seems as interested in the search as Travis, maybe more. "Over here. Over here," and he steps to a hand-drawn map of the cemetery framed on the wall, plots marked off in squares and rectangles and triangles, a crowded landscape. Each plot is numbered.

"Here you are right here." An index finger on the map. "X-marks the spot. Not far at all. Not far at all. It will be my pleasure to show you." And before Travis can say no thank you, the sexton turns and heads for the door, card in hand. He'd wanted to find the plot himself, wander around, sight-see and take stock. He doesn't know how the Hemperly plot will measure up. The sexton must be clairvoyant because he fires back, "So few members come in these days, and I don't get to do this as often as I'd like," and there's a plea in there somewhere.

"Lead the way," Travis says.

Back outside the building, the cars lean into the brick culverts.

"Is there a funeral today?"

"If only that were the case." The sexton eyes a cloud with a wistful look. "The re-enactors are back. I prefer to keep my distance." He makes a flat statement that he doesn't elaborate. Before Travis can ask, the sexton cautions urgently: "Be wary of the fire ants." And he points to a mound squashed behind a tire of one of the leaning sedans, the red SUVs, the ants frantic with the work of bugging out. "I urge you to keep an eye out. Their bites are quite painful."

He hadn't noticed before. The small mounds are everywhere, on every plot and the brick walks between. Small and not so small red heaps pile up against granite and the concrete boundaries of the plots, in the grass, too, popping up over the interred, a chaotic and unregulated colonization. The sexton starts down a brick walkway at a brisk pace. The mausoleums have given way to headstones in this section. He stops beside a well-maintained plot, grass finely trimmed. Not a weed. Not a leaf. The headstone is large but unadorned, an urn on each end. Two footplates right where you'd think they'd be. No fire ants, either, no red mound.

"This is the Margaret Mitchell plot," the sexton says. "Our most popular. Visitors come from around the globe to see this headstone. Travis steps up. Headstone tourism? That seems a grim hobby. The paparazzi have arrived on the scene a little late.

Travis thinks of Charlie. He hasn't returned to Westview since they laid his plaque. His brother's loss is a lifelong wound, but he's never seriously considered visiting Westview Cemetery, even though it's not far from the College. He wonders if his father makes the trip.

The sexton starts for the far wall of the cemetery. "Not far," he beckons. "Not far." He repeats everything twice, an unusual tick. Travis jogs down the brick to catch up. The walkway declines with accompanying erosion, flowing sand and soil, the red clay exposed, and the mausoleums give way to headstones that lean this way and that.

The Hemperly plot is down-market, apparently. Travis antic-ipates and hopes that it isn't the shabbiest one on the block. The sexton stops and looks down at the card.

"Here it is," he says with a flourish. "Here it is."

Travis steps beside him. The weedy square has a single obelisk in its center, HEMPERLY chiseled onto the granite beneath the pyramidal point. Before it, three small headstones lined up in a row, with four more behind the spire monument, seven in all, and not one of them plumb. "Children?" he blurts in surprise. The little headstones have chiseled dates: birth and death. Travis does the math. Only two of them lived to see three years. The plot is full of toddlers and infants.

"And four adults," the sexton points to the card matter-of-fact-ly and a faded pencil illustration of their placement. "Two on ei-ther side of the obelisk."

This is not what he expected at all. The granite names are fading. Infant. Infant. Infant. Infant. Infant. Infant. Zoe.

The sexton notes the tragic loss, as he puts it, and asks Travis for details he does not have. "Illness." He flips the card over. "Scar-let Fever most likely by the dates, but it's hard to say really. Epi-demics were common in those days." And then the sexton adjusts into a formal stance. "I'll leave you to your reflection," he says. "It was a pleasure to meet you. Please stop by anytime. Anytime." And he turns back toward the building.

"My reflection," Travis thinks but isn't sure where to start. So many children. So much death. He has no connection to the names on the headstones and might as well be standing before any of the plots. He takes a step up and into the tall grass, careful to step between where he estimates the caskets are placed. The obe-lisk has withstood a century of weather, coal soot from the chug-ging trains and now whatever's in the cloud of auto exhaust that overhangs the city. The pyramid point is smooth, but the spire itself has the patina of age, the elements slowly working to fade the inscription on each face. Augustus. Hatty, beloved wife (the mother of the children, Travis figures, considering the dates). Hel-en, unbeloved apparently (his great-grandmother?), and Charles

190

E., the last casket buried, 1964, the year after Travis was born. This must be Suitcase Charlie, and he imagines the portrait of his great-grandfather, his annoyed expression. The small headstones of the children lean, knocked off-kilter by the slow churning of continental drift. No, this isn't what expected at all. His grandmother can shine some light here. Good thing she's still around to ask. He'll have to have lunch with her after he returns from the mountains. But one family mystery at a time, he tells himself. No clues here. Just eleven sad burials, relatives long gone and forgotten, and he realizes that he has wandered into a thicket of reflection, just as the sexton predicted.

A breeze on the back of his neck brings both a chill and an incremental change of the season. The rail yard clanks and then a tremendous crash and a shudder as something large hits the ground, a freight container dropped onto a rail-car, or maybe there's been an accident over behind the wall. He's not a praying man but it seems like the thing to do, so he gives it a shot, bowing his head and closing his eyes. He doesn't know what to appeal for, and nothing comes. He has seen what he came to see and has gotten his fill. Move along, move along. One last look at the headstones and he leaves the buried past behind and gets back to the more cheerful activity of recreation and trots down the brick path and back the way he came. The weight of the little headstones begins to fade as he moves back uphill and into the big money plots on the crown of the cemetery land. He returns to the asphalt road and gets back to running, first through the crowded mausoleum 'burbs, then the road declines, segregation begins, and the monuments change again. The Jewish section with its closely packed sepulchers, the African American section with its sparse monuments, the headstones becoming more modest as the elevation decreases. A few quick clouds pass overhead, their shadows dragging over the cemetery, and up ahead is a large monument, notable for both its size and apparent planning. Most of the cemetery has been laid out haphazardly, but this area has been designed to purpose. It is the tallest monument yet, much taller, another obelisk but several stories tall with the road splitting and going around, circling it.

Travis slows to a trot when he reaches the shadow point of the spire, broad and long on the road. Carved in the center of the spire, the chiseled words tell the story: OUR CONFEDERATE DEAD, withstanding the years, but still slightly fading. And the confederate dead are there, or at least their headstones are, row after row of round-topped marble stones surround the obelisk in ranks, a roll call that spreads in every direction, all of them the same, Arlington-like without the vast numbers. It seems to him there should be more, what with the mortality rates of the war. Care for the returning Confederate dead must have been low on the collapsing Confederacy's to do list. He runs past the regimental headstones and after a while comes upon a grassy field free of monuments. Except one. The tomb to the unknown soldiers stands alone, a monument behind a gated wrought iron fence. It's the same dead lion for sale in miniature on the gift shop shelves. Grisly thinking to imagine what's been buried underneath here. The sculpture of the beast is dead on its side, laid out on a pedestal, Confederate battle flag underneath, flagstaff broken. Another monument heavy with solemnity yet not a particularly well sculpted one, he thinks. He appreciates the vision of the artist and the symbolism works, yet his execution displays an unsteady grasp of both proportion and zoology, which makes the lion unrealistic in form, and it seems unlikely that the sculptor would have taken the occasion to make a bold artistic statement. He stops equivocating: it's just a bad sculpture.

A snare drum gets his attention, a tattoo rat-a-tat-tats on down the hill. Travis answers the call and starts off again—an easy run today with all the stopping and starting—and then he sees a mob at the far end of the cemetery, standing behind a grove of elms in what must be the potter's field. Down the hill and around he runs and comes upon the crowd, all facing away from him. Thirty or so people gather together, the women in hoop skirts, the men in coats with tails and a few stovepipe hats, all of them with their backs turned to him. It makes little sense until he sees the gallows and then it makes no sense at all. He has happened upon a public execution. His head hums. It's a hanging. He doesn't know whether to go for the law or just feel out-of-place or just feel underdressed for the occasion.

Seven white men stand in a row on a low platform, thick nooses dropping around their necks from the scaffold that stretches above their heads from one tree to another. Most of them have beards. It's a military execution by the looks of it, with a tribunal in Confederate butternut, officiating. The commander must be the one with the snappiest uniform and longest beard, a puffy man with a paunch. He stands next to the young drummer. Travis slows to a walk and approaches quietly. He is the only person in modern dress. This must be the reenactment the sexton mentioned, and he again thinks fondly of his Viking days. Is anyone capturing this on film? He looks for a video camera, can't see one, and he notices that one of the re-enactors standing at the back of the crowd is African-American, a young man who notices him and turns his way. His eyes widen and he breaks away and heads over. He is a few feet away when Travis realizes that he is one of his students.

"Professor Hemperly! Hello," he says in a hushed tone. "What are you doing here?"

One of his students. Travis reaches for a name, but none comes. "I'm just out for a run in my kicks," he says.

"Kicks? What are kicks?"

"My running shoes. What's going on here?"

"Civil War reenactment." the student says and begins a tale of a stolen locomotive and captured spies. "They were hung here in 1862. This is an anniversary. What do you think?" He pulls at his cotton shirt. "One hundred percent period-accurate." He shows off his loose trousers, his suspenders and brogans.

"A slave?" Travis asks.

"Oh, usually I'm a member of the Massachusetts 54th, the all-black regiment. Did you ever see *Glory*? We do movies sometimes and sometimes just have commemorative events, like today."

"Really?" he says. "Do many African-Americans participate?"

"About a hundred of us the last time we got together. Most stick to the 54th. But I've got my slave costume, too, and get called for that from time to time. It's easy money. Re-enactors are fanatical about detail, and the record says that "negroes" attended the execution. At $25 an hour, it beats working security at the High."

On the platform, one of the condemned steps forward to speak. He is eloquent and says that he is not afraid of death, that he is no spy but simply a soldier performing his duty and that he has no hard feelings for the South or its people. They have been deceived by their leaders, and their rebellion is useless and hopeless. They would live to regret their part in this and the country would be reunited. The flag of the reunited country would fly over his grave. Travis thinks he's pretty gracious, considering the circumstances, but his words do not go over well with the crowd.

"Kill the damn Yankees!" from somewhere inside the pack.

"Kill 'em! String 'em up!"

And then the whole crowd begins to jeer. The commander draws his sword, raises it, the drummer boy begins the countdown drum and when the commander lowers his sword the drumming stops abruptly. The platform falls away and the prisoners fall and jerk around until they hang limp.

"Um . . . " Travis says.

"Oh, that's not real." The student whispers. They're rigged. It's all part of the show."

The crowd cheers and someone breaks out a flute and it begins to whistle "Dixie" and the drummer joins in. Everyone begins to sing. I wish I were in the land of cotton. A few energetic yippees are thrown in, and Travis wonders if that's the way it really went down. It seems more like a recreation in a bad film to him, despite all the attention to the costume detail. At the back of the crowd, a heavy yet well-dressed gent turns their way.

"Toby! Get back over here, boy!"

"Yassa, Massa!" the student says. "Yassa!" He rolls his eyes at Travis. "I'll see you in class tomorrow, prof." and he runs back to the happy crowd. Travis takes one step back. As a former re-en-actor himself, he can appreciate the activity, but he was getting a paycheck for playing dress-up. These gents and their ladies and the confederates up front are here on their own time. He begins to mull the oddness of it, and then: pain.

The ants began their charge as soon as his shoe landed on the mound, and the first bite snaps up his spinal cord and explodes in his brain stem. Then more, one two three four five six seven, and Travis hops and yells, ants scrambling across the shoe, the short sock, and some on his leg. Everyone turns. The hanging Yankees raise their heads.

Chapter Twenty-four

$\mathcal{R}$emus is a kindly darkie by design. He is fixed the way that Mr. Chandler wrote him, and he can't be any more or less than that. He has to be true to his nature, even if someone else made it up. But after recent events, he is less inclined to just get along. Despite being born into bondage, he has spent his long life looking on the sunny side. *Der ain't no bad wedder*, he's always said. *Jest dif't so'ts er good wedder*. But even Auntie Sun doesn't shine like she used to. There's too much junk in the air these days. All these cars. They're worse than the trains used to be, chugging in and out of town, smoke boiling up from the smokestacks and blowing soot all over the place. He's been standing here at the crossroads all day holding up his sign and dodging the cars, and now the sun is beginning to set over the west end of West End, dropping down over behind the shopping mall. He doesn't have a lot of time.

His stay in the calaboose has left him out of sorts. They let the crazy nigger go after a few hours but kept Remus locked up for three days. Three days in a cage. Drunk and disorderly, they said, but he wasn't drunk, he was just drinking. He lost his Styrofoam cup during the scuffle and is now using his hat, which is a problem because of the holes, but he's put in a paper sack lining and that works alright. In his other hand, he holds a sign on a piece of cardboard he found in the side lot of the fire station, although he doesn't know how to write, just knows how to make his mark and a few things he's picked up, like a cent sign: ¢. He's drawn a big one with a piece of coal he found on the railroad track, scrawled it across the corrugated ridges. He's been walking up and down the lines of cars with it since the shadows were at their shortest. Now the sun is falling fast, and there are more cars on the road as they pull up the hill from the school, everybody going home at the end of the day.

There's a routine to it. He holds up his sign to as many drivers as he can get to before the light turns green and the cars accelerate and pass him by until the light turns red again and the next cars slow to a stop, rolling up to the red light and the others backing up behind. One, two, three, four, five. And then he starts all over again, walks up to the first one in line and tries to catch the driver's eye, but he can't because the man is wearing dark glasses on his eyes, like a blind man. He sits with his head straight forward looking at the nothing across the street, even though Remus is standing there two feet away. But his window is down.

"Eb'nin', Mr. Man. He'p ole Remus dis eb'nin'?"

The driver says nothing. He just looks out the windshield. And there really is nothing to look at, just the entrance to the access road. Remus knows, he's been looking at it all day long himself. So he says it again a little louder. Evening, Mr. Man. Help old Remus this evening? The driver says nothing. Remus stands his ground and waits a little more. He holds his sign higher and gives it a little shake. Still, the driver says nothing.

"W'at make you hol' yo' head so high?" Remus asks, but still not a notice. Then he mumbles to himself, "You ole scribble-scrabble."

This gets his attention. The man turns his head. "What did you call me, old man?"

"You ole scribble-scrabble," he says a little louder as he steps down to the next car in line. It feels good to speak up. He's been smiling for so long that his mouth hurts. From time to time he dwells on back-in-the-day, back when he was famous and everyone knew him and loved him. And now just look. His reflection in the window of the next car, a big gal behind the wheel who's all dressed up. Her hair looks like there's a big spider on her head. The cars've got tin plates on the back, letters and numbers stamped on them and fixed on the bumpers. This gal has a tin plate on the front of hers that doesn't have numbers, just letters that he can't read because he can't read. DIVA. Maybe it means she works for the city. She's wearing dark glasses too, and he extends the sign closer, sees it reflected in her side window. Most people who help him out with spare change are the people he can look in the eye. Her car looks brand new. You'd think that the new cars, the cars with the shine, would help him out, but it's always the cars with a little wear to them. The dressed-up gal doesn't pay him any attention either. Her window is rolled up and her door locks go *thunk-cabunk*.

"Miz biggity," he mumbles. "Miz high n' mighty."

She doesn't have any idea who he used to be and wouldn't care if she did. He's been longing for how it used to be all day. It gets him like that sometimes, and when he gets into that sort of mind, he always misses the critters, misses Brer Rabbit and Brer Fox. Brer Terrapin and Brer Bear and Brer Turkey Buzzard, too, but Brer Rabbit the most. Wasn't anybody who didn't know who they were either, all of them in high cotton together. But at least Remus is still around, at least he can say that. Brer Rabbit and Brer Fox are gone-gone. With the way the city's built itself up, they've probably run off to the deep woods. Only critters he sees these days is Brer Squirrel in the daytime and Brer Rat in the nighttime. But they're not as sociable. It's just not the same.

The crossroads is on a rise, and he's got a good view of the shopping mall across the interstate. The parking lot is big and empty. There are some cars parked down front near the front door, but most of it is just land that they tractored flat and paved over. And it's good growing soil underneath too, or used to be. It used to be the big apple orchard. He'd help himself to one every once in a while. Good soil everywhere around here. He kept a little vegetable garden when he stayed over in the cabin behind Mr. Chandler's house.

The sun has settled on the roof of the mall, and purple spreads out behind, but mean-looking clouds are catching up to it and are beginning to block it out, making the dark come early. They're real thunder-boomers too, big and high like giant anvils, their bottoms blue-gray and weighted down with water. The one on the left lights up, a yellow flash that tears through the bottom side of the cotton boll. And it doesn't take long for the rumble to come, and the cloud roars at the shopping mall. The paper lining his hat is folded in on itself, and the coins rattle around at the bottom when he shakes it. He takes a quick count and then counts again to make sure. They want five dollars to let him stay at the church for the night. And they won't let him in if he doesn't get there before the cut-off at sundown. Another flash inside the cloud and another thunder rumble, and if he doesn't get there before they shut the door, he's going to have to spend the night out in the rain. He counts through the bag again, the case quarters and then the dimes and nickels. A few copper pennies. It's not that he minds the rain so much, but there's a cold snap on the way. He can smell it in the air, see it in the sky. He can feel it on the inside. They won't let him build a fire anywhere around here, and there's not enough good wood to pick up, anyway. People get mad at him when he goes into their front yards looking for firewood. There's some trees along the train tracks, but the last time he stayed down there they beat him up and painted his hair orange. And he doesn't have any matches, besides.

The green light stays on longer now that there are more cars on the road, and they pass in a long line. He waits on the curbstone for the light to turn red again, holding his sign in front of him. He tries to look each driver in the eye, but not a one of them turns his way. There's a little click whenever the traffic signal changes color, one click for yellow, another click for red, something going on up inside the signal box hanging over his head. With one click the cars speed up, trying to get past the yellow light and then another click and one more gets past, running through the red light and the car behind rolls to a stop at the line. Remus takes a step off of the curb and into the street, a white man behind the wheel of this one, and not wearing sunglasses. It's hard to figure the white folks these days. There aren't many of them driving around the neighborhood any more. He hasn't seen more than three of them today and they all passed him by, too, but a man gave him a dollar bill just the other day. Remus holds up his sign, and the white man looks at him and there's that moment when he thinks that he just might give him something but he only takes his hands off the wheel, turns them up, and shakes his head.

Another rumble over the shopping mall and raindrops start to dot on the road. Headlights begin to flip on around him, the lights of the car next in line shine, and raindrops fall in the beams of light. Remus steps on up to the window, the rain running down it, too, and the driver rolls it down. He leans his head out.

"Better get on to the shelter, old man."

The rain picks up. Remus pushes his hat forward.

"You don't have enough to get in, do you?"

"Dat's de long en de short 'n it," Remus says and shakes the hat. The coins clink and jingle. He didn't feel the raindrops at first, but now they tap on the top of his head, and he could sure use his hat. The man leans back inside the car and jostles with a billfold. When he leans back out, he's got a five dollar bill in his hand.

"Here you go, but you'd better get a move on. They're going to lock the doors in just a little while." He points at the setting sun and drops the bill down into the hat.

"Bless yo' soul," Remus says and pulls the bag from the hat and places the hat on his head. He wipes the rainwater from his spectacles but it doesn't do much good.

"You'd better go straight there," the man says. "Don't stop at the liquor store now."

"No, suh," Remus says and thanks him again. And now the rain is really starting to come down and the sun almost swallowed by the clouds. The signal box overhead clicks and then clicks again and Remus tips his hat to the man as the car rolls past, his window rolling back up. Then the next car in line is a big truck, one of the ambulances from down at the Gradies. A black gal driving and a white boy on the other side. The truck horn blares. "Get the hell out of the road!" she yells and lays on the horn. The rain falling in front of the headlights picks up and now it's really coming down. Remus steps back up to the curb and the ambulance roars past, tires splashing the forming puddle at the curbside. The church isn't far, just right around the corner. He can see the steeple from here rising from over behind the mall.

It's not such a long row to hoe, and then he'll be under shelter. He can cut through the mall parking lot and get over there in no time. Thunder rumbles overhead, and it begins to rain like the sky had been turned to water.

Chapter Twenty-five

*T*he office doors of the history department faculty run off of a narrow back hallway in Garvey Hall, popping up on the left and right between cork board rectangles that are not updated regularly. The linoleum floor shines this evening from the recent pass of the buffing machine and the late night labor of the custodial staff—the college's least visible and least compensated employees. They clock in on the vampire's time schedule, slogging through the buildings, sweeping and mopping and buffing and initiating the trash's final journey from the wastepaper baskets in the offices to the Atlanta city dump across town. But for the most part, Garvey is empty at night, and this is how Kwasi Kalamari likes it. The Dr. is in this evening, having made it inside the building just before the raindrops began to fall. He gets more work accomplished when the students aren't around, and with everyone gone he can also abuse his privileges on the department's copying machine without the chair interfering and chastising. It's a bonus that she suspects that he's the one who depletes the printer paper and empties the toner bar, but she can't prove it. She confronted him about it in the lobby just yesterday. But Kalamari is careful. There is no proof, nothing but the accusation. He just looked her in the eye. His: wide and innocent. Hers: narrow and searching, looking for evidence of culpability and giveaway body language. They locked in eyeball confrontation before the bulletin board until she blinked and backed down, as always.

Kalamari settles into the chair behind his desk. The window to his office opens from the bottom and swings out in a vertical slant, but it's closed this evening or almost. It won't shut completely. The latch won't catch. Raindrops tap on the magnolia tree and the accompanying wind makes the big leaves rattle. Cool air blows in through the gap and onto the open wound scabbing over, and it throbs, the pulse of his heart on the back of his head. Police brutality, he thinks. It couldn't have been any more blatant. His longest dread is now gone and he feels its absence like a missing limb. His arm is still sore from the tetanus booster that the careless sister down at the hospital gave him a few days before, driving the needle deep and striking bone. It shouldn't have to be such a struggle, he thinks. Police brutality, plain and simple. Things will never change.

Overhead, one of the fluorescent light tubes is dark and the other hums in sketchy health, but it's still too much light for him. The harsh white glare is ugly and unnatural, and he prefers the golden forty-watt glow from the articulated brass desk lamp. Desk lamp on, overheads off. Last night's stick of incense has burned down to a stub in the whittled wooden tray and needs replacement. He pulls the desk drawer out and rustles around until he finds the box and retracts a purple stick, places it in the holder and fires it up with a flame from the Olympic lighter he found lying on the asphalt as he hustled over from his parking spot, the interlocking circles of world cooperation defaced by tire tread. A thin wisp of smoke rises, spicing the air jasmine next to the boom box. It is the one item that does not belong among the artifacts in his office, a holdover from the Reagan 80s, and its polystyrene casing mars the feng shui harmony. Everything else in the office has hand-crafted energy. The Gle Mu and Gle Gon masks on the wall, their long faces with mouth's open in small O's, reacting to a particularly well-placed retort. The wood cut prints from the Pueblos Negros: The figures in a canoe. The big-eyed fish. There's a fu-fu bowl on the carved table of the elephant with its curling tusks, a pricey item that should bring a stronger connection with Mother Africa than it does, having been bought on his last trip over and shipped back at great expense. But every time he looks at it he remembers the unpleasant hassle it took to pick it up from the Atlanta airport, after having been lost and then found and then lost again by Delta freight and circumnavigating the globe. Twice.

Still, most of the office is in tune with the actual earth. Except for the boom box—his one capitulation to the modern western tradition. It fills a good quarter of the desktop, the molded plastic casing approximating forged steel but not fooling anyone, and it flies the flag of cheap consumerism and sweatshop economics. Kalamari presses the power button and the red eye glows on and the music plays from the CD spinning in its guts, a melodic *a capella* male voice calling and the village chorus responding in indigenous harmony. The radio spots should be coming up soon. He reaches for the organizer next to the incense burner, thumbs through the pages, and stops. The broadcast times are written down in his tiny longhand, and he checks the hour on his father's wristwatch. The watch needs a new band, the worn leather strap is cracked from age and tearing near the dial from everyday use. It will break sooner or later, but replacing it would eliminate the connection. He never saw his father without it, and the strap is marinated in his sweat. That is its value, its worth. It runs a little slow.

A flash of lightning outside the window and then the thunder a few seconds after. The wound throbs. Police brutality. Plain and simple. No one did anything. They just stood around and watched the Man beat another brother down. There's never an amateur video cameraman around when you need one. The wound throbs. It used to be that you knew who was on one side and who was on the other, even the brothers and sisters who couldn't or wouldn't protest were on the same side—even if they didn't agree on tactics. There was a shared understanding of who was oppressed and who was not. Not so these days. Too many brothers and sisters have been seduced, their African essence diluted, and he glares at the boom box. But the revolution is coming. He knows this. The street soldiers are gathering, and he is gathering them, difficult to assemble though they may be. Engaging the community has become a side-struggle. That is why he is here tonight. He is in the office this evening to prepare for community outreach. It is time for the panel to discuss the word once again, and this should be a platform for unification and recruitment, an opportunity, but Longman is in charge of getting the message out, and he isn't a serious brother, just one more corrupted black man and not capable for the essential purpose at hand. He has never put real effort into advertising for the panel, otherwise it would be standing room only. The Hall of the Inward Journey will seat a few thousand, and true, the seats are uncomfortable and the acoustics terrible, yet with proper promotion it should overflow like a mass meeting. It is difficult to find sufficient assistance nowadays.

And speaking of that, the new hire turns his stomach. He does not approve of Longman adding him to the dais, but Longman did an end-run around him and spoke to the Chair first, and it's no surprise that she thought it a good idea. Kalamari dislikes Europeans of all stripes, to begin with. The only item he allows into his apartment that is the color white is the toilet paper—he is not a racist, however. He is a *racialist*, as he confidently explains whenever he is challenged on the point. If he is prejudiced, he is just being sensible. Ethnocentric. It is just natural. Go to any lunch room in any high school in the country and note the seating patterns. You will find the black students sitting at one table and the whites at another. Black people cannot be racist anyway, and he instructs his students well on this fact. We do not have power, and power is required to be racist. And even if we did have power, we could not be racist. We are a wise and intuitive people, and it is not within our spirit.

In the lobby down the hall, a key slips into the main door and jiggles as someone fiddles with the lock. His colleagues are rarely in after hours. It's probably the cleaning crew, he thinks, and this is confirmed when he hears the housekeeping cart roll in and the custodian behind, whistling "We Shall Overcome," just like last night. Kalamari inhales the soothing incense fumes and meditates while he waits for the quarter hour and the radio announcement, the lights low, the incense mellow and an occasional opening of an office door, dumping of a trash basket, shutting of the door, the custodian whistling as he makes steady progress down the hall. When the cart finally wheels up, Kalamari opens his eyes. The pushcart fills the doorway, the custodian behind. Mid-thirties, Kalamari guesses. His body shape suggests a steady toxic diet. His yellow shirt provides a pleasant contrast.

"How are you this evening, sir?" the custodian asks, not unforced. His golden tooth catches the light.

"I'm blessed," Kalamari answers. The wound throbs, and a question comes to mind.

"Brother, when was the last time you suffered from the hand of our oppressor?"

"Sir?"

"When was the last time you were beaten by the police?"

The custodian pauses. "I'm a church-going man, sir. I don't mess with all that."

"Yes, but certainly you have been the victim of police abuse. You are a black man in America."

Another pause. "Well, there was that one time. But I was young."

"Driving While Black?" Kalamari gives a guess.

"I takes the bus, sir."

Kalamari nods in approval at the mention of mass transit.

"They did do my cousin real bad when he was down, though. You need your trash emptied tonight, sir?"

Kalamari does and invites him into the office. The custodian steps through the doorway and makes quick work of it, pulls the plastic liner from the wastebasket and replaces it with a new one. Kalamari leans back in his chair, hands clasped.

"Have a good evening, sir."

"Stay strong, my brother."

The custodian gets back to the spiritual as he pushes the cart on to the next door. Kalamari checks his watch and looks at the time. It's just before the quarter hour. The boom box sits in the shadows, red eye glowing. He presses the button for FM Radio, and the music of the motherland stops abruptly, replaced by the set station. And he is right on time. Dance music is winding-down, and the DJ begins to talk over the end of the song: "*And now for our community service thangy, brothers and sisters, boys and girls. Come on down to Bankhead this Saturday and volunteer to help put up a new playground in Bowen Homes. That's right, something for the young 'uns. Come on now. Set your alarms early and get out of that bed when the rooster crows. The fun starts at 8:00 on de dot! Don't need to bring nothin' but yo' beautiful self!*

Home Depot is going to provide it all, from the swings and the monkey bars to the shovels and the Co-Colas. And it's time to beautify Sweet Auburn once again. Ebenezer is having another trash pick-up jubilee on Saturday afternoon. Didn't they just do this? I guess this is the post-Olympic clean up. Let's make the ATL look pretty even when all those Olympians aren't around, shall we? Meet in the big parking lot at high noon. And it's that time again: Hosea Williams is going to feed the hungry once again this Thanksgiving, and you know he is, but he ain't gonna feed 'em all by himself. He needs your help. The annual Thanksgiving Dinner for the Needy needs volunteers. Take down this number, now: 404-666-3339. That's 404-NO NEEDY. Give 'em a call and get your volunteer on. V-103 will be down there, too, and you know we will, so come on out and help us give out the turkey birds. And finally, there's a heavy panel discussion down at Morris Brown College this weekend—"Nigga: I'm Talking To You, Sucka!" Those academic brothers are getting it on! Okey-dokey, back to the paa-tay after 'these important announcements' as the saying goes. Bootie-shake! Bootie-shake! Y'all don't go nowhere."

Lightning flashes, the radio crackles, and a jingle begins advertising a hair relaxer. That's it? Kalamari blinks, his peace of mind ruined. That's all? He didn't even announce the date and the time of the program. The wound throbs. It is a constant frustration: there is never anything serious in the media. It is all trivia and misinformation. Volunteering is all well and good—he has volunteered his entire life—but he is trying to elevate the discussion. It should not have to be such a struggle. He shouldn't have expected more in the first place. Not even from a brother. He has to serve his corporate masters. Water rises to its own level. What else did he expect? As always, the truth is found on AM radio, he thinks. The public access stations. All things considered, he's amazed that they let the voice of the people be heard at all, even though they've ghettoized the means. The AM audience is small but a beacon for those committed to right thinking. He's a regular call-in contributor to "Street Soldiers" himself and has even been down to the station a few times. He punches the AM button. Thumb and forefinger on the serrated groves of the knob, and he dials past the stations: ... *"found my thrill"* ... *"Christos de Jesus"* ... *"another disappointing year"* ... *"on Newstalk 750!"* ... *"nig—"* ..

. His fingers stop dialing at this one. Did he hear that correctly? The speakers snap, crackle, and pop. Kalamari dials it back. It's a faint signal. . . . *"are listening to WC"* . . . His thumb turns the knob forward a fraction. . . . *"on Conf"* . . . *"alk Radio,"* and he's captured the station. The signal is weak, just within reception range. Static crackles over the tinny voice.

"Next caller, go ahead," a white man's voice, one of those with a white citizen's council drawl.

"I mean, I think you're absolutely right, Henry. They're lucky to be here. I'm not trying to justify slavery, but it was the law of labor at the time, like you say. Without the rule of law, we'd have anarchy. It doesn't make sense to judge what our ancestors did based on our standards of today. That's ridiculous. It's like getting mad at the blue laws. The law is the law. I mean, come on. Would they rather still be in Africa, sitting in a grass hut with a bone in their nose?"

Somewhere deep inside Kalamari's brainpan, a switch trips in power failure. "Uh-uh," he shakes his head. "Uh-uh." The talk show host speaks.

"So you're saying that they are trying to revise history?"

"That's exactly what they're doing. They're trying to make it sound like all white people owned slaves."

"I can't say enough how important it is for us to remember our history, not as the media and the schools misrepresent it, not as the blacks want to try to make it look. We need to stand up and remember who built this country. Remember that you have the right to say what you want. It's called freedom. Remember this fact: it is not against the law to be prejudiced. It is not against the law to be a bigot."

"I ditto that, Henry."

"Uh-uh," Kalamari's head still shaking, speech centers still shut down.

"Don't forget that. All of you listening in. Thanks for calling this evening. Okay. Don't have anyone in line here. I know you're out there, and we're having a good discussion tonight, as always. I want you to be part of it. You know the number. Pick up the phone and give me a call." And then, just in case anyone out there happens to be tuning in for the first time, he gives the number.

Kalamari grabs a Dixon Ticonderoga from the UNCF coffee cup next to the telephone and scribbles the digits across the open page of the organizer. Someone picks up on the first ring.

"WCTR. Thanks for calling in." A different white man's voice. "Name please?"

"Kalamari," Kalamari barks.

"Kalamari? Like the squid?" he asks.

Kalamari grits his teeth. "K-A-L-A-M-A-R-I, he spells it out. KA-la-MAH-ree. *Dr.* Kalamari."

"Like the squid."

"Yes," Kalamari fumes. "'Like the squid.'"

"Pro or con?"

"What?"

"Pro or con. With the discussion topic. Are the blacks today lucky that their ancestors were slaves?"

"Absolutely, positively con!"

"I like kalamari," the white man says. "One of my favorite appetizers. You're up next, buddy." And the phone line goes blank in his ear as he's put on hold.

Buddy? Kalamari starts. The sting is sharp. No one has ever called him this diminutive before. All his years of education, his book, his lifetime of teaching and service, and they still call him out of his name. The wound throbs. Two clicks in his ear and then he's on the air.

"Next caller, go ahead," the talk show host says.

"No, no, no, no, no, no, no, no, no!" Kalamari boils over.

"I take it that you disagree?"

"No, no, no, no, no!"

"You don't disagree?

"No!"

"Well, what's your position, then?"

Synapses return to normal function, and all cylinders begin to fire. Where to begin? he thinks. Where possibly to begin? Five hundred years of slavery and oppression. Rape. Torture. Lynching. Immolation. Subjugation. Humiliation. An entire culture stolen. Terrorism and murder at the hands of these Europeans, at the hands of this white man at the other end of the telephone. He is on the line with the devil himself. In person. The red fiend with horns on his head, trident in hand, and whip-tail swishing. Brimstone rising from the surrounding rubble. His father's voice in his ear, his father, who worshiped the god of the oppressors: Get thee behind me, Satan!

"Devil!" Kalamari exclaims, and he steals himself for the confrontation at hand. He is going to face him down.

"Devil?" the host says. "The last time I checked, my name was Henry Hemperly." He chuckles at this.

"Racist devil!" Kalamari adds an adjective then changes up the noun: "Racist cracker!" There's no denying it, despite the effort he puts into maintaining daily balance, he has lost his cool and the visceral boil blocks his thoughts. Repeated clicking from the other end of the line and over the boom box speaker too. The host speaks emphatically:

"I told them to fix this button! God-almighty-knows!"

"Evil incarnate!" Kalamari cries as the host shouts over:

"I'm hardly a racist. I'll have you know that my son teaches at the black college downtown. The problem with you people is you call anyone who disagrees with you a racist. And you are clearly the racist here, sir. I have never been called a cracker in all my life. Mr . . . Kalamary—what kind of name is that, anyway?"

"Outrageous!" Kalamari sputters. "Can't you see . . . the twisted logic . . . ! It's evil! You're evil!" More clicking on the other end of the line, but he has assembled the tools he needs to carry the day, or at least this conversation. "The problem of evil . . . !" he attacks, when the sky outside the window lights up, the administration building across the street flashes in the crack of lightning and the thunder just overhead. Just like that, the room goes dark. The phone goes dead.

The power is out.

"The problem of evil . . ." Kalamari blinks into the darkness.

The hall lights, the desk lamp, the eye on the boom box, all gone. The only thing left, the red tip glow of the incense stick. Another lightning flash and thunder shakes the building. Blue light bathes the office once, twice. The masks of his ancestors cast quick shadows toward the door and then back to the pitch black dark.

Chapter Twenty-six

George Hemperly clutches the wall sink beneath the bathroom mirror, both hands gripping the cold white porcelain, and he gags in paroxysms of retching that make the dog bark. Spats of oyster phlegm miss the bull's-eye drain hole and lump around the basin, and something else is in there, too, a different, darker color. Is that blood? Yellow eyes widen in alarm until he realizes that he is just coughing-up coffee. He gives the coffee cup on the side table a hard stare, its state flag emblem, the Confederate battle flag, the stars and bars reduced to curving logo status now. Back to the mirror and he begins yet another day trying to reconcile the reflection of the unkempt man in the bathrobe with the man he is in his mind. His Johnny Weissmuller pecs have long-since collapsed. And then there's the daily decay of his face. Is his nose larger? Are his wrinkles deeper? He maps out a plan for this morning's grooming. The open holes in his head get the worst of it. His eyes. His mouth. The monstrosity of age spreads from them in deep and permanent grooves. One long black hair sprouts from the bridge of his nose, beanstalk-like. For the first time, he notices all the hair sprouting from his ear canals. How the hell did he miss that before? And he wonders how long it's been there, how long he's had this slip in grooming. Maybe he's been living alone in the woods for too long.

There are some tweezers around here somewhere, he thinks, and glances around the cedar wood bathroom, opens the glass cabinet door, but there is nothing on the shelves but more medication, amber plastic pill bottles guarding the drugs from the rays of the sun. The hair hangs out of his ears like weeds. They didn't even pass through a gracious gray stage and went straight to thick-shafted old-man white. Maybe he should go for the pliers in the kitchen drawer. When he retired and moved to the mountains, he thought he was walking out of the office and onto an easy street of his own paving. The bumper sticker on the CJ-5 said it all: *Even A Bad Day Fishing Is Better Than A Good Day At Work*. He scouted the land and built the cabin himself in this unspoiled wood on the narrow mountain lake. The rainforest: oaks and maples and hemlocks that hadn't seen a saw. The rhododendron and mountain laurel sealed the deal. He cut in his own road and was careful to follow the contour of the earth and only had to remove two trees to build the place. Not so easy to get back in here. He has to put the Jeep in four wheel drive to get in and out when the snow comes.

George turns his head, eyes into corners, and finds a better angle. The hairs have grown over the cusp of the lobe and out. Henry's son said he was bringing a woman up with him. All George wants from her is an acknowledgment. Some lasting eye contact, a passing touch of the hand, anything that indicates that he's still got a little of the old magic left, a little attention that makes him feel like he's not yet completely out of the game. But his eyes are bloodshot this morning, the old sparkle covered with gunk. And those hairs. He needs to put some effort into grooming his face before they arrive. To hell with it, he thinks. He'll yank them out after he takes a shit, but first he leaves the bathroom, grabs his grandfather's 30-30 and totes the rifle out onto the deck for a smoke.

The lake is steaming. Morning fog as the planet warms. The sun lies low between two mountains across the water, centered in the cleavage. A few clouds drift, and their shadows drag across the calm water. He sets the rifle stock-down, barrel next to his eyeglasses on the rail, water drops on the lens from last night's rain. The view is still spectacular. It always is, even after four years, sixteen seasons, the same view from the same overlook—but only if he stands on the wooden planking just so, angling his line of sight away so that he can't see the construction to the right. When he moved to the Blue Ridge, there weren't any buildings intruding on the serenity, no fish cabins, much less houses. Then the Atlantans arrived, and now his once peaceful mornings are filled with Mariachi music. He looks at the sun and gauges its height on the horizon. The Mexicans should be arriving any time now. George pulls a cigarette from a fresh pack and reaches for the rusted Zippo on the railing. The lid scratches open, and he lights up. If they think that they can just come in here and destroy his peace and quiet, then they have another thought coming.

He knocks last night's raindrops from the seat of the plastic chair. When he sits, his bathrobe absorbs the remainder, the water cold on his bare ass. He doesn't have to wait long. Here they come, the pickup truck's engine grinds through the trees over the call of the birds. Tires crush through the gravel rocks, and the lake water amplifies the crunch. Six Mexicans sit in the bed, three on each side. And they've already got that music going, the happy horns and Spanish that he can't understand, a party at a wetback rodeo. The truck parks next to a dead trunk and underneath a widow-maker. The boss man, the young white guy with the orange hard hat, steps out of the cab and stretches, arms up. Good morning, you son of a bitch. The Mexicans climb out of the back and get right to work like always, three walking over to the blue tarp that covers the timber wood. They all dress like cowboys, blue jeans, checkered shirts, cowboy boots too. Mustaches all. The guy in the Stetson stands over by the power pole, his nail gun pointing down at the mud.

George holds the cigarette between thumb and forefinger, smoke curling up. He gives it a long pull, lets it dangle, and reaches for the Winchester. It's a heavy bastard. They've been together for a long time. He carried it with him everywhere he went down in Haylow, padding down the sand roads and crunching through the underbrush, the stock heavy on his shoulder. He grabs his eyeglasses from the balustrade, knocks the drops from the lens, hooks the stems over his ears and lifts the business end of the rifle toward the Mexican labor. The barrel moves from one illegal to the next, targeting them in-between the prongs of the sight and the bead at the end of the barrel. They are all moving targets except for the one in the Stetson. The pin covers his mustache as George draws a bead on his head.

"Boom," he jerks the barrel up high as if he'd fired off a

round—the .30-30 kicks like a son of a bitch—then he turns toward the lumber pile and aims at the one bending over.

"Boom." He jerks the barrel up again.

$\mathcal{T}$ravis is hoping for a romantic mountain getaway, but Ying and Yang have other ideas. The Volvo drives north on the interstate, past the concrete barrier of the perimeter highway and into the galaxy of sprawl beyond, leaving the metro area behind. Meggan sits in the side seat in black blouse and new blue jeans. The dogs ride up front, too. She insisted, and that's no problem, Travis said. One sits in her lap, the other squeezed into the floorboard. Their little eyes target him, beady and protective. Travis steers with his left hand and scratches his ankle with his right.

"You know, it's *Yin* and Yang," he glances at the Jack Russell in her lap, shedding all over the car, the white hairs airborne.

"What?" she pulls the vibrating dog closer.

"It's . . . he rethinks it. Her eyes are wide, and they shine. She is so beautiful.

". . . Nothing."

"So what's your uncle like?"

"I haven't seen him for a long time, not since my brother drowned."

"Your brother drowned? I didn't know that. I'm sorry."

"Thanks. It was a long time ago," and Travis notes the irony of proximity: the exit to the lake is just ahead. He has no desire to go down that road again, and the beater Volvo continues north, skirts the machinations of the chicken cartels in Gainesville with their schemes of global domination, and climbs in elevation up into the foothills. Traffic is light, tractor trailers heading north mostly, and the vehicles change the farther they get upstate, the sedans and coupes of the city replaced by pickup trucks and Jeeps, red with black trim being a popular color. Travis gives Meggan the back story. He's never known this side of the family well, having shifted to his mother's people after his brother's death and the following divorce. But he's been getting a big dose of Hemperly family history lately. He tells her about the ax murder story, the dead man chained to the tree, and he voices his suspicion.

"I think it might have been a lynching," he says.

"A lynching? Really? Wow, that's weird."

They stop at a rest area to give the dogs a walk. There's a convenient parking spot in front of the info building, and as soon as Meggan opens her door, the dogs launch for the picnic tables and don't return when called. When they finally get back on the interstate, an hour has passed. But there is no hurry, and traveling with no expectations of time is emancipating. Travis returns to small talk.

"Remember when we went to Blood Mountain?" he asks and smiles at the memory.

"We went to Blood Mountain?" she says. "You and me? When?"

"Back when we were in college." A hint of distress in his voice. "Don't you remember?"

"Oh, yes. I remember that," she says unconvincingly. "We had fun. It was such a beautiful day."

The disappointment comes in a wave. The dog in her lap raises its head and begins to growl at him, unprovoked. "Good boy," Travis says, and Ying (or is it Yang?) barks sharply. A lull in the conversation arrives, but the moment is saved by the Blue Ridge Mountains. "Look, there they are." Travis points out the windshield.

The mountains are veiled on the horizon and rise in ever-growing humps. They are, in fact, blue. At least from here. Travis reaches for a descriptive adjective: amazing, fantastic, fabulous, extravagant, magnificent, brilliant, dramatic, dazzling, breathtaking, astonishing, marvelous, wonderful, exciting, incredible—none of the words in the thesaurus do them justice. The Blue Ridge Mountains are off-the-beaten-path impressive. They are not on the rotation of routine images of American natural beauty—not the Grand Canyon, not Yosemite, not Rushmore, not the Badlands—and they are all the more spectacular for it. Abrupt mountains heavily forested. Fast water over slippery rocks. Blue nature.

"Wow," Meggan says, eyes out the windshield. "That's a sacred place."

That's the word he's looking for, he thinks. Only from a poet. Another half an hour up the road, and they're surrounded by the mountains and the Cherokee National Forest, evergreens everywhere, rushing rivers and streams, tall hemlock and rhododendron and mountain laurel, spring water dripping over stone outcroppings the size of the Volvo, the size of his apartment building and on up the size scale.

Meggan points the spring water out to the dogs and the one in her lap puts his nose to the window glass, tongue wagging. Dog hairs drift and cling, and Travis shifts into low gear as they start up another switch-back, a steep climb up and over a summit and then they zig and zag down the backside of the mountain. Up and over, up and over, altitude climbing. It's getting colder. Travis asks Meggan if she needs to get her coat from the trunk, but she doesn't and she says that she enjoys the cold on her skin. In his peripheral vision, he checks for nipple swell.

The beater Volvo crests the next summit, and the road becomes a long straight-away, down a steep angle. And then there's something harsh in the air. Meggan leans forward.

"What's that smell?"

Travis shrugs and sniffs, the mechanical stink burning in his nostrils. He downshifts and rides the brakes down the long decline. Something litters the road up ahead, black strips and chunks, and as they roll into the debris field, he rolls down the window to take a look.

"Looks like rubber," he says, as they roll through exploded bits of tire. Up ahead on the right, a tractor trailer truck has taken the runaway truck ramp, run off of the road and up a sharp dirt incline. The truck has jackknifed, the cab plowed into the dirt bunker piled up at the far end of the ramp, the last thing between the truck driver and certain death from a plunge off the side of the mountain. The door to the cab hangs open, and the driver is crouched on all fours. He looks underneath the truck.

"Wow," Meggan says. "He was lucky."

*B*y the time they finally find his uncle's place, the sun is dropping behind the mountains. George's directions up were clear enough, but the terrain is tough and the roads aren't well marked, and it gets dark here earlier than it does in the city. Travis turns off of one gravel road and onto another, and then rolls up to what must be the place. Not much to mark the entrance, just a POSTED: NO TRESPASSING sign. Gravel pings on the undercarriage.

"I hope this is the right place," he says and considers his uncle's caution: When the paved road stops, you stop. Don't drive where you're not supposed to be. He's looking for an A-frame cabin, and there's one at the end of the rutted road, so this must be the place, and the beater Volvo crunches to a stop and parks next to an old Jeep. Yang gets out first and heads for the hills, Ying not far behind, scampering over the gravel on short legs. Meggan yells "Boys!" with concern in her voice. "Come back! Travis, help me! Get the leashes!" They set off down the gravel drive after the dogs. When they return, Meggan leading with the dogs now leashed, George is standing in the floodlight under the eave. The surrounding dark makes the cabin look like a deep sea submersible.

"Well, it's about time y'all got here." George is expansive in burgundy sweater and blue jeans. "I know I'm off the beaten track, but Atlanta isn't that far."

"Uncle George." Travis walks over, shakes his hand.

"Travis, I haven't seen you since you were knee-high to a pup." His uncle has a firm handshake. George looks Meggan over. "Who's the little lady?" His boots crunch the gravel as he steps up to her and plants his eyes on her chest. "My God, she's a pretty one."

"I don't think it's been that long, Uncle George." Travis says. "This is Meggan."

George doesn't bother to disguise his ogle. Meggan holds out her hand.

"Pleased to meet you," she says.

George embraces her in a bear hug. "I'm a hugger," he says. And this he proves by duration of embrace. Travis counts the seconds: Tick. Tick. Tick. Ying and Yang walk up to George, tongues out. And not barking, Travis notes.

"Howdy boys," he bends over and scratches one head then the other. A blue tick hound comes around the side of the house, tongue wagging.

Meggan takes a step back, pulling the two dogs back, their hackles up. "Easy boys." Ying and Yang do their thing, Yang growls and Ying barks, invading another dog's territory and being bold about it, strength in numbers and all that. Meggan shushes them but they don't listen.

"This is Stonewall," George says. "It's alright. He's not a biter." The hound walks up to Ying and Yang, stepping carefully, and there's a tense moment before they get down to the business of sniffing genitalia and making friends.

Meggan reaches out and pats the hound on the head. "You're a pretty fella."

"The hound that won't bark." George shakes his head. "Stoney!" he yells, and the blue tick begins to yelp. George rolls his eyes. "All the good money I gave for that dog. Y'all come on in. I've got some ribeyes ready to throw on the grill."

Travis pulls his duffel and Meggan's vintage Samsonite suitcase from the trunk and follows his uncle into the cabin, Meggan behind. The layout is simple: a living area and kitchen on the bottom floor with bedroom and bathroom in the back. Up the narrow steps is a loft. The weathered beams overhead are hand cut, the imperfection adding character. A fieldstone fireplace on the far wall. Meggan inhales. "Smells like cedar."

It looks like his uncle is still painting. Everywhere he looks, there is a fish in a frame. Travis doesn't know fish himself, other than canned salmon and tuna that he buys from the supermarket. He lugs the luggage into their bedroom and Meggan follows. Most of it is filled by a king sized bed. Travis asks which side she prefers and she says it doesn't matter.

After a quick unpacking, they put the leashes back on Ying and Yang, who are busy running around sniffing everything, and they take the dogs for a quick walk down to the lake. It's not far, and there's an obvious path to the small dock, even in this dark. The moonlight helps and the stars too. Ying and Yang zip here and there, sniffing this and that. The thrill of the new smell. Travis observes that it was good to get the dogs out of the house, and Meggan agrees. They step out onto a plank dock. There's a small boat tied to a broken cleat, a skiff made of metal, dark green hull distressed, a rowboat with two oar locks and a small Evinrude cocked horizontal, propeller out of the water. A rusted tackle box, a fish net, and a good two inches of water near the outboard that needs to be bailed. Overhead, the stars turn. Hale-Bopp is brighter than the last time he took the time to notice. Meggan takes in a deep breath, holds it in for a few seconds, and lets it out slowly.

When they return to the A-Frame, steak is in the air. Three ribeyes sizzle on the charcoal grill. "Beer's on ice," George stands by the Webber Kettle and points to the large blue cooler beside the sliding glass door.

"I've brought a bottle of wine," Travis offers. "Pinot grigio. Napa Valley."

"Y'all go ahead with that." George says. "I'm a Budweiser and bourbon man, myself." He picks up a rocks glass from the side table, lifts it in toast to the gallon of Jack Daniel's on the bench, and takes a sip. "Mixers are in the cooler."

"I'm in," Meggan says.

Travis says he's no spoil-sport and retrieves two more rocks glasses from the cabinet to the left of the refrigerator. When he steps back onto the deck, Meggan is standing close to his uncle, both laughing. Ying, Yang, and Stonewall know what's-what and they sit patiently in a row before the grill, ranked from tallest to shortest and alert should any of the ribeyes make a break for it.

"How do y'all like your steaks cooked? I like mine bloody." The cigarette bobs between his lips. They dine in the dining room. Over dinner, Travis and George catch up. They talk about the matriarch, of course, Grandma Rosa Lee. George says that he's been meaning to get down to see her. Travis detours into his Viking adventures and George retorts with fish stories. Meggan sips whiskey and laughs at the punch lines. When his uncle asks what it's like teaching black students, Travis gives what is becoming his standard reply: They're all good students. This is misinformation, of course. Some are solid and some not so, exactly like their white counterparts, but he feels a need to advocate for them around certain demographics.

"Well," George says.

After cleaning up, they leave Ying and Yang disappointed behind the sliding glass doors. Meggan doesn't want them outside unleashed. The air is nippy out on the deck. Crickets and tree frogs have the cabin surrounded and chant in the dark. George lights a yuppie log in the chiminea and gets a fire going. He pulls broken up branches from the galvanized tub and stuffs them down the clay chimney. The dry wood catches and flames flicker high, crackling and shooting sparks. Then he grabs the bourbon and freshens-up the rocks glasses all around with sloppy, generous pours. Travis pulls three more Buds from the cooler.

Meggan asks if she can turn off the lights so they can look at the stars. "It's inside the door," George says. "A double-joint switch."

Travis gets up and flicks the switch, and then they're all in the dark, the only light pollution coming from the rising fire. The moon is waning, is just a sliver, and the sky is clear. A sip of whiskey and a good scratch on his ankle, and then Travis's eyes adjust to the low light. The star field is brilliant overhead, with the wispy arm of the galaxy wheeling across the sky. Meggan sits on the bench seat, Travis and George in the white plastic chairs, heads dropped back and looking up as the earth moves into the asteroid field.

"Look! There's one," and she points up, index finger tracing the trail of a meteor. "It's the Perseids!"

Travis has had three sips, no, four, of the bourbon. He feels warm inside and a little woozy too. He angles the chair closer to the chimenea, the flames shooting from the top. Another meteor streaks across the sky. This isn't a bad way to live, he thinks.

"That's spectacular," he drops his head back and takes in the stars. Another sip of bourbon and a swig of beer to chase it. Barking down by the lake.

"So," George pauses as he looks over his shoulder and then lights another cigarette. "You said you wanted to hear about Haylow."

"You went down there, right?" Travis asks. "Grandma Rosa Lee said you did. She said it was where you started smoking."

George laughs at this and smoke jets through his nose.

"Yeah, I spent my summers down there when I was a teenager. Ran the commissary for my grandfather, your great-grandfather."

"Suitcase Charlie?"

"Suitcase Charlie, yes. Charles E. Hemperly." Another look over his shoulder at the barking dark. "Is that my dog?"

Travis says that it's all a big mystery to him, Haylow, the turpentine farm, and his great-grandfather.

"Well, there's no mystery to it, but I'm glad to tell you." He looks over his left shoulder and then his right. "Where's my bourbon?"

Travis points at the rocks glass by the chair leg.

"Thanks." He reaches down for his drink. "Let's see... Huh. Your great-grandfather acquired enormous acreage in pine land in Clinch County in the early 1930s, right on the Florida border. He got it primarily from tax sales, people who owned it before the Great Depression but couldn't pay. George looks across the cove. "Then he started working it for turpentine." More barking. down by the lake. He inhales through his nose slowly and yells: "Stony! Stop messing with that snake!"

They sit under the stars. Two meteors streak. Then one more. Travis prompts him: "Anything else?"

"Let's see . . . " George says. "There were the trains."

"Trains? A train came through?"

"That's what it was. A railroad junction. The Seaboard Coastline and the Southern. It was that and our turpentine farm, just a village, if that. There was one white family—my grandfather and me—and the blacks who lived in the quarters a mile away. It's all swampy land, but it wasn't water all the time. The further east you went down the railroad, it became *The* Okefenokee Swamp. And it was water and wet snakes and gators.

"I came in on the picture in the mid-30s. I'd take the Coastline down from Atlanta. It was an all-day ride. It'd take ten hours to get down there. You'd leave at eight o'clock in the morning and get down there at six o'clock at night. And you'd have to tell the conductor to stop the train. There was no stop there. If you wanted to catch a train out, you took a bunch of newspapers and built a fire on the track when you heard it coming. And they'd stop."

"You're kidding me," Travis says. "No station?"

"No. They had a little old shed. And a water tower. That was it."

"What'd you do?" Travis knocks back the beer bottle, the beer cold going down.

"Mostly I ran the commissary. We'd buy materials and foodstuffs for the blacks and keep books on 'em and subtract it from their turpentine gatherings for the week."

"No other white people?" Meggan asks.

"No. Just us. Well, there was this one guy, a big Swede." George pauses and wrinkles bunch on his forehead. "I can't remember his name. The overseer. He was a sorry son of a bitch."

Quarters? Overseer? It sounds like the vocabulary of slavery to Travis, and he takes a sip of bourbon, an image of Tara in his head. Some days at the college, he feels like he's wandered into a racial thicket. Other days, he's just a working stiff and could be teaching anywhere. And his family is more eccentric than he'd realized.

George gets back to it. "The old man had about twenty-five or thirty blacks working for him. Half of them were the chippers and the other half the dippers. The chippers had cutters. They called them cutters, big weird-shaped knives with five pound weights on the bottom."

Travis asks what for.

"So they could hit the tree harder. That's what they did, cut streaks in the pine trees. They'd start at the bottom of the trunk and put in what they called a cut, and they put a metal cup in there and metal runners to run the turpentine into it. After a month or two the cups would fill up, and the dippers would go into the woods and put the cups into a big barrel. That's how it worked. The chippers and the dippers. And for some reason, the chippers were the meanest of the lot. There was just a lot of meanness down there."

"Meanness?" Travis asks, but George keeps going.

"We'd take the mules and the wagon into the woods on Friday and they'd dip all the cups and put them in a big barrel and then we'd take it into Valdosta 40 miles away to the distillery and they'd distill it. It was called WW. Water White, the best grade. And they'd pay in cash for it right there and distill it into turpentine. We had a still on the place at Haylow ourselves, but for some reason it didn't work so we stopped that crap."

"Did my father ever go down there?"

"Henry?" George pauses. "He might have come down there once, I think. He would have been just a boy."

"So what about the African-Americans? What was it like for them?"

"Terrible. Absolutely terrible. I don't see why they didn't all run off. I wouldn't have put up with that crap for ten minutes. They had enough to eat and that was about all. And that was questionable at times. A lot of work, and nothing else."

Travis says that it sounds like there wasn't a whole lot to it.

"There damn sure wasn't." George hits his beer. "It was an isolated place." Another sip of bourbon. "No electricity. Well water. Outdoor plumbing. Snakes everywhere you looked. Cottonmouths. Rattlers."

"I like snakes," Meggan says.

"You wouldn't like these," George draws from his cigarette. "To my mind, a moccasin snake is the worst kind of snake available. He won't warn you. He'll just hit you. A rattler will at least give you a clue." Another sip. "Boy, they had 'em down there in Haylow, God-almighty knows. And nobody seemed to object to it. I can't believe how people lived down there. Compared to my life today, I wouldn't even think about it. But I was a city kid, and it was all a big adventure, you know."

"No electricity?" Travis asks.

"Not at first, the REA was put through while I was there. But we only put it to the still and the store. Didn't have any light in the house."

"No light in the house?" Travis scratches his ankle. These bites are going to get infected.

"No. The old man didn't want any."

Travis takes advantage of the segue. "So, why'd they call him Suitcase Charlie, anyway?"

George smiles at this. "Granddad always carried around a suitcase full of money. That's how he got the name."

"Why?"

George gives Travis a 'my nephew must be a half-wit' look. "To grease the wheels." He takes a sip of bourbon, cigarette hanging from his lip and bouncing up and down as he speaks. "Your great-grandfather was not a humanitarian. The milk of human kindness did not flow in his veins. He had a quick temper. Red-headed. But he knew a lot about money. You know he was in the legislature, right?"

"I've seen his portrait," Travis says.

"He was elected to the Georgia legislature in nineteen thirteen, and the last session he was in was 1954. So he served something like forty years. He had some clout at the capital. He even got them to pave the state road to Valdosta, the road from nowhere to nowhere, they called it. But they didn't like the old man down there. He wasn't from the county, and they just thought he was a rich man from Atlanta and they didn't like him. He was meaner than shit, anyway."

"If they didn't like him, how'd he get elected?"

"Well, the suitcase helped. You don't know much about politics, do you, nephew?"

"I work my side of the street and you work yours," Travis says.

"Fair enough. I don't know how the hell he lived down there. But he loved it." George points at Hale-Bopp. "That comet is the damnedest thing I ever saw."

Travis is pretty sure that his uncle is holding back, and he wants to ask more pointed questions, specifically, if his father witnessed a lynching there. He needs to get George alone.

"Well, enough about that," he says. "There's one thing I've been wanting to ask you since we arrived."

"What's that?"

"Is the fishing any good around here?"

"Are you kidding me? You've got to hide behind a tree just to bait your hook."

"I saw you have a boat down at the dock. You want to go fishing tomorrow?"

"Now you're talking," George turns up his glass and finishes it off. "But what about Meggan here?"

"Pass," she says, reaches out and touches George on the forearm. "You two go ahead. I wanted to take the boys for a hike, anyway."

Moment of truth: the sleeping arrangements have not been discussed, but there's only one bed, the setting is romantic, and Travis is a little drunk. There's not a lot of room in the room with the king-sized mattress, just a narrow channel around the breadth of the comforter. Meggan has traveled its limits and stands in the dark in front of the window, looking out and up at the fingernail moon. Travis turns the knob of the fish lamp on the night stand, and the shade glows orange. Her black blouse is gathered at the hip, accentuating her bottom half, her blue jeans form fitting and giving her a fertile look. Travis walks over and puts his hands around her waist and kisses the side of her neck. A hint of patchouli.

"What'cha looking at?" he slurs.

She says "Nothing," and he keeps his hands on her waist as she turns around to face him. He slips his thumbs into her jeans, draws them against soft buttocks underneath, and gets a piece of panty. Hands under her shirt and fingertips tracing lightly up the small of her back. She lifts her head and presents her mouth for kissing, eyes closed, bourbon on her breath. Her lips are soft. There's a little tongue action in there, too, and he tries to inhale, tries to pull the air from her lungs into his lungs, and then they'll trade and he'll breathe his into hers, but it's a no-go.

Meggan puts a hand on his sternum and pushes. Travis takes one step back, and he's against the bed, legs against the comforter. She drops to her knees perfunctorily, tugs the zipper of his pants down, reaches a hand into his underwear, pulls it out, and gets to work. So much for romance, he thinks, and sucks in his gut. He has imagined this moment with her—or one like it—for at least a decade, but now that it's here it doesn't match his expectation of tender intimacy: Meggan with her eyes closed, her head working up and down mechanically, like a bobble head. Still, it isn't that bad. He does a Kegel, moves his crotch forward hoping to add a little length, and he makes a few encouraging grunts.

"You like that, baby?" She speaks with her mouth full as she plugs away. "You like that?"

Another grunt from Travis, a code used by the ancients. Meggan is in control and runs the show. After a while she either gets tired or figures that her toil isn't going to bear any fruit, so she takes a breather and unbuttons his pants, yanks them down his legs and they bunch-up over his loafers. He slips out of his shoes, sock feet on the hardwoods, and his pants in a wad. Meggan stands up and drops trou too, unbuttons her jeans, grabs them at the waistline, a hand on each hip, and works them down, first the left side and then the right, yanking the tight denim over her thighs in increments, pushing pants and panties out of the way. Then she turns toward the bed, her back to Travis. Her blouse is wrinkled at the bottom hem and dog hair everywhere, and she leans across the comforter, face down, arms outstretched, hands sliding toward the pillows as she presents rearward, her bottom up.

"Turn out the light," she says. "And do me doggie-style."

Chapter Twenty-seven

*T*alk about a hangover. Travis wakes up, head pounding. The sun is harsh through the window and the flimsy curtains, and the UV rays burn his cheek. Where is he? The ceiling fan overhead doesn't turn. Dust gathers at the edges of the blades, the cobwebs drooping. And then he remembers and turns his head on the pillow. Meggan is sleeping with her back toward him all the way over at the other end of the big mattress. He reaches out to touch the mole between her shoulder blades but can't. And then his headache surges with the effort: boom-boom-boom.

He stumbles from the bed and into the kitchen in search of healing coffee and finds a full pot, a glass carafe in a coffee maker on the kitchen counter. The coffee mugs are in the cabinet just above, the logical place. Travis grabs the closest, a white mug with St. Andrew's Cross. A month ago he wouldn't have thought a thing about it. Now he's got all this new stuff in his head. The state flag controversy is everywhere he goes, even with a hangover.

George and Stonewall are out on the deck, his uncle with a cigarette hanging from his lips. The wreckage of last night's binge is in evidence: empty beer bottles lined up neatly on the railing, labels ordered. Cigarette butts on the deck. Blue sky and a few wispy clouds over the mountains. Mariachi music from across the lake where they're building a house. A rifle leans against the balustrade.

"About time you got up," George says. "We've got to get going if we're going to catch any fish. They knock off in the afternoon."

Travis groans. "I'd forgotten about that," he says. "I hope you don't drink decaf. Do you have any cream and sugar?"

"Hell, no." He raises his coffee mug, the stars and bars forward. "I like my joe strong and black, just like my women."

It's an old joke, corny with age and sliding toward the dustbin of outdated cultural humor. Last night's drinking binge didn't do much to settle Travis's curiosity about Halo. In fact, it turned it up a few notches. His suspicion that there is something ugly about all this has been a slow grower, stunted by too much shade and not enough water, but things are beginning to come to light. And something stinks. Still, triage is in order.

Travis thinks *oh my God, my head, my head*, and steps to the railing. Boom-boom-boom. He sees vomit in his future. He looks down at the rifle, barrel pointed up to the sky. The wooden stock is scared from use and age. It looks like it should be in a museum, a relic of the Wild West. Initials are carved parallel to the rifle butt, carelessly dug into the stock with a knife. CEH.

"Was that Suitcase Charlie's?"

George looks across the cove at the construction. "Can you speak Spanish?"

"*Un poco*," Travis raises his free hand and pinches an inch of air between thumb and index finger.

"What the hell does that mean?"

"A little."

"I don't really mind the Mexicans," George says as if Travis had asked. "Not like some do up here. They're hard workers, and I can't fault a man for wanting to make a living. But I don't like it that they don't speak English. And I don't like their music."

In rebuttal, happy horns blare from across the cove and there's an enthusiastic *Ai-ee!* Travis's headache surges. "The sooner we get out there, the better." George nods at the lake.

"Do you have any aspirin?"

"You can pick some up when you go get the worms and some biscuits for breakfast. The bait shop is right up the road." Travis puts a hand to his head. "And pick up a six pack, too. Bottles."

When Travis opens the door to the bait shop, a little bell tinkles. The three white guys stop talking and look him over. Two good old boys in muddy camouflage overalls and a string-bean goth behind the counter, pale face, black shirt, long black hair and an ear ring. Travis speculates: deer season? He doesn't know the schedule. He tries to make friendly and says howdy. The goth says howdy back, and the hunters just look at him, so he gets down to business and asks for the worms. "Worms in the ice cream cooler," the goth directs with dirty fingernail. "In the back." And there's quite a selection: large, medium, and small wrigglers in sturdy cardboard containers. Last night's night crawlers, and Travis wonders who collects them, thinks that if he doesn't pick up another contract at the college maybe he can transition into that line of work. He hasn't been fishing since his father burned the cabin cruiser and doesn't remember the strategy of bait selection, if he ever knew. He grabs a cardboard cup of X-tra large night crawlers, opens the lid, and the dark soil inside is damp. He digs a finger in and unearths a big fat worm the size of a finger. His nausea is on the march. This should do it. He replaces the lid and grabs a container of regular worms, too. The two guys in camo are giving him the hairy eyeball, he can feel them on his back. Travis tries to access whatever Southern accent is left inside of him, tries to pass for a local, but he doesn't know the particularities of the native idiom, so he just goes with Hollywood sitcom Southern. "How y'all this mornin'?" He places the night crawlers and a six-pack of Budweiser on the counter and then grabs three bacon egg and cheese biscuits from the rack. Local fare wrapped in wax paper. "These biscuits any good?"

"Is that all?" The goth behind the counter enunciates. He keeps his head down and won't look him in the eye. Bait and beer and biscuits in a brown paper sack.

"I'll take some aspirin, too," Travis drops the middle syllable.

*T*he boat leaks. Travis bails it out with an empty bucket of chicken before they leave the dock, but the water is back by the time they arrive at their destination: a fallen hemlock in a brush heap that George says the fish like to hang around. George had the rods and reels in the boat when Travis returned with the bait. Meggan had already left with the dogs, hiking around the lakeshore, she said. George says that she didn't even want a biscuit. She took a banana. "A banana for breakfast," he says and shakes his head in wonder. He maneuvers the boat a little ways from the sunken tree, kills the Evinrude, and tells Travis to drop anchor. "There's a lot of little ones around in here, but that black water by the tree is where they're at." He points. "I caught a bass here a few weeks ago. He was about four pounds."

"How deep do you think it is here?" Travis eyes the water and wonders aloud.

"About three feet." George holds up a boxy orange life vest. "You need a Mae West?" Travis rolls his eyes, then George gets personal: "I didn't hear the headboard banging last night. And I was listening for it."

This is the first time Travis has been alone with his uncle as an adult, or perhaps ever, and he'd assumed that they'd continue along their established pattern of uncle/nephew discourse. Travis wants him to come clean about Haylo and Suitcase Charlie, doesn't want to tell him that he's offended, even though he is. "We had to be quiet for the dogs," he demurs. He opens the paper sack and passes a biscuit. "Here's your breakfast."

George takes it. "Thanks. So. Is she any good?"

"You know, Uncle George. I really appreciate you having us up. You've been a gracious host, but you're really crossing a line."

"Sorry about that. Don't mean any offense."

"None taken."

"She looks like she's good, though."

"How long have you been alone up here?"

"Too damn long, apparently." George flips the cooler open. "You ready for a beer?"

"Good God. I've still got a hangover from last night. And it's not even eight yet."

"This'll cure it. Just pound it down."

"No thanks. Maybe later."

"Well, I'm having one. Beer and biscuits. The life of a fisherman." He twists the bottle cap and toasts the lake.

"Uncle George, Meggan is really special to me."

"Okay, Travis. I'm sorry. And I mean it. I sincerely apologize. I was just trying to bond with my nephew. Give me the bucket. I'll bail for a while."

"Thanks for saying that." Travis reaches behind him and grabs the bucket. The waxy cardboard is buckling. "I'm not sure how much life the Colonel has left in him." There's a pause, a bit of unexpected family fealty going on here in the boat that Travis didn't expect. He'd just come up to get some answers. He chews this over and reconsiders priorities.

George mumbles, "She does look like she's good, though."

"All right," Travis says. "I'll take that beer."

George pulls a bottle from the cooler and passes it. "Chug it. You'll feel better."

"You're the doctor." Travis twists the top and turns the bottle up. He empties half of it before he chokes, and wipes his mouth with the back of his hand.

"So what is it you wanted to ask me?" George asks.

"You caught on to that, huh?"

"Well, you weren't so subtle. 'What I really want to talk about is fishing.'" George laughs.

"I figured you were holding back with Meggan there."

"Listen, Travis. I don't know you well, but you are family. There are some things that should stay in the family."

"Like what?"

"Well," George says. "Pass me those night crawlers." He picks up his rod and reel. "Let me get a line in first."

Travis opens the paper sack, pulls out the container.

"Thanks," George takes them. "I said last night that your great-grandfather wasn't much of a humanitarian." He opens the lid, sticks two fingers into the soil. "What I meant to say was, he thought that the 13th Amendment was more of a suggestion than Federal law."

"The way you talked about it made it sound like slavery."

"That's about what it was. It was the perfect slavery set up. *Good God!*" George pulls a night crawler from the container, a pinkie-sized worm that squirms between his fingers. "What are you trying to catch? A shark?"

"Porpoise," Travis says.

"Illegal." George studies the twisting worm. "We pull a porpoise out of this lake, the Game Warden will be down on us in a minute."

"We pull a porpoise out of this lake, we'll be in the newspapers."

"Pass me the regulars," George points at the sack.

Travis pulls the other container, and they trade. He shifts to Southern dialect: "I ain't afraida' no worm," He digs fingers into the container. "Gonna' catch me a big ole' fish." He extracts a night crawler and impales it on his hook. George takes a sip of beer. He has to reach backward to root through the tackle box, pulls out a ratty sun hat and fits it on his head. A little more digging through disorganized compartments and tangled monofilament. "Damn. We came out with no good hooks." They both go about the business of baiting the lines and casting. It's been a while for Travis, and he winds the reel, pulling the line back.

"Like this," Georges makes an invisible cast with his free hand. From the side. Use your wrist. Travis tries a few more times, and soon both lines are in the water, the red bobs near the sunken tree.

"All right, shoot," George says.

"Well, not long after Charlie died, my father told me he was down at Halo and saw a man who had been killed with an ax. He'd been chained to a tree. And he said you were there, too. It didn't occur to me at the time, but now that I remember it, well, I was wondering if y'all saw a lynching. But when I asked dad about it, he said he didn't remember it, didn't remember telling it to me, either. Can you help me out? Were you there?"

George removes his hat, scratches his head, and replaces the hat. "That crap went on down there all the time," he says. "The klan was very active. They'd ride through the quarters at night. On horses. Night riders, we called them."

"Horses?"

"I can still hear their hoofs beating on the sand roads. They burned a cross once down by the Coastline shed. I watched it from the front porch. That big fella, that Swede, he was in the klan. We had this fella, this black. Damon was his name. He walked up from Jasper, Florida, all the way to Haylow, to get a job with the old man, and one day he and that Swede got into some kind of an argument at the commissary. I was sitting out front, drinking a Coke. And we had a puller handle, which was as long as this fish rod. You'd put a hook on the end so you could reach up high, ten feet. And I heard them shouting inside the store and so I went to go inside and here comes Damon running out. The Swede had the puller handle. It was solid oak, and he was beating the hell out of the fella, right in the head. That was some sorry business."

Well, there it is, Travis thinks. George looks him directly in the eye, and then they sit in the quiet for a little while. There's a chop out in the main channel of the lake, but it's calm over here. George turns up his bottle, and Travis follows suit. His head is feeling better.

"How about Suitcase Charlie? Was he in the klan?"

"Well, he was in state politics. Listen, there was just a lot of meanness down there. That was some wild country. People went armed. We went armed."

"Why?"

"Like I said, there was just a lot of meanness."

"When was the last time you were there?"

"Haylow? Hell, not since the '40s. Probably about the time the war ended."

"Why'd you stop going?"

"Girls." George says. "I got older, and Atlanta became more interesting to hang around in than that farm. There weren't any girls down there."

"Do you think that it's all still down there? The house? The quarters?

"I don't know. There might be something left. But the old man died and we sold the land to the Langdales. Why?"

"I was thinking about going down there," Travis says. "Maybe I'll make the drive down there next summer and see what's left. Can you draw me a map?"

George looks around. "Don't have anything to draw on here."

Travis pulls the last biscuit from the bag and flattens the paper sack. There's a pen in the tackle box, so George pulls it from the lures and tangled monofilament and gives it a go, begins by sketching the railroad junction and then the house. Then the commissary. Then the quarters.

"There wasn't much to it, like I said." He sketches it out and ends by writing the title, HAYLOW, GA in scratchy script. Then he underlines it.

"I thought it was spelled H-a-l-o."

"Yeah, everybody does. Here you go. It was something like this. Don't hold me to any of it. There just wasn't much to it. He reviews his work. "Oh, yeah. The swamp was this way." And he adds that.

His uncle has laid it all out for him and he's even drawn him a map to follow. What to do now? Travis cranks the reel and winds the line back in, the fat night crawler slides away from the uninterested fish. The monofilament winds on the reel, and the line drags back over to the boat. He cranks and cranks, and when the line drops straight down, the worm leaves the water and hangs limp on the hook at the end of the rod. He's a goner. Time for a trade-out. But Travis gives it another cast, his best one yet, and the worm sails in a graceful arc, the reel spinning, and the worm plunks down close to the log, the red bob floating. It's coming back to him, now. Before the next thought has time to arrive, the bob dips into the water. A pause, then a second dip, and then the how-to returns from somewhere deep inside. He flicks the lever, locks the line, and waits for the third dip. Wait for three. He doesn't know why, but that's what the voice inside tells him to do. And then when it comes, yank the rod hard to set the hook.

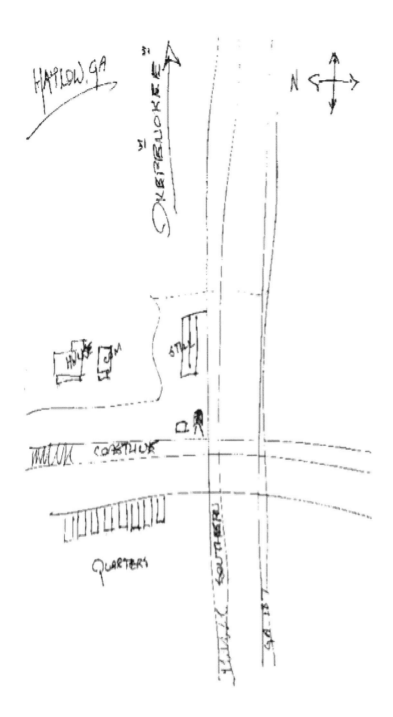

Chapter Twenty-eight

News of death comes abruptly when by landline, at least for Travis—more-so than being on the scene and witnessing the demise himself. The realization of Charlie's death had been a slow process, a stair-stepping downward into increasing fear and panic, beginning with his initial lack of alarm—he laughed when Charlie first hit the water—that grew into a rapidly escalating dread. Hope of rescue turned to full-blown horror as the seconds ticked by, each tick keeping Charlie under water for longer than Travis could hold his own breath. Time became unreal. Out-and-out. And then denial began as he leaned over the gunwale, the chop gently rocking the cabin cruiser as he gaped at the widening circle where his brother had hit the water. Charlie dead? He had just been standing next to him and laughing about the turd in the head.

It happens like this: George is standing in the kitchen, telephone receiver to his ear, the cord tangled up and swinging. Travis and Meggan sit on the loveseat in front of the fire in the fireplace, a good blaze going as all three quarter-logs catch. Ying sits in his usual berth in her lap. Yang sits at her feet and licks his balls. Their bags are packed and wait by the door, ready to go. "No shit?" George says and not long after he hangs up the phone, placing the receiver back into its cradle on the wall. "Your grandmother's dead," he says, pulls a hard pack of cigarettes from the kitchen counter and taps it on a knuckle as he walks through the sliding glass door out onto the deck.

Travis's jaw drops. Meggan reaches out with a comforting touch. "Travis, I'm so sorry," she says and her hand is warm on his forearm. He blinks a few times and then says wow.

"We were just talking about her last night," Meggan says. "How weird is that?"

Travis feels disoriented, so he stands up, but still feels disoriented. Ying and Yang both look up at his face, un-hostile for the first time. Is that sympathy in their eyes?

"Give me a minute," he says and follows his uncle outside. George's back is turned and he looks out over the lake. Bad weather is rolling in, storm clouds everywhere and making the water murky. Soggy cigarette butts at the bottom of the balustrade. Empty bottles of Bud still line the drink railing, dead soldiers. Stonewall sits at his uncle's feet, snout up. George strokes his head briskly and then scratches the sweet spot under his jaw. Travis walks over, arms crossed against the chill.

"This is some shit, isn't it nephew?" George's eyes are red. He blows smoke.

"How did she die?" Travis asks.

"Henry said a chandelier fell on her."

"*What?*"

"That's what he said. While she was eating brunch. Your father's already contacted our attorney. It looks like we'll be owning an old folks home soon." He turns his head to the construction across the lake.

"You okay?" Travis asks.

"Thanks for asking. She was a tough old bird. I thought sure she'd make it to a hundred. I probably should have made it down to see her more often than I did." George takes another drag from the cigarette. "A Goddamned chandelier. Can you believe that?"

Chapter Twenty-nine

A modest crowd gathers at Druid Hills Baptist for the funeral service. Travis's grandmother outlived most of those who would have attended to pay their respects. Still, there's surviving family and a shuttle bus of residents from Piedmont Lake. Travis, Meggan, Henry, George, and relatives from the other side of the family up in one of the Carolinas. The funeral director. A scattering of people that no one knows. The only person missing is Travis's grandmother herself, but she's close by, sealed in the casket in the back of the hearse parked under the awning and out of the rain. Despite the unhappy circumstance, there is no keening. No wailing. No caterwauling, either, nothing like Charlie's funeral decades before—the only funeral that Travis has attended previously and his only comparable reference. Like Charlie's funeral, there is no body to view this time around. There is only the decorative register to sign and send best wishes to the surviving family, but the fabric-covered log is just part of the package deal and once shut, will never be re-opened.

The rain slows everything down, including Travis and Meggan. He steers the beater Volvo down Ponce de Leon Avenue and through the storm to the big church across from Plaza Drugs. There aren't many cars in the lot and he finds a parking space close to the back entrance, next to the shuttle bus. It's a good thing he thought to bring an umbrella. He opens the car door and deploys the umbrella with the push of a button, the rain beating on the black fabric, and circles the car to Meggan's side. She usually prefers to walk in the rain, she says, but not when it's like this. They splash through a big puddle and underneath the portico. Out of the downpour, Meggan gives her hair a shake and combs fingers through to fix it back. The hearse is shiny and freshly waxed, untouched by the raindrops pounding above. A rent-a-cop from the

Atlanta Police Department wears yellow rain gear and leans on the seat of his motorcycle while thumbing through a paperback, bending to keep it dry. George smokes a cigarette over by the back entrance to the sanctuary. They walk over, Travis shaking the dripping umbrella. George's eyes are red. Travis puts a hand on his shoulder and squeezes.

"How are you holding up?

George looks at the hearse. "She had a long life. I'll take 96, myself." He nods back toward the doorway. "It's the second room on your right. I'll be back in in a minute."

George Hemperly. Sorry I didn't spend more time with you. Don't hold it against me.

Travis deposits the dripping umbrella in the circular stand just inside the door. He knows this church from his childhood, when he used to come with his grandmother on babysitting weekends. It still smells the same, like newly opened pages of religious tracts. But he doesn't remember the layout or which hall goes where. Crosses on the wall to the left and the right, then a bulletin board with purple construction paper announcements of upcoming events. They walk somberly and side-by-side past these and down the hall and into the reception room.

They are the last to arrive. Travis looks over the room. Elderly women gather around a white grand piano, blue-hairs from Piedmont Lake. He recognizes one of them from the lunch with his grandmother. A few relatives from the other side of the family he knows but can't remember names. He'll have to introduce Meggan in a way that prompts them to provide one. And there's an old black man sitting on the couch, a cane by his side. He's the guy who feeds the ducks. His father is here, too. Henry stands beside a table to his left with a woman Travis doesn't recognize and talks with a man in a black suit and a prominent forehead.

"Hey, isn't he the guy on that billboard?" Meggan asks.

"That's my father," Travis says, just as he meets Henry's eyes.

"Travis." Henry steps forward, hand out. Their hands clasp in a misfired shake. "Thanks for coming, son. This is Dorothy." He introduces the leathery woman with a pricey dyed-blonde hairstyle. Travis shakes her hand and thinks: boob job. He introduces Meggan, and Meggan is pleased to meet them both. "Call me Dot," the woman says.

His father looks tired. He looks older, too. No reason why he shouldn't, Travis thinks. He is older. Still, it surprises him. His face looks thin. His teeth are bleached unnaturally white. Travis says that he's sorry that it took a funeral to get them together, but before he can continue the excuse, the man with the big forehead steps forward, his expression solemn. He is the funeral director, he says, and he is sorry for Travis's loss. Travis thanks him for his condolence, and yes this is a sad occasion and yes what a tragedy and yes the weather is terrible. Henry asks Travis if he will be a pall bearer, and this brings a twinge. They've been there before, although it was a risky choice when Travis was young. He almost dropped his end of the casket. But yes, of course, he says.

Henry Hemperly. Goodbye, Mother. You're going Home. John 3:16.

The funeral director needs to speak with Henry about a few details, he says. His father seems to be in charge here, George apparently abdicating the traditional role of the older brother for a smoke. Meggan looks over the room and says that she could use a drink. Travis agrees and wonders if George has a flask that he would share. He looks down at the table. The log book of guests is open, and there's a powder-blue fountain pen between the pages. He lifts a corner and flips through the empties. Looks like it can handle a thousand mourner funeral. More. Ladies first, so he tells Meggan you first. She grabs the fountain pen:

Meggan Ragsdale. Everything happens for a reason.

She hands the pen to Travis. He scribbles his name and then pauses to read over the entries. What to say? Rest in peace? No. Go with God? No. You will be missed? None of them seem right.

He wants to capture his turmoil but it's not ordered enough to allow for translation into English. Finally he scribbles:

Travis Hemperly, Grandson

And he drops the pen between the pages.

The room has been designed for standing, and there are not a lot of places to sit, so stand they do. A big parlor with four exposed support columns and a low ceiling. Bead-board painted white. A long couch along this wall and a short couch along that. The mourners and visitors collect in distinct groups. The Piedmont Lake visitors by the piano, the Carolina relatives by the long couch. The black guy who feeds the ducks sitting alone over there. Travis and Meggan step over to the relatives from the other side of the family, two couples, on the low end of elderly. They all know his name. Warm handshakes all around, and Travis introduces Meggan. No luck on getting names in return, and he explains away his bad memory. They are congenial about the slight and upbeat considering the circumstance. Both men wear American flag pins on their lapels and both abruptly volunteer that they dislike the President of the United States of America. Travis looks at Meggan. Meggan looks at Travis. And then Travis thanks them for making the drive. Then it's on to the group of old women, the surviving members of his grandmother's Sunday school class, they say. Travis recognizes Ina from lunch a few weeks before and thanks her for coming. She seems pretty nimble without her scooter. She introduces Travis to the others and tells them that he teaches at the black college. The other women think that it's wonderful that he would do such a thing.

Ina Short. Vengeance is mine, sayeth the Lord.

Travis pulls Meggan over to the old black gentleman sitting alone on the white couch. Everyone ignores him, and Travis wants to make an extra effort to make contact. He introduces Meggan, but the guy's not much of a talker and doesn't seem interested.

Then the pastor walks into the reception room and calls everyone's attention. He's young, about Travis's age, Travis figures. He stands with his fingertips together prayerfully, and announces that the service will begin shortly, if they could please move into the sanctuary. There's a bottleneck at the door, the mourners at once crowding through in baby steps, and the sanctuary is just down the hall. Travis ordered an arrangement of lilies over the phone and hopes they don't look too cheap. He checks them first thing when they enter into the open cathedral. They're on the left side of the pulpit, not too shabby, and there are three other floral displays. He remembers Charlie's funeral, a better attended affair. There were more Hemperlys then, more friends and family and a bigger crowd, and the air was thick with sorrow and grief, or at least that's how he remembers it. Thick with it. A jam of grief. A molasses of grief. The service today is more like an impromptu family gathering in black.

The absence of a body to view brings grim speculation to mind about the condition of her earthly remains. The chandeliers in the dining room were enormous, Travis thinks. She must have been squashed flat. And of course, there's a bit of relief too. It could have been him. There hasn't been much time to reflect on the loss of his grandmother, just a few days, and he's been busy with classes and grading essays since they returned. And then there's what George told him about Haylow. The lynchings. The klan. He knows he's lost something but isn't sure what. He feels grief, but not strongly. He feels loss, but of what? It occurs to him for the first time as he stands in the big echoing room, pews ranking back, that if he does not sire a son, he will be the end of the Hemperly line. That's a painful epiphany to have at a funeral, he thinks. Meggan's shoulder presses against his shoulder, her head back as she looks up. Stained glass circles the dome above the balcony.

The funeral service is short but seems long anyway. Immediate family sits on the front row, and Travis and Meggan settle in on the hard pew, Dorothy and then Henry. George next to Meggan. They are not there to mourn, the pastor says, but to celebrate Rosie Lee's transition to Glory. "Rosie Lee?" Travis thinks. No one ever called her that, not that he remembers. The pastor gets the larger family narrative right but misfires on the specific details in an attempt to comfort with intimacy: His grandmother is "Rosie Lee." George is "Georgie." Henry is "Hank."

After the service ends, there isn't much dawdling. The attendant from the funeral home keeps the schedule and hurries the mourners to the graveside service. Once outside the church and under the awning, they jockey for position in the processional to Oakland Cemetery, yellow rectangles placed in the windshields saying FUNERAL. Travis and Meggan hang back under the awning. Meggan steps up to the hearse and peaks into the back, her hands up to her face to shade the light.

"Travis? How tall was your grandmother?"

He holds a hand out mid-sternum. "About here. Why?"

"Come here and look."

*T*he rain lets up, but not much. The procession drives to Oakland Cemetery, headlights on, flashers blinking, windshield wipers working back and forth. The cop on the motorcycle leads the way, then the long black hearse, Henry, George and Dot in the limo, the Carolinians, the shuttle bus. Travis and Meggan bringing up the rear. The cop slows at the red light intersections and hits his siren a few short beats and the motorcycle escorts them through, his grandmother released from municipal laws in death.

It doesn't take long to get to the cemetery. The short processional rolls underneath the brick arch and through the wrought iron gates swung wide, and it creeps down the narrow cemetery road and into the cluster of gray monuments and white oaks, leaves on the ground and wet.

Everything has been prearranged.

When they reach the administration building, the cars pull over on the brick shoulder and park bumper-to-bumper. The sexton steps from under the portico arch, an umbrella over his head. He speaks to the funeral director behind the wheel of the hearse and points down a brick walkway. There's a green awning set up over the family plot. Travis can see it from here. The rain is light now, mostly dripping from the oaks' high limbs, and everyone gathers at the rear of the hearse. The funeral director gives out positions: Henry and the director up front, Travis and George in back. The sexton volunteers help should they need any, but there are only four handles on the small casket. The sexton drops his jaw and then closes his mouth in a pout.

Getting the casket to the plot is wet work. The pall bearers jostle about, everyone serious about the activity yet no one really knowing how to go about it, excepting the funeral director, who gives instructions: He opens the rear door to the hearse and swings it wide. Travis and George step up and grab the brass handles. It's a small casket, a child's casket, and this brings a quiet alarm at what must be inside. The funeral director says *on three*: One, two, three, and they pull, the casket sliding out and the pall bearers get their footing with the load. The sexton advises that they be careful when they hit the brick. The rain has made it slick. He leads the way down a narrow brick walkway, the shuffling pall bearers following. Travis whispers to George for an explanation.

"The plot was full. There was only enough room for a child's casket. But this is where she wanted to be buried."

"How'd they fit her inside?" Travis asks, horrific scenario in mind.

"Folded her in half. I could sure use a smoke."

"Folded her in half?" Travis asks. "Seems like that would be illegal."

George shrugs. "It's not."

"Couldn't they just have cremated her?"

"She wasn't of the cremation generation," he says. "She really wanted to be buried here. Henry said she was very specific about it. I might not have been the most attentive son, but I'm not about to argue with my dead mother."

It's awkward going. The casket is heavy, the brick walk slippery, the rain cold on his face, but no trip-ups, and the small procession proceeds past the monuments and headstones, makes the left turn and then over to the green canvas shelter set up over the plot. A strange interior decoration underneath with the Hemperly monument in the center, its tip touching the canvas, and the small gravestones of the children all around. Some whispering about this as the mourners assemble. A hole has been dug, a mechanism in place, an iron rectangle with a wench stuck into the ground, a retractor into the chest of the earth. The pall bearers jockey the casket into the hole, the funeral director giving instructions in a quiet voice. The casket is set into place. Everyone tries to crowd in underneath the awning and out of the rain, all of them packed in close. Travis and Meggan shoulder-to-shoulder, his leg against one of the little headstones. Meggan looks down, eyes on the inscription. The pastor steps forward, a Bible in hand. Ashes to ashes. Dust to dust.

 $\mathcal{T}$he brief service ends with a thud. After the words are spoken and the casket lowered, the mourners wander back down herringbone brick to the line of cars parked along the narrow alley and leaning into mossy gutters. Everyone is quiet. George and Henry stand by the hole and look down. There's a little friction between the brothers. George thinks a wake is a good idea and wants to go to lunch, yet Henry is a teetotaler. He doesn't drink alcohol and disapproves of those who do. He wants the wake to be alcohol-free, as commanded by Scripture, he says. George wants a drink and argues that nowhere in the Bible is there a commandment to abstain, but Henry shoots back that he should treat his body like a temple and his is no temple. George doesn't know his Gospel well enough to site chapter and verse in rebuttal so loses by default. In the end, it's no contest. George might be the older brother, but who is it that took care of their mother while he spent his time fishing up in the mountains? They settle on a meat-and-three off of Ponce de Leon, a Tea Room that serves just that, beverage-wise: tea. Coffee, lemonade, and whatever kind of Coke you want, too, but no booze. George grumbles.

Only the immediate family and their escorts go to the wake: Henry, Dot, Travis, Meggan, and George as fifth wheel. The rain breaks by the time they get to the restaurant, and the sun shines through in a few spots. The hostess ushers them to the big round table by the street-side window, the Ponce de Leon traffic rolling by. George whispers to Travis as he takes his seat: "Is that a hooker on the corner?"

"You like them strong and black, right?" Travis answers and encourages him to invite her in as his date. George says touché, nephew. The menu is basic Southern fair: fried chicken, black eyed peas, greens and creamed corn for Travis and some Jimmy Carter Custard for desert. There's a trick to ordering the food. A textured plastic glass in the middle of the table is full of short pencils appropriate for the golf course. There's a green menu pad, too. "You fill out your order and give it to the waitress," Henry says. "Isn't that neat?" He's been here before and knows how it works. They used to come here on Sundays after church, he says, and George remembers and admits begrudgingly that the Tea Room was a good choice, a good fit to memorialize their mother. Dot exclaims on the quaint restaurant, the signed and framed photos of city and state paparazzi, and the yellowed newspaper clippings from *The Atlanta Journal* and *The Atlanta Constitution* from back when the city could support two separate newspapers. The waitress arrives, a white woman with water, a clear plastic glass for each of them, and she asks them what else they'd like to drink. Henry wants sweet tea, and it's sweet tea all around until they get to George, who orders a bourbon anyway and winks at the waitress. No-can-do she says as she collects the green order tickets.

I've got a question," Travis clears his throat and addresses the table. "I've been trying to clarify some of the family history lately," he looks at George, "and I was surprised by the headstones of the children back at Oakland. I haven't heard about them before. Who were they?"

Henry speaks in authoritative radio voice: "Those were Grandfather Charles' and Grandmother Helen's children," he says. "They were taken by the typhoid back around the turn of the century."

"All seven of them?" Travis asks. "She had seven children?"

"Eight, including our father," Henry says.

"That's not right." George says from the window. "Four of them were Gus and Hattie's. Three of them were Charlie and Helen's. And it wasn't typhoid. It was scarlet fever. Or was it yellow fever?"

"No," Henry disagrees. "They were all Grandmother Helen's."

"You don't know what you're talking about, little brother," George escalates.

Henry is affronted. "I talk about the importance of knowing your family history all the time, George. We discuss it nightly on the radio. Maybe you should listen in, sometime."

Meggan jumps in between and plays peacemaker: "It was a tragedy, either way. Imagine, so many children. How horrible." Dot agrees with her but mitigates the heartbreak by pointing out that the blessed little angels are now sitting by the side of Jesus. Travis says that it's a shame that they can't ask his grandmother. Before George can come back at Henry, the waitress returns with the tea, five glasses on a tray.

Fortified with a sip of sweet tea, Travis proceeds with the wake proper and steers the discussion. He suggests that they go around the table and everyone provide a remembrance. He raises his tea glass into sunlight. "I'll start. I didn't used to like iced tea because my introduction to it was through Grandma Rosa Lee. She used to make a gallon jug of tea with only two tea bags. Two. For years I believed that iced tea was bitter brown water that I couldn't stomach, and I could never understand why anyone would drink it."

"Those gallons of tea got us through the Great Depression," George says, and Henry agrees.

They continue around the table counterclockwise. Meggan says that she never met her but wishes she had. She sounds like quite a woman. George goes next and turns to Henry.

"Remember when we cleaned out the freezer in the Prado house?" Henry laughs. "Talk about scars of the Great Depression," George says. "She bought a big box freezer to save food, and she hoarded it. Froze everything. It didn't matter how little.

And she never cleaned it out. Ever. She thought that once frozen, all you had to do was to thaw it out, and it would be good as new. She had food in there dating back at least to the Eisenhower administration." He laughs at this. "After we moved her to Piedmont Lake, Henry and I cleaned it out. We emptied out all of that decades old, freezer burned, carefully wrapped in tin-foil food, and we found a frozen egg in the back of one of the shelves that someone had written a date on with a magic marker." He takes a long sip of tea in pause.

"Well," Travis asks. "What was it?"

"Nineteen fifty-eight!" And everyone laughs.

"And George fried it up right there," Henry says. "Cracked it open on a skillet and fried it sunny-side up!"

"Oh my Lord." Dot holds a hand to her mouth. "Did you eat it?"

"Gobbled it down right there." George pats his stomach.

"Really?" Travis asks. "Is that safe?"

"Well, he did take a bite of it. A small bite," Henry clarifies.

"I offered to share it."

"What did it taste like?" Dot asks.

"Absolutely nothing," he says. More laughter around the table.

It's Dot's turn. She straightens her back and adjusts her shoulders. "Henry and I would drive into the city once a month and take Mrs. Rosa Lee to Sunday service at Druid Hills. That was always such a blessed occasion. I will cherish those memories forever."

"That's nice," Meggan says.

Henry goes last, and his voice doesn't seem put-on, Travis thinks: "Mother started working for Co-Cola in the forties during the war. She started as a secretary for the branch manager, then they talked her into moving up to personnel after that woman who had the job killed herself."

"Killed herself?" Meggan asks.

"I'd forgotten about that," George says. "She had the idea that they were going to make her the new president, and when they didn't, she shot herself right there in her own office. So then they came to mother and asked her to take her job."

"George talked her into taking it," Henry says.

"They really wanted her, but she didn't think she could do the work." George rolls his eyes at the thought. "Tell the rest of it," he prompts with his chin.

Henry takes a sip of tea and adds a pause. "This was some job for a woman back then. After that, she hired every secretary that Coke employed for the next twenty years. She hired Coke's first black lady secretary." Henry looks at Travis. "This was during the sixties. They didn't want to hire her, but mother took her in there and told them to hire her and they did hire her. The first black secretary at Co-Cola. Your grandmother did that. Got them to hire the first black secretary at Coke. Lester Maddox even wrote an editorial in the newspaper criticizing them and saying that Coke forced her to hire a black woman. But it was the other way around."

"Who's Lester Maddox?" Meggan asks.

Travis shifts in his seat. His grandmother was a Civil Rights pioneer? He's never heard this before, either. His father and George have probably been talking. The story smells like they're telling it for his benefit. Strange that it isn't in the family folklore, but maybe it was. He's been away for years. Maybe it just never came up. He wonders if there's any way to verify.

The waitress approaches carrying a large, round tray, her hip leaning to one side to help balance the weight. A short black woman brings up the rear, a second tray of food held up high. "Who got the country-fried steak?" she asks, and George pokes an index finger up to the ceiling as the meal is distributed, vegetables individualized in small white bowls. Then she asks if they need anything else. Henry asks for more sweet tea, and she says that she'll bring a pitcher for the table. Travis eyes the Coca-Cola wall clock. He's on a countdown. The panel at the college is this evening.

"Let's say the blessing," Henry says as if it's the normal next thing to do. Travis can see giving thanks if the meal was on the house, but they're paying for it themselves. Henry's left hand is already in Dot's, and he reaches to his right, his palm open and waiting for Travis's hand. Some jostling around the table as Meggan and George catch on too. Travis wonders if his father and Dot hold hands when it's just the two of them. Maybe they do. He and Meggan join hands and then his other in his father's. The dwindling Hemperlys sit in a circle, holding hands. Henry clears his throat, returns to radio voice, and dictates a business-letter:

"Dear Heavenly Father,

Thank you for the bountiful meal we are about to receive. We are grateful for your blessing, grateful for family gathered here today, and we ask that you embrace those who we've lost. Please prepare a special place for Rosa Lee Hemperly, mother, grandmother, and devoted believer. Hold her close to your bosom.

Amen."

Amens seconded all around the table. Henry squeezes Travis's hand before he lets go. Travis squeezes Meggan's before he releases hers, and so on all around the table and back to Henry. George says that he appreciates Henry's prayer but using their mother's name and God's bosom in the same passage wasn't the best choice.

"You need to grow up, George," Henry stabs a fork into his collards for emphasis.

"Calm down, little brother. I'm just trying to lighten the mood."

Travis considers his father and uncle. They've been bickering on and off since the funeral. The thought develops until he applies it to his own circumstance. What if Charlie hadn't died? What sort of relationship would they have had? He picks up his spoon and taps it on his plastic iced tea glass, *thock, thock, thock*, and raises his voice. "I'd like to make a toast." He lifts his iced tea high. All eyes on him now.

"To Grandma Rosa Lee."

Plastic glasses go up all around the table. Meggan, George, Dot and Henry join in the toast. To Mrs. Hemperly. To mother. To Mrs. Rosa Lee. To mother. And then a second toast comes to mind before he thinks it through and takes present company into account. Travis raises his glass higher.

"And to Charlie . . ."

Meggan and Dot follow suit and lift glasses in toast, but George's eyes widen, and his teeth clinch in sudden grimace as he looks at Henry. Travis hadn't intended to summon Charlie, but now he's at the table anyway. There's no seat for him though, so he just hovers above the cornbread. Henry doesn't move, doesn't look at Travis. He just looks straight ahead, his glass still raised in toast to Rosa Lee, his shame suddenly exposed, but only to half the table. Meggan doesn't know. Nothing from Dot that he can tell. Looking in her eyes is like looking out a window. She's only heard whatever version his father told her. They hold their glasses up in earnest toast, waiting. George's eyes fix on Travis, and he pleads with his retinas. Please don't do this. His gaze is full of intent, as protective as one brother can be for another. Henry sits tight, his glass still raised, but his hand shakes a little and a sip of sweet tea splashes on his plate, just missing the drumstick. All the turmoil is back. All the years Travis has spent away from these Hemperlys, holding onto the truth. He looks around the table. George still pleading. His father still still. And it comes down to this. It's up to him. He can either increase the torment and destroy the peace or let it pass. Paper it over. He's spent twenty years standing up for the truth, standing up for Charlie, who hovers and waits. The dwindling Hemperlys and their dates wait for him to finish his toast. The Hemperlys and their history. George pleads. His father sits. Deep down, Travis has always known there was only one choice, only one way to fix this tragedy in family history. It's always been in front of him.

". . . tragic accidents both," Travis gets onboard.

"May they rest in peace," Henry completes the toast.

And they leave it at that.

Chapter Thirty

Walk, Travis, walk. Briskly. He's running late, but it's too late to back out now. It's the first time he's returned to the college green since the interview. The rain quit, and the sun came out during the wake but now it is dropping behind Dubois Hall and resting on the hipped roof of the tower. And he hasn't been to the Hall of the Inward Journey before, a name that suggests both enlightenment and pretense, he thinks. But Longman told him where it was, just up the hill and to the right, and the campus isn't that large anyway. Still, he prefers to be on time, and that's the impression he wants to leave, particularly this evening during his first extracurricular event.

He parks close to the rising Humanities Tower, under a light pole and beside the big green dumpster, an iron rectangle that's filled to the brim with construction debris. The mercury vapor lamp overhead blinks on, even though it's still light out. The shadow of the tower falls across the parking lot. Compared to Garvey Hall right there, the new building looks huge, impressive, even though it's not half-built. He's watched it shoot up to the sky over the past few weeks, has seen it grow from the trench work of foundation laying to the geometric I-beam framing, and now the first few floors have been filled in with walls of granite, the rest of it an iron skeleton next to the boom crane. Progress, Travis thinks. The Liberal Arts move toward the 21st century, and it gladdens his heart. How lucky for him to land a job here and now, at the beginning of the renaissance of the humanities, and he imagines a future in which his older self—now safely tenured and ensconced on the faculty here—thinks back to this very moment, and he smiles at the prophecy of telling others that he remembers back when they built the tower. What a mess that was.

But first he's got to make a good impression at this panel. And he is running late, even when adjusting for CPT. There is a curious orientation to time on campus. The meetings don't begin when scheduled. It doesn't matter how large or how small a gathering. Travis is usually right on time and the first person in the room. His esteemed colleagues will mill about for an extra ten or twenty minutes before a meeting gets underway. Nevertheless, he's probably still late this evening, even allowing for that.

He adjusts his necktie, straightens his coat, locks the car behind him and steps across the shadow of the tower and into what's left of the sunlight. Garvey Hall crawls up the hill behind him, poorly maintained as always. The new tower is just in time. Garvey looks beat. It has collapsed from fatigue and is exhausted from decades of climbing the hill with little support and has flopped down into the middle of the road, parched, and begging for water. He wonders what they'll do with it once all of the Humanities departments have moved into the new building.

So Travis hustles up the hill to the Hall of Inward Journey and tries one last time to think of something to say. With his grandmother's unexpected death and the trial of getting her in the ground and grieving, he wasn't able to spend the time planning a proper presentation, not even a last-minute bullet list of points. He functions more efficiently when he prepares in advance, but he's got nothing, and he's late. What can he possibly contribute to this discussion? Should he say the word aloud in front of this audience or just go with the "N-word"? It's probably a bad idea all around to use the word itself. His colleagues will likely bandy it about with ease. But his melanin deficiency is particularly acute at this moment. And let's face it, after the revelations in the mountains, he feels a new awkwardness in taking part. Suck it up, Travis. Suck it up, he tells himself, and then he takes a big breath and does just that, climbs the hill to the college green, turns right at Dubois Hall, and hustles past the Klan Bell.

The Klan Bell. He still doesn't know what to make of it. College lore says that it's to be rung to gather all students and faculty together should the Ku Klux Klan attack the college. He still doesn't know what to think about this. Is it a historical fact? Fanciful folklore? Just plain paranoia? Maybe all three. As he hurries past the big brass bell, Haylow comes to mind, the slavery dynamic down there and what George said about the klan. The Night Riders. Maybe he could work this into his presentation somehow? But this gets a quick veto. Maybe the smart thing to do is to just sit on his hands and say nothing after all.

He trots up the front steps of the Hall of the Inward Journey and under the stained glass arch, through the double doors. His footfalls echo down the hall to the auditorium. Fingers on the brass plate and he gives the door a gentle push, but it creaks as it opens anyway and the noise echoes throughout the big room: three rows of audience seating, and a big proscenium stage. He doesn't think to catch the door, and it bangs shut behind him. Loudly. Heads turn, look, and then back to the student behind the podium stage right. The proceedings have begun.

The student doesn't miss a beat as he reads words of introduction from index cards. There's not much of a turn out tonight, about twenty in the audience scattered across the seats. Longman, Kalamari, and Tigony sit behind a table stage left. And something smells good. On top of the long table to his right rest two hot trays, lids ajar, Sterno flames purple. Smells like fried chicken, Travis thinks, as he hurries down the aisle, up the steps and under the proscenium arch quickly, his body language telegraphing *Don't mind me, I'm not really here*, and he takes the empty seat, turns to them and whispers, "Sorry I'm late. My grandmother died."

Skeptical looks from Kalamari and Tigony. Longman whispers his condolences.

The student with the index cards introduces Longman, who leaves the table to introduce the panel. He steps behind the podium.

"Good evening," he greets the scattered audience.

"Good evening," the audience responds in monotone.

Longman thanks the student for his kind introduction and applauds him. Travis, Kalamari and Tigony do the same. Then he turns back to the audience. "How are you niggas doing tonight?

I'm talkin' to you, sukka!"

The audience responds favorably. Travis shifts around in his chair and feels a pull in his stomach. Hunch confirmed: participating is a really bad idea.

Longman counts on his fingers: "Nigger, Nigra, Negro, Nigga, Niggaz, The N-Word, whatever you call it, we have had to contend with this word and its variations for all of our lives. It won't go away, and it never will. But we rarely address it seriously or discuss its place in contemporary culture in any substantial way. Everyone gets wound up, and we just argue about it among ourselves." He points to the left of the auditorium to a student in necktie sitting on the front row. "You think that the word is offensive and its use is an expression of self-hate." He points to his right at a student with his feet up on the chair in front. "You don't see what all the fuss is about. Which one of you is right?"

"I am," yells the student with his feet up.

"This is what we've come together to discuss tonight. Let me introduce our esteemed panel: Dr. Kalamari is a long-time member of the history department here at the college and the author of *The Street Soldier Revolutionary Handbook*. Some of you are using his text this semester. Applause through the crowd. Dr. Tigony is a specialist in Black Male Studies, and we thank her for joining us, as always." Obligatory clapping here. "And Professor Hemperly joins us for the first time. He is new to the history faculty at the college and an authority on the Viking Era. I'm sure he will put that knowledge to good use for us tonight." Travis gives a wave. Someone in the audience asks, "Who?"

"Here's how it's going to work," Longman says. "Each panelist will present, and then we'll have a question-and-answer period. Afterwards, a buffet-reception at the back of the room."

Travis has seen Tigony infrequently since the interview. The few times he has passed her in the hall he has waved and nodded and tried to make a connection as she's one of the few white faculty. They have a common trait. But she ignored him then, and she's ignoring him now. On the table before her, a neat stack of papers. Looks like twenty or so pages, Travis figures. Is she going to read the entire paper? Longman said ten minutes.

Longman moderates: "First we'll begin with Dr. Tigony." He begins an intro clap. Tepid response from the students. Kalamari checks out his fingernails. Longman takes a step back and gestures to the podium, palm up. "Anne."

Tigony leaves the table, paper in hand. The hardwood stage creaks as she steps toward the lectern, denim dress whipping. Longman continues applauding, solo now and she passes a good head beneath him. "Thank you, dear ones, for attending tonight," she begins. A little bit of feedback as she adjusts the articulated stem of the mic.

Travis turns to Kalamari. It's just the two of them now, and he reaches out colleague-to-colleague. Kalamari hasn't seemed to care for him since he arrived, and Travis has wondered if he can repair the bad start. Might as well give it a shot now. He leans over and panders in a whisper. "Dr. Kalamari, I'm considering using your book next semester."

Kalamari turns, tilts his head forward, slides his glasses down to the end of his nose. "Be respectful, Mr. Hemperly. Don't talk during the presentation."

Ouch, that stings, Travis rubs his cheek, and thinks that the slap might have left a mark. Longman returns to the table, and the folding chair creaks when he sits back down. He leans and whispers, "You're next."

Tigony's voice echoes through the big room. The acoustics aren't very good, at least from up here on the stage, Travis thinks.

"I'm glad to be here this evening, and I would like to thank Dr. Kalamari for his hard work in putting it together." She turns and claps in his direction, and the students follow along. Longman sits on his hands and smiles. "It is an honor to have been invited." She turns back to the auditorium and holds a hand above her eyes to shield the glare as she scans the audience. "Dear ones, thank you for attending this evening. I recognize several of you, quite a few of you have taken my class at some point and know that I begin each semester with a testimonial. For the benefit of those who do not know me, I have had the honor of serving on faculty for more than a decade, yet I have to acknowledge that as a white American, I stand before you a racist. This is my burden, and I try my best to atone for it daily."

Longman and Kalamari watch Tigony's back attentively. Travis does the same but tunes out as he's on a countdown. Ten minutes left before he has to have something to say, and he's got nothing. Perhaps it's proximity to the college green, but he feels the same anxiety that gripped him before his interview a few weeks before, a performance anxiety that paralyzes his mind. With all that's happened over the weekend, he hasn't had the chance to mull over a presentation as he'd intended and now that he's on looming deadline, he doesn't know what he could possibly say on this topic. He has nothing to pull from but personal experience and not much of that. Occasionally he's thrown together with a white male he doesn't know—that time he road back to town with the tow truck driver or that time he was backpacking—and said stranger would drop the word first thing, as if it were a chummy icebreaker. Come to think of it, it always made him feel the way he does now, unsure of how to proceed. So there's that, if he chooses to speak from a confessional angle.

He doesn't want to contextualize the word historically because he doesn't have the authority and because he doesn't want to step on what Kalamari or Longman might be prepared to say.

Most of Tigony's presentation is a testimony about entrenched white racism, and she doesn't actually discuss the word itself much. This is probably a smart way to go in this circumstance, he thinks, and tunes back in to catch her conclusion: "That's why I call for a complete ban on the word in every possible use. That's why I begin all of my classes with a small symbolic ceremony to bury the word. Many of you here have participated." She calls out to students in the audience. It is my hope that this word will leave the lexicon, will be banished forever from common usage, and that this panel will no longer be necessary. Thank you."

The students applaud, a polite response, and then Longman joins her at the podium.

"Thank you Dr. Tigony." He applauds for a few more claps.

"Next up, Professor Hemperly from the History Department. Hemperly. Nigga, I'm talking to you, sukka!"

More tepid applause. Travis swallows his growing panic, leaves his chair and walks over to Longman.

"Help me out if I crash and burn here," he says to Longman, who laughs and gives him a pat on the back. And then he's on his own. He steps up to the podium, heart pounding in his head, reaches for the mic, and greets the audience with a feedback squeal so loud that students cover their ears. The horrendous sound echoes around the auditorium. He adjusts the mic again and the howl returns, worse the second time around. It's a sustained tone that rises and falls in pitch, rises again. Longman steps up and they both adjust. The noise is squared away, and a few students rub their ears. A few mumbled complaints come too.

"I apologize for that," Travis says and takes a deep breath: "Thank you Professor Longman, and I'd like to thank Doctors Kalamari and Tigony, as well." He claps his hands, and the lone applause echoes through the auditorium. He looks back. Kalamari leans forward, elbows on the table, and frowns. The students look up, expectantly. What to say next? "I would like to begin with a quick testimonial myself," he says and veers off-topic. "My grandmother passed away this weekend. She lived a long ninety-six years of Atlanta history and experienced the turbulent century firsthand." He pauses for effect or sympathy or just to drag out the minute. "I want to honor her memory by sharing with you one of her accomplishments. She worked for the Coca-Cola Company here in Atlanta for fifty years. And in that time, she was able to contribute to the struggle for civil rights herself. She played a central role in the company hiring its first African-American secretary. It wasn't a popular position for her to take, and she received criticism both inside and outside the company," he wings it. "It wasn't easy, I'm sure."

"Don't you mean 'administrative assistant'?" a student on the front row asks.

"Excuse me?" Travis pulls at his necktie.

"You said 'secretary.' Don't you mean 'administrative assistant'?"

"'Administrative assistant,' yes. That was what I intended to say." The audience is silent. "Thank you for the correction." Another student up front yawns.

"She worked for Coke for forty years and played a part in integrating the company."

"How do you know she did this?" yelled from the back. The acoustics are terrible.

"Well . . . it's part of my family history." Travis doesn't mean to sound defensive but does, anyway.

"How do you know it's true?

"Well, it's what I was told."

"Yes, but how do you know that it's the truth?"

"I don't have any reason to suspect that this isn't, wasn't, a factual recollection about the past." Travis tries to encourage a give-and-take in the classroom, and that can be like pulling teeth. *Now* they want to talk?

"How do you know it's not just a story that white people tell themselves to make themselves feel good?"

A student in the middle range chimes in: "I thought you said she worked at Coke for fifty years. Now you say forty. Which was it?"

"What does any of this have to do with the N-word?" another shouts.

At this point, Kalamari has had enough. He rises from his seat so violently that it tips over behind him and bangs loud on the hardwoods. Reverb through the auditorium. Travis turns. Kalamari stalks over to the podium. Not a glance at Travis, and he grabs the stem of the mike and bends it down.

"Brothers, you are all facing a grave danger here!" And he commands that they follow him outside. Travis is comfortable with the sudden interruption as it gets him off the hook, but not for long. He turns toward Longman, his eyes telegraphing, What's going on? Longman shrugs. Kalamari leaves the podium, hops off the stage, and trots down the aisle to the entrance at the back of the chapel. Along the way he again commands again for the students to assemble outside. They stand from their seats, confusion in the auditorium now.

He pauses by the door and motions them to follow, hand brushing away the air.

"There is no time to waste! Assemble outside!" The students leave the seats, and make some hubbub, some restless talk, but they follow orders. Travis, Longman, and Tigony rise from the table too and step down from the stage. Outside, the sun sets, a brilliant violet sky to the west behind Dubois Hall. Mercury vapor lamps on tall light poles spark to life, light shining down. When Travis steps outside the main door, Kalamari is standing beside the Klan Bell. He grabs the rope, pulls the clapper, and the bell begins to ring. *Clang, clang, clang.* It's louder and deeper than Travis thought it would have been, and peels over the college green, a warning system from the 19th century. The students turn their heads this way and that. "All brothers assemble!" Kalamari yells over the clanging. Students begin to file out of Dubois Hall across the green and the dorms down the hill empty out, too, the students scratching their heads: What's going on? A few trot over, and a crowd begins to grow. More students begin to come up the hill from the shoebox dorms, walking underneath the artificial light shining overhead. What do you know? Travis thinks. It works. He turns to Longman.

"Is this part of the program?" he asks and takes a step down to get closer to the growing crowd. Longman puts a hand on his shoulder and stops him.

"Hang back a minute," he says, and Travis does, steps back up to where he was before.

Kalamari yells: "Brothers!" Then he gives it a few more rings. *Clang, clang, clang.* "Brothers. We are in jeopardy. We are in jeopardy tonight! You all know what this bell is for. That it is only to be rung should the KKK come to campus and try to destroy us. Brothers, that threat is here! Right this minute! We have an infiltrator from the Ku Klux Klan among us!"

Travis thinks: Uh-oh, and he takes a step backwards.

"And he's standing right over *there*!" Kalamari points a finger at Travis. "*Hemperly!*" he yells. "I know who you are!" He pulls the rope and rings the bell. *Clang, clang, clang.* A few more students show.

"Brothers! This is the son of the devil himself!" The dorms have emptied out with fire drill curiosity. The crowd spills over onto the college green. "Five hundred years of slavery and oppression, brothers. Don't forget. Their methods may have changed, but they still seek to put you in chains. He is trying to shackle your mind and return you to bondage!"

Longman chews on his lip, his brow bunched up in wrinkles, and that's a worried look if Travis has ever seen one. "I think it'd be a good idea if we stepped back inside," Longman says and reaches back, a hand on one of the doors. Travis thinks: This is nonsense, and he turns to the crowd and gives a smile—it's more of a grimace, really—and he shakes his head in disagreement.

"Don't be fooled by that smile!" Kalamari points for emphasis. "Smiling faces, sometimes they don't tell the truth. Smiling faces tell lies, and I've got proof!"

Longman grabs Travis by the collar, and the knot of his necktie pulls up hard into his throat.

". . . choking me," Travis chokes.

"Come on," Longman pushes the door open and pulls him through. Travis stumbles on the steps up. The door shuts behind them. There is no one else is in the hallway. Everyone is outside. Kalamari's voice is still loud outside but muffled now.

"What's he talking about?" Travis adjusts his necktie and clears his throat.

"Don't know, but he's riling up the crowd. That's never a good sign, historically speaking." He looks back toward the Hall of the Inward Journey. "This way," he points.

"This is ridiculous. Let's go back outside, and I'll explain it away." But he keeps walking.

"You've had your nose too deep in the books, my friend. Crowds don't work that way," Longman says. They reach the auditorium doors. Longman pushes them open and steps inside. "I think the best idea is for you to get out of here. Now. There's a stairway over here that leads down to the back entrance. Come on!"

Students continue to gather around the Klan Bell. It is mounted on brick piers. Kalamari takes advantage, bends a knee, and hoists himself up. He wraps an arm around the brass as best he can and clings. The students have already lost interest. The crowd dissipates quickly.

"Brothers!" Kalamari shouts. "Don't let him get away!" He points a finger back at the building, but there are only a few students left. And they're beginning to make tracks.

"I'll give you extra credit!" Kalamari incentivizes.

The closest student stops, turns, looks up at the clinging prof.

"How much?" He steps forward.

"Run, Travis, run. "Quickly," Longman says. Travis steps inside the auditorium and Longman slams the doors shut. He reaches for the long table beside the door, the one with the hot trays. "Help me move this table to block the door," Longman says as he heaves and lifts the end of the table. The hot trays jump, knocking the Sterno flames askew and the silver lids off, chicken wings piled high in the trays. He drags the table over before Travis can get to his end and jams it under the brass door handles. Travis's heart pounds in his ears. "I think you're right," he says. "Will that hold the door?"

Longman starts down the aisle, Travis right behind. He's fast for such a big man. "Quickly!" he motions, and Travis doesn't waste any time. There is pounding on the other side of the blocked door. They reach the stairwell together and start down the steps when the door below bangs open. They're coming in the back entrance too, Travis thinks. He and Longman reverse tracks, run back up the steps and back into the auditorium just in time to see the table blocking the door tip forward. He jumps back into the stairwell and hears it crash to the floor. The hot trays clatter, chicken wings scattered, and flaming Sterno splashes napalm-like across the hardwoods. Footsteps still clopping up from below: bam, bam, bam. "The balcony!" Longman says. "Quickly!" and they take the stairs up, bounding two and three at a time. Below them, the footfalls come closer but step into the auditorium and not up to the balcony level. As soon as Travis and Longman enter the balcony, they drop down to their knees and out of sight. Travis follows Longman, who crawls underneath the railing running the length of the balcony edge. Voices below echo up. "Fire!" someone yells in the empty auditorium. "Get a fire extinguisher!" Kalamari's voice. Lots of commotion from the rear of the auditorium and Travis smells the smoke.

"The window," Longman whispers and goes for the window bank at the other end of the balcony. He crawls quickly for such a big man, too. They get to the window without notice and are in luck. It's cracked open already and slides up when they both push the sill up, although it makes a dreadful scrape as it slips in the channel.

It's dark out, and there's nothing up there but Hale-Bopp. The window opens from the second floor, the drop to the grass below about twenty feet high, Travis figures, high enough that it would give him pause, but it doesn't this evening and he doesn't hesitate. He doesn't even look at Longman, just whispers, "I'm getting the hell out of here," and is up and over the sill. He lands in a crouch, his feet on the grass. Street lights to his right and to his left, but he's dropped down into the dark space in-between. There isn't anyone around. Then Longman drops and lands beside him, a big man falling heavily, and he cries out when his feet hit the ground. Travis hears the crack.

Longman sits up, puts both hands on his knee, and rocks back and forth on his butt. "Of all the luck," he whispers.

Travis asks him if he's okay.

"I don't know. Of all the luck," he whispers again and then, "Longman, Longman, Longman!" and he shakes his head. He tries to stand but winces and plops back down. Travis says let me help you.

"I think this is the end of the adventure for me," he says.

He points down the empty cul-de-sac, the road running down the hill toward the Humanities Tower as the pain drives him to the brink of melodrama: "Go ahead. Save yourself," he winces, then:

"I'll be okay."

Travis thanks him, and they clasp hands. "There's one good thing," Longman says. "This year's panel will be a memorable one. Keep to the shadows. Hurry. You're almost home-free. And good luck."

Thanks, Travis says, and then he sets off into the dark, alone. He counts the streetlights: one, two, three, four of them between here and the Humanities Tower, its superstructure unlit and ghostly. No stars out and no moon either, good conditions for a prison break, Travis thinks. He runs in a crouch along the hedge next to the wrought iron fence. Lights off in all the buildings. He scurries from dark spot to dark spot, crouching along the way. It's not far to his car. No noise behind and no one around. The streetlights are the only worry, their yellow beams casting down and lighting up the street in oval pools. If he can reach the construction area, he should be safe. Three street lights, then two, then one, and he's at the cyclone fence. Fingers in the wire diamonds, as he hoists himself up and over and into the hard hat zone, drops down beside a red wheelbarrow and tries to fit into its shadow. So much depends upon this wheel barrow, he thinks. It's the last lighted spot between him and his car. He stops to catch his breath. His heart rate slows. The Humanities Tower rises beside him, straight up to the starless sky. How quickly things change, he thinks. Not an hour ago he was musing about the possibility of being a long-term member of the faculty here, and now this. Then he makes his move and is soon in the dark shadow of the tower. Almost there. Almost safe.

He creeps low along the side of the building, shoes in the mud, probably ruined, he thinks but will worry about that later. And there's his car, parked by the big dumpster and directly under the street light, which shines brightly onto the dull paint. Why'd I have to park under that light? he thinks. He takes a quick survey of the lot, looks it over in case anyone is lying in wait, makes a move to the cyclone fence when he sees a figure kneeling next to the dumpster and staking out his car. Damn, he thinks. He's stuck here. There's no place to go.

Then someone steps around the far end of the building at

the other side of the parking lot. A big man who leans against the brick and begins to yell, "He's over here!" he waves and repeats. "Over here! Come on!" Longman's voice. The crouched figure behind the dumpster stands up and runs toward the voice, clearing the way. Travis moves quickly and he's up and over the fence. His feet hit the ground running, keys fished out of pocket and he's in his car.

Almost safe.

The Volvo cranks on the first turn, and tires squeal as he peels out of the space.

Almost safe.

Longman is still leaning, still yelling, still waving, but the hound dog pursuer puts on the brakes, turns, and starts back toward the Volvo. Travis uses swing-set logic and leans back and forth over the steering wheel to make the car go faster.

It's not even close. The Volvo zips by his pursuer, makes the turn at Garvey Hall, and speeds toward the guard shack. The undercarriage hits the speed bump and bottoms out. Sparks fly. He's almost out of this. The way is clear. Then it's not. The campus cop on duty steps from the guard shack and square into the crosswalk, arm raised, hand up flat in stop sign, blocking escape. No way around. Travis steps on the gas, grips the wheel. The guard stands fast. Travis shuts his eyes and braces for the impact, squeezes his eyes tighter and holds. The distance vanishes . . . and he's clear. He made it. In the rear view mirror, the campus cop steps from the guard shack and back into the crosswalk, raises a hand to his mouth and shouts.

"Hey! Slow it down!"

Chapter Thirty-one

Sanctuary, sanctuary. Travis needs to find sanctuary. And fast. The beater Volvo speeds off the campus, freedom bound. The campus recedes behind him, no cars in the rear view mirror giving chase. Go, go, go. His foot down harder on the gas pedal and his heart pounding away. Everything is different around here at night, the streetlights shining in the dark and not a lot of traffic around, just a few cars passing in the oncoming lane.

The Volvo trucks up the hill, and he closes in on the traffic signal at the top. Red means stop. An old man stands in the street and holds a cardboard sign. Travis swerves to miss him, busts the light, turns onto the interstate highway, and accelerates down the entrance ramp. The Volvo merges with the eastbound traffic, slows to match its speed, and the surrounding cars bring relief. Safety in numbers. He begins to breathe easier and goes with the interstate flow, just another car on the road. There's only one place to run, so he heads that way, drives past the Cabbagetown exit and continues a few stops down to Meggan's. By the time he reaches her door, his pulse has relaxed. Ying and Yang are on guard dog duty as always, and they sound the alarm, nails scratching the hardwoods and barking on the other side of the door when he approaches the stoop.

He doesn't have to knock. Meggan opens the door and holds the dogs back. She's still wearing black from the funeral, but she wears black all the time, so.

"I'll bet you didn't think you'd see me again so soon." Travis steps into the living room and embraces her, arms around her shoulders. She returns a light hug and then he gets a pat on the back. "I could use a drink," he says, reaches down and pets Yang and then the jumping Ying.

"That wasn't very long."

He's not sure how to reply to this: His presentation was cut short because they discovered that his family has a racist past and then they chased him off the campus?

"It was canceled," he says. "Power outage."

"Oh. That's a shame."

"Can I stay at your place for a few days?" he asks. It might be wise to avoid the apartment for now. "I'm serious about that drink," and he steps into the kitchen, Meggan and the dogs following behind. The kitchen is dark, the only light small from underneath the vent hood. In the sink, light on glass: bottles of booze upended, bottle caps on the counter. Vodka. Bourbon. Scotch. Gin. Muscadine Schnapps. All the liquor dumped down the drain. Travis stops.

"What's this?"

"I'm not going to be able to help you out with that drink," she says.

"Are you okay?"

"Travis, we need to talk."

A sick feeling in his gut. "Okay. Let's talk." His voice is hitched up a little. She looks so beautiful in the dim light, her hair down.

"I've been thinking. Your grandmother's funeral made me realize a few things and I . . ."

"It made me realize a few things too," he interrupts, the end of his family line surging and that feeling in his gut, sinking.

"Well." She says. "This is awkward. We're not here for very long. And . . . Well, I don't think we're working out."

He didn't see this coming, and his jaw jerks with the impact. "What do you mean we're not working out? We just had such a good time in the mountains and went to such a nice funeral."

"I just don't want to settle," she says.

Ouch, that hurts, and he winces at the uppercut. "'Settle?'" he says. "What do you mean 'settle?'"

"You're a nice guy, Travis. But I'm looking for something more."

"Something more? What do you mean something more?" His thoughts double back and come twice. "We've only been going out for a few weeks," he pleas, and as the words leave his mouth, he knows that they're not going to turn this thing around. "Meggan, I think we've really got something here."

"My name's not Meggan," she says. "It's Margaret. I'm sorry. I think you should go." She looks down at the dogs and says cheerfully, "Say goodbye, boys." Ying and Yang are uncharacteristically quiet and say nothing.

Travis feels as if he has been hit on the head with a cinder block, and his brain doesn't work so well. "What?" he says. "What?" And then there's his heart again, pounding in his chest. It's getting quite a workout this evening. This can't be happening, he thinks. This can't be happening. Bottles emptied in the sink and she looks resolute with her arms crossed. He's not going to be able to change her mind with words here in the kitchen, and then he recovers from the blindsiding enough to catch his falling dignity. "It's been a long day for both of us," he says. "I know that I'm at my emotional wits' end. Let's give it a few days and talk later," and he makes his way quickly back toward the front door. Let me get out of here before she vetoes the idea, he thinks. Meggan stands in the kitchen entrance and leans against the wall, arms still crossed. "See you later, boys," Travis says and lets himself out, pulls the door closed, takes three steps toward the beater Volvo when behind him the deadbolt locks with a click.

It's the now that consumes everything: all of his thoughts, the firing of his atria, the diameter of his arterial walls, the blood flowing to his brain. His heart hurts inside his chest. His car weaves over the center line as he steers back onto the interstate. He drives with both hands on the steering wheel, both of them tremoring on the leatherette cover. What happened? Did she really just dump him? He reviews the past three weeks to look for clues, but none come to him.

He drives back to the apartment—to hell with staying away. He's got nowhere else to go. Let them come. He doesn't bother to turn on the lights, steps into the bedroom, drops his clothes, skips the PJ's and crawls underneath the covers on the mattress and curls up in fetal position, head on the pillow and knees to his stomach.

*T*ravis either doesn't have dreams or doesn't remember them, he doesn't know which. This isn't how it's always been, and every now and then he awakes and strains to recall if there's been a thought in his head over the hours of the previous sleep. This morning, he's got a few impressions: Complete darkness. No ground under his feet. He's falling but doesn't know if he's falling up or down or sideways. There is nothing more. When he opens his eyes, there's no telling how long he's been out. He didn't note the time when he came in and now the sunlight is streaming in through the window, red numbers blink at him from the alarm clock on the floor. Did the power go out?

He teaches on Mondays, Wednesdays and Fridays, and today is Wednesday. His first class is at eight, and by the look of the sunlight outside, he's missed it. He pulls sweat pants and T-shirt from the hamper, and consults the brick of coffee in the refrigerator, makes a fresh pot, leans on the countertop, and sips from an Olympic Games coffee cup. Where did he get this? he studies the colorful logo. The clock on the microwave blinks, too. Thoughts don't come, his eyes half-lidded and head catatonic, even after all the sleep. Everything has collapsed around him. He feels the downward trajectory of it all, the debris sliding down along the declining slope.

*E*ventually, the caffeine does its job. After a little while he's able to put his thoughts into some kind of order and attend to them. The protestant work ethic inside of him urges obedience. He has a responsibility to teach his classes, a responsibility to teach his students. He must serve his profession. But who is he trying to kid? If he's a no-show, then his students will just be glad for the day off. They'll be happy for the unplanned extra time, an unexpected bonus to their day. At the least, he should telephone the history department secretary—administrative assistant, he corrects himself—and let her know that he won't be able to make it in. After last night's escapades at the panel, he'll take a few days off and maybe it will all blow over.

Travis piddles around the apartment in a zombie lurch for a few hours before it occurs to him what he needs to do. It's obvious, really, when he finally figures it out. He has to drive south. He has to drive down to Clinch County and see for himself if there's anything left. It will give him something to think about other than Meggan and the trauma of loss. It's been pulling him all along, anyway. He wants to find the Hemperly house, wants to see if it's still standing. The commissary. The turpentine still. The railroad crossroads, too. But most of all, he wants to see the quarters.

An hour later, and he's on the road. He drives outside of the perimeter highway and leaves the metro area behind, rolls through the long stretch of suburban wasteland, his head numb, hands on the wheel. In his condition, he probably shouldn't be operating heavy machinery. He drives through the subdivision belt surrounding the city and eventually the trees begin to outnumber the people, woods to his right and his left, and then he can't avoid it any longer. Meggan has left him. Meggan is gone. He has had this experience before, riding in a car driving south and feeling hollow from loss, and he broods on the sorrow all the way to Macon.

The first world recedes behind him and gives way to the developing world. Travis doesn't realize it at the time, there is no sign, no warning to alert him. He's just another traveler on the road. The locals have a perception that he lacks, and his car and license tag give him away. A quick calculation and he estimates about three hours before he reaches the bottom of the state, but he's never been good at math. The farther south he drives, the less developed the landscape. Occasional gas stations and fast food joints of familiar order huddle around the exits, surrounded by farmland and forest and dependent on interstate traffic, first world outposts on the frontier. Long stretches between exits, and when he passes the overpasses, there is nothing to exit for. No fuel, no, food, no sights to see, just a state road on an overpass. Cities give ways to towns. Towns give way to villages. But even these fade the farther south he goes, replaced by local establishments. Barbeque houses and restaurants without quality control mechanisms in place. The fading blue roofs of the falling Stuckey empire. He travels where the fast food chains fear to tread, and it occurs to him that he is traveling back in time. The interstate highway is a river into the past, the road exits are tributaries spaced farther and farther apart and leading to farmland isolation. He is surrounded by the agrarian southland that he apparently has in his blood, but he's not sure how the world works down here. The harvest has passed for some of the crops, he notes. Fields on either side of the road are harrowed earth, upturned dirt prepared for the next planting season. What could it be? There's no telling. A red biplane above the field over there flies low over leafy rows of who-knows-what? Cotton? Marijuana? Then a cloud streams from its belly and trails behind, dusting the crops below. He's never seen that before, a biplane outside of a museum that he remembers, and this gives a thrill as the plane lifts in a graceful turn, double wings leaning as it comes back at the field from the other side. A second cloud streams from the plane and drops poison down onto the next row of crops. Travis thinks: maybe there are options besides teaching for him? Maybe he could get into that line of work.

Another hour down the road. Travis has lots to think about but not much to look at, and he drives along in a trance, studying the insects smashed on the windshield. When the farmhouse appears on the left, he hasn't seen anything for so long that its very appearance makes him sit up straight. A stately Victorian house in decay. It's the biggest place he's seen. A hipped roof. Two dormers. Two brick chimney stacks. Six spindled columns supporting the front porch red-rusted roof. The clapboard on the side of the house is falling apart, and the whole structure is engulfed with saplings and seedlings, brush and a small tree or two, one growing up through the shattered shingle roof. It's not the antebellum mansion of his imagination, but it's the grandest structure he's come across in a while. What a shame to let a place like that go, he thinks, a once grand plantation house overcome by vegetation and time, and he wonders if the Hemperly House in Haylow will be the same. The period is right. Turn of the century. The fields around the house are giving way to the approaching forest wood, which grows into the abandoned farmland, and before too long the fields end, and pine woods grow up to the shoulder on both sides of the road. The virgin-growth forest is long gone, a few spots here and there that could be parts of the original chaos somehow overlooked by the clear cutting frenzy. But the farther south he gets, the more the trees are ranked in ordered rows, like orchards. Pine trees categorized by size. Youthful trees to his right, toddler saplings to his left.

*H*aylow was full of meanness and snakes. That's how George described it. His whole story was thick with it, an enduring dream of slavery time. Back at the college, Kalamari believes that the characteristics of race are essential to the core of being, Internalized. Genetic. Unavoidable. Does this drive his eccentricity? The man probably has his reasons, yet they sure make him peculiar. He has called Travis a "European" since day one, and takes as gospel that Travis is a representative of white supremacy. But Kalamari is of his father's generation and a prisoner of the hand he's been dealt. And speaking of his father, he is as unreconstructed a racist as there's ever been, yet something deep inside prevents him from admitting it. There are no epiphanies in his future. He believes skin color establishes a social hierarchy that is indisputable, and Travis can't be sure but suspects he justifies this convenient pecking order with his religion. That's an ugly thought. Both have dedicated their later years to squeezing a simple answer from a complex question. Doing so is therapeutic for them somehow, but now he is just guessing. Who knows what they really think? They're driven by emotions that he just can't gin-up himself.

Meanness, George had said. Haylow is filled with meanness. What did he mean, exactly? It was more than a synonym for racial conflict. If meanness is there outside the windshield, he doesn't see it. There's nothing down here, just the pine trees and insects. He gets back to considering the bugs on the windshield and becomes aware. A haze crosses the road up ahead, a shadow on the air. He squints and wonders. What is this? Air pollution or maybe smoke from a burning, maybe a forest fire, but the haze doesn't behave like smoke, and the closer it gets, the darker the shadow becomes. He remembers and pushes the switch to roll up the window as the Volvo hits the wall of gnats and crosses over the line.

Chapter Thirty-two

The gnats are a real problem. Travis can't see the road. He turns on the headlights and the windshield wipers. It's a good thing he got the window rolled up, and he wonders if they can get in through the a.c. vents, but they don't.

The swarm thins by the time he reaches Valdosta, although it's still a menace. The first world has returned, too, with a WAL*MART and strip malls and a courthouse square downtown. Valdosta State College on the outskirts. Maybe he'll stop by on the way out and see if they're hiring, he thinks. He refuels the Volvo before the final push east, stands beneath the awning of a gleaming service station, nozzle in the hole, gallons ticking past. As he squeegees dead insects off the windshield, a cloud of gnats shows great interest in his head. He waves a hand to shoo them away, but they are determined. Some strategy is in order before he gets back into the car: he yanks the door open quickly and slams it behind him so they won't get inside, but some do anyway. A quick drive through the old part of town, and he stops for lunch at a diner across from the courthouse square. When he walks in, everyone looks up. The booth by the window is empty. He eyes the torn cushion and slides in the other side and spreads the state map across the tabletop. They're a friendly people down here, or at least his waitress is. The middle-aged white woman keeps refilling his coffee cup and messing up the cream/sugar mixture just after he gets it right. On the front of her T-shirt, the bug-eyed Olympic mascot gives a thumbs-up sign. Even down here, he thinks. She says she's lived in Valdosta for all of her life, but she's never heard of Haylow. She doesn't know the swamp all that well though, if that's where he's headed. A gnat lands on her lower lip. A tiny whine bugs his ear. He bats it away and asks her how she can stand them. You just get used to it, she says.

Haylow is no longer on the state map, if it was ever there to begin with, and George's map isn't much help, either. GA 187 does run from east to west. A train track parallels the state road, too, but there isn't a railroad symbol running down from Atlanta into Clinch County. There isn't a railroad junction. There isn't a Haylow, or at least no easy way to find it. He eats a burger and makes a plan, but it's not much of one: drive east until a railroad track crosses the road, or turn left when he runs into the swamp.

When he leaves the diner, the gnats have knocked off for the afternoon siesta and aren't as bad. Blue sky is everywhere, but clouds gather over past the courthouse dome.

A quick open and shut of the car door, and it doesn't take long to get out of town. He circles the square before he gets the direction right and drives past vacant storefronts. Downtown commerce has left for the big box stores on the bypass, and then he's on the main road and rolling through the black side of town. Small houses close together on both sides of the road. People out on front porches and sitting in the shade. An old man waves as he drives past. After that, he's surrounded by pine again, their peculiar ranking in rows, the orchard order, all the saplings the same height. An insect hits the windshield. Then another. So much for cleaning it off. A logging truck passes in the oncoming lane, its load of trunks shifting, and that's the last of the traffic. There are no other cars, just the empty asphalt stretching out the windshield and receding in the rearview mirror, the two lanes divided by the dash-dash-dash of passing-lane paint, long faded. The road is so straight for so many consecutive miles that something seems wrong.

George was right. There isn't a whole lot to it. A sand road every once in a while. And plenty of sand running off into the brush, as if the gnats caramelize seasonally and fall to the ground. Another bug hits the windshield. The splotches are evenly distributed across the glass. Travis turns on the wipers to clean them away, but the reservoir is empty now and they just smear. Two buzzards on the road up ahead, feasting on roadkill. An opossum, it looks like. He slows and honks the horn, but they don't leave their lunch until he's right on top. He takes a risk and rolls the windshield down. Maybe the inside gnats will exit. Heat and wind on his face. A fast bird he can't identify, fast but not fast enough. It flies low across the road and thunks on the grill. Feathers in the air. That can't be a good sign.

Travis drives east for half an hour. He feels numb. Everything has gone so badly. He has been dumped. His career might or might not have collapsed. He reaches for clarity, but there is none and none coming. He drives deeper and deeper into the unpopulated interior, when suddenly the ordered woods on either side of the road give way to jungle chaos: the trees grow where they want, scrub brush and palmetto fronds, too. Then the swampland begins. Bog water pools around the pine trunks. Spanish moss hangs from the tree limbs.

There hasn't been a road on his left for a while now. Maybe he's passed it. His foot eases off the accelerator, and the Volvo coasts using the built-up momentum. Another mile down, and there's a road up ahead to the left. It's a paved road, too. Anticipation makes him lean forward over the steering wheel. This is a good candidate, not quite forty miles. He pulls the turn signal lever down and makes the left turn. The Volvo clumps over the railroad tracks, tires over the rail. Travis hits the brake and stops in the middle of the track, no trains coming, and he can see for miles on either side. The bait shop sack with George's map is on the passenger seat. His uncle's scratchy pen-work shows a dog leg turn, and that's exactly what this road does. It makes a sharp left in front of a battered double-wide trailer and then a sharp right. Is this it? The Volvo makes the dog leg and Travis looks for the Hemperly house. According to the map, it should be right here, but there is only the thick wood, a screen of trees, patchwork grass and sand. He pulls the Volvo off of the shoulder before the dense pine thicket, turns the ignition off, sits back in his seat and wonders. The dog leg turn is here, but there's no house. It might be farther up the road, but he didn't cross a southbound track on the state road. There is a north/south rail line but no railroad junction. And dog leg turns are common. Maybe the track was taken up? But that doesn't make sense. Atlanta is crisscrossed with unused track. If they lay dormant in the city, why spend the time and effort to take them up down here in the middle of nowhere? Still, he's got to start somewhere. It's time to do a little field work, he thinks, and he swaps out his loafers for his kicks, opens the car door, and the gnats fly in.

The air is fragrant with pine. Sweat under his arms, too. If he had never traveled out of state, he'd probably ignore the humidity. Like the waitress, he'd just be used to it. But the air is thick with it. It's hot. It's sticky. His shirt is already wet. And good Lord, the insects are terrible. A mosquito lands on his forearm, and he slaps it into a bloody skid. A quick look around for Posted signs, but it's okay to trespass, apparently. He does a 360 and surveys the scene: Rough grass and brush, water pooling in spots. The dark trees and the double-wide trailer over there. A junk pile mixed with the thinning trees on the other side of the car. The wood here is wild, bog everywhere, as if the earth has sprung a leak and is sinking. What to do now? He starts by assuming that George's map has some accuracy to it, which would place the railroad crossroads right over there, about a hundred yards.

Travis crosses a plowed-up field, large furrows with big clods of dirt and dips full of water. He walks around the largest patch of swamp yet and over to the straight iron rails. It's a standard issue train track: two rails over creosote cross-ties, all on a bed of gravel that extends a few feet on each side into the grass. Travis looks up and down the track. It's the same view both ways, the two rails running to the vanishing point in the distance, trees on the left but the right was clear cut not too long ago, it looks like. And there's still no cross track. Altitude-wise, he must be close to sea level. The track is built up on a gravel foundation, the rails high and dry, but the earth beyond is wet on the other side of the track too. He can see the Volvo from here, small over by the wood thicket. He listens for a train, but none are coming, and he'll be able to tell in plenty of time to step off the track before getting flattened. The track is as long and level as the state road next to it. He begins his march, looking left and looking right. George said that there was a water tower. He doesn't see one. He doesn't see anything. It seems like there would be some evidence of a tower, but there is nothing. The only sound: his shoes when they hit the gravel between the ties, and he walks west for a while. Nothing. Nothing. Nothing. Something at his feet. What's this? An iron rectangle, a flat plate, lies between two of the ties, each end driven into the wood with a spike. Why is this here? He wonders. It serves no purpose that he can see, other than a marker, but marking what? He looks west up the track. He looks east down the track. He looks south, and then he sees it: the flat run of grassy swampy scrub for about a hundred yards and then the pine canopy begins again, but there's a cleft in the trees. He turns around. It's the same thing on either side, a split in the trees to the north. There was another track here, he thinks. And now that he looks for it, there's gravel in the grassy scrub to the north and to the south, too. This is it. He's found it.

"Welcome to Haylow," he greets himself.

It looks like Haylow died on the vine, he thinks, and what remains of the settlement is sinking into the advancing swamp. If his great-grandfather had planned to create his own kingdom, his own town, his own empire, it hadn't turned out that way. The seed of a settlement had been planted, a turpentine farm at a railroad crossroads, but it didn't flourish, having succumbed to who-knows-what? Bad planning? The swamp? The KKK? Travis shakes his head and swats at the gnats. There's not even enough remaining of the railroad junction to get the armchair archaeologist in him worked up. From what he can see, all that's left of Haylow today is the story. What happened?

There's only one place to go. Might as well give the door a knock and see if the population is home today. Travis makes his way back across the dirt field. Dirt clods break as he crosses back over the upturned field, dodging water and the swampy spots, then across the dog leg, across the patchy grass and up to the screen door of the double-wide. The trailer looks like a fake house, and the two plastic deer in front of the window don't help. The sun hasn't been kind to the shingles, and they've faded to the color of yellow that summons nausea. There's a tin shed roof bolted to the side, a sedan parked in the shade underneath. The screen door is torn at the bottom, the decorative aluminum curls bent out, and it rattles when he knocks. He takes a step back and waits. Then he knocks again. The woman who opens the door is thin and wrinkled, thick glasses on her face, old lady hairdo askew. Travis introduces himself and begs her pardon. He tells her that he's driven down from Atlanta, that Charles Hemperly was his great-grandfather and used to have a turpentine farm here. He asks if she knows anything about that.

"Charlie Hemperly?" a gravelly male voice from inside. "I knew Charlie Hemperly!" he yells. She speaks quietly: please come in, and she opens the door wide.

The trailer smells of mothballs. There is so much to look at all at once that he can't take any of it in. Floral doo-dads everywhere. Floral prints on the walls. Brass plate clocks with glass covers. A ten point buck clock. A John Wayne clock. A Jesus clock. Crystal crosses on each side of the door. Tables covered with figurines and ceramics: faux-cake stands with faux-cakes, faux slices cut out. Glass candles. Bobbles. Thingamabobs. Doohickeys. Junk. There's a shotgun beside the door, stock on the carpet, barrel pointing up at the antler rack. She leads him in the next room. A big man, an old man, relaxes on the gold couch beneath the back window, a green nasal cannula drooping from his nose and into the oxygen tank next to the TV. He's got a nasty pink scar on his check, a long vertical cut from temple to chin. Travis wipes his feet on the mat and steps inside. A floral-patterned area rug on the carpet. He steps over to the big man and extends his hand for a shake. "Thanks for inviting me in. I hope I didn't catch you at a bad time."

"Lamberson," he says, his handshake soft.

Travis reintroduces himself and says again that his great-grandfather used to own the property here and run a turpentine farm. Did he know anything about that?

"I used to work for your granddaddy," he says.

"Great-grandfather," Travis corrects and thanks him again. "They've told me that his house was around here somewhere."

"It's in our backyard. You parked right in front of it."

That's strange, Travis thinks. He didn't see anything but the trees. He asks if he'd be willing to talk to him for a minute. The woman takes a seat in a fabric chair with floral print. "Lamberson. That's Swedish, isn't it?" Travis asks.

"That's what they tell me," he draws mucus in his throat and coughs into his fist. "I used to work for Mr. Charlie." Lamberson hacks another productive cough and the cannula swings.

What luck, Travis thinks and apologizes for interrupting his TV. *The Wheel of Fortune* jingle plays in the background, and the colorful wheel spins on the screen.

That's alright," Lamberson says and tells the woman to turn the sound down and get their guest some sweet tea. Travis isn't thirsty but something inside him instructs him that it's rude not to accept the hospitality, so he says thanks and explains his purpose. He has driven down from Atlanta to look over the old place, was just curious about it. It sure is remote out here, he says.

"That's how I like it," Lamberson says and coughs again. Travis is concerned about his health and says so. He doesn't want to cause him any problems, but the old man waves away the thought and says that he'll just pace himself like always. It's not a problem. "You like this show?" He nods toward the colorful wheel that spins as the audience whoops it up. The quiet woman walks over to the set and turns the knob. Travis mourns his stolen TV and says that he doesn't really know game shows. The old man leans back. "Well," he says.

Lamberson is eight-six years old, he says, and he was born here in Haylow. They've been together for sixty years, man and wife, and there aren't many people who can say that. He and his wife are the last surviving members of the town. If you wanted to call it a town, and he snorts at this. More of a crossroads, he says.

"Why'd you stay all this time?" Travis asks the obvious question.

"Don't know where else I'd live."

"*We'd* live," the woman, his wife, leans forward and puts a hand on his.

Better you than me, Travis thinks. He's always had access to people and cultural or historical opportunities, even as a Viking at L'Anse Aux Meadows. Travis has a slough of questions to ask and he sure wishes he'd brought a tape recorder.

"When your granddaddy came here, there weren't nothing here but the railroad. He got the land and had it in his mind that he was going to build his own town. I don't know why he'd think that anyone would want to live out here in this swamp, but he did. For a while it looked like he might just pull it off. He had clout up at the state capitol, and even got us a post office. My wife was the post master."

"Sure was," she nods. "I liked doing that."

"Post office?" Travis says. I didn't think that there was anything else here but the railroad."

"Well, there wasn't much. There was a little old store by the Coastline track. That's where the Post Office was."

"So there was another railroad line?"

"Sure was. But they took it up."

"Why?"

"Don't know why. They just did. After that, everything began to dry up."

Travis asks about the scar.

Lamberson traces a finger over the pink line on his cheek. "That happened in the commissary. I had an argument with one of the chippers, and he took at me with a cutter."

"You were lucky."

"He was lucky," the woman says.

"Oh, it's not that bad. You shoulda seen the other fella. He ended up with the short end of the stick." Lamberson scoots around on the couch and inhales a few deep breaths. "It was after that I stopped working for your granddaddy. The other blacks told the old man that if he didn't fire me, they'd all leave. So he did. This was during the war, and workers were hard to find. The blacks knew this, and they exploited it. Anyway, that's when I got into the bee business."

"The bee business?" Travis takes a sip of tea.

"The bee business. Decided to go to work for myself."

"How'd that go?"

"Went okay. Not at first. Had to buy the honeybees on credit, and didn't nobody have any money, not down here, anyway."

"We worked like blacks," the woman says.

Worked like blacks? Travis thinks. The Lambersons have updated their vocabulary with the times, it sounds like, but there's still a giveaway in there somewhere. *Worked like blacks* seems a linguistic fart.

"My uncle George came down here when he was a teenager. He ran the commissary. Do you remember him?"

"Oh sure, I remember George. He was always walking around with that rifle and chasing the gals."

"Chasing the gals?" Travis asks. "He said there weren't any women down here."

"Well, there weren't, except for some of the black gals that stayed in the quarters. Some of the workers had their families here."

This comes as a surprise, and Travis blinks. He asks Lamberson if he remembers his father, Henry, but Lamberson says that he doesn't remember him and the cannula swings.

"Is there something you wanted to ask me, son?"

Might as well get it out there, Travis thinks. "My father told me once that he came down here, and he saw a man who had been chained to a tree and murdered with an ax. I've been trying to find out if that was true. And I'll be honest with you. That's why I made the drive."

"Why are you worried about it?" Lamberson inhales through his nose, a deep breath but a wet one.

"Well, sir. I'm not worried about it. I was just curious."

"Sounds to me like you're worried about it."

Travis pauses. His grandmother used the same words. Is he worried about it? He leans forward, elbows on his knees and turns his hands palms-up. "It'd just be a help to know. That's all."

"I wouldn't know anything about it." Lamberson looks him in the eye.

"But it did happen?"

"Listen here. Why are you asking?"

"Well, George said that there was a lot of the klan down here, and I was wondering if my father saw a lynching, that's all."

"The klan? Down here?" Lamberson laughs.

"Well, that's what he said. He said that they were very active."

The temperature in the room drops, and Travis feels the frostiness on the back of his neck. Lamberson coughs, phlegm in hand. "I think maybe it's time for you to go."

Back outside, Travis stands in the front yard, and the gnats descend. How to get to the truth? It's not much of a leap to imagine teenage George trying to romance the African American girls. But he was so definite about the klan, and Lamberson bristled at the suggestion. He swats his way back to the car.

The beater Volvo is sinking. Travis walks up to the back tire and looks down. Water has sprung from the porous earth, about an inch underneath, the same for the front tire. The ground was dry when he parked the car, now the sand squeaks with every step.

Behind the car, the woods are dense and dark, but now that he looks for it, there is something back there behind the dark screen of trees, ruins enveloped by the forest. Travis steps into the woods, moving the brush aside. Lamberson was right. He'd parked the Volvo directly in front of what's left of it. Not much of a plantation house, Travis thinks. The wood becomes thick fast here, growing up at the end of the sand shoulder, tall pines and saplings and some Spanish moss, too. He has parked not twenty feet away from the ruins of the house, yet the wood is so thick that it's hard to make out. Travis looks for snakes. Once he's in, the trees thin, the wreck of the house is clear, the collapsed front porch, the chimney and the shingled siding.

What a disappointment.

He hadn't actively imagined what the house would look like,

but now that he's found it, he realizes that what he had in mind was, if not more commanding, at least less primitive. The Victorian farmhouse he'd passed outside of Valdosta comes to mind. He's never seen a house so crudely built. It's a collapsing shack, a window on each side of the door, one for each room. The trees have moved in. They grow up around and through the ruins. This was what he had expected the quarter houses to look like. Porch collapsed. Roof collapsed on the right side. The backside of the house is down, too. It has been consumed by the woods. Travis steps carefully, makes his way past the pine trunks. The wooden beams rotten and shingles scattered about and dissolving into the brush. The front door is a dark rectangle, and he thinks of snakes. Moccasins. Rattlers. The shingles break under the weight of his shoes and pop. He sticks his head inside, and his eyes adjust to the dim light. Wooden floor bowed up. Brick fireplace empty. No furniture. Even the windows are primitive. He doesn't go further, stands in the doorway. If this was a plantation house, then it wasn't much of a plantation.

There's almost nothing left of the commissary. It looks like a rectangular junk pile. The Hemperly house or shack or whatever was still identifiable as a house, but the commissary is just a heap of wood and rusted barrels, shingles and bent metal. He steps onto a beam, but stops when he hears a rattle. Then another. He steps back quickly, backs up a few feet but doesn't see the snakes. They're in there somewhere, though.

Across the grassy back yard, Lamberson's double-wide trailer stretches across an island dry of land. The back door creaks as it swings open. His big frame fills the doorway. No nasal cannula hanging from his nose. He's off the oxygen and holds onto the door jamb with effort. He motions Travis over. Travis steps from the brush.

"You find what you're looking for?" his voice wheezing and full of fluid.

Travis looks back over his shoulder. "I'm not sure."

"Listen. You seem like a nice fella, and I know you come a long way."

"I'm just trying to find out about my family."

Lamberson waves the thought away. "I just didn't want to talk mean about your granddaddy. You want to know about the klan?" He shakes his head. "There weren't no klan down here." He takes a deep inhale, his breathing labored. "Everybody down here was black except us. What do you think we did, dress up in bed sheets and go over to the quarters to burn a cross like they do in the movies?" His face is red with the effort, the scar on his cheek heated.

"I don't mean any disrespect," Travis says. "That's just what he said."

"George was a storyteller even back then. I don't know why I'm bothering to tell you this. You don't know a Longleaf from a Loblolly." He shakes his head. "You're off the map down here, sir. This ain't the city. There ain't no law down here, never has been. I'm the law. You're the law. The niggers are the law. Whoever has the gun is the law."

"Or the ax?"

"Now you're getting it." Lamberson wheezes.

They part with a handshake. Lamberson says that the quarters are down the sand road that crosses the cut where the Coastline railroad used to be. He points a thick finger at the woods. "About a mile past the track." A gnat feasts on the soft wet meat at the corner of his eye. Travis asks for permission to poke around. Lamberson says to go ahead. He'd be careful for the snakes if he were him, though.

About a mile. That's all he has to go. He gets back in the Volvo, rolls down the window to let the gnats out. There's no use in keeping up the façade of a gnat-free environment, and he is beginning to get used to them just like the waitress said. The sand road leaves the highway about thirty feet behind him, over toward what must have been the post office. Not much of a building. The tires get fair traction on the sand, and puddles wait here and there in the pine straw. The Volvo wasn't made for off-road travel, the undercarriage low to the ground, and Travis drives slowly, wheels rolling over the sand and into the growth of the cut where the track used to be. He looks north and south, and it's easy to see from here, the scar through the woods not yet healed. Eventually the two sides will grow back together, the forest whole once again, but it'll take a while.

The going is easy for a ways after he crosses the cut and Travis follows the tire ruts until they begin to fade. The sparse grass becomes aggressive, spreads and conquers until the road disappears as the forest reclaims the territory. Pine straw carpets the ground and saplings have grown and scrape the undercarriage. He slows the Volvo to a creep, inching deeper down the abandoned road, deeper into the advancing swamp until a rear tire begins to spin, and then he's not going anywhere.

Great. Now what? He'll have to walk back to the trailer to call AAA. He gets out of the car to inspect the damage. The left rear tire has punctured the earth and is in a bog. He'll have to find something to stick under the tire and use for traction, but there is nothing here, just the wood and the overgrown sand road with thickening saplings and brush. He could hike back to the trailer, but if the quarters are up ahead, he can pull a plank from the ruins, so he sets off bushwhacking through the scrub brush. Both George and Lamberson said that they were about a mile from the house, and the running has given him a sense of how long it takes him to cover the distance, but the dense thicket slows him down. It would help to have a machete, he thinks, both to hack through the brush and provide the comfort of having a weapon. No law but whoever has the weapon. It doesn't look like anyone's been back here for a long time, and then Travis realizes that no one knows he's down here. Not Meggan, not his father or George. He didn't tell anyone about the trip. Lamberson knows, but he's not in any shape to leave the trailer. An unsettling tingle in his neck.

He could get injured and die back here, and no one would know. He'd just disappear.

$\mathcal{H}$e sees a tin roof first, rusted dark red, trees before and around it, all surrounded in creeping green overgrowth. He bushwhacks toward it, and the saplings and brush blocking the sand road begin to thin and clear. Ten more paces and he no longer has to dig his way through the brush. The road has returned. It's overgrown and there are wet patches here and there, the swamp intruding. Travis walks along the green strip in the center and treads into the quarters. Pine trees surround on the left and the advancing swamp on the right. The buildings are organized, like a small abandoned subdivision: four cabins on this side, four cabins on that side, front porches facing each other. The quarter cabins haven't been consumed by the wood, as the Hemperly house had. They are still standing, all of them. There's nothing about the modern world here. It might as well be 1896. Or 1796.

There's a small clearing between the cabins. Sand mostly but some brush, some wet, and a big wooden barrel in the center of the open space. Travis steps into the center of the clearing. They're all the same: brick piers, brick chimneys, slanted tin roofs, front porches. A second room, a kitchen, built onto the back with stovepipes poking from the tin roof. Large window holes with no glass. Dense green overgrowth from the woods on the left, leafing vines engulfing the kitchens and climbing up onto the rooftops. The cabins to the right are sinking into bog water. Sparse trees behind them as the land turns into swamp, the Okefenokee advancing. The Coastline track was close, the cut in the trees still visible to the north. Cords of rotting logs are stacked on the front porches, unused firewood. Not what he expected at all. The cabins are smaller than the ruins of the Hemperly house, but not by much. There must have been a little community back here, primitive but private, only one road in.

One of the buildings is different from the cabins. No front porch on this one, just a doorway with no door. A ball of spinning gnats in the air close by, the excited insects coming closer. Travis ducks the bugs and walks over to the building at the head of the cabins. A red tin roof but pitched like a house roof. He pokes his head in. Windows on the right and left, no glass, shutters open, gray light in the dim room. He closes his eyes for a moment, opens them, and they adjust. There's not much to it: two folding chairs standing, one tipped over, a stack of folded chairs by the door, and look at the rust. A Christ-less cross on the wall.

George didn't draw a church on the map, and it's the last thing he expected to find. The Holy Ghost is long gone, he thinks. Who knows when he made his last visit? The shell of the church is on the high ground, the driest patch of land in the quarters. Travis closes his eyes and drops his head, and there's nothing but dark and a few vague shapes. Then he thinks of Meggan. Of Margaret. He's not a praying man but considers it. Brush rustles in the forest behind, and a twig snaps. The accompanying voice is high-pitched but gravelly, vocal cords strained:

"Well, Mr. Man, I speck you done come ter de een' er de row."

Hackles rise. He's all alone back here. If anything were to happen, he could be in real trouble. He turns toward the scrub and raises an arm up in defensive posture. A rabbit and a fox step from the palmetto brush, both wearing threadbare hand-me-downs. Their shirt sleeves are rolled back and trousers rolled-up too, at the ankles. No shoes. The rabbit's shabby waistcoat is unbuttoned, the vest hanging open. Smoke curls from the bowl of his corncob pipe. The fox standing behind him is a good head taller, more when he straightens his posture. Suspenders hold up his pants, which are clearly a few sizes too large. They both look up at him, unafraid. How easily they stand on their hind legs. The fox speaks next:

"Look et 'im. He dunner wat minnit gwine ter be de nex, do he?"

Travis chokes then yelps and retreats a step. His hand grips the door frame, palm on the rough wood, and a splinter drives in. The Coastline cut stretches in either direction, cleaving through the pines, and the swamp beyond. His mind cannot accept this.

Something has happened in his head.

The rabbit takes a step forward, grabs the corncob and pulls the pipe from his mouth. "Now you see how de lan' lay?"

Travis shuts his eyes and shakes his noggin. "This isn't real," he says, squeezes his eyes tighter then looks again. They haven't moved an inch. The rabbit's ears are turned forward and the fox is panting now, his tongue hanging from open jaws. Sweat stains their shirts at the arm pits, and their clothes make the air prickly. The rabbit takes another step forward, points the pipe's stem up at Travis' head.

"Mr. Man, I'm gwine ter larn you ef hit's de las' ack!"

Epilogue

*A*n opening day demands ceremony, and the new building on campus is no different. The new tower behind Garvey Hall rises toward the sun, which is blocked by clouds on what otherwise would be a brilliant spring afternoon. The spring—when a young man's heart turns lightly to thoughts of love. An older man's heart, however, turns to thoughts of conquest and domination. At least in this case. The provost of the college stands beneath the bronze statue of Reverend Dr. Martin Luther King, Jr., in the center of the crowded plaza, a security guard to his right and back up to his left, revolvers holstered on hips. The day has finally arrived, and there's quite a turnout. Students, faculty, staff and administrators fill the plaza and overflow into the street, which has been closed for the occasion.

The provost had spent no small amount of time making his case before the board of trustees, the purse strings held tightly in their fingers. He stood smartly at the head of the long mahogany table and made his case by PowerPoint presentation, projecting charts and graphs of the future onto the screen: the humanities are obsolete. History, literature, music, art. They are all impractical. Behind-the-times. Downright prehistoric. The liberal arts might have been a necessary component of an earlier education, but this is a different time, a different world, and they hardly reflect the needs of today's workforce. Particularly for these students. He should know. He was dean of the business department for a decade. To build a tower to the humanities is a giant step backwards. They might as well build a tower to alchemy and teach the students to turn lead into gold. What today's student needs is an education in the principals of commerce and marketing, as well as a solid tutoring on business fashion. People defer to a man in a suit and tie, after all. Doesn't matter what's inside the suit. The white folks have been getting away with this for years. Just look around the room, he gestures. The board members look around the room and see that it is so.

The provost was persuasive, and the day is here for the opening ceremony. The weather has cooperated and brought all the symbolic elements of rebirth: Robin's-egg-blue sky. Pink and yellow pansies in glorious bloom. Birds and bees present and accounted for. It's a wonderful day and quite a day for the opening, the provost thinks. He stands in the shadow of the statue and coordinates the proceedings. MLK Plaza teams with untapped energy. The local news is there, too. The cameraman hefts the camera on his shoulder, his eye to the eyepiece and pointed at the Egyptian obelisk, the satellite van parked up the hill and ready to broadcast. There's even an official from the mayor's office shaking hands. It's quite a turnout. A platoon of students stand at the ready for their march up the hill to the new tower. They line up in squads ten students long, all of them wearing business suits of varying quality and cost and fit. Each wears a necktie, red being the preferred color, and all hold a leatherette briefcase with the college logo emblazoned in gold.

Such is the solemnity of the event that they're not even talking among each other. This is what progress looks like, no one can argue with him about that. Across the street and behind Garvey Hall, the newly titled Citadel of Business rises high and casts the humanities building in a permanent shadow. The Citadel of Business. Just think of it, the provost thinks, and the thought makes him giddy. The building is ready to open. All that's left to do is the punch-out list and the landscaping. Once the provost sealed the deal, he scheduled the ceremony first thing before the humanities faculty had a chance to return from spring break and organize a protest.

Before he can give the order to start the march, someone starts making a racket on the sidewalk over in front of Garvey Hall. Who is that? he wonders. One of the history faculty. What's-his-name? Kalamari, the one with the dreadlocks. He holds a protest sign aloft and shouts at the top of his lungs. Some example he sets. He can't make out the sign. Something about capitalism. The cameraman turns his camera toward Garvey Hall and the one-man protest. This is just a disgrace, the provost thinks. His point is proved, his efforts justified. He turns to campus security in the shadow of the statue and take-down ready. Good thing he thought to bring them. Heads are turning now, and Kalamari keeps screaming who-knows-what. Security steps forward, first one and then the other, hands reaching for pistols on hips, eyebrows up.

The provost gives the nod.

Acknowledgments

This novel was a long row for me to hoe, and I have more people to thank for their support and generosity than I can remember. If your name isn't here, please let me know.

First and foremost is Anthony Grooms, who pointed me down this road to begin with. I'm grateful for his support and friendship.

Irene Hatchett and Shay Youngblood read early drafts pulled from a sprawling manuscript of shifting POVs. Their encouragement came when I'd all but dropped the project.

The Hambidge Center for the Arts and Bob Thomas. My residency gave me the setting, solitude and time to shape the manuscript into something coherent.

Rebekah Stewart and Brigadoon Lodge (brigadoonlodge.com) graciously allowed me to hole up in a cabin to finish drafting the novel. And it's the best fly-fishing east of the Mississippi.

A squad of sharp-eyed readers including Lisa Aloisio, Lisa Orten Cross, Amy Foster, Carol Raybourn, Donna Smith, and Steve Weeks.

Joe Taylor and Livingston Press, who endured an avalanche of galley edits with grace and good humor. Thanks, Joe!

Anna Schachner and Lydia Ship at The Chattahoochee Review.

Off-stage help includes but isn't limited to: Bob Butler; Andy Aloisio & Thom Aakre at KDA Communications; Natalie Bard at the Royal Gorge Regional Museum & History Center; James Louis, head of the North Jersey History and Genealogy Center; Lil, Jack, Travis, Bill, Judy, Margot, and Brandon Stewart; Will Wright; Charles McNair; Charles Fox; Lain Shakespeare and The Wren's Nest; The Drinking & Thinking crew: Tony Grooms, John Holman, and Ravi Howard, who provided a writer's community when I needed it most.